Gérard de Villiers

CHAOS IN KABUL

Gérard de Villiers (1929–2013) is the most popular writer of spy thrillers in French history. His two-hundred-odd books about the adventures of Austrian nobleman and freelance CIA operative Malko Linge have sold millions of copies.

Malko Linge, who first appeared in 1964, has often been compared to Ian Fleming's hero James Bond. The two secret agents share a taste for gunplay and kinky sex, but de Villiers was a journalist at heart, and his books are based on constant travel and reporting in dozens of countries.

On several occasions de Villiers was even ahead of the news. His 1980 novel had Islamists killing President Anwar el-Sādāt of Egypt a year before the event took place. *The Madmen of Benghazi* described CIA involvement in Libya long before the 2012 attack on the Benghazi compound. In the same way, *Chaos in Kabul* mixes fact and fiction to vividly reflect the current upheaval in Afghanistan.

ALSO BY GÉRARD DE VILLIERS

The Madmen of Benghazi

CHAOS IN KABUL

A MALKO LINGE NOVEL

Gérard de Villiers

Translated from the French by William Rodarmor

Vintage Crime/Black Lizard

Vintage Books

A Division of Random House LLC | New York

A VINTAGE CRIME/BLACK LIZARD ORIGINAL, OCTOBER 2014

The Library of Congress Cataloging-in-Publication data
Villiers, Gérard de, 1929–2013.
[Sauve-qui-peut à Kaboul. English]
Chaos in Kabul : a Malko Linge novel / by Gérard de Villiers ; translated from the French by William Rodarmor.
pages cm.—(A Malko Linge novel)
1. Undercover operations.
2. Spy stories. I. Rodarmor, William, translator. II. Title.
PQ2682.I44S46 2014 843'.914—dc23 2014030511

Vintage Trade Paperback ISBN: 978-0-8041-6933-2
eBook ISBN: 978-0-804-16934-9

Book design by Joy O'Meara

www.weeklylizard.com

Printed in the United States of America
10 9 8 7 6 5 4 3 2 1

PART ONE

CHAPTER 1

Doha, Qatar
January 2013

The sun was just rising when the Qatar Airways flight from Islamabad landed at the Doha airport. It was 6:03 a.m. The plane had taken off from Pakistan a little more than three and a half hours earlier.

There were now four flights a week on a brand-new Airbus between the capitals of Pakistan and Qatar. This was a big improvement over Pakistan International Airlines' old puddle jumpers and their haphazard schedules. As a result, the plane was full of Pakistanis, rich businessmen and poor job seekers. The Qatari rarely traveled to Pakistan. With only a quarter of a million native-born citizens, Qatar focused on exploiting its gas reserves and the one and a half million Pakistanis, Indians, Filipinos, and Bengalis who did the work that kept the country running.

One of the first passengers to reach the immigration counter was a young man with a neatly trimmed beard wearing an ill-fitting suit, no tie, and a brown coat. He was tall and thin, with a shock of black hair, a prominent nose, high cheekbones, and a sharp, heavy-lidded gaze.

The Pakistani passport he handed the Qatari immigration officer was in the name of Gulbuddin Askari, businessman from Quetta, in Baluchistan.

"Where are you staying, sir?" asked the officer.

"At the Four Seasons," the traveler answered in excellent Arabic.

A rich businessman, then. Located on the corniche along West Bay, the Four Seasons was the best hotel on the peninsula. The immigration agent smartly stamped Askari's passport. Wealth was appreciated in Qatar. Besides, the black crocodile leather attaché case the Pakistani was carrying showed definite class.

Pulling a small roller suitcase, the man calling himself Gulbuddin Askari made for the taxi stand, yawning widely. He was short of sleep. He'd come from Quetta the evening before and slept only three hours in a small hotel near the Islamabad airport before getting up at one thirty in the morning for his flight. He barely noticed downtown Doha's skyscrapers glittering in the morning sun.

At the Four Seasons, Askari was grateful to reach his room. The first thing he did was to unfold a small prayer rug, face Mecca, and spend a long time praying. Then he got undressed, took a shower, and stretched out on the bed.

His meeting wasn't until that evening, but it was essential that he be clearheaded. His soul at peace after a fervent prayer, he quickly fell asleep.

The fuselage of the private Grumman jet bore no markings beyond "Brown & Root, Inc." in small blue letters above the airstairs. The plane landed at Doha airport at 5:45 p.m., twenty minutes ahead of the flight plan given to the Qatari authorities. A business flight from Dallas, with a refueling stop in Madrid.

Besides the crew, there were two men on board. On landing, they handed the immigration service American passports in the names of Carl Gorman and James Ganlento. A pair of ordinary businessmen, a little weary after their seven-thousand-mile trip.

Less than an hour later, they were settling into their rooms—at the Four Seasons.

At 7:30 p.m., Askari appeared at the entrance of the bar and was immediately spotted by the two Americans. The white-haired man calling himself Ganlento stood and approached him.

The men exchanged a long handshake. They had already met three times before, and they liked each other.

"I've reserved a private dining room in the Fortuna," said Ganlento. "Shall we go there, or would you like to have a drink here first?"

"Let's go to the restaurant," said Askari. He didn't drink alcohol and was uncomfortable in public spaces with scantily dressed foreign women.

The men headed for the Italian restaurant, the pride of the Four Seasons. Their table was already set, with wine, mineral water, and fruit juices. Before sitting down, Ganlento turned to his companion.

"Carl, I'd like you to meet Mullah Abdul Ghani Beradar. He's a member of the *shura* in Quetta and has Mullah Omar's full trust."

He then turned to the young Pakistani.

"Mullah Beradar, this is Carl. I'm not authorized to reveal his identity, but I can say that he has come from Washington especially to meet you. He's very close to the president and is here on his behalf."

The two men shook hands. The white-haired man—who was actually Clayton Luger, the CIA deputy director in charge of clandestine operations—gestured toward the dining table. The men sat down and helped themselves to drinks. Luger had asked the restaurant that they not be disturbed and had a silent buzzer under the table to summon the waiter.

Luger now turned his blue eyes to the mullah. He was a big man, taller even than the young Afghan, and his white hair inspired respect.

"Who on your side knows about this meeting?" he asked.

"I was sent by Mullah Omar himself. Nobody in the supreme *shura* knows about it."

"What about the Pakistanis?"

Beradar hesitated slightly before answering. It was an open secret that the Taliban's Quetta assembly was carefully monitored by Pakistan's Inter-Services Intelligence agency. It was even said that an ISI officer sat in on all its meetings.

"They know I'm here, of course," he admitted.

"What do you plan to tell them?"

"That I came here to meet some Americans to ask that the drone strikes in the tribal areas be stopped, as part of an eventual accord. They know that this is under discussion."

Luger nodded approvingly. It was a credible cover story. As the CIA deputy director, he was in charge of the supposedly clandestine program of killing al-Qaeda and Taliban leaders with drone strikes. The program cost far less than traditional military operations, produced better results, and was strongly endorsed by the White House. President Obama never hesitated to sign an executive order in support of the operations, though unofficially they didn't exist.

With the Pakistan question resolved to the two Americans' satisfaction, the men started on their appetizers.

They had chosen to meet in Doha instead of Dubai because the ISI didn't have a network here, whereas the Pakistanis were particularly well informed in Dubai. Given what was to come, it was essential that no one know of National Security Advisor John Mulligan's presence here.

Mullah Beradar had finished his plate of fried vegetables, and Luger gave him time to drink some mango juice before asking, "What's your opinion of the Chantilly meeting a few weeks ago?"

At the initiative of the French government, representatives of various factions in the Afghan conflict had met in a Chantilly hotel for informal talks in late December 2012. They included representatives of the Quetta Taliban, the Massoud Tajiks, the Afghan government, and the Karzai opposition, but no one from the Haqqani network, and no Pakistanis or Uzbeks. The goal had been to find a way to resolve the conflict without too much damage.

"We didn't make much progress," Beradar said with a frown. "There were two main sticking points: the withdrawal of coalition troops—"

"We have made progress there," Luger pointed out.

The Pashtun smiled. "Yes, but only between ourselves. Nothing official."

"We have given you our word that we will leave by the end of 2014," insisted Luger. "We will keep our promises."

"I can confirm that for the White House," said Mulligan, breaking his silence.

"I don't doubt you," the mullah said smoothly. "But what if President Karzai asks that some troops stay after 2014? You would find yourself in an uncomfortable situation."

A silence followed, eventually broken by Clayton Luger.

"President Karzai can't run in the presidential elections set for April 2014," he said. "He'll be out of the game."

Mullah Beradar shook his head, smiling. "We don't trust Karzai. That was the second point raised at the Chantilly meeting. As long as that man is around, we can't foresee any agreement. He'll either rig the election or run one of his loyalists, who will then do whatever Karzai says."

"Why do you hate him so much?" asked Luger. "After all, he's a Pashtun like you, from the Popolzai tribe in Kandahar."

"Hamid Karzai is a corrupt man and a traitor," said the mullah sharply. "If he doesn't leave in time, he will wind up like Shah Shujah."

That was the worst insult anyone could hurl at an Afghan. Shujah had been put on the throne by the British occupiers of Afghanistan in 1839. When the foreign troops left, the Afghans lynched him. Forever after, he was seen as the model of a traitor to his country.

"You're very hard on Karzai," said the CIA deputy director with a slight smile. "He isn't our unconditional ally. After all, he's the one who stopped the coalition offensive in Kandahar in 2010. It would have done you tremendous damage."

Beradar grimaced scornfully. "Karzai is a good tactician. He pretends your leash on him is longer than it really is. He also tries to appease us. But we aren't fooled. He knows that nothing can happen in Afghanistan without us. He is a weak, hypocritical man, which you yourself recognize."

Luger went back on the offensive. "President Karzai has his faults, but I don't think he wants to see a bloodbath in Afghanistan."

"We don't either," said the mullah, "and we aren't trying to seize complete power. All we want is our legitimate place at the table."

"I can understand that," said Luger cheerfully. "And now I think it's time to tackle our dinner."

He pressed the hidden buzzer, and in moments, two Pakistani waiters came to clear the appetizer plates and bring in the entrées. When they did, the three diners were in an innocuous discussion about the fall in Kabul real estate prices caused by the many foreign companies leaving ahead of the coalition's imminent departure.

The dinner plates had long since been cleared, but the men hadn't touched the dessert, an excellent tiramisu. The mullah, because it contained alcohol; the two Americans, because they were focused on their topic.

The meeting had been difficult to arrange, and it had to produce results. But they were going around in circles. The mullah kept dodging, coming back to his usual positions. His two interlocutors were becoming visibly annoyed.

"We aren't enemies, as you know very well," Mullah Beradar reminded them. "In 2000 we were the ones who responded to your request to eradicate poppy farming. It was the Taliban's way of showing that we were reliable partners."

The national security advisor looked at his watch.

"I'm very sorry, but we have to take off in an hour at the latest," he said. "I have a meeting with the president in Washington tomorrow morning. I came here to try to find an area of agreement.

"As you said, we were friends back in 2000. We can be friends again, under certain conditions. Here are ours. The first is very simple: the movement headed by Mullah Omar must formally and in writing renounce terrorism, meaning al-Qaeda."

Beradar drew a notebook from his pocket and started taking notes.

Mulligan continued. "The second point is just as important: Afghanistan post-Karzai must remain an Islamic republic, not an Islamic caliphate, even if the Taliban movement participates in political life.

"We very much hope to have a candidate who will bring about

some national unity between the Pashtuns and the former members of the Northern Alliance. This will avoid bloody clashes between Tajiks, Uzbeks, and Pashtuns. We aren't asking to participate in the elections, only to vet the candidates who represent your way of thinking.

"In exchange, we are willing to take Mullah Omar off our blacklist. What do you think?"

Mullah Beradar finished taking notes and looked up.

"That's not a very generous offer," he said in a neutral tone.

"But can you agree to the main points?" asked Mulligan.

"I don't think there's anything unacceptable in your plan," said the cleric. "But you haven't mentioned one thing: How many soldiers would you be leaving in Afghanistan after 2014? You know that the presence of foreign troops is a red flag for us."

Mulligan was unruffled.

"The president now feels that six thousand troops would be enough to continue training the ANA"—the Afghan National Army.

"That's still too many," said Beradar, shaking his head. "There can't be any troops left in the country."

"This is something that can be discussed," said Mulligan. "Let's be clear. I know you don't have the military strength to seize Kabul or any of the big provincial cities, even if coalition forces aren't present. But the U.S. doesn't want to see a terrorism campaign launched right after our departure. It would make us lose face."

"I understand," said the mullah, smiling amiably. "But you haven't addressed the Karzai issue. The engagements we have reached can be enacted, but only on one condition: that Hamid Karzai is no longer part of the Afghan landscape, in any capacity."

"You commit enough attacks!" snapped the CIA deputy director. "Why don't you eliminate Karzai, if you hate him so much?"

Mullah Beradar smiled regretfully.

"We don't have the means," he said. "He rarely leaves his palace, where he is very well protected. Anyway, you brought him in after the Bonn Agreement in 2001. It's up to you to rid us of him."

"How? We can't very well put him on a plane and dump him in the ocean. He is the president, after all. He may have been elected by fraud, but he was elected."

The Afghan made a vague gesture. "That is a process we don't care to be involved in. We know that you dislike Karzai as much as we do. Even his fellow Pashtuns don't like him. All I can say is that for Mullah Omar, this point is nonnegotiable. Karzai must be gone before any agreement between us can be reached. As long as he is in place, there's no use having any further talks. Karzai isn't our problem; he's yours."

Beradar turned to Mulligan and added, "I apologize for being so blunt, but I am expressing the will of our leader, Mullah Omar."

A long silence followed.

Luger realized that further discussion was pointless. He forced a smile and said, "Thank you for making your position clear. We will consider the Karzai question carefully."

Beradar stood up and the Americans followed suit. After lengthy handshakes, the three men left the private dining room. The mullah slipped away toward the elevators.

"So do you think we've made headway?" Mulligan asked Luger when they were alone.

The CIA deputy director nodded thoughtfully.

"I think we may have the makings of a solution here, provided we can resolve the Karzai problem. The Taliban are taking a more moderate position than they have in the past."

Mulligan's head jerked up in surprise.

"Moderate? They're throwing acid at girls who want to go to school!"

"I meant moderate politically. They aren't demanding total

power. They're prepared to leave room for the Tajiks, the Hazara, and the people who aren't too compromised by Karzai. That could mean an almost peaceful transition."

Another long silence followed, broken by the national security advisor.

"Clayton, do you have any ideas about how to solve the Karzai problem?"

"A few, and none of them very good. It's a political matter that only the president can decide. But I'll try to think of some practical solutions."

In fact, the CIA deputy director had only one in mind, and it posed a major ethical dilemma. Since September 2001, the United States had killed many of its adversaries, including Osama bin Laden.

But never a sitting president.

CHAPTER 2

His Most Serene Highness Prince Malko Linge, Knight of the Order of the Black Eagle, Margrave of Lower Lusatia, Knight of the Royal Order of Seraphim, and Knight of the Order of Malta—to cite just some of his titles—looked out his library window at the silently falling snow that since last night had been covering all of Burgenland.

He was lost in thought.

The music coming from the ballroom reminded Malko that his castle had guests tonight. Some twenty squires from neighboring estates had come to Liezen to eat braised venison with chestnuts prepared by his faithful old cook, Ilse, who had preceded it with a mountain of charcuterie. All washed down with beer and Steinhäger gin.

People had started dancing after dinner, but Malko discreetly slipped away, leaving his guests in the hands of his fiancée, Alexandra, who looked dazzling in a mauve Azzedine Alaïa gown.

For some reason, he wasn't enjoying the party as much as he should. It was the manifestation of his worldly public life, that of a somewhat impoverished Austrian nobleman who somehow managed to preserve his station in ways unsuspected by the hoi polloi.

Very few people knew of Malko Linge's connection to the CIA as a highly skilled freelance operative. In exchange for taking insane risks, it allowed him to pay the castle's bills. As he watched the snowflakes fall, Malko found himself thinking that every stone of the old place was soaked in the blood of those who died so he could live and enjoy it. The swirling wall of white flakes gradually covering the courtyard cobblestones seemed to be cutting him off from the world.

Malko wasn't feeling himself this evening. He downed his glass of Russky Standart and was about to rejoin his guests when a warm body leaned against his back. He had no trouble recognizing Alexandra, whose heavy breasts pressed against his alpaca jacket.

The young woman slipped an arm around his waist, pulling him closer.

"This is certainly the first time I've ever seen you go into the library alone," she murmured teasingly.

They had often made love in that room, and a fair number of Malko's other conquests had lost what remained of their virtue there. In spite of Alexandra's fierce jealousy, he sometimes couldn't help yielding to his predatory instincts.

"It was too noisy in the ballroom," he said. "I'm glad you came to join me."

He rested his hand on the young woman's, which was firmly pressed against his belly. She put her lips against his neck.

"I counted the women guests, and they were all present, so I went looking for you. What's the matter?"

"Nothing, exactly. I just needed some time to think. I was remembering Tunis. I don't like what happened there. A lot of people died for nothing."

"That was far away," Alexandra answered lightly. "Now you're home, enjoying life, and life is good. Your guests find you charming and brilliant, and they envy me."

"You know this is all going to end someday," he said. "You'll get that bad phone call . . ."

"Not necessarily. You can always shake off your spooks and come live with me. I have a big, beautiful home and a vineyard that can easily support both of us without your having to risk your life every three months."

"You'd want me to leave Liezen?"

"Why not? Even if you kill ten times more people for the CIA, you'll never be able to restore this castle completely. It's a money pit, and you know it."

"It would break my heart to leave Liezen," he said, shaking his head. "I'd rather burn it down."

Alexandra burst out laughing.

"What a good idea! It would make for a terrific bonfire. We could throw one last party and dance in the courtyard while the castle burned."

Malko wheeled on her.

"Stop talking nonsense! Come on, let's go back. Our guests will think we have bad manners."

Alexandra didn't budge, blocking his way instead. In a low voice she said, "Let's imagine that I'm one of your women guests and you found me here, all alone in the darkness. What would you do?"

They weren't exactly in darkness and he could make out Alexandra's voluptuous curves perfectly well. He never wearied of her, in spite of his exotic adventures. Standing slightly akimbo, she gazed at him, looking as sexy as the devil.

She came closer, leaning gently against him, and murmured, "So what would you do with this new, unknown woman? You might sit her on the sofa, put on some music, and tell her how charming she is."

As she spoke, she pulled him over to the red velvet sofa that had hosted many of their embraces. She sat down beside Malko, gazing at him.

"Personally, I think you might start by kissing her, to see how far she's prepared to go. That would be a good beginning, don't you think?"

Her lips met Malko's, and her tongue darted into his mouth. She was relaxed, and he could tell that she was getting excited.

The kiss went on and on.

He stroked Alexandra's heavy breasts and could feel her nipples harden under his fingers. Now getting excited in turn, he slipped his hand to her knees and under her dress, which gave a highly erotic rustle as it slid up over her stockings.

The young woman pulled her mouth away.

"Now I think you should take her panties off," she murmured. "That's a good test. If she squeezes her thighs together, it means she still needs a little more champagne."

Malko's fingers were already stroking Alexandra's thighs. She wasn't squeezing them together—quite the contrary. When he reached the edge of her string panty, she raised her hips slightly so he could slide it down. It was soon a crumpled ball of black lace on the carpet. She spoke approvingly:

"See? Who dares, wins."

She eased herself down on the cushions to give him access to her already wet pussy.

His gloomy earlier mood forgotten, Malko was caught up in an erotic and romantic rush. He felt Alexandra stroking his alpaca trousers, then delicately unzipping them. His fiancée's warm hands made their practiced way into the opening and seized his prick.

For a few moments, only sighs and the rustle of clothing could be heard. Then Alexandra moved slightly to see if the prick now rising from the alpaca pants was properly stiff. She brought her mouth close to Malko's ear and sweetly said, "I assume that your conquest was well brought up, and that she learned to use her mouth properly in finishing school."

As she spoke, she went down on her knees in front of him. When Malko felt Alexandra's warm mouth close around him, he thought he would faint with happiness. Eyes closed, completely relaxed, he gave himself over to her. He put his hand on the nape of her neck to guide her a little. A little later, he felt resistance and let her come up for air. She again brought her mouth close to his ear.

"Your lady love has done a fine job of preparing that thing, and I think she deserves to have it deep inside her. Honest pay for honest work . . . It's up to you to lead her on, to anticipate her desires. For her to fully enjoy what's coming, I think she might want to kneel on the sofa, like this."

Alexandra stood up, turned away from Malko, and knelt on the red sofa, her chest against the backrest. Stepping behind her, he had only to loosen his pants and lift her mauve dress over her hips, then press his cock between her cheeks. It easily found her pussy when he bent his knees a little. With hardly any effort, he sank into her to the hilt. She raised her hips, the better to receive him.

Grabbing her waist, a happy Malko slid in and out of her. Alexandra sighed with every thrust, giving deep little moans.

This lasted until Malko felt his climax approaching. Alexandra could sense it too, from the way he was clutching her hips and the quickening tempo of his thrusts. Turning her head, she said, "You've gone this far; you can afford to get rough with her. She wouldn't dare complain."

It was an explicit invitation.

Restraining his climax, Malko pulled out, then pointed his cock higher. Finding her hot ass was enough to make him lose what remained of his restraint. Grasping his cock firmly, he set it against the tight opening and shoved.

Alexandra gave a hoarse growl as he sank deep inside her. Then her hips began to sway while Malko pounded as hard as he knew how.

When he came, his yell seemed to shake the falling snowflakes. Good thing the library door was closed . . .

The two of them stayed that way for a long time, feeling dazed. Then Alexandra turned to him.

"I think you should apologize for your roughness now. She may never have been taken this way before. Kiss her hand and get her a glass of champagne. She deserves it."

Malko eased out of her.

They quickly straightened their clothes and left the library hand in hand.

Malko's old butler, Elko Krisantem, saw them entering the ballroom and came over with some glasses of champagne on a tray.

Alexandra drank hers down and gave Malko a sly look.

"Thank you for that pleasant interlude, sir. I must go join my husband now."

She moved away toward a group of their guests.

Malko was putting his glass down when his cell phone beeped. A text message appeared on-screen:

I need to see you in Washington asap. JM.

He put the phone in his pocket. "JM" was John Mulligan, the White House national security advisor. He called Malko only for extremely delicate missions.

And extremely dangerous ones.

CHAPTER 3

The weather in Washington was no better than it had been in Austria. Snow silently swirled along Sixteenth Street to a White House no doubt busy preparing for Barack Obama's second inauguration.

Malko released the window drapes in his room at the Hay-Adams and looked at his watch: exactly 1:00 p.m. It wouldn't do to keep John Mulligan waiting. The national security advisor was a powerful figure in the White House. He was the man who knew the deepest secrets, who directed the United States' *real* policy, and who helped the president make decisions that weren't always endorsed in the sainted halls of Congress.

Malko had flown from Vienna to New York on Austrian Airlines, then taken the train to Union Station. His reservation at the Hay-Adams, the fanciest and most expensive hotel in town, turned out to be an elegant suite. That meant the Americans would be asking him to do something very difficult. Along the Potomac, they didn't throw money out the window.

Malko took the elevator downstairs to the hotel dining room, whose maître d' approached with an ingratiating smile. Just then, the door curtains parted, admitting a very tall, white-haired man wearing a black down coat. When he spotted Malko, he strode over, smiling.

"Malko Linge?"

"Yes."

"I'm Clayton Luger, deputy director. I work with Ted Boteler. He was supposed to come today, but he has the flu. Follow me!"

Boteler, whom Malko knew well, ran the CIA special operations group, in charge of undercover missions.

Luger led him to a booth at the very back of the room.

"I'm sorry. I should have been here to meet you, but traffic was bad. John should be here any moment. Care for a drink?"

Malko was served a glass of Stolichnaya but barely had time for a toast when a tall, redheaded man crossed the room to their booth, moving like a charging elephant. The national security advisor.

Mulligan and Malko exchanged a long handshake.

"It's nice to see you back in Washington," said Mulligan, sitting down.

After some small talk, they ordered: New York steaks for the two Americans, rack of lamb for Malko.

It wasn't until they'd finished their salads that Mulligan turned to Malko and asked, "Does anyone know about your trip?"

"Your immigration officers certainly do," said Malko. "They questioned me quite carefully, probably because of the upcoming inauguration. Why do you ask?"

"This meeting must remain absolutely secret. I didn't even enter it in my appointment book. It concerns an extremely sensitive subject."

Because of the time difference, Malko was starving, and he was afraid Mulligan might tackle his subject immediately. Fortunately that wasn't the case, and they took the time to enjoy their entrées.

Finally, the security advisor pushed his plate back and said, "You were in Afghanistan three years ago, as I recall. What do you know about the situation there now?"

"Only what I read in the newspapers," said Malko. "Not great, it seems."

"That's an understatement. We're in deep shit there, and President Obama wants us out. No troops after 2014. We've already evacuated four hundred combat positions all over the country. We can't move any faster."

"What will happen after the coalition troops leave?"

"That's the number one problem. Word on the ground is very bad. Every time we leave a place, the Taliban move in. They're clever. They don't play a public role, but they control everything, under the table. When villagers have a legal dispute, they don't turn to the official justice system, which is totally corrupt, but to the Taliban, who are honest."

"What about Karzai?" asked Malko.

The American gave a harsh laugh.

"He's nothing but the mayor of Kabul now. Never leaves his palace anymore. He'll take a helicopter to travel twenty miles, and that as rarely as possible. He's surrounded by family leeches and people so corrupt it would curl your hair. His whole entourage is rotten."

"What will happen after you pull out?"

"The regime should be able to hold Kabul and the cities," said Mulligan. "But nobody can gauge the police and ANA soldiers' loyalty to the government. Today they'll fiercely defend the smallest checkpoint; tomorrow they might change sides and disappear. And in that case, the regime could collapse in a few days. Like in Vietnam."

An ugly memory for the Americans.

By the time their coffees arrived, Malko still didn't know why Mulligan had summoned him to Washington so urgently. After all, there wasn't much he could do to settle the Afghan problem.

"If you don't mind my asking, what is on your mind, John? I don't imagine you called this meeting to give me a lecture on geo-strategy."

"No, I just wanted to give you the big picture. Now we get to the tough part. And everything I'm going to tell you is top secret."

Mulligan lowered his voice.

"A week ago, we had a secret meeting with the Taliban in Qatar. I went there under an assumed name."

"You did?" Malko asked in surprise.

"Yes. The Taliban wanted to be sure that the American government was really behind the negotiation, that this wasn't just a CIA trial balloon that the White House would immediately shoot down. So Clayton and I made the trip to Doha together."

"What came of it?"

"An outline of a plan to end the crisis," said Mulligan vaguely. "It still has to be ratified by Mullah Omar's *shura* in Quetta."

"What about the Pakistanis?"

Mulligan grinned sarcastically.

"If the Taliban sign, the Pakistanis have to agree. They've got them by the balls."

"And what about the Karzai government?"

Malko felt Mulligan stiffen slightly, and he understood that they were getting to the heart of the matter.

"The Karzai government isn't aware of this démarche," he said. "And it won't be."

"But they talk to the Taliban too," Malko objected.

"Of course. Karzai is doing everything he can to win them over. Remember, he was very close to them in the beginning. They even planned to name him ambassador to the United States! Their connection only began to fray after September 11, when we drove the Taliban out of Kabul with the help of the Northern Alliance. After that, Karzai became the Taliban's nemesis. Initially because of his support for the coalition, and later because of his government's corruption."

Clayton Luger broke in. "Did you know that one of Karzai's brothers siphoned off nine hundred and sixty million dollars from the national bank by authorizing loans to his friends? They promptly ran off to buy real estate in Dubai, while remaining officially insolvent in Afghanistan."

"So why are you leaving Karzai out of the talks?" asked Malko.

A long silence followed, eventually broken by the security advisor.

"For the reasons I'm about to explain. As I said, we're facing a dilemma. The president wants to disengage from Afghanistan as quickly as possible."

"The Agency has already pulled more than a thousand operatives out," said Luger. "We only send our 'newbies' there now."

Mulligan resumed. "Every report that crosses my desk says the same thing. Once the last coalition troops leave, the Afghan National Army will fall apart. It already has a 27 percent attrition rate every year. Police, same thing. The Taliban have completely penetrated them. Which means we might wind up leaving with our tails between our legs, like in Vietnam. That's something the president wants to avoid at any cost."

"So you're in a tight spot," said Malko. "Do you have a solution?"

"The Taliban suggested one to us. Even though Karzai's weak and corrupt, they're afraid of him. So they suggested a negotiated settlement that would ensure a peaceful transition."

"They'd be giving up their claim to power?" asked Malko skeptically.

"No, they want some power, but they're prepared not to take it all—at least, not the moment the coalition leaves. If the Taliban are in control of Kabul a year after we leave, we save face.

They'll be wielding the real power, of course, but officially, the new Afghan government will be holding the reins. Even if this doesn't fool anybody. After all, nobody blamed the Russians when the Taliban hung President Najibullah three years after they left."

Mulligan fell silent, then ordered another cup of coffee. The Hay-Adams dining room was emptying out. Some people were going back to work, others up to comfortable rooms where their lovers waited.

"And what's the price for the Taliban's indulgence?" asked Malko.

"Hamid Karzai," said Mulligan.

In the silence that followed, the two Americans' tension was almost palpable.

"So you're dropping him?" Malko asked carefully. "That should be easy. He's powerless without you."

Mulligan gave him a long, meaningful look.

"That's impossible, politically," he said. "We've been singing his praises to the world for the last decade. Officially he's our ally, through thick and thin."

"And unofficially?"

Mulligan's face betrayed nothing.

"He has to go."

This time, the silence that followed was even longer, eventually broken by the national security advisor.

"That's the mission I would like to assign you. To get rid of Karzai for us."

Malko felt a wave of vertigo. He never imagined that Barack Obama would go this far.

"Does the president know about this?"

Mulligan didn't blink.

"He has given me carte blanche. He doesn't want to know the

details. He just wants a guarantee that his administration will never be connected to this affair."

Malko was silent for a few seconds, unsure that he'd really heard right.

"What exactly do you have in mind?" he finally managed.

Luger leaned across the table.

"We considered several options, but the only effective one appears to be physically eliminating Hamid Karzai," he said in a low voice. "That's Mullah Omar's bottom-line condition for striking a deal with us."

The national security advisor spoke again.

"As I said at the start of this conversation, the president doesn't want to hear about that country anymore. My job is to work out an honorable transition, and for that we need the Taliban."

It all felt so overwhelming that Malko found himself unable to speak for a few moments. A representative of the president of the United States was asking him to assassinate the president of Afghanistan in order to please the Taliban.

And he wasn't dreaming. He was in the Hay-Adams Hotel, a stone's throw from the White House, in Washington, D.C. . . .

"If the Taliban are so eager to get rid of Karzai, why don't they do it themselves?" he asked Mulligan. "They've completely infiltrated Kabul, and they have plenty of means at their disposal."

The CIA deputy director answered for Mulligan.

"They have tried," said Luger. "Several times. They launched a mortar attack at a meeting Karzai was attending. And they recently sent a young Taliban messenger with a bomb hidden in his crotch that severely wounded the head of the NDS"—the National Directorate of Security.

"Karzai is paranoid. His movements are never announced in advance.

"He got rid of his Blackwater people and replaced them with

bodyguards from his tribe. He always wears a bulletproof vest under his robes. In the palace, every item is examined. Cell phones are forbidden. Aside from his intimates, Karzai hardly sees anyone."

Mulligan paused.

"I'll repeat my question," he said. "Will you undertake this assignment?"

Malko wanted to rub his eyes in disbelief.

"John, this mission is impossible," he said. "The Agency has everything it needs in Afghanistan. You operate a fleet of drones that can hit anything. What can you expect from one man against the Karzai machine? Besides, you know I'm not a killer."

"Are you turning it down?" asked the American sharply.

"No, I'm just voicing the questions I have to ask myself. I know Afghanistan, but that isn't enough for a mission like this."

"You wouldn't be alone," Luger immediately said. "We have a small asset in place who's never been connected to the Agency but has served us on many occasions. He'll be at your disposal."

"What kind of asset are you talking about?" asked Malko.

"A private contractor named Nelson Berry," said Luger. "He's a South African who set up a protection company for foreigners. Afghans also occasionally use him for risky jobs, like delivering currency in unsafe areas. We've asked him to carry out several 'gray' sanctions in the past, and he's always performed well. These days, his back is against the wall because he has high expenses and his customers are leaving Kabul. He contacted me to see if I had anything for him."

Malko was surprised.

"And you trust this man Berry enough to make him such an offer?"

"Yes, we do," said Luger. "He's been killing all his life, in South Africa and elsewhere. It will be up to you to convince him, with an irresistible offer."

"Do you think he has the means to assassinate Karzai?"

"I don't like the word 'assassinate,'" said Mulligan with a frown. "We're sidelining him, for reasons of state."

Sidelining . . . as in forever.

Malko looked at his two interlocutors in turn. They were perfectly serious, focused on their request. He really was being asked to kill the president of Afghanistan.

As if he could guess Malko's thoughts, Mulligan said, "You're the only person we can make this offer to, because of your capacities as a mission leader and because of the trust we have in you. You won't be responsible for the outcome, of course, but if you succeed, you'll be doing our country an enormous service. I certainly understand your scruples, but eliminating Karzai will prevent many deaths."

Malko was feeling boxed in. This proposal wasn't being made casually.

"Aren't you worried that Berry will just take the money and run?" he asked.

"I don't think so," said Luger. "I've been his handler myself. He says yes or no and names his price."

"Even for an assignment like this one?"

"For him, this would be a mission like any other," said Luger. "Just a little harder."

Malko could feel himself on a slippery slope. He tried to snag a rock to keep from going over the cliff.

"What role would the Kabul CIA station play in this?" he asked.

"It won't know the real purpose of your assignment. We'll tell the station people that you're coming to continue the negotiations with the Taliban that we began at Doha."

"With someone in Kabul?"

"Yes. Our Taliban friends gave us the name of a person you will meet, one Mullah Musa Kotak. Under the Taliban, he was the minister for the promotion of virtue and prevention of vice. Karzai named him to the High Peace Council, a thing he set up to bring in Talibs who might still be useful. Kotak is in close touch with the Quetta *shura*. He'll be told about your arrival."

"A former Taliban minister, and he's still in Kabul? That's amazing!"

The security advisor smiled.

"As you know, nothing is simple in Afghanistan. Kotak's a committed Talib, but the Karzai people have never given him any grief. He has a lot of influence within the Taliban. He might be able to help you."

In the face of Malko's silence, Luger added, "One other person may also be of help: we have a source within the NDS. He can give you information without asking how it will be used. He's also somebody who needs money. But you have to be very careful in contacting him. His name is Luftullah Kibzai."

The three men were now the only people left in the Hay-Adams dining room. Mulligan ostentatiously looked at his watch and said, "I can't stay with you any longer. The president is expecting me in half an hour for Chuck Hagel's debriefing. He just returned from Kabul, as it happens."

"Are you going to tell him about this conversation?" asked Malko in surprise.

"Absolutely not," said Mulligan.

Malko was starting to feel trapped. The tense silence lengthened, broken only by an occasional tinkle of glasses from the bar. Malko could feel the Americans' eyes on him. The men asking him to assassinate Hamid Karzai were honorable, honest, and clearly patriotic. In this muted, elegant setting, the whole thing seemed crazy, but there was no way to avoid the reality. He was being asked to become a killer for hire, like one of Israel's *kidonim*, for the most powerful nation on earth.

Malko understood his interlocutors. The United States couldn't afford to lose face. Even if this was a gamble, it had to be attempted.

"Very well, I accept the assignment," he said, "but on one condition."

"What?" the two men asked simultaneously.

"I'm doing this for free," he said. "I won't receive any compensation from the Agency. But if something happens to me, I want your word that I'll be given the honors I deserve, and not considered a gun for hire."

What might have been a tear appeared at the corner of Mulligan's eye.

"Malko, I swear that if anything happens to you, God forbid, you'll be buried in Arlington Cemetery in the company of those who gave their lives for our country."

CHAPTER 4

A machine gun protected by sandbags stood on the roof of the little Kabul airport terminal, manned by a lone helmeted Afghan soldier.

Along with the many combat helicopters parked at irregular intervals along the single runway, it was the only tangible sign of the war raging in Afghanistan. Just two civilian planes stood in front of the blue-and-white-striped terminal.

Gone were the flags of the various nations of the ISAF—the International Security Assistance Force—that once flew at half-staff when one of their troops was killed.

As Malko stepped down the stairs from the Flydubai Boeing 737, he spotted a white Land Cruiser a few yards away. A tall man in a down jacket with a pistol on his hip got out and approached him.

"Are you Malko Linge, sir?"

"That's right."

"I'm Jim Doolittle, one of Warren Michaelis's deputies. The COS asked me to meet you. Come with me, please."

Malko climbed into the Land Cruiser. Seated in back were two impassive Marines in full combat gear: helmet, M16, hand grenades, pistol.

Doolittle explained their presence. "We always have to have an escort in town," he said. "We go out as little as possible."

They drove over to the terminal, and Doolittle dropped Malko off at an empty garden opposite the building.

"Give me your baggage claim tickets and your passport, and wait here, please."

Doolittle's SUV had the permits required to park next to the terminal. The unwashed masses, on the other hand, were kept at a distance behind the first checkpoint, more than five hundred yards away. The terminal entrance was protected by coils of razor wire and guarded by soldiers, fingers on their AK-47 triggers.

The fear: car bombs.

Slumped on a park bench, Malko huddled in his cashmere overcoat. He had dozed on the flight from Dubai to Kabul and still felt bleary-eyed from the long trip.

Around him, the landscape of snow-covered mountains looked like the Alps.

A fairyland.

Once his Boeing 737 had crossed the crest of the mountains, it had descended to the plain on which Kabul stood at an altitude of fifty-nine hundred feet. Close up, it looked like less of a fairyland: around downtown the city spread like a cancer over the barren hills in vast shantytowns without water or electricity. The slums looked like the *morros* of Rio de Janeiro, minus the sea and the sun.

It was thought that Kabul had three million inhabitants, but nobody was really sure. The number could be higher. The last census had been taken forty years earlier.

What struck Malko was the silence. The last time he was in Kabul, coalition planes were constantly landing and taking off amid a hum of activity. Today there were no Americans left—they had pulled back to Bagram Air Base, forty miles from Kabul—and the only planes on the runway were C-130 Hercules turboprops in Afghan colors. A French contingent was stationed at the airport to oversee the return home of its last units, but it was nowhere to be seen.

As Doolittle drove out of the airport, Malko noticed that the controls weren't very strict. But the car still had to stop at the first checkpoint, then at a second, on a roundabout dominated by an old MiG-21 that looked ready to take off. As they swung onto Airport Road, the arrow-straight route downtown, Malko turned to Doolittle and asked:

"What's the mood in Kabul these days?"

"It's cool," said the American. "The ANA and the police run the city. There aren't many shootouts or kidnappings, just a car bomb from time to time."

Traffic was relatively light. A green Afghan police pickup with a dozen men in back roared past them. As before, the dusty avenue was lined with fruit and vegetable sellers.

You didn't feel you were in danger.

Ten minutes later, they reached the Massoud monument. The roundabout was dominated by a column with a big ball on top and hung with two enormous pictures of Ahmad Shah Massoud, hero of the Panjshir Valley and the Northern Alliance. Al-Qaeda agents had assassinated Massoud in his headquarters in September 2001.

Doolittle was soon forced to slow down. Downtown, the traffic was terrible. They made their way between rows of concrete walls twenty feet high topped by coils of razor wire. Punctilious checkpoints slowed the traffic further.

The only cars on the road were Toyotas, of every year and model, with both right- and left-hand drives.

"Seems like a lot of Toyotas," Malko remarked.

"About three-quarters of a million, sir. They come from the four corners of the earth."

Malko noticed many more flat Tajik *pakol* hats than he had on his last visit. One would think that the Tajiks controlled Kabul, which must get under the skin of the Pashtun majority.

Every thirty yards or so, they saw a man armed with an AK-47, in or out of some sort of uniform, guarding something or other. It made Kabul look like a city under siege.

"Are you still operating out of the Ariana?" Malko asked.

"Affirmative, sir."

The Ariana was a former hotel near the American embassy. It stood at the end of an avenue interrupted by roadblocks where the French embassy was located; it had once served as the Taliban's headquarters. The Ariana was the CIA's Maginot Line. With Agency numbers melting away and its case officers ordered to keep a low profile, not much was going on here.

The SUV was now moving at walking pace around Zarnegar Park through a flood of vehicles that included a few yellow taxis. There were no stoplights, just policemen in tattered gray uniforms waving little red disks to direct traffic.

A dense crowd, nearly all men, flowed along the sidewalks, with the occasional handcart adding to the chaos.

Despite the apparent calm, Doolittle watched the crowds of people as if they were wild animals. A little girl in rags with enormous eyes approached and extended a dirty little hand, her pleading face pressed against the bulletproof glass.

Piteous.

Doolittle gave her an angry glance.

"You've got to be careful, sir," he said. "A kid will ask you to lower your window to give them money, then toss in a grenade."

No risk of that happening with the Land Cruiser. Its windows were two and a half inches thick, and too heavy to be rolled down.

When Malko spotted the Kabul Serena Hotel, he noticed something new: a high wall had been erected between the hotel and the one-way street in front.

The Land Cruiser drove up onto the sidewalk, first passing a barrier of black-and-white metal tubes, and continued along the hotel wall. Three more checkpoints followed: the first to make sure the vehicle was authorized to enter the Serena, the second to run a mirror under the chassis. The third checkpoint, for passengers, was behind a pair of heavy sliding gates.

Driving military vehicles and wearing police uniforms, the Taliban had attacked the Serena in 2008 and killed half a dozen people. An investigation later showed that the head of the commandos, who died in the attack, had regularly enjoyed the hotel spa while scouting the area.

Passing the last gate, the Land Cruiser pulled up under the awning at the entrance to the hotel. A staffer in a turban greeted them with a broad smile.

"I'll wait here, sir," said Doolittle. "The COS wants to welcome you."

Malko had met Chief of Station Warren Michaelis three years earlier. He was a tall, lanky American who must now be near the end of his tour.

"Okay. I'll check in and come back out."

The hushed Serena lobby didn't exactly feel like party central. A few guests lounged on red benches around the central fountain. Malko checked in and went up to his room, number 382. He dropped off his things and went downstairs.

Getting out of the Serena was easier—just one checkpoint—and the Land Cruiser was soon back in the infernal traffic, made worse by the absence of stoplights. Power blackouts had become so common, the lights were simply switched off.

Eventually, they reached the avenue with the embassies of France and the United Arab Emirates. It was bordered by stone walls twenty feet high. Doolittle pointed down the street to a building topped by a kind of watchtower with a corrugated iron roof.

"We're almost home!" he said.

To reach the Ariana, they first navigated chicanes of concrete blocks that narrowed traffic to a trickle. These were followed by sandbag emplacements manned by Nepalese soldiers in black uniforms, weapons at the ready. The men were protected in turn by a guard tower with two heavy machine guns.

The walls around the compound were plastered with signs in English and Dari forbidding taking photographs, slowing down, and getting out of a car unless ordered to do so by the guards. Violators, they warned, would be shot on sight.

Doolittle zigzagged through the chicanes. The traffic barrier protecting the entrance to the Ariana was lowered, admitting the SUV to the hotel courtyard.

At the entrance, they again had to show their papers, and Doolittle phoned the CIA station chief from the guard post. He turned to Malko and said, "Mr. Michaelis is expecting you, sir. I'll accompany you because you don't have a badge."

The inside of the hotel hadn't changed since Malko's last visit: white walls, shabby rooms, electrical wires running every which way, and doors protected by electronic locks. Everybody carried photo badges well in evidence, including two embarrassed-looking Afghans. That was understandable: if the Taliban identified them, they could have their throats cut.

Every floor had a metal detector so sensitive that a paper clip would set it off.

Warren Michaelis was standing in front of his third-floor office in shirtsleeves. He extended a hand to Malko.

"Welcome back to Kabul! If you'd come a few months later, you would've missed me. I'm going home for good in June."

The station chief's small office had chicken wire over the windows, to protect against hand grenades. Maps covered the walls.

"Langley alerted me that you were coming," he said, "and said that your activities here had nothing to do with the station. Just the same, I've been told to be at your disposal. Is there anything you need?"

"Not for the moment," said Malko. "I'm here to make contact with some 'respectable' Talibs, to save the station problems with the Afghan government."

"That's not a bad idea," Michaelis said with a sigh. "Karzai is on the warpath, accusing us of colluding with the Taliban to extend our stay in Afghanistan. Actually, Washington doesn't want a single American on Afghan soil after December 31, 2014. You needn't tell me anything about your assignment, but I'll give you my cell numbers, as well as Jim Doolittle's. I've asked him to drive you around during your stay. I've also prepared a local phone for you, with a SIM card that can't be traced."

He handed Malko a bare-bones Nokia with the phone number printed on it.

"I have to leave you now," Michaelis said. "I have a meeting at ISAF. But let's have lunch together."

A half hour later, Malko was back at the Serena. His room overlooked a garden that still had some snow in it and came with a minibar that held only nonalcoholic drinks. The Serena chain had been bought by the Aga Khan and didn't serve liquor.

Using his personal phone, Malko called Nelson Berry, the man he hoped to persuade to kill Hamid Karzai.

A deep voice promptly answered.

"*Baleh.* Salaam alaikum."

"I'm looking for Nelson Berry," said Malko.

"Speaking. Who are you?"

"I'm a friend of Sherwood"—Clayton Luger's work name.

"Are you in Kabul?" asked the South African.

"I just arrived. Can we meet?"

"Sure. Where are you?"

"At the Serena."

"Good. In a half hour, walk out of the hotel and turn right. At the next intersection, there'll be a checkpoint with some police cars. Pass through it, walk another twenty yards, and wait there. A gray Corolla will pick you up. The driver's name is Darius Gul."

CHAPTER 5

Night was falling when Malko left the Serena, but the weather was pleasantly warm. He passed the police checkpoint at the next intersection and spotted Berry's car. It was an old gray Corolla with chipped paint and a cluster of artificial grapes hanging from the rearview mirror. The bearded Afghan at the wheel cracked open his door.

"Darius?" Malko asked.

"*Baleh.*"

When Malko walked around to open his door, he got a surprise: it weighed a ton.

Armored!

That was unexpected, for such an old car.

The Corolla took off sluggishly, its engine straining at the weight, and merged with the dense throng of Toyotas.

They turned onto Sharpoor Street, a wide avenue with a long wall twenty feet high on the left. It was broken only by a few entrances guarded by watchtowers, blocks of cement, and razor wire.

Darius, who hadn't spoken, waved at the complex and muttered, "NDS."

That was the National Directorate of Security, the domestic intelligence service. Oddly enough, it wasn't located within the city's fortified Green Zone. The Taliban would attack it with a car bomb from time to time and be mowed down by the guards.

It kept the NDS agents on their toes.

The Corolla passed in front of the enormous Iranian embassy and angled right. Here the street was lined by modern houses, several stories high, painted in garish colors and protected by armed guards. Afghans dubbed these monuments to bad taste "poppy palaces," because they were often owned by drug traffickers.

The car turned into a side street, jouncing along the muddy road. They passed a series of houses, each uglier and more imposing than the last. Darius stopped at a green metal gate protected by an enormous steel beam and two sinister-looking guards carrying AK-47s and wearing black vests with spare magazines. The gate opened and the Corolla pulled up in front of the house.

Inside, he led Malko to an office with several computers on a table piled high with files. A tan leather sofa stood next to a low table holding a folding AK-47.

The man who rose from behind the desk was a giant, standing nearly six foot three. His hair was an odd, orangish color, as if dyed. His massive shoulders and biceps strained against a black T-shirt. Sharp eyes, a pug nose, and a prominent chin made him look a bit like Quentin Tarantino. The hand he extended to Malko was practically a club.

"Nelson Berry," he said.

"Malko Linge. Sherwood sent me."

"Any friend of Sherwood is a friend of mine," said Berry. "Care for a *dop*?"

"Vodka, please."

Berry walked to a bar at the back of the room, poured them both some Tsarskaya, and raised his glass.

"To Afghanistan!" he said. "A beautiful country. Too bad I'll have to leave it soon."

When Berry sat down on the sofa, his pants hiked up, and Malko glimpsed a GK ankle holster with an automatic. The South African also had a Beretta 92 at his waist and a couple of clips.

Berry downed his vodka and glanced sideways at Malko.

"When was the last time you were in Kabul?"

"Three years ago."

"It's changed a lot since then," Berry said. "The coalition troops have pulled out and set up shop at Bagram. The Afghans are in charge of security in town."

"How is that working out?"

"It's okay. The Taliban don't want to cause *too* much chaos. They're keeping the pressure on the Karzai government, but they leave foreigners alone. You can walk the streets without fear of being shot or kidnapped, except maybe by thugs."

"The Serena looks more defended than before," remarked Malko.

"Yeah, it's one of their regular targets. Some Taliban hardliners want to drive the foreigners out of the country, but they're a minority.

"But from the business side, Kabul is chaos. Half of the houses around here are for rent. The other security companies have packed up, and there's no work left. I'm one of the last, and I don't know how long I can hold out. When the businesspeople leave, they don't need us anymore. The Afghans give us work from time to time, but they only pay pennies on the dollar.

"I was renting this house for fifteen thousand dollars a month. I got it down to eight thousand, but even at that price my expenses are too high. So I hope you've got good news for me, meaning a well-paid job. Sherwood has always been tops."

"That's the case, pretty much," said Malko cautiously. "It involves a 'neutralization.'"

"I've done plenty of those, but the Agency has changed. Outside of Kabul they're making like Special Forces and do the jobs themselves."

Berry sounded resentful.

"This action would be in Kabul."

"In Kabul? There are no Taliban targets here except for the washed-up guys Karzai has taken in."

"This doesn't involve them," said Malko, proceeding carefully. "This is a very focused, dangerous job. Extremely dangerous, actually."

"Okay, *bra*, we're not here to make snowballs," said the South African with a sigh. "Give me the whole story."

"Karzai," said Malko.

Berry gave him a look of surprise.

"How does this involve Karzai?"

When Malko didn't answer, the South African swore softly.

"Holy shit! You don't mean . . ."

"Yes, I do."

A long silence followed, eventually broken by Berry.

"If business were better, I'd pour you another vodka and we'd part friends. Only I'm in a bind. I don't even know how I'm going to pay next month's rent. But do you have any idea what you're asking? Even the Taliban haven't been able to attack Karzai, and they've got people everywhere."

Malko almost felt relieved.

"I understand," he said. "Forget about it."

Berry roused himself.

"Hang on a minute! I didn't say no; I just need time to think if this thing is doable. Give me two days. And I warn you, if I say yes, it's going to be very, very expensive."

"I don't think that'll be a problem."

"Karzai's got a very long arm. He controls the NDS and has lots of connections. And especially, he's extremely distrustful. Have you seen the station people, by the way?"

"They sent a car to pick me up at the airport."

"Do they know about this Karzai thing?"

"No. Officially, I'm here to negotiate with the Taliban."

Berry smiled ironically.

"Everyone's negotiating with the Taliban, even Karzai. Best not to tell the station anything."

"Why not?"

"You know a guy named Mark Spider?"

"No, I don't."

The South African poured himself another vodka.

"He's an Agency man, the one who brought Karzai on board in 2002. He was station chief here twice. Karzai owes him big-time and Spider does everything to protect him. He's gone back to Washington, but he still has people at the Ariana. If they get even a whiff of a threat, they'll warn Karzai. So be very, very careful."

Malko made a mental note of this detail, which Clayton Luger had forgotten to mention: that Hamid Karzai had moles within the CIA!

Malko needed to be sure he knew where he stood with Berry.

"Do you think this project is feasible?" he asked.

The South African gave him a chilly smile.

"Everything's feasible. It's a question of means and money. Luck, too. Okay, I—"

A ringing phone interrupted him. Berry had a brief conversation in Dari, hung up, and turned back to Malko.

"They've already searched your room at the Serena."

Malko felt an unpleasant chill run down his spine.

"Who did?"

"The NDS. It's normal; they do it to all the new arrivals. Do you have anything compromising?"

"I don't think so."

"It's no big deal," said the South African. "But I'll give you a secure local cell phone, just in case. They tap a lot of lines. Do you have contacts in the Taliban?"

"Just one," said Malko.

"Hang on to it! You never know, it could be useful. All right, I think we've said everything that needs saying. Just the same, I've got a housewarming present for you."

Berry went over to his desk and came back with an automatic pistol in a GK ankle holster and a folded sheet of paper.

"Here you go. It's a GSh-18, the model the Russian special forces use. Can't be traced. Strap it on your ankle. And this is the weapons permit that goes with it. It'll spare you some hassles."

Malko was dumbfounded.

"How did you get your hands on this?"

"I have a guy at the Interior Ministry who sells them to me for ten thousand afghanis," said Berry casually. "Fill out the form in your name. If you're stopped, the registration number will tell them where it's from, and they won't ask any questions. Do you need a car?"

"Not for the time being," said Malko.

Berry nodded approvingly.

"You're right to keep a low profile. In any case, everyone in town's gonna know who you are very fast." He stood up. "And if anybody wants to kill you, it'll be easy."

"By the way, is the Atmosphere still open?" asked Malko.

It was the only hot spot in Kabul, a restaurant-nightclub-café with a pool and music where the expats hung out.

"Yeah, but it's fallen off. The chow's lousy, and not many people go there anymore."

Malko suddenly thought of the young South African woman he'd once had a passionate fling with in Kabul. As a fellow South African in the city, maybe Berry knew her.

"Do you know if Maureen Kieffer is still in Kabul?"

Berry let out a roar.

"You know her? Yeah, she's here, and she's struggling, just like me. There's no market for armored cars anymore. Hell of a boss girl, isn't she?"

Berry gave Malko a crushing handshake and walked him out to the gray Corolla.

When Malko walked in, the hotel's metal detector started to beep, and he quickly pulled out his weapons permit and the magnetic door key that showed he was a hotel guest.

Once in his room, Malko dialed Maureen Kieffer's cell number, which he still had.

Amazingly, she picked up on the third ring.

"Maureen?"

"Who's calling, please?"

"Malko."

There was a long silence, than a joyous shout.

"Malko! Are you in Kabul?"

"Yes. What about you?"

"I'm still here, but I'll be going home soon. I don't have as much work as before. Everybody's leaving."

"Can we get together?"

"Of course! Are you at the Serena?"

"Yes. Want to have dinner at the Atmosphere?"

It was the place where they first met.

"We can do better," she said. "We'll go to the Boccaccio. I'll pick you up around eight. I'll phone from the car and you can come down. With the checkpoints, it's too complicated, otherwise."

Maureen Kieffer seemed more mature than the last time they were together. Two deep wrinkles framed her mouth, but she could still fill a sweater. She was wearing black cargo pants and boots. They shared a long hug, and when Malko brushed her large breasts, he felt a stirring of desire. She was as sexy as ever.

Malko's foot bumped into a folding AK-47 on the floor of her car.

"I better get going," she said. "Otherwise, they'll start shooting at us. They're so damned jumpy!"

"But your car's bulletproof," remarked Malko.

"Yeah, but then you have to touch up the paint."

She shifted into first, and the three-ton SUV lurched forward.

A quarter of an hour later they turned into the rutted alley where the Boccaccio stood. There was virtually no traffic in Kabul at night, except for green police pickups and a few taxis. Also no pedestrians, though the fruit and vegetable sellers kept their stands brightly lit in the faint hope of attracting customers.

Unlike other Kabul restaurants, which preferred anonymity, the Boccaccio displayed its name on a marble plaque atop a concrete security barrier.

The dining rooms were full of Afghans and foreigners, including a few Americans who had permission from the embassy. The black stone walls gave the place an exotic look, as did the Russian waitresses, whose skimpy outfits would give a Talib a heart attack. You got the feeling they weren't here just to wait on tables.

Maureen and Malko were led to a table in the back room, and a young waitress came to take their order.

"Champagne!" said Malko.

Here, alcohol was served.

A bottle of Roederer Cristal arrived in a few moments.

"I see that you haven't forgotten what I like," Maureen said with a grin. "The restaurants get their supplies from the embassy cooks, who steal from the diplomats."

They clinked glasses.

"I never thought I'd see you again," she said. "Anyway, I'm heading back to South Africa soon. There's nothing left to do here."

They ordered what turned out to be some very decent carpaccio and pasta.

People were talking loudly, and the atmosphere was animated.

Maureen lowered her voice.

"The boss is a crook," she said. "He cheated a lot of people, and he did time in Dubai, but at least it feels cheerful here."

By the time Maureen and Malko were finished, the room was emptying. Afghans started work very early in the morning, and people didn't stay up. Besides, darkened streets weren't exactly inviting, even though police cars were parked at checkpoints at every intersection.

"Want to go back to my place?" asked Maureen.

There weren't more than a half dozen cars in the little street. The avenues were deserted, and once you were off the main arteries, the pavement was terrible. You'd almost think the city was abandoned. At each checkpoint, you had to slow down and switch on your dome light.

The usual wartime routine.

Maureen pulled up in front of her guesthouse and honked. Two Afghans carrying AK-47s and wrapped in heavy *patu* cloaks against the night cold opened the double gate.

Soon they were in the apartment Malko remembered from his

previous visit. The living room had a big flat-screen television, lots of rugs, and a long sectional sofa. A wood fire in the fireplace warmed the room. It felt very civilized.

Without a word, Maureen pulled her cashmere sweater over her head, revealing a much more feminine lacy black bra. Then she sat down to take off her boots and cargo pants. Her black string panty matched her bra perfectly and quickly came off as well.

She stretched voluptuously before disappearing into the kitchen. When she came out a few moments later, she had a bottle of champagne and her eyes were bright with excitement.

"Get undressed," she told him. "I'm going to hose you down."

Malko knew her habits and didn't argue. He undressed, helped by the young woman, who seemed eager to see him naked. That done, she propped him in front of the fire on a stack of big cushions, then leaned over and started to masturbate him. When she was satisfied with the result of her efforts, she jumped up and said, "Whatever you do, don't move!"

Maureen's plan was simple: she was going to spray Malko's belly with champagne, the way they did at Formula One finishes. But just as she picked up the bottle, they heard a scratching at the door, followed by a few low words in Dari. Maureen stopped what she was doing and answered, also in Dari. The door opened to admit a small girl in a head scarf, who ignored the fact that her mistress was naked, as was Malko.

"What's the matter, Narifar?" asked Maureen.

The little maid said a few quiet words, then backed out of the room.

"What's going on?" asked Malko.

"There's a guy hiding in the alley," said Maureen. "He's on a motorcycle."

CHAPTER 6

Maureen put on a robe and set the champagne on a cof-fee table. She then picked up her Kalashnikov and left the room. Not knowing what else to do, Malko put on his pants.

She returned a few minutes later, followed by her two Afghan guards. They were frog-marching a skinny and clearly terrified young man between them. One of the two spoke to Maureen in a respectful tone, and she translated for Malko.

"They say he was lurking in the alley. He must have followed us from the Boccaccio."

"What does he want?"

"We'll ask him."

She said a few words in Dari, and a guard took a curved dagger from his belt and set it against the man's throat. He shrank away from it in fear. Maureen said something to him sharply, again in Dari.

"I told him to tell the truth," she said to Malko, "or we'll cut his throat."

When their prisoner remained silent, one of the guards grabbed his hair and yanked his head back. He screamed and immediately started talking. Maureen translated as they went along.

"He says someone ordered him to follow you. Apparently he was waiting in front of the Serena, though I didn't notice him. Says he was tipped off from inside the hotel, which is how he knew when you were going out."

"Who is this 'someone'?" asked Malko.

"An NDS guy who hires him to tail people. They meet at a restaurant where a lot of cops go."

She gave a crisp order, and the two guards led the young man out of the room.

"The NDS seems to mistrust you," she said. "They're on edge these days. Were you aware of this?"

"I know they're interested in me," said Malko, remembering the search of his room.

His mission was off to a great start. Maureen let her robe fall to the floor and came over to gently rub her body against Malko. The contact with her warm skin immediately gave him an erection, which the young woman happily seized. When she judged it firm enough, she pushed Malko over to the sofa and fetched the champagne.

She popped the cork, shook the bottle, and aimed it at Malko's belly. When she slipped her thumb aside, a flood of champagne washed over his stomach and cock.

Now satisfied, she set the bottle down, kneeled on the carpet, and started licking the champagne off Malko's belly. Then she turned to his stiff cock, first licking it like a cat, then suddenly taking it in her mouth.

Afterward, she shifted onto the sofa, while continuing to lick him.

"There are two things I love," she said with a sigh. "Good champagne and sucking a man with a stiffy. Now it's your turn."

She lay back, spreading her legs to reveal a tuft of reddish hair. Malko moved on top and sank deep inside her.

Maureen bounced to his rhythm, tightening her thighs around his hips and giving a little cry with each of his thrusts. It felt delicious.

With a hoarse shout, Malko came.

"Lucky I had some champagne in the house," she said with a cheerful laugh a few moments later. "God, it's good to fuck!"

"Is your maid used to seeing you with men this way?"

Maureen laughed again, heartily.

"Sure. I have two Uzbek girls. They're as quiet as mice, and they live ten times better here than in their villages. Besides, they're illiterate, so they're discreet."

She was already getting dressed, first putting on her panties, then her black cargo pants. She pulled on her sweater without bothering with a bra.

"What are you doing?" asked Malko.

"I'm escorting you back to the hotel. You seem to have some enemies in Kabul. I don't know what you're doing here, but you'd better be careful if you want to leave in one piece!"

The temperature had dipped a few degrees, but the sky was still an astounding cobalt blue.

It was three o'clock in the afternoon, time for Malko to meet Mullah Kotak, the former Taliban minister Mullah Beradar had named at the Doha meeting. Thanks to some mysterious connections, Mullah Musa Kotak had managed to stay on in Kabul and was now a member of the High Peace Council, an organization created by President Karzai as a channel to the Taliban.

Malko didn't know if Kotak was aware of the Americans' plan, but he would always be a useful contact. He apparently spent every afternoon at the Wazir Akbar Khan mosque, in a building on the mosque grounds.

Jim Doolittle, the case officer who had picked Malko up at the airport, drove Malko there in a white CIA Land Cruiser. There was no point in hiding his movements. The fact that his room had been searched and his dinner date followed showed that NDS agents were keeping an eye on him. Plus, he had obviously been spotted at immigration. The NDS must figure he had come to talk with the Taliban. Malko was happy to let them think that.

The Land Cruiser stopped next to a fence, through which Malko could see a bare garden and a shabby-looking modern building.

"This is the mosque, sir," said Doolittle. "I'll wait for you here."

Malko got out and took the path inside. An open area in front of the mosque was covered with worn carpets. In it, a man wrapped in a *patu* lay on his back, talking on his phone. Others were kneeling and praying.

Malko walked around the building to the rear of the mosque. A young Afghan with round glasses appeared, wearing a *shalwar kameez*—traditional tunic and trousers. In English, he asked Malko what he wanted.

"I'm here to see Mullah Kotak."

"Follow me," said the man.

Malko entered a large room with a hard dirt floor, cob walls and ceiling, and a few pieces of rickety furniture. Shelves of books covered one wall, and a couple of computers stood on the desk.

At the back of the room, a fat man propped up on cushions on the floor was eating. He gave Malko a happy salute.

"Salaam alaikum! I heard you'd arrived in Kabul," he explained in fluent English. "Did you have a good trip?"

"Excellent," said Malko to the mullah, who waved him to a nearby cushion.

"One of the faithful just brought me some stew. It's lamb with candied fruits, and absolutely delicious. Would you like a taste?"

Malko politely declined, and Kotak went back to eating greedily. Between bites, he said, "Life is so hard that whenever Allah sends me something good, I enjoy it to the fullest."

The cleric was so fat, he had to lean over just to reach his plate. Kotak looked like a harmless little Buddha, but he had harshly applied sharia law when the Taliban ruled from 1996 to 2001.

He finished eating, drank some fruit juice, and fell back on his cushions with a happy smile.

"I am not the imam of this mosque, but I come here every afternoon to see people and receive visitors. My apartment is too small and far from downtown. What do you think of Kabul today?"

"It seems pretty quiet."

The mullah gave a laugh that ended with a slight belch.

"President Karzai's people claim that our Taliban friends aren't in the city. They say they're all out in the provinces and that the ones who come to launch attacks are from Logar or Maidan Wardak. It's almost true."

"Why 'almost'?"

Kotak laughed again.

"Because in Kabul, the Taliban are everywhere! We've infiltrated all the ministries, the army, the police, the bazaar. We know everything that's going on." He lowered his voice. "There are even Taliban in the president's entourage, though he won't admit it."

He heaved a heavy sigh and continued.

"If only Allah would rid us of this cowardly, corrupt man, this traitor to his country!"

He paused, clearly giving Malko a chance to take the hint. When he didn't, Kotak went on.

"I don't know what you've come to do in Kabul, but if I can help in any way, it would be an honor and pleasure. Are you planning to go to Quetta?"—the seat of Mullah Omar's *shura* in Pakistani Baluchistan.

"I don't know yet," said Malko cautiously.

The cleric made a gesture that was almost a blessing.

"In spite of my modest position, I have many friends around the country. If you want to travel there in safety, I can help you."

Their eyes met. Kotak's gaze was impenetrable, but Malko understood from this brief conversation that the Taliban had just "approved" him, as Clayton Luger had predicted. It also meant that they might be able to help him in case of trouble.

"Thank you very much for your welcome," he said.

The cleric struggled to his feet from the worn carpet and took Malko's right hand in both of his.

"Please come back whenever you like!"

Once back in his hotel room, Malko took stock. He had one last contact to make: Luftullah Kibzai, the CIA's mole inside the NDS. Going to his office was out of the question. Though instructed not to, he would have to telephone him.

The number rang for a long time before an almost inaudible man's voice answered with a few words in Dari. When Malko spoke, his accent must have shown him to be a foreigner, and the man continued in English.

"Who are you?" he asked.

"I'm a friend of Sherwood's, and I just arrived in Kabul. Can we meet?"

There was a long silence on the line, as Kibzai hesitated.

"We could have dinner at the Sufi," he finally said. "It's in the Taimani neighborhood. Around eight o'clock."

"Perfect," said Malko.

Night was starting to fall, and Malko had nothing else to do. The Serena was three-quarters empty and the bar didn't serve liquor, so he fell back on watching CNN. Among other things, he learned that Lance Armstrong had admitted to doping in his Tour de France races.

Malko was still watching the news when Berry phoned.

"How's it going, *bra*?"

"So far, so good," said Malko.

"Let's meet tomorrow morning. Pick you up at the same place, at nine o'clock?"

"That works for me."

The South African was apparently starting to find the idea of assassinating President Karzai appealing.

CHAPTER 7

The Sufi's nearly empty dining room lay in a gloom pierced only by the gleam of the candles on its tables. A waiter in an embroidered vest led Malko past a big stove to a second room, where a man spotted him and waved.

"I'm the person you are meeting," he said, as if afraid to say his own name.

"You're Luftullah Kibzai?" asked Malko.

"Yes," the NDS agent breathed, looking like a deer caught in the headlights.

Kibzai ordered for them both, glanced around, and spoke in a low voice. "I have to be careful. For some time now, President Karzai has been angry with the Americans. I have an advantage because officially my job is to maintain relationships with my opposite numbers in the CIA, and to oversee the negotiations over the return of the Bagram prison to the Afghan authorities."

"What's the situation in Kabul?" asked Malko.

"There aren't any more large-scale attacks," he said. "Though a few weeks ago a female suicide bomber blew up a minibus with seven South Africans who were working as pilots for NATO. Otherwise, the streets are quiet. The army controls the city."

"So everything's fine," said Malko.

"No, it isn't. At the NDS, we're worried. The Taliban have

sleeper agents everywhere. They know everything. They even knew the security plans of the last *loya jirga* assembly.

"They can infiltrate and strike at will. We discovered there's a huge traffic in stolen uniforms. You can get a pair of military boots for three hundred afghanis—about six dollars. A uniform costs five hundred afghanis; a coat, two thousand. With that you can outfit people very easily."

Kibzai reminded Malko that every Afghan family had members on both sides, and the dividing line could be pretty porous. Three months earlier, a sergeant who'd been in the army for four years drove to the Ministry of Defense at the wheel of a general's car. It had an "A" pass on the windshield, which exempted it from searches. Once he was inside, he detonated two hundred pounds of explosives. It was later discovered that his cousin was an important Taliban leader.

Under a surface calm, Kabul was apparently seething with violence.

The restaurant started filling up, mainly with Afghans. Malko lost his appetite when his entrée came: a glutinous mass of rice and tough chunks of mutton. Pushing his plate aside, he asked, "Does President Karzai really know how bad the situation is?"

"Of course!" said Kibzai. "We give him alarming reports every day. For example, he knows that south of Kabul members of the Haqqani network secretly force members of the police and the army to sign statements declaring their loyalty to the Taliban. With that kind of document, they've got a hold over them. They're ruthless, and people are afraid of them. Not long ago, the Taliban approached a truck driver who delivered merchandise to the ISAF in Bagram. They asked him to bring in a large, remote-controlled explosive device. He refused. The next day, they strangled his son.

"And three days ago, a woman came to our headquarters and killed a Tajik officer who had been arresting Taliban leaders. She showed the NDS guards all the right passes, walked into his office, pulled out a gun with a silencer, and shot him twice in the head. Then she calmly strolled out. We still have no idea who she was."

"Are you frightened yourself?" asked Malko.

The Afghan nodded. "Of course, because I'm known to be close to the Americans. If the Taliban take power, I won't be able to stay in Kabul. I already don't dare visit my home village. The Taliban are in charge there."

"It sounds as if the Taliban are everywhere," concluded Malko.

Kibzai nodded again, sadly. "Yes. The provinces are falling one after the other. The Americans have evacuated Kunar, in the northeast, and government officials don't go there anymore. Close to Kabul, the Taliban have taken over Logar Province. Except for the big towns during the day, they control everything. The governor doesn't dare leave his residence.

"It's even worse in the south. They completely control Kandahar Province; Helmand, too. You can't use the Herat-Kandahar-Kabul highway anymore. I'm told they're infiltrating around Bamyan, cutting the road to the west. The only safe one is the Mazar-e-Sharif highway through the Salang Tunnel, because it's in Tajik territory."

"So what keeps the Taliban from coming out into the open and taking power?" asked Malko.

"They lack enough matériel for a direct confrontation with the army and the police," said Kibzai. "They've only got a few mortars, machine guns, grenades, and explosives. But they're prepared to die.

"President Karzai is smart and very cautious. Plus he's protected by the Americans. They don't like him, but they need him. If he were out of the picture—because he'd been killed or left the country—everything would collapse, probably in a few days. The Taliban already have a working underground organization, so they would quickly take over."

Malko was feeling more and more perplexed. From what Kibzai was saying, the American plan to get rid of Karzai so as to strike a deal with the Taliban was a delusion. Once again, it looked like the Americans were being fooled. Only this time it wasn't some CIA station chief but the president of the United States.

"So if I understand what you're saying," Malko asked, "Karzai's death would be a victory for the Taliban?"

"They're going to win in any case," said Kibzai with a bitter smile. "They're Pashtuns, and the Pashtuns have always run Afghanistan. Besides, they have Pakistan behind them.

"Anybody who wants to control Afghanistan has to do it through the Quetta Taliban. And the Taliban have developed a more sophisticated approach than when they took power the first time, in 1996. They'll go slower and won't be so brutal, so as not to alarm international public opinion. When the last American leaves, they will complete their takeover."

Malko suddenly found himself wondering if even attempting this mission was a good idea. The problem was, he would have to return to Washington to persuade John Mulligan to change his mind. Communicating through the Kabul CIA station was out of the question.

Kibzai was studying him.

"If you don't mind my asking," he said, "what are you doing in Kabul? There are already so many of you CIA people here."

"I've come to make contact with some Taliban who don't want to be officially connected to the Agency. I've already met with Musa Kotak. Do you know him?"

"Who doesn't?" said the Afghan with a smile. "He's a very powerful man. He was part of the ruling circle during the 'black years.'"

"How is it that he hasn't been bothered?"

"He's one of the people Karzai protects, to keep a channel to Quetta open. Kotak holds a major trump card: he knows everybody who collaborated with the men in black, and he manipulates them. For a Talib, he is a moderate, like Mullah Mansur, his old mujahideen comrade-in-arms against the Soviets. But his friends keep a close eye on him."

"Why so?"

"The Taliban hardliners don't trust him. I'm sure they've placed their people in his entourage."

"What's the relationship between Kotak and Karzai like?"

"They have regular contacts, to pass messages. And there's still a chance that if Karzai felt all was lost, he could turn against the Americans and hand the country to the Taliban to save his skin. Afghanistan has already witnessed about-faces like that. It wouldn't surprise anybody. They would just hang the seconds-in-command."

As Kibzai talked, thoughts were clashing in Malko's mind. President Karzai trusted Mullah Kotak, who was working behind his back. It was likely that Kotak already knew about Malko's plan. But didn't the Americans want to get rid of Karzai precisely to avoid a betrayal on his part?

"You have to move cautiously," Kibzai was saying. "The Taliban aren't a unified block, and only the Pakistanis know exactly who is who. Musa Kotak is powerful, but he doesn't control everything."

"I'll be careful," Malko assured him. "I have a question: Do you know if your NDS colleagues are interested in me?"

"Of course they are!" said the Afghan with a grin. "We have a special section that deals with foreigners suspected of being here on 'unofficial business.' I'll try to find out more, and we can meet again here in two days, if you like. It's best not to use telephones. The Russians trained us very well."

The NDS agent, who had cleaned his plate, looked at his watch.

"I have to head home now," he said. "I live far away. I'll see you here in two days."

As Malko watched Kibzai leave, he wondered what he was getting himself into. Not only did his mission seem impossible, but there was nobody here he could trust. Maybe he would know more tomorrow, after his meeting with Nelson Berry.

Malko found himself secretly hoping the South African would turn his offer down. That would solve a lot of problems.

CHAPTER 8

Nelson Berry greeted Malko in full combat gear, with a pistol on his hip.

"I had to get up very early, to deliver some money in Logar for people who work for the coalition," he explained.

"Couldn't they go themselves?"

"No, they're scared. It's dangerous to go walkabout with ten million afghanis in cash. There are plenty of roadblocks, even without the Taliban. But they don't dare attack us."

Berry paused. "Want some coffee? It's American."

"No, thanks."

Looking pleased with the success of his delivery, Berry flopped down on the sofa next to Malko.

"I've thought it over," he said. "I'll take the job."

When Malko didn't react, Berry turned to him in surprise.

"Aren't you pleased?"

"Yes, of course I am. What are your terms?"

The South African smiled.

"When you hear them, you might want to say no."

Malko remained impassive.

Berry might be a killer, but he was also a good negotiator.

"I'm listening," said Malko.

"I want a million dollars in front money, and three times that much when the job's done."

"That's a huge amount of money!"

"For a job you can't give to anyone else. You know that as well as I do. About the front money, I need five hundred thousand in cash here, and five hundred thousand to be paid to my bank in Dubai. I'll give you the account number.

"I won't be keeping all that money, by the way. I have to pay off people big-time to get information, and I'll be risking my neck every time I approach someone. If Karzai gets wind of this project, I'm a dead man."

He paused again. "Are we agreed on the price?"

"I'll transmit your proposal," said Malko cautiously, "and give you an answer within twenty-four hours."

"Okay," said Berry. "I don't start working until the money's paid. If I weren't at the end of my tether, I'd never take this job. It's much too risky. Karzai's still very powerful. Plus, you never know who's on your side here. Pashtuns have treachery in their blood."

"Do you have an idea about how to do this?" asked Malko.

The South African looked at him sharply.

"I know how *not* to do it, and that's by attacking Karzai in his palace. The security there is intense. Now that he's kicked the Blackwater guys out of Afghanistan—too trigger-happy—he's protected by men from his home village. Real bulldogs. Illiterate Pashtuns, and you can't bribe them. There's always two of them in his office when he has a visitor, fingers on the triggers.

"The Taliban have tried to get suicide bombers into the palace and never get past the front door. Last year one blew himself up after he was searched."

Malko had heard about the assassination attempt. It had nearly killed Asadullah Khalid, the head of the NDS.

"They took all the usual precautions, of course," said Berry.

"Put him up in a guesthouse, made him change his clothes in a room that had surveillance cameras, to make sure he didn't have any explosives. He took off his clothes and put on the ones the NDS gave him. The cameras didn't show any explosives, so they took him in to see Khalid."

When they embraced, there was an explosion, said Berry.

"The Talib had hidden an explosive behind his balls," said Berry. "Out of modesty, the surveillance cameras only filmed him down to the waist. Khalid was badly hurt and hasn't been well enough to return to his job at the NDS. His deputy, Parviz Bamyan, is running the show."

"So what options does that leave you?" asked Malko.

"The only way to hit Karzai is to shoot him during one of his trips to the airport when he goes abroad or out to the provinces."

"If you could find a position along his route, would you have a chance?" asked Malko.

"He's got armored Mercedes that'll stand up to everything short of an RPG-6," said Berry. "Plus the motorcade uses three of them at the same time, so you never know which one Karzai is in. And the NDS closes off the whole route."

"Isn't there some other way?"

"Sure, send him a chick with a bomb in her pussy!" Berry laughed loudly. "I'm kidding. His wife is a doctor who lives at the palace, and he doesn't chase women.

"So that's it. The ball's in your court now. You bring me the money, and we agree on the rest; then I'll really start thinking. And now, I'll have you driven back to the Serena. Be careful!"

Malko had called Warren Michaelis an hour earlier about using the CIA's secure communication links, and the station chief now welcomed him warmly.

"I gather you want to call Langley."

"Yes. I need to talk to Clayton Luger."

"No problem. Come with me."

Michaelis led him to a guarded, bunker-like room with digital code access at the end of a hallway. Once inside, he pointed to a green telephone.

"That's a secure line to Langley. I'll leave you to it."

Michaelis left, closing the door behind him.

Malko couldn't help thinking that while the line might be secure against outside eavesdroppers, the station itself probably recorded everything. But if he wanted to communicate with Washington, he didn't have any choice.

The deputy director answered but stopped him as soon as Malko gave his name.

"Call me back on 8453," he said. "I'm not free here."

Malko did so.

"Have you made any progress?" Luger asked.

"A little," said Malko carefully. "It's a tricky situation, and I wonder if you aren't taking the wrong tack."

There was a long silence on the line.

"I thought the basic issue was settled at our meeting," Luger eventually said. "What do you need?"

"A million dollars up front, half of it in cash. For the balance, I'll text you an account to credit. It's in Dubai."

"Okay, okay, don't say too much. There's no problem with your request. I'll give the station instructions. Anything else?"

"The weather in Kabul is nice."

"Keep me posted," said Luger, and hung up.

Once again, Malko found himself thinking he didn't like this mission. It certainly wasn't the first time the CIA had wanted to kill a political opponent, but in the case of Karzai, he wasn't sure it was the right approach. The Americans didn't grasp how devious Afghan thinking could be.

Michaelis was waiting for Malko in his office and greeted him with a smile.

"Is all well at home?"

"Seems to be," said Malko.

The station chief was clearly curious about his conversation, but Malko said only, "You'll get instructions to give me five hundred thousand dollars. How is that handled?"

"We don't work with the banks here. When we need cash, we send a message to Dubai and the money comes to Bagram. You should have it in a day or two. But watch out for the NDS. They won't like you talking to the Taliban, and they might try to give you trouble."

"What do you mean?"

Michaelis shrugged.

"I don't know. Plant drugs in your room, stage an accident. Get some crazy guy to attack and stab you. It wouldn't be anything direct, but it could hurt."

En route back to the Serena, Malko found a text message that had come in while he was at the Ariana:

I have to talk to you. Maureen.

He phoned her, but when she answered, the racket at her end was so loud he could barely hear.

"I'm in the workshop," she yelled. "I'm doing a rush job."

"Can I come see you?"

"No problem. You have a car?"

"Yes, but the driver's an American."

"I'll never be able to tell him the way. Wait in front of the Serena. I'll send my car and driver. It'll be half an hour."

Maureen's driver took Malko to her guesthouse, then to the workshop.

The place was full of Afghans, all busy welding. Malko spotted the young woman crouching near a smashed Toyota, also welding. She was wearing fatigue pants and a tight pink tank top. She stood and pushed her goggles up onto her forehead.

"I'm sorry," she said. "I've got an urgent repair job, and my guys can't handle it on their own. But I'll take a tea break with you."

She put down her welding goggles and torch and walked ahead of him into her apartment. To a little Uzbek maid, she shouted, "Chai!"

"Are you making headway in your business?" she asked when they were alone.

"Yes, some," he said. "Incidentally, I wanted to ask you something. Do you ever work on Karzai's armored vehicles?"

She laughed.

"I'd love to, but an American outfit got the contract, and they're milking it. Besides, he uses imported Mercedes. In the old days, when Blackwater handled his security, the guys would bring me their Toyotas for repairs. That's all over now. Anyway, Karzai doesn't go out very often, and only to the airport. There's no chance he'll ever wear out his Mercedes."

"They're heavily reinforced, aren't they?"

"It's the M-Class model," she said. "I once inspected one, for fun. It would stand up to anything."

"Even an RPG-7?"

"No, probably not. And the Taliban now have RPG-27s, which are much more powerful. Besides, if you pack seven hundred pounds of explosives in the car next to it . . ."

"Why are you asking me this?" Maureen wanted to know. "Are you planning to blow Karzai up? It'll win you a lot of friends."

She was joking, and Malko made no effort to set her straight. But suddenly, she turned serious.

"Actually, why *are* you asking me all these questions? Why so interested in Karzai's cars?"

"Just idle curiosity," Malko assured her. "By the way, you sent me a text saying you wanted to talk. What about?"

"I got a strange message about you," she said, "and I wanted to warn you. It has me worried."

CHAPTER 9

Malko felt uneasy. Maureen Kieffer was a no-nonsense woman. If she was worried, it wouldn't be without reason.

"What's going on?" he asked.

"An Afghan I know called me this morning. He talked about you and our dinner at the Boccaccio. He wound up saying that it would be best if I weren't seen with you."

"Who is he?"

"A guy I've dealt with a few times, an NDS agent. I think he's in love with me."

"What do you think this means?"

"That the NDS is watching you? I don't know, but I bet you do."

The unspoken question was clear. Malko decided to tell her part of the truth.

"The CIA and Washington asked me to come here to make contact with certain members of the Taliban."

"That would explain it," she said. "Contacts between the Taliban and the Americans are Karzai's nightmare. If the NDS is suspicious of you, watch your step. They can mess you up in very nasty ways."

Which was pretty much what Warren Michaelis had told him.

"I'll be careful," Malko promised, "and we'll be discreet. Do they have ways to retaliate against you?"

"In Afghanistan, if the president doesn't like you, anything's possible. They can expel you from one day to the next, even if your papers are in order. I'd hate if that happened. Anyway, there you have it; I wanted to warn you. I'm going back to work now."

"Why does the NDS handle this sort of problem?"

"It's the only agency that hasn't been infiltrated by the Taliban. The NDS answers directly to Karzai. Its agents are his muscle, and they're good at their job. If the Taliban ever come back to power, those guys better hop on the first plane out of here. Otherwise they'll all be hanged, after being tortured."

Which didn't tell Malko who had tipped the NDS off about him.

The young South African woman was looking at him anxiously. "I really have to leave you now," she said. "I need to finish fixing that car, and it's gonna take me half the night. My driver will take you back. Be careful! You can't trust anybody here."

She kissed him, pressing her body against his, and smiled.

"I'd still like to enjoy you a little more while you're in Kabul."

Malko had been turning in circles since the previous evening. He'd had no word from Michaelis, and without any money, he couldn't contact Nelson Berry. He didn't feel like going out for a stroll, and the Serena's nonalcoholic bar was depressing, so he spent his time shuttling between his room and the dining room. Finally, his phone beeped: a text message.

A courier will be at your place in an hour. WM. That had to be the money destined for Berry. Malko dialed the South African's poppy palace, and an Afghan answered in strongly accented English: "Commander not here. In Wardak until tomorrow."

A short time later, a young CIA case officer brought Malko a briefcase full of hundred-dollar bills in plastic wrappers from the Arab Bank in Dubai.

"It's five hundred thousand dollars, sir," he announced. "I have a receipt for you to sign."

Malko initialed the form next to his name. As much as anything, the CIA was one big bureaucracy.

"Did you go to Dubai to get this money?"

"Affirmative, sir. It's easiest, and we come back through Bagram. There are special flights that aren't subject to Afghan inspection. I make the trip often."

Once alone, Malko closed the briefcase, wondering what he was going to do with the money until the next day. The safe in his hanging closet was much too small. He wound up stowing the briefcase inside his suitcase, which he locked. It wasn't much, but it was better than nothing.

He now had just one meeting left: his dinner with NDS agent Luftullah Kibzai.

Inside, the Sufi was as dark as ever. Malko sat down at the same table as before. There were even fewer people in the restaurant than there had been the last time.

Kibzai showed up ten minutes later.

"I'm taking a big risk by contacting you," he said in a tense voice the moment he was seated.

"Why?" asked Malko.

"I was able to see part of your file. You were right; you were targeted. We have been tracking you since you arrived. A team was waiting for you at the airport."

Malko felt an unpleasant prickling on the backs of his hands.

So it wasn't his visit to Musa Kotak that had sparked the surveillance, he realized. And that raised a lot of questions.

"Why would they do that?"

Kibzai lowered his voice even further.

"I don't know. Our agents don't usually follow CIA people; there are too many of them. You were targeted specially. The order came from the head of the agency. I have the feeling they already knew something about you."

Malko felt a chill. The Afghans didn't have a crystal ball, so the information could only have come from Washington.

"Do you know anything more?" asked Malko.

"No, and I'm going to ask you not to contact me again, except in an emergency. I could get in very serious trouble. It might already be too late."

He seemed panicky.

Malko was starting to understand the warning given to Maureen Kieffer. The Afghans were doing whatever they could to isolate him. And this was probably just the beginning. The NDS had surely noted his visit to Nelson Berry. What would they make of that?

This was no longer an impossible mission, he thought. It was a suicide mission. He would have to warn Washington as soon as possible, he decided.

The NDS agent put the menu down.

"Would you mind if I left now? I'm not hungry, and I only came because I promised."

"That's all right," said Malko. He wasn't hungry either.

After a weak handshake, Malko watched Kibzai slip out like a shadow. There was nothing left for him to do but call Jim Doolittle and be driven back to the Serena.

It was eight in the morning when his cell phone rang. Nelson Berry apologized for calling so early.

"I got in at two a.m. Did you phone yesterday?"

"Yes, I did," said Malko. "Send me Darius, please."

Malko would have to tell Berry about the NDS surveillance. It might upset him, maybe even make him back out of the whole project. But he didn't have any choice.

Malko took the briefcase with the five hundred thousand dollars downstairs and left the hotel. The day was chilly, and he drew his cashmere coat a little tighter. Past the police checkpoint, he spotted the Corolla. He got in and laid the precious briefcase on the floor.

Darius was as silent as ever. They drove down Sharpoor Street, first passing NDS headquarters, then "poppy palace row," eventually reaching the rutted road that led to Berry's house. Suddenly Darius slammed on the brakes and uttered a brief curse. The jolt made Malko look up. A car was stopped across the road.

Moments later, both the Corolla's front doors were yanked open at the same time. Malko saw men with guns, their faces hidden by ski masks.

One grabbed Darius by the arm and threw him to the ground. When he tried to get up, the man pistol-whipped him, and he collapsed. The masked man immediately got behind the wheel, while a second climbed in the backseat and jammed his gun into Malko's neck. Malko wasn't even carrying the pistol Berry gave him—not that it would have done much good.

The man at the wheel shifted into reverse, and the Corolla jounced backward out onto Sharpoor Street. Not a word had been spoken.

He'd been kidnapped!

CHAPTER 10

Malko didn't dare move. At least he hadn't been shot immediately. That was a good sign.

Continuing down Sharpoor Street, the Corolla passed any number of armed guards, none of whom paid it the slightest attention. Twenty minutes later, after a complicated route through back alleys, the car entered a small courtyard. Several men immediately surrounded it.

Malko was taken out and searched and relieved of his cell phone.

Another man took the briefcase with the money and led him into a kind of workshop. Once they were sure he wasn't armed, they sat him in a corner of the workshop and talked briefly in Dari or Pashto, behaving as if he wasn't there.

One of them came over and slipped a canvas bag over Malko's head, blindfolding him, then tied his hands behind his back. Two men raised him to his feet, forced him to walk a few yards, and shoved him forward. When his head hit a metal floor and his legs were lifted up, he realized he was being stuffed into a car trunk. The lid slammed. He had trouble breathing and was very cold. He felt the car start and drive out to the street.

Who had kidnapped him?

The car drove on a bumpy road for a while, then on pavement, then on bumpy road again. When it stopped after what felt like half an hour, he felt both relieved and frightened, wondering what would happen next.

The trunk was opened and two men helped him out. When one removed his improvised hood, he saw the lights of Kabul in the distance. They were at a farm on a hillside, and the air was chilly.

His kidnappers, who were still masked, hustled him around behind what looked like a farmhouse and brought him to a well. They looped a thick rope around his chest, lifted him over the edge of the well, and pushed him out. Malko found himself dangling in space, being lowered along damp stone walls.

The descent didn't take long. Five or six yards down, his feet touched the bottom of the well. It was dry, thank God!

They untied the loop and pulled up the rope.

In the darkness, Malko could make out a man sitting on the ground: a youngish Afghan with a full beard and deep-set eyes. He gave a surprised look at Malko, who clearly wasn't Afghan, and said something in Dari. Malko answered in English, but the man shook his head. He didn't understand. As they sat looking at each other, suddenly everything went black. The kidnappers had covered the well, plunging them in darkness.

Malko shivered. The temperature was icy. He would've wanted to talk to his companion in misfortune, but the man crouched against the wall seemed to be dozing.

How long would he be down here?

Why the kidnapping?

And above all, would anyone be looking for him?

His head bandaged, a shaken Darius told Nelson Berry what had happened.

"They were waiting for us," he said. "They knew we had money. They were bandits."

"What about the car?"

"They drove off in it."

The South African couldn't understand it. There were certainly robbers in Kabul, but how could they know Malko was carrying a lot of money? It was very strange.

Berry was now out five hundred thousand dollars in cash, plus the armored Corolla, which was easily worth a hundred thousand. Why kidnap Malko? There was only one possible answer: ransom. So the kidnappers would be demanding ransom, but from whom? Malko didn't live in Kabul, and they didn't know about his connection with the CIA. Nor would the Corolla's license plate lead them to Berry. The car was registered in the name of an Afghan who lived in the Emirates.

"Darius, we've got to get all the people we know working on this," he said. "I'll go see my pals in the police. Maybe they'll know something."

Warren Michaelis dialed Malko repeatedly, but the calls immediately went to voice mail. He also tried the Serena, but Malko hadn't been seen at the hotel since that morning. Clearly something had happened to him, but no assaults on foreigners in Kabul had been reported. The local hospitals would have noted the presence of a non-Afghan.

"We're going to the NDS," said Michaelis.

That was the only agency with the technical means of locating Malko's cell phone. Their Russian training would come in handy.

Nelson Berry was in a funk. Despite his many connections, he hadn't gotten any information. There had been no sign of Malko since that morning. Just then, his cell rang. Maybe he would learn something, he thought.

A rough-sounding man spoke, in Pashto.

"Is Malko Linge your pal?"

He so butchered the Austrian's name that Berry had to make him repeat it twice before he could answer yes.

"We have him," said the man. "If you don't give us fifty million afghanis, we'll cut his throat. You have until tomorrow. After that . . ."

The man hung up.

Berry looked at his cell. They must have found his number in Malko's phone. But they couldn't know that Malko wasn't actually a pal of his.

The South African quickly sized up the situation. He had no intention of paying any ransom, and it probably wouldn't do any good anyway. There would be bargaining, of course, but Berry wasn't prepared to waste even a tenth of that sum in a lost cause.

He wondered who could help him. Contacting the Kabul CIA station was out of the question; they would ask him too many questions. There was nothing he could do for Malko except to haggle over the size of the ransom, to gain time.

He tried to call Malko's number back, but without success. No number had appeared on-screen when the kidnappers phoned him.

Berry walked over to the bar and poured himself a shot of vodka. It was too bad. He liked Malko, and the Austrian could have earned him a lot of money.

Just the same, he decided to try one thing. Using a special phone, he dialed a number in the United States. An anonymous voice instructed him to dial a code, which he did, getting a second voice mail. The first was just a cutout.

"Our friend has been kidnapped and there's nothing I can do," said Berry. "You better alert whoever needs to know."

Clayton Luger would have his own ways of taking action.

The cover on the well was moved aside, admitting a dim, grayish light. Malko looked at his watch, which they'd neglected to take from him.

It was 7:00 a.m.

Next to him, his companion in misfortune was curled up and appeared to be sleeping. Malko felt as if he'd spent the night in a refrigerator. He was shivering. When he looked up he saw something being lowered from the top of the well. It was a cardboard box with two bowls of *palau*—rice mixed with pieces of mutton, the national Afghan dish— and two bottles of water.

Malko was so hungry that he devoured the food, but the rice was cold and didn't provide much warmth. When he finished eating, he turned to his companion.

"How long have you been here?" he asked in English.

The man shook his head, not understanding, so Malko tried the word for "here," one of the few Dari words he knew. Holding up his fingers, he asked, "*Inja*?"

This time, the man understood. He held up five fingers on his left hand, and four on his right: nine. So you could survive nine days in these conditions, thought Malko.

He wondered who would be working on his behalf. Maybe Nelson Berry, and maybe the CIA.

Standing at his office door, Walid Varang greeted Warren Michaelis with a broad smile. The Afghan was the third-in-command at the NDS.

When they shook hands, Varang's wrist displayed a Rolex watch worth a million afghanis. It clearly was the fruit of admirable thrift, since his salary was only fifty thousand afghanis a month. When the Directorate seized a shipment of heroin, part of it always went missing, and most of that went to the higher-ups.

"We've located Malko Linge's cell phone," Varang announced.

Michaelis felt a huge wave of relief.

"Where?"

"In Chehel Sotoun." A very poor neighborhood, a slum without running water or electricity. "We'll go there together."

Waiting in the courtyard were three Fords crammed with armed men. The lead car held the technicians whose job was to locate the cell phone. They drove along the Kabul River for a few miles, then climbed a hillside on a slick, muddy road. The cars passed squalid hovels under plumes of charcoal smoke, a few women in blue burqas, and men with pushcarts.

Halfway up, they stopped. Varang got a message on his radio and turned to Michaelis.

"We're very close," he said.

They all piled out, and the NDS agents took positions around their chief. The technicians set up their gear in a small intersection with no shops nearby, only houses. Thanks to the cell phone's built-in GPS, they could pinpoint its location within a few yards. Suddenly two of the technicians walked over to a garbage bin, frightening some stray cats in the process.

One man kicked the bin over, spilling its contents.

Michaelis watched as the Afghan bent and picked something up, which he brought over to them. He immediately recognized the Nokia he'd given Malko.

"The signal hasn't moved since yesterday," said Varang. "I

think whoever kidnapped Mr. Linge threw away his phone here, to cut the trail. This is as far as our investigation can take us."

The two men exchanged a long look, and Michaelis understood that Varang thought they would never see Malko alive again.

CHAPTER 11

Warren Michaelis gazed thoughtfully at Malko's Nokia. Once its battery was charged, he would know what numbers had been called, which might give him a lead.

The NDS agents climbed back into their cars, leaving him alone in the intersection. He eventually got in and turned to Varang.

"What can we do?"

"Not much," said the Afghan, shaking his head. "At the NDS we don't deal with street crime, which seems to be the situation here. But criminals don't usually attack foreigners; it makes for too many complications. This is a strange case."

"Do you have a theory about what happened?"

"No, except that Mr. Linge was almost certainly kidnapped. Otherwise, we would have found his body by now. Unless . . ."

Varang left the sentence unfinished, then continued.

"You might ask the Interior Ministry. They handle political offenses and extortion. Unless you know something more specific, that is."

Which meant that Varang thought Malko might have been kidnapped in connection with his CIA activities. As it happens, Michaelis was wondering the same thing. Could the Austrian have been seized and forced to reveal what he was doing in Afghanistan? If that was the case, the attack could have come only from President Karzai's entourage—and they would never find him. If the Taliban were involved, they would have already taken credit for the kidnapping.

Varang dropped Michaelis off at his Land Cruiser.

"I'm very sorry," he said. "I really would have liked to help you. I'll send a bulletin to all our offices, in case we hear anything."

Once back in the Ariana, Michaelis summoned the case officer who'd been detailed to deliver the five hundred thousand dollars. The young man confirmed that he had given the cash to Malko in person.

Just whom was the money for? Michaelis wondered. The Taliban, according to Malko. Even if there were a way to identify the recipients, the CIA station people weren't authorized to contact them.

Michaelis sat down to draft a report for Langley. He didn't know what Malko Linge's mission in Kabul was, but it was off to a very bad start.

Nelson Berry saw an unknown number appear on his cell phone and answered. It was the same man with the Pashto accent as the day before, one of Malko's kidnappers.

"Do you have the money?"

"It's impossible to get that much money together quickly, and you know it," said the South African. "Let's meet so we can agree on a reasonable price."

"Ours is the reasonable price."

"In any case, I need to be sure he's still alive," said Berry, changing tactics. "I want a photo of him with a copy of the day's newspaper."

"We're not taking any photos," said the Afghan sharply. "I'll send you something else: an ear."

"You don't even know who I am," said Berry.

"True, but we can send it to the Serena, and they can pass it on. You've got until tomorrow."

He hung up.

Berry wished he hadn't taken the call, because he now faced a new dilemma. If he didn't do something, this would end badly. The best solution was to alert the CIA, but that meant revealing his contact with Malko, which he didn't want to do.

Berry decided to wait until the next call. They never killed hostages quickly, he told himself. Or maybe Malko was already dead, in which case it wouldn't make any difference.

Another cold night had passed when a faint glow lit the upper walls of the well. Looking up, Malko saw a man leaning over the edge. He said a long sentence in Dari. Malko's companion started, said a few words, then painfully got to his feet. A rope with a loop was already being lowered. The prisoner took it and wrapped it around his chest. Before he could say anything, the rope tightened and he was hoisted up to ground level. He scrabbled on the stone wall with his feet, as if to help himself rise faster.

Malko felt a stab of envy. His fellow hostage was free, his ransom probably paid. That might turn out to be helpful, he realized. The man was sure to be questioned by the police, who would learn that Malko was being held and come looking for him.

He looked up again.

The Afghan had now reached the edge of the well. The kidnappers who had hauled him up pulled him over, and he disappeared from sight.

Now Malko felt even lonelier. The presence of the other man, even though he couldn't communicate with him, had been some comfort.

Suddenly he heard the sounds of a heated argument in Dari. The voices grew louder. This was followed by silence, an angry yell, and the sound of pleading.

The two gunshots startled him.

There were no more sounds from above. The cover was put back on the well, and Malko was again in darkness. He no longer envied his companion, whom the kidnappers had obviously killed, maybe because the ransom hadn't been paid. It didn't make his own future look very bright.

Trying not to think, Malko huddled against the wall in an effort to keep warm. If only he could communicate with his captors, tell them whom to contact to negotiate his ransom. Because if nothing happened, he might suffer the same fate as the Afghan. He could always refuse to take the rope, of course, but they would just shoot him at the bottom of the well.

Reza Assefi, the Interior Ministry's special counsel, bowed deeply to Warren Michaelis. In Kabul, the Americans still ruled the roost. The previous month, the CIA had delivered three hundred and seventy-five million dollars' worth of gear purchased from Rosoboronexport, which sells military Russian matériel, to outfit the Afghan police: AK-47s, night-vision scopes, communications material, and Jeeps.

Those kinds of presents can buy lot of friendship. Without American dollars, the Afghan police would be getting around on bicycles. Some of this gear was resold to the Taliban by corrupt cops. Others took their shiny new toys and switched sides. In a way, the American aid helped pretty much everybody.

In keeping with Afghan custom, Assefi and Michaelis politely inquired about each other's families, drank tea, and discussed politics and the weather. At last, the CIA station chief was able to get around to the reason for his visit. A man connected with the Agency had come to evaluate the situation in Kabul, he said, and had disappeared.

They found his cell phone in a garbage can, but no ransom demand had reached the U.S. embassy. Michaelis thought it obvious that Malko would have told his abductors whom to contact.

A warm smile firmly in place under his handsome, well-trimmed mustache, Assefi listened.

"That's terrible," he said. "You should have come to us sooner."

"Would you have been able to do anything?"

"I don't know, but we could have launched an investigation," said Assefi, immediately backtracking. "As it happens, we're handling a similar case right now. There might be a connection. Wait a moment."

Assefi stepped into his office and made a call. Minutes later, a secretary in a head scarf brought him a thick folder.

"Here we go," he said, opening it. "Ten days ago, a young banker named Gulbuddin Mohammadi was kidnapped as he left the bank. Next day, a man called his wife and threatened to kill him if she didn't pay a million afghanis. The woman didn't have that kind of money, so she contacted us, and we put a tap on her phone.

"This didn't get us anywhere, unfortunately. The kidnappers used hidden numbers when they called, and by the time we could pinpoint the call, it was too late. From their voices, we guessed they were Pashtuns. We searched our records but didn't find anything. These groups often form and split up quickly. They're people who come to Kabul in search of work and are trying to get by."

"So you weren't able to identify them," said Michaelis.

"No, unfortunately."

From the police official's somber tone, Michaelis sensed he hadn't heard the end of the story.

"Did the wife pay the ransom?"

Assefi shook his head.

"No. She put their house up for sale but couldn't find a buyer. And this morning we found her husband's body in a vacant lot in the Pashmina Bafi neighborhood with two bullets in his head."

Michaelis was shaken.

"What do you suppose happened?" he asked.

"Gangs like this aren't very organized," explained Assefi. "When they realize they aren't going to get a ransom, they kill the hostage, then pretend they haven't."

"We absolutely must rescue Malko Linge," said Michaelis.

"It's surprising that you haven't gotten a ransom demand," said Assefi. "They do this for money. It's either that, or something else is involved. . . . We'll open an investigation in any case, starting from the last time Mr. Linge was seen."

"He left the Serena two days ago, in the morning."

"Ah, you've given me a lead!" said the Afghan. "I'll have the hotel staff questioned, and keep you posted."

This meant they would round up some unlucky bastards, tear out their fingernails, and beat them to a pulp. Afghan police methods were pretty crude. The only reason they didn't use electric shocks on prisoners? Too many power outages.

Reza Assefi stood up.

"I will keep you informed every hour," he said warmly, eager to still be deemed worthy of the Americans' three hundred and seventy-five million dollars.

Michaelis left the ministry feeling depressed. Knowing the Afghan police's limited abilities, he didn't think there was much chance of their finding Malko.

Back at his office, he passed word to the telephone operators to immediately route to him any call involving a ransom demand.

All he could do now was pray.

On the seventh floor of CIA headquarters in Langley, Clayton Luger was feeling grumpy. He hadn't gotten any news of their operation since Malko's phone call from the Kabul station.

From his office window, Luger could see the ugly cafeteria and the parking lots, coded blue, green, yellow, and purple. People with offices on the Potomac side had a beautiful view across the green space and the river.

A secretary knocked on the door and put a freshly decoded message on his desk.

"It came via Doha," she said.

When Luger read the message, he could feel the blood drain from his face. It had originated in Kabul and reached him through a series of cutouts:

> Nelson Berry reports that Malko Linge has been kidnapped by persons unknown.

"My God!" Luger exclaimed.

His stomach in a knot, he phoned his secretary.

"Get the Kabul station on the line!" he snapped. "Warren Michaelis. If he isn't there, have him traced."

His phone rang a few minutes later.

"This is Michaelis," said the station chief. "I just got a flash."

"What happened to Malko Linge?" Luger demanded.

Michaelis was speechless for a moment, then stammered, "You know about that?"

"You're the person who's supposed to tell me what's going on!" barked the deputy director.

"I just sent you a message," protested Michaelis. "You should get it any minute now."

"Well, I haven't. So what's going on?"

"Somebody kidnapped Malko Linge two days ago. All we know is that he was last seen leaving his hotel. We don't know if this is connected with the assignment you gave him."

"I don't think so," said Luger. "Did you get a ransom demand?"

"No, sir."

"We've *got* to find him. Do whatever's necessary. And keep me informed!"

Nelson Berry was preparing a transfer of currency to Logar when Darius came into the office.

"I might have some news, Commander."

Berry looked up. He hadn't heard from the kidnappers and was starting to worry.

"Is it about the kidnapping?"

"No, about the Corolla. I talked to a couple of car dealers, because I figured the thieves would try to sell it. It's worth a lot because of the bulletproofing. I just got a call. One of the sellers in Qala i Dawiat has an armored Corolla for sale. He's asking three hundred thousand afghanis."

The used-car bazaar was located on a hillside north of the airport. Its dozens of sellers had every model of Toyota available.

"Did you locate him?" asked Berry.

"Yes. He said he didn't have the car but could have it brought if I wanted to see it. He's got a display space, the third lot on the left as you enter the Qsaba car dealers area."

"Good for you!" said the South African approvingly. "When are we going?"

"I told him we would come around five o'clock."

"That's great!" said Berry. "Go tell Rufus and Willie they're coming along. You bring the seller to us, and we'll all come back here together."

Rufus and Willie were former South African mercenaries who often worked for Berry.

"Very well, Commander," said Darius. "But if the men who stole the car are there, they're sure to be armed."

"We'll be armed, too," said Berry grimly.

As Darius was leaving the office, Berry's phone rang.

"It's me," said the kidnappers' spokesman. "Do you really want to see your friend alive? We're tired of waiting."

"We're getting the money together," said Berry. "But it'll only be thirty million afghanis."

"Then we'll kill your friend."

But the Afghan said this without much conviction, and Berry felt he was hooked. Thirty million afghanis was an enormous sum.

"Don't be stupid! If you kill him, you won't get anything!"

"Okay, we'll give you until tomorrow." The kidnapper hung up.

If his expedition went badly, Berry figured he could always hand the problem off to the CIA. They could afford thirty million afghanis.

CHAPTER 12

Musa Kotak had spent the last half hour on the phone. He'd gotten a message from Mullah Beradar in Quetta, who'd heard about Malko's kidnapping. Clayton Luger had asked the Taliban to help rescue him.

Naturally, Kotak started by trying Malko's cell phone, but without success. He then alerted all his contacts. The Taliban had a network of informers throughout the city, and nothing escaped them. They were everywhere, in army and government circles, among police and criminals alike. If Malko had been kidnapped by gangsters, word would reach them. Even crooks were afraid of the Taliban.

Berry and his crew drove for several miles through the industrial wasteland north of the airport. Berry was at the wheel, with Darius next to him. Rufus and Willie rode in back with folding AK-47s in their laps. The road hadn't been repaved since the dawn of time, and the ride was torture. The four men in the Land Cruiser were shaken, not stirred.

Turning off the highway, they passed under an archway announcing the Qsaba car bazaar. The road climbed through a kind of no-man's-land, with car sellers on either side displaying their vehicles. Berry's group passed a herd of sheep and a refugee camp before reaching the main business district.

Hundreds of vehicles were lined up on lots of various sizes.

All Toyotas.

Suddenly, Darius cursed. He had just spotted the gray Corolla on a lot to their left. The car was parked in front of a shuttered building, the plastic grapes still hanging from its rear-view mirror.

Two men were standing next to it, bearded Afghans in brown *patu* cloaks.

Darius turned to Berry.

"Commander, if those are the guys who stole the car, they're going to recognize me."

"In that case we'll shoot first," said the South African.

They stopped a few yards from the stolen Toyota, and Darius and Berry got out. The men in *patus* looked at them but without any sign of recognition.

Darius went over to them, his hand on his heart.

"Salaam alaikum," he said politely.

"Alaikum salaam," one of the two answered. "Are you the man who wants the car?"

"My boss here wants it, but I'll be driving it."

"Does he have the money?"

"Of course," said Darius.

There were practically no formal vehicle sales in Afghanistan; it was too complicated. You simply paid for a car, and the registration stayed in the original owner's name.

"We want to see the money first," said one of the men.

"It's with my boss in the Land Cruiser," said Darius coolly. "If we can agree on a price, I'll go get it."

The man in the *patu* didn't object. Taking precautions was standard procedure.

Darius first walked around the Corolla, to confirm that it was indeed his car.

"Can I get in?" he asked.

"Go ahead, but make it quick."

The men in *patus* seemed nervous.

Darius climbed behind the wheel. Nothing had changed. When he opened the glove compartment, he saw that the registration papers were still there. The key was in the ignition. He turned it and the engine came to life.

One of the thieves immediately came over and aimed a big pistol at him.

"Don't do anything stupid, brother. If you try to drive off, I'll shoot you."

"I just wanted to see if the engine sounded okay," Darius assured him. He revved the engine and switched it off, then casually ran his hand under the dashboard. When he found the small button he was looking for, he pressed it. This activated an antitheft system he'd rigged that disconnected the ignition. Unless you knew the trick, you couldn't start the car.

Darius straightened in the seat and got out.

"It runs all right," he said, "but it's too expensive."

"What are you offering, brother?"

"Two hundred thousand, tops."

The man spat on the ground in disgust.

"May Allah curse you! This car is a marvel. Besides, it's armor plated and the engine is new."

"I'm only paying two hundred thousand, not an afghani more."

"You're nothing but a dog!" said one of the men.

Darius smiled slightly.

"Then I'm sure you'll sell it, but not to me."

Without another word, he went back to Berry and reported.

"I set the antitheft system," he said quietly. "It won't start anymore. They're going to be in trouble."

Berry and his team drove to the upper edge of the market, then turned around and came back down. When Berry reached the lot with the stolen car, he slowed.

The Corolla was still there, but now its hood was propped up. One of the thieves was bent over the motor; the other was sitting inside the car.

Berry pulled into the lot.

"Let's go!" he said.

The two thieves were so absorbed in trying to get the Corolla running that they didn't notice Berry's men until the last minute.

Darius came over with a big smile and asked, "Having a problem, brother?"

The Afghan didn't turn around. So he didn't see Berry before he grabbed him, carried him bodily to the Land Cruiser, and threw him in the back.

The two mercenaries got out in turn. When the man at the wheel of the Corolla looked up, he found himself staring into the barrel of a gun. He went for a weapon, but Rufus threw him to the ground and Willie kicked him in the jaw. Then they dragged him to the Land Cruiser and tossed him in on top of his partner.

In the meantime, Darius got behind the wheel of the Toyota and flipped the circuit breaker hidden under the dashboard. Within half a minute, he was driving out of the lot and down toward the main highway.

Berry climbed into the SUV and followed him while Rufus and Willie trussed up the thieves crumpled in the back.

The operation had taken less than two minutes, and nobody seemed to have noticed. Berry had successfully recovered the armored Toyota and captured two men who surely knew where Malko was being held.

All he had to do was make them talk.

Huddled at the bottom of the well, Malko heard the cover being moved aside. He saw a black circle—the sky—then one of his kidnappers' heads. The man leaned over the lip of the well and shouted a few words in Dari.

Malko was shivering and hungry, even though he'd been fed an hour earlier. He felt as if he were freezing from the inside. How long could he endure these conditions? he wondered.

A second man's head appeared, also shouting something Malko couldn't understand.

"What is the problem?" asked Malko in English.

But the kidnappers clearly didn't understand him.

A few moments later he saw the rope drop down the well and land beside him. They obviously wanted him to come up. Malko hesitated to take it, remembering what had happened to his fellow hostage. But if he didn't, his kidnappers would just shoot him. Reluctantly, he tied the rope around his chest.

It immediately tightened and they started hoisting him. At the top, he was roughly grabbed and hauled over the lip of the well. Malko's legs were so shaky, he almost collapsed when the rope was untied.

Around him stood three glowering bearded men. One waved a gun under his nose, then pressed the barrel against his forehead. The cold steel gave Malko a jolt of adrenaline. They were going to kill him!

The two others continued shouting, and one started kicking him. They seemed angry, but Malko couldn't figure out why. He tried again to speak to them in English, but that was useless. Something was going on, and he didn't know what it was. As they kicked and punched him, he clung to the lip of the well so as not to fall.

Circling around him, the three bearded men seemed unsure of what to do next. One came over and yelled something in his face. This time, Malko caught the word "Toyota."

Something had happened to the stolen Toyota, but what?

Eventually they left him to argue angrily among themselves. Malko took the opportunity to look around. He noticed that the farm was surrounded by high brick walls.

A metal click made him jump. One of the men had just cocked his pistol. No doubt about it: they had decided to execute him, like their other hostage.

Suddenly Malko had an idea. They hadn't taken his pen and notebook, so he wrote Warren Michaelis's phone number on a piece of paper. He handed it to one of the men and said a single word: "Dollars."

And prayed they could read Western numerals.

Their quarrel stopped abruptly and the three men peered at his message. Then the argument resumed, more calmly this time. One of the kidnappers came over and shouted at him, in Dari of course. Malko repeated the word "dollars."

It was the same word in both languages.

Given the total lack of communication, the discussion ended. Finally one man tossed the rope to Malko. He was apparently headed back down the well and wasn't going to be killed right away. He was almost happy to step over the lip and be lowered on the rope.

Going down, however, he felt even colder than he had up above. Fear had made Malko forget how chilled he was.

Now he prayed with all his might that they would call Michaelis. The CIA had the means to negotiate with his kidnappers and would do everything it could to save him.

Reaching the bottom, Malko untied the rope and huddled against the wall, unable to stop violently shivering. Without his cashmere coat, he would have already died of hypothermia.

A shout made Malko look up. A man leaning over the lip of the well tossed something that bounced down the walls and landed at his feet.

It was a small, brown, and round.

A hand grenade.

CHAPTER 13

The Land Cruiser pulled up in front of Berry's poppy pal-ace, and he and his fellow mercenaries dragged their prisoners out of the car, shoving them through the small basement door.

Rufus and Willie hauled the two Afghans into a workshop and started systematically and methodically beating them. For some minutes, the only sound to be heard was the dull thud of fists on flesh. When one man slumped to the dirt floor, he was hauled back to his feet and beaten some more. Their lips smashed, eyebrows split, and noses broken, the Afghans endured their punishment stoically. If they had fallen into the hands of the police, they would have suffered the same softening-up treatment. It was the local custom.

Darius had parked the armored Corolla and was now watching the scene in silence, smoking a cigarette. During a pause, he remarked, "I don't think they're hitting hard enough, Commander. Let me take over."

"Be my guest," said Berry, who was leaning against a workbench. He himself hadn't touched the prisoners yet.

Darius took a metal cricket bat from a corner of the room and started whacking the two men on the back and kidneys, while eloquently cursing them in Dari.

Feeling relieved, he finally put down his bat and lit another cigarette. The two men lay sprawled on the ground, bloody and mute. Resigned. Fatalistic.

Berry, whose Dari wasn't good enough to conduct an interrogation, turned to his driver.

"Tell them we don't want to hurt them. We just want the man they kidnapped and the money he was carrying. If they lead us to him, we'll spare their lives."

Darius translated, and the men struggled to their feet. The older of the two answered briefly.

"He says they got the Toyota from two guys who promised them money to carry out the kidnapping. They say they don't know what happened to the foreigner."

Berry was unimpressed.

"Tell them that they're lying and that I don't like liars," he said flatly. "Ask them again."

When Darius did so, the older man answered plaintively.

"He says he's not lying," he translated.

Berry calmly walked over, drew his Makarov, and put the barrel on the top of the younger prisoner's head. He aimed the automatic straight down and pulled the trigger.

In the small room, the sound of the shot was deafening. The bullet tore through the victim's skull, ending up somewhere between his lungs, and he pitched forward as if struck by lightning. Berry slipped the safety back on and holstered his gun. The second prisoner was now staring up at him in terror.

"Tell him I'm going to continue the interrogation. The first time he tells a lie, he'll suffer the same fate. Does he understand?"

Darius translated and the surviving prisoner stammered something.

"He understands," said Darius.

"Does he know the kidnappers?"

The prisoner nodded.

"What are their names?"

"Abdul and Zarnegar."

"Have they killed the hostage?"

He wasn't sure. "When they left to try to sell the Toyota, he was still alive."

"Where?"

"On a farm."

"Is it far from here?"

"Not far."

The prisoner used the word *nazdik*, which could mean anything from five hundred yards to ten miles.

"In an apartment or a house?"

"He's down in a well," he said, and described the farm and the well.

It was a clever system; the police could search the farm without finding anything.

"How many men are there?" asked Berry.

"Two, maybe three," said the prisoner. "The owner of the farm is there; he's supposed to get part of the ransom."

"Do they have weapons?"

"A Kalashnikov and some pistols."

"Where do they sleep?"

"At the farm."

"You're going to take us there."

At this, the prisoner looked upset.

"I don't know if I could find my way there," he said. "It's complicated."

"Darius, tell him that if he doesn't take us to the farm, I'll kill him, just like his pal," said Berry. "It's late, so we won't go there tonight, but tomorrow at dawn. Tie him up good!"

Darius was happy to oblige and lashed the prisoner's wrists to the workbench. There was no danger of his escaping.

Maureen Kieffer was so distracted she couldn't concentrate on her welding work. She hadn't heard from Malko for two days now. She had called a friend at the Serena several times, but without any luck. She didn't dare contact the CIA. They wouldn't tell her anything, anyhow.

No report of a foreigner being kidnapped had appeared in any of Kabul's twenty newspapers.

She didn't know where to turn.

Warren Michaelis was going through the memory of Malko's Nokia. Among the few numbers listed, one of them gave him a start. He checked it against a database, and a photograph of Nelson Berry promptly appeared on-screen.

The CIA station chief swore under his breath. So Malko was in contact with Berry! That couldn't have anything to do with the Taliban. He knew the South African well and had even worked with him in the old Blackwater days. The Agency had used Berry to discreetly eliminate some double agents and Taliban infiltrators, and for some even dirtier tricks. But Michaelis didn't like the man. He considered him a killer for hire and had cut off contact.

Other Americans and Afghans continued to use him, however, because he controlled a small group of expats—South Africans, mainly—who were prepared to do most anything. Berry was even suspected of working for some big drug traffickers who hired him to protect their shipments.

In short, Berry was off-limits, yet Malko had been in touch with him.

Was the Austrian acting on his own, or was he following orders? If the latter, Michaelis should have known about it.

For the moment, however, what mattered was finding him, and Berry might have some information. Michaelis dialed his number and left a message to call back immediately.

Michaelis was about to leave the Ariana when his personal cell phone rang: an unknown Afghan number appeared on-screen. He answered, feeling somewhat surprised. Very few people knew his private number.

An Afghan man said a very long sentence in Dari that Michaelis had trouble grasping. His Dari was far from perfect, but he caught the words "hostage," "dollar," and "tomorrow."

"Wait! Wait!" he shouted into the phone.

On his landline he called his secretary.

"Tell Wardak to get in here right away!"

Amin Wardak, one of his Afghan deputies, burst into the office moments later. Michaelis held the cell phone out to him.

"It's a man who only speaks Afghan," he said. "I think it's about Malko Linge."

After a long exchange in Dari, Wardak turned to the CIA station chief and said, "He says they're holding a foreigner. They will kill him if they don't get a ransom of fifty million afghanis. They plan to execute him tomorrow morning at the hour of the first prayer."

Michaelis felt his blood run cold. He had found Malko but was now in danger of losing him for good.

"Tell him it's too late to get so much money together. He has to wait until tomorrow. And until noon, not the first prayer. He'll get what he's asking for."

Wardak relayed the information, then put the phone down.

"He said he'll call back tomorrow."

"What was that reference to the first prayer about?" Michaelis asked. "Are they Taliban?"

"No, they're trying to make us think so. They're common criminals. That's even more dangerous. When they don't get a ransom, they often kill the people they kidnap."

"We'll pay the damn ransom, for Christ's sake!"

"Be careful, sir. This will be very tricky. We should get the police to handle the operation. Otherwise, we might lose both the money and the victim."

"I'll phone the NDS first thing in the morning," Michaelis promised. "I'm not going to get any sleep tonight."

At least he was reasonably sure of one thing: Malko was still alive.

Malko's frozen hands clutched the grenade his captors had dropped down to him. It was a little American grenade, its pin still in place. Why had they given it to him?

Intimidation?

He could pull the pin and try to throw it up when his kidnappers removed the well cover, of course. But if he missed and it fell back down, he'd be blown to bits. In short, there was nothing he could do with it.

The cold seemed to have gotten even worse. Malko was now shivering constantly and was only dimly aware that he hadn't been fed. He was so chilled that he didn't feel very hungry, though he knew he was getting weaker. Between the cold and the fear, he was sure he wouldn't be able to sleep. But then, sitting on the damp ground with his head on his knees, he gradually dozed off.

"Walid, I'm in contact with Malko Linge's kidnappers," announced the CIA chief. "How do I proceed?"

It was 7:45 a.m., and Michaelis had phoned the NDS official before he left for the office. They had to act fast.

"Come to my office in an hour," said Varang. "We'll go to the Interior Ministry together. They have more experience in dealing with this kind of problem. You can't just hand over the ransom, because if you do, you'll never see Mr. Linge again. The exchange has to be very carefully worked out. But at least you've picked up the trail. It's clearly a case of extortion."

When Berry and his men opened the workshop door, the thief was snoring.

"Wake him up!" Berry ordered.

Darius did so by kicking the man hard, then hauling him to his feet. Between the dried blood on his face and his grossly swollen lips, he wasn't a pretty sight.

The South African went to stand in front of him and said, "You're going to take us to the farm. If everything goes well, you'll go free. But if the prisoner is gone or dead, you'll become a *shalid*"—a martyr.

The man was led to the Land Cruiser and put in the passenger seat, his hands still bound. Darius got behind the wheel, an AK-47 beside him on the floor. Berry and the two South African mercenaries climbed in back, along with what they needed to assault the bandits. They even had an M16 with a 40 mm grenade launcher, which could splatter bad guys all over the landscape.

"Which way do we go?" asked Darius.

"Take the Nangarhar road," said the prisoner. It was the way to Jalalabad.

They crossed the city center and headed east, generally following the Kabul River. After a mile or so, the prisoner pointed to a track that climbed a barren hillside on the left.

"I think it's there."

Berry, who was sitting behind him, jabbed his gun in the prisoner's neck.

"You think, or you know?"

"It's up there," he blurted. "In the village of Tara Khel."

It was a big village spread across a stony plateau at the foot of the mountain. The track snaked around ravines and cliffs. They were now out in the middle of nowhere, about ten miles from Kabul.

And they had a problem: the white Land Cruiser stuck out like a sore thumb. They could only pray that Malko's kidnappers didn't spot them. If they did, they would have all the time in the world to cut his throat. Around here, a white SUV was bound to arouse suspicions, but Berry hadn't wanted to take the armored Corolla. That would have been worse, because the kidnappers knew it.

The track got even bumpier, and Darius was forced to slow down. As they neared Tara Khel, the prisoner said, "Turn right toward that big farm."

An even worse road led to a large, isolated farm with high brick walls. They pulled up in front of a green metal door. Darius stopped, and the five men got out of the SUV. Berry pushed on the door, but it was locked.

He aimed his pistol at the lock. Behind him, Rufus and Willie stood poised on either side of the prisoner, weapons at the ready.

"Okay, let's go!"

Berry shot the lock and kicked the metal door open. Driving the car thief ahead of them, the three South Africans rushed inside.

The farm consisted only of a low building with an old Corolla parked in front.

A few seconds later, the farmhouse door was opened by a man with an AK-47. He had no time to use it, however. Rufus stopped and fired the grenade launcher. Its 40 mm projectile hit the man right in the chest, literally blowing him to pieces.

A second man appeared and was immediately cut down by the raiders. Stepping over his body, the three South Africans entered the farmhouse, leaving Darius to guard the prisoner. They found a man at a table, eating. He quickly raised his hands as high as they would go. Rufus and Willie searched him—he wasn't armed—and forced him onto the floor.

The South Africans then searched the house without finding anything. They went outside and ran over to Darius and the prisoner.

"Make him show us where the well is!"

The terrified Afghan led the way behind the house. The South Africans found the circular well, its opening sealed by oilcloth held down by planks.

They tore off the boards and the cloth, uncovering a dark, round opening.

Berry leaned over the lip and called, "Malko!"

The bottom of the well was dark, and he couldn't see what was down there. After a few moments of silence, a feeble voice answered, "Yes, I'm here."

"He's alive!" Berry shouted.

When they hauled Malko out of the well, Berry swore softly in Afrikaans. He wasn't a softhearted man, but seeing Malko made him revert to his native tongue. The Austrian was as pale as death, his face gaunt under a four-day stubble. His cashmere coat looked several sizes too big for him.

He opened his eyes and attempted what he probably thought was a smile. "You got here just in the nick of time," he muttered.

The men half carried him to the SUV parked outside the walls. Malko wasn't able to stay upright in his seat, so they belted him in.

Their Afghan prisoner had been anxiously watching the scene unfold.

"Is everything okay, Commander?" he asked in Dari, and Darius translated.

Berry shook his head and said, "Bad luck, buddy. We need your seat, so we have to leave you here."

Pulling out his Makarov, he shot the man in the head. The impact sent him flying backward as his skull exploded.

"Go get the guy in the farmhouse," ordered Berry. "We're taking him with us."

Then he dialed Warren Michaelis and held the phone out to Malko.

"Talk to him!"

When Michaelis saw Berry's number on-screen he figured he finally might get some news. He answered the phone.

"Hello, Warren?" said Malko. "It's me. I'm okay."

"Good God, Malko! Where are you?"

"In Nelson Berry's car. He rescued me."

"All right. Come to the Ariana. I'll alert the checkpoints. Give me the car's license number. Do you need a doctor?"

"Yes."

"Everything will be ready when you get here. Are you far away?"

"I don't know."

Michaelis hung up with a huge feeling of relief.

And quite a few unanswered questions.

CHAPTER 14

When Malko opened his eyes, it took him a few seconds to realize he was in a hospital. Nelson Berry had driven him directly to the Ariana, where Warren Michaelis was waiting. Berry then delivered the man they found in the Tara Khel farm to NDS headquarters.

Meanwhile, the station chief drove Malko to the American embassy and checked him into the infirmary reserved for sick or wounded embassy staffers. Everything there was American: doctors, drugs, and nurses. Also, it was in the Green Zone, and safe.

Glancing down, Malko saw an IV plugged into his left arm; glucose, probably. He was having what felt like an out-of-body experience: he was very weak, but his mind was completely clear. The room was so warm that the cold that had been part of his every waking hour in captivity had dissipated.

The door opened and a man in a white coat with a stethoscope around his neck came in.

"Hello, I'm Dr. Perkins," he said, extending a hand. "You weren't looking too great when they brought you in. You must've had quite an ordeal. Tell me what happened."

Malko managed a smile.

"For four days I was only given water and rice to eat," he said. "I wasn't mistreated, but I was very, very cold."

"We'll have the test results tomorrow," said the doctor, "and see if you picked up any bugs from the water. It looks to me as if you lost a couple of pounds a day, which you should be able to gain back pretty easily. What mainly weakened you was the cold. You need a week's rest and a lot of steaks. Tomorrow we'll do a full body scan. Until then, just take it easy and get as much sleep as you can."

That advice was hardly necessary. Malko's eyelids were already drooping.

He was nearly asleep when the door opened again.

"Feeling better?" asked Michaelis.

"I'm fine," mumbled Malko. "I just need a few days' rest."

"Forget it. Perkins isn't letting you out of here for a week. Anyway, there's nothing you have to do right now. I called the Serena and told them you were traveling.

"And I've got good news: my friend Walid Varang at the NDS just called. The man Nelson Berry turned over to the police has confessed. To get enough money to finish his farmhouse, he would rent his well to kidnappers to hold their victims. The NDS asked the Interior Ministry that he be transferred to their custody."

"What about the five hundred thousand dollars?"

"Vanished, for the time being. But that's not what matters. The main thing is, you're alive."

"I wouldn't expect too much from that interrogation," said Malko. "It was an ordinary kidnapping. They wanted money."

"Well, we'll see," said Michaelis. "By the way, here's your cell phone. We found it in a trash can. Here's a charger, too."

He set the Nokia on the bed.

"Thanks," mumbled Malko, already drifting off.

Soft daylight filtered through the frosted-glass windows. Malko looked at his watch and couldn't believe what he saw: it was 1:45 p.m. He'd been asleep for fourteen hours!

Moments later, the door opened and a nurse entered with a cart bearing his lunch. Malko realized that he was starving. He practically shed tears of joy to see a rare New York steak with French fries. He could have eaten the plate. Too bad the coffee that accompanied this feast tasted like old socks.

Now feeling much better, Malko checked his phone's in-box and found a series of increasingly anxious messages from Maureen Kieffer.

He immediately called her.

"Malko? What happened to you?"

"I had a very strange adventure," he said. "I was kidnapped."

"You were damned lucky," she said after hearing the story. "Usually they kill the people even after the ransom is paid. Where are you now?"

"At the American embassy, in the infirmary."

"I hope you remember that you owe me a dinner," she said teasingly.

Malko suddenly perked up. "Want to come share mine this evening? They aren't discharging me anytime soon."

"They'll never let me in."

"I'll arrange it," he promised. "Come whenever you like. They bring me dinner around eight o'clock."

Down in an NDS basement, Mossein Ravash regretted renting out his well. For hours, he had been beaten with fists and metal bars. Then they stretched him out on a bloodstained wooden table, tied his arms and legs down, and pounded his belly and groin.

Yet he had already told them everything he knew, which wasn't very much. He'd only been providing a service. His Pashtun interrogator now picked up a knife, came over, and breathed stale onions in his face.

"Brother," he said sarcastically, "if you don't tell us everything you know, I'm going to slit you from here"—he put his finger on Ravash's navel—"all the way down. And believe me, it's going to hurt."

From the man's expression, Ravash knew this was no idle threat. He desperately racked his brains for something to tell him. The police had already identified all the culprits, so there wasn't much left.

Suddenly he recalled a conversation he had overheard between two of the kidnappers.

It might just save his life.

As he repeated the conversation between the two thugs, he knew he'd caught his interrogator's attention. The Pashtun flashed an evil smile and went upstairs to report.

Maureen showed up five minutes after Malko's dinner arrived: spare ribs and broccoli and a bottle of California wine.

Shrugging off an enormous down coat that made her look like a blimp, the young woman stood revealed in all her glory. She was wearing a tight black sweater whose buttons down the front looked ready to pop off, and tailored black leather pants stuffed into fur boots.

She came over to Malko and pressed cold lips to his.

"You'll have to forgive me for not wearing stockings!" she said. "Winter isn't quite over yet, and it's cold in the evenings. When you come to the house, it'll be different."

"I'm too weak to do anything," Malko assured her. "I just wanted to see you."

"Me too," she said. "I was really worried, you know. In Kabul, when people don't pick up the phone, it usually means they're dead."

They arranged the dinner plates in front of them, and Maureen opened the wine.

"To us!" she said.

The California wine was fine. They were both hungry and ate quickly. Then Maureen sat on the edge of the bed and ran a hand gently over Malko's cheek.

"You look nice with a beard."

"I feel scruffy," he protested. "As soon as I get out of here I'm going to make myself look human again."

Maureen leaned closer and brushed her lips against his. She prolonged the kiss, finally darting a tongue into his mouth that tasted of California wine. Malko felt something like a shock of static electricity. The young woman's breasts were pressed against the sheets. He first stroked around them through the cashmere sweater. When he brushed a nipple, it immediately hardened under his fingers.

She started. "Cold weather makes me very sensitive," she murmured.

Malko was already undoing the tiny buttons, and the sweater parted to reveal a generously filled black bra.

They had stopped talking. He conscientiously encircled her beautiful breasts, gradually shifting the bra aside.

Though seemingly content, the young woman suddenly jumped up. "Wait!" she said.

Her breasts swinging, she marched over to the door to lock it but unexpectedly bumped into a fat black nurse who had come to retrieve the dinner cart. At the sight of the bosom yearning to breathe free, the nurse rolled her eyes.

Maureen didn't turn a hair.

"I was about to call you," she said smoothly. "We're finished."

Taken aback, the nurse grabbed the cart and fled from the room as if she had Beelzebub nipping at her heels.

Maureen calmly locked the door, came back to the bed, and leaned over Malko.

"Are you feeling any better now?"

She finished unbuttoning the sweater and offered her breasts to Malko, who playfully squeezed them and brushed their nipples. Smiling, Maureen slipped her hand under the sheet and touched his chest.

"You lost some weight," she said.

Her hand wandered over Malko's body. But when it reached his belly, he flinched.

"I'm still sore all over," he explained. "I was lying huddled up twenty-four hours a day."

She gently began to massage him with a circular movement. Very gradually, her hand drifted lower. When the tips of her fingers reached Malko's groin, she asked, "Do you still hurt there?"

He was starting to get an erection. The young woman's fingers now wrapped around the base of his cock and moved up the shaft a little.

Maureen gently pushed the sheet aside and let out a little cry. "It's true, you're really skinny!"

Her mouth moved down to Malko's left nipple. When she teased it with her tongue, he again felt that little electric shock.

By now, she had taken his prick in her hand and was gently stroking it.

"I'd say you're on the road to recovery," she said. "You seem even stiffer than before."

With Maureen gripping its base, Malko's prick was now standing at rigid attention.

"You'll have to be satisfied with my mouth tonight," she said. "I don't have the energy to get undressed."

Malko didn't speak.

Maureen bent her head and very gently took his cock in her mouth. He lay back with his eyes closed, savoring every second of delicate pleasure. While he played with her breasts, Maureen sucked him in her special way. Each time he twisted her nipples, her tongue got more active, until the moment she finished him off. As if he were being drained by a succubus, he grunted briefly and exploded in her mouth.

Feeling exhausted and happy, he took Maureen's hand and squeezed it.

"You could make a dead man come!" he said.

"Don't say things like that!" she exclaimed, making a funny face. "Talk about death, and you'll make it happen."

She'd gotten up and was putting on her bra. She calmly buttoned her sweater and leaned close to Malko.

"Next time we'll go to the Boccaccio, and I'll hose you down afterward."

Still strapped to the wooden table, Mossein Ravash was shivering with cold, unable to sleep. But he was feeling pleased with himself at having stopped the interrogation. Afghan cops were quick to use torture, but when the "customer" talked, he usually pulled through.

He heard footsteps and turned his head to see his interrogator, who had left nearly two hours earlier. The Pashtun was carrying a kind of black bag and approached Ravash from behind. Standing above him, he unfolded the thing he was holding: a hood with a drawstring. He quickly slipped it over the prisoner's head and tightened the drawstring around his neck.

Jerking against his restraints, Ravash shouted, "What are you doing, brother?"

The Pashtun didn't answer. He took a cord with a slipknot from his pocket and wrapped it around the prisoner's neck. Then, using all his strength, he strangled him.

Ravash didn't even have time to be afraid. He tried to tense his muscles, but the cord dug into his flesh, crushing his larynx and carotid artery. With his lungs starved of air and his brain of blood, he struggled for a few moments more, then gave a final shudder and went limp.

The interrogator waited a while longer to be sure Ravash had stopped breathing, then untied the cord and removed the hood. The strangulation marks were barely visible.

Leaving the way he'd come, he went up to his office to draft his final report. It stated that the prisoner had suffered a heart attack during enhanced interrogation. It happened all the time.

A half hour earlier, the interrogator's supervisor had listened to his account of the confession and consulted his own superiors, then decided that Mossein Ravash had to die. His secret was too explosive for him to be allowed to live.

CHAPTER 15

"You look in great shape, Malko! No one would ever guess you just spent four days down a well!"

Malko smiled at the station chief's somewhat forced cheer. Fresh from his rest at the embassy, his first visit had been to Michaelis.

"Did they find the money?" he asked.

The station chief shook his head. "Not a cent. And we'll never know if it was taken by the kidnappers or by the Afghan police."

"Then you'll have to bring me another five hundred thousand dollars from Dubai."

"I'll take the necessary steps," said Michaelis with ill grace. "You still need it, right?"

"My mission hasn't changed," said Malko. "As you know, I was kidnapped while bringing the money to its intended recipient."

"Nelson Berry?"

Malko met Michaelis's eye. "What makes you say that?"

"I found his number in your cell phone. Which poses a small problem. We stopped dealing with Berry some time ago, on orders from Langley. He's one of a number of people we no longer hire because of his dubious activities. He's occasionally been known to protect poppy shipments."

"That needn't concern you," said Malko. "I've been in contact with Berry, and at Langley's request. And I'll remind you that my activities in Kabul have nothing to do with your station. So you don't need to worry about fallout from them."

Michaelis flushed slightly, opened his mouth, then closed it again. He'd been put in his place, well aware that he couldn't oppose a decision by Clayton Luger.

In no mood to prolong the meeting, Malko stood up. "I'm counting on you to have the money brought to me at the Serena. If you have any questions, you can ask Langley for a new authorization."

Even after his rest in the infirmary, Malko still felt pretty shaky. He was eating normally again, but his bones didn't seem to have completely thawed.

Time to get this assignment back on track, he thought. He would start by contacting Mullah Kotak. But first he had to thank Nelson Berry. Without him, he might still be at the bottom of the well.

The South African had told Michaelis how he'd gotten involved in the kidnapping, when the Pashtuns found his number in Malko's phone and called him, and what he'd done next.

"You saved my life, Nelson!" said Malko warmly, when he came on the line.

The South African took this with his usual aplomb. "If I hadn't found you, the station would have taken charge."

Malko had just hung up when Michaelis called.

"We have some news from the NDS," he said. "The owner of the farmhouse wasn't able to tell them anything more. They roughed him up a little too much, and he died of a heart attack during the interrogation."

That was a sad funeral oration, but for Malko, the incident was already ancient history. This was Kabul. The city wasn't really dangerous, but sometimes it had bad surprises in store.

When Malko entered Musa Kotak's quarters at the mosque, the fat cleric struggled to his feet and hurried over to him.

"My dear friend!" he exclaimed, taking Malko's hand in both of his. Kotak's somewhat protruding eyes seemed to radiate kindness. He led Malko to the back of the room and sat him on some cushions, next to a tea tray.

"I prayed to Allah a great deal for you," said Kotak, as he and his belly settled themselves on the cushions. "When I heard you hadn't returned to the Serena, I got very worried."

"How did you know about that?"

"I have friends everywhere," said the mullah with a beatific smile. "I first did some checking on my side, but I didn't get anywhere. Now I understand things better."

"They were just crooks," said Malko reassuringly. "Thugs who wanted to make some money. I was locked up with a young Afghan banker, and they shot him when his family couldn't pay."

Kotak's chubby face looked grave.

"I think there is more to this than money," he said mysteriously.

"What do you mean?"

The cleric took a sip of tea before answering.

"After you were rescued, I continued looking into this business. Did you know that the NDS interrogated the owner of the farmhouse where you were held?"

"Yes, I was told that he died while being questioned," said Malko. "Heart attack, apparently. But I don't see that he would have anything to tell them."

"That's not quite correct," said Kotak. "It's true that he died in NDS custody, but not of a heart attack. He was strangled, on orders from above."

"Strangled!" exclaimed Malko. "Why?"

"Because without realizing it, he told them something very important."

"About me? I never even saw him!"

"That's true. But what he told the NDS agents was critical. Apparently the kidnappers discussed you in front of him, and they revealed that the kidnapping was done to order. They'd been told to kidnap you and, once they got the ransom, to kill you. A murder disguised as a botched kidnapping. It wouldn't have attracted any attention, because it happens often enough."

"But they really did want the ransom," Malko insisted. "They even tried to get it from the CIA."

"Of course! The ransom was their premium for the operation—which wound up costing the people who ordered it nothing."

"How can you be so sure of all this?" asked Malko skeptically.

"We have informers in the NDS. One of them read the report written by the interrogator. It says that the farm owner talked and was then executed. This report went directly to the head of the NDS. To his deputy, that is, since we managed to put Asadullah Khalid out of action."

"Who ordered those men to kill me?" asked Malko. "They didn't know me."

"We did some investigating and found that this gang often works for a certain Babrak Parwan. He's a big drug trafficker who has a fancy poppy palace here in Kabul. When they're not kidnapping people, the gang handles his drug shipments. They do whatever he tells them to."

"Even assuming that's true," said Malko, "what does this drug trafficker have against me?"

"I'll let you guess. Parwan is a member of the Popolzai tribe, and a distant cousin of President Hamid Karzai."

Kotak fell silent to give his dramatic revelation time to sink in. Malko was shaken. Not for a moment had he considered that there might be a connection between the kidnapping and his mission in Kabul. What Kotak had just told him opened some very dark new vistas.

"In other words, you think President Karzai gave the order to eliminate me? But why?"

Looking like a cat playing with a mouse, the cleric smiled again. "I can only think of one reason," he said. "He heard about your intentions. Since he can't oppose the Americans openly, he used the gang, Afghan-style."

"This is very serious!" said Malko.

The mullah nodded his round head. "True enough, but there's worse. It means that someone has learned your plans. And if we don't discover who that is, we are heading for disaster."

Malko was speechless. This was an absolute catastrophe. It was so easy to get rid of somebody in a city like Kabul—especially if that somebody didn't know where the attack was coming from.

"Are you positive about what you're telling me?"

Kotak nodded sadly. "I'm afraid so. It's a miracle that the farm owner revealed what he did. Otherwise, I would have been as much in the dark as you, and the next attack might have been worse. Now we have to figure who the 'mole' is."

"It won't be the CIA," said Malko. "They don't operate that way."

"Also, they don't have the local connections," added Kotak.

"It isn't the people I met with in Washington, either. And the NDS agents who searched my room at the Serena wouldn't have found anything compromising."

"I doubt that an official agency is involved," said the mullah. "I can only think of one group: the people in my circle who oppose this plan."

"You mean within the Taliban *shura*?"

"That's right. There are a number of factions in Quetta. Some feel that we should deal with Karzai and persuade him to step down. I think they are wrong, because it's not just Karzai. His entire clique will fight to stay in power."

"Are you suggesting that someone in Quetta warned Karzai about my plan?"

"It's not impossible," admitted the mullah. "He has his contacts among us. Everybody plays his own game."

"In that case, I'm in very serious danger."

The mullah gave a short, bitter laugh.

"Yes, but it's nothing personal! Karzai doesn't even know you; he just wants to hang on to power. Besides, you work with the CIA, so you are officially untouchable. But you still must be extremely careful."

"Could that drug trafficker you mentioned be acting on his own?"

"No, he would never attack a foreigner, especially not one close to the CIA. But here's another possibility. Maybe Karzai's CIA friend Mark Spider heard about the project and warned him. Let me think about this. When I know something, I'll text you."

CHAPTER 16

The dining room in the Jardin de Taimani was full. The recently opened French restaurant attracted many expats and few Afghans.

Maureen Kieffer was practically dressed for summer, with a long gypsy skirt and a yellow sweater so tight that it precisely outlined her nipples. She was watching Malko eat, almost tenderly.

"You really are doing a lot better!" she said. "I put a bottle of champagne on ice for us."

She was eager to get Malko home, but as they were drinking their coffee, a tall redhead with green eyes made her way to their table.

"Alicia!" Maureen cried.

The two women air-kissed, and the newcomer joined them.

"This is Alicia Burton," said Maureen. "She's an American reporter. She's also very brave: she lives alone at the Gandamack Lodge."

"Quite unusual, a woman alone in Kabul," remarked Malko.

"So what do you do?" Alicia asked.

"I'm a political observer for the European Community."

"Do you have a place in town?"

"No, I'm at the Serena."

An eager expression flitted across her face.

"You should invite me over so I can take a bath," she said. "At the Gandamack, we don't have hot water that often."

She gave Malko a bright, meaningful look. She was shamelessly flirting with him right in front of Maureen Kieffer, who kicked him under the table.

Despite the pain, Malko gallantly said, "Come on by. I'll be happy to let you use my bathroom."

He was rewarded with another kick.

"I'm afraid I didn't catch your name," said Alicia.

"Malko Linge."

"I hope we run into each other again."

She shook hands and walked away, swinging her high, rounded ass.

"What a slut!" hissed Maureen. "I thought she was going to duck under the table and give you a blow job! She sleeps around a lot."

"Is she really a reporter?"

"Yes, she is. She used to have a boyfriend with the CIA, but they had a fight. She also screwed a couple of the Blackwater guys. But really—she's got some nerve!"

Maureen paused.

"You ready to go?"

The beeping of Malko's cell phone woke him. The night before, Maureen had proven every bit as exciting as his fantasies. She'd started by squirting him in the face with champagne, to discourage him from ever seeing Alicia Burton again. After that, things improved significantly. Maureen enjoyed making love as much as ever, and it was very late when Malko got back to the hotel.

Checking his cell, he found a long text message:

You have a meeting with a friend who can tell you some interesting things. Come tomorrow at 6 pm to the One Star Petroleum station in Kotali Khayr Kana. It is on the Salang road, 12 km from downtown.

Malko had finished reading the text when the room phone rang.

"A young lady is here, asking for you," said the desk clerk.

A woman's voice chirped in the handset: "Malko! I'm not disturbing you, am I? It's Alicia Burton."

That was unexpected.

"What a pleasant surprise," he said. "I was just about to come down for breakfast. Would you care to join me?"

"Love to! I'm starving!"

When he met the young reporter in the lobby, he realized that she was hardly starving. Her eyes had a definite come-hither look—with emphasis on the come—and her miniskirt ended well above her knees. Good thing she was wearing a long sheepskin coat over it; otherwise, she'd be attacked at the nearest street corner.

They settled in the breakfast room and chatted about this and that until Malko signed the check.

"Will you treat me to a bath now?" asked the young woman.

Malko smiled diplomatically.

"You can use my whole room, actually; I have a meeting I have to go to. Come on upstairs."

Alicia followed him to his room and tossed her sheepskin coat on a chair.

She turned to Malko and said, "Thank you."

Then she leaned into his arms and stuck her tongue down to his tonsils, while doing a furious bump and grind against his crotch.

By dint of great effort, Malko managed to pull away a few inches. Alicia looked at him mischievously.

"No matter what happens, when I tell Maureen that I came to see you, she'll assume we slept together. So we may as well!"

Well, it was direct at least. Stepping close again, she wrapped her arms around his neck.

"In any case, turnabout is fair play. Maureen stole one of my boyfriends, a guy from the embassy, so . . . It's because she's got big tits. I don't have big tits, but I'm told I'm a good fuck."

Unbuttoning her blouse, she said, "Take a look!"

She wasn't wearing a bra, and Malko could see she had small, pointed—and perfectly acceptable—breasts.

She walked over and locked the door, then came back to him.

"I'm going to take a bath now. Afterward, I hope you behave like a gentleman."

She scampered into the bathroom and closed the door, leaving Malko nonplussed. Either Alicia Burton was a charming ditz or she had something in mind. Malko opted for the second possibility, so he didn't go downstairs for the meeting he'd invented. He wanted to see what kind of stuff the exuberant reporter was made of.

Alicia came out of the bathroom bare breasted, with a hotel towel around her hips and an impish smile on her lips. When she spotted Malko in the armchair, her smile widened.

"Ah, you really are a gentleman, I see!"

She came over to sit on the arm of the chair. The towel slid down to her upper thighs, revealing the warm-toned bush of a true redhead.

She leaned over and kissed him. Once again her tongue played a manic dance in his mouth, and she shuddered when he stroked her bare chest. Then she slipped to the floor, dropped the towel, and attacked Malko like a good little worker bee, respectfully taking his cock in her mouth while caressing herself. The woman knew how to multitask.

Malko relaxed and enjoyed himself, while thinking—as Bill

Clinton reportedly did—that he was not having sex with this woman. Taking refuge in the presidential maxim, he let Alicia do as she pleased. He only gently held her neck at the very end, helping her ensure that he was good to the last drop.

Which he was.

Apparently satisfied, she jumped up and led Malko over to the bed.

"Tell me all about yourself!" she said, much more familiarly now. "What are you doing in Kabul?"

Malko immediately knew he'd been right to behave like a gentleman. Alicia Burton hadn't yielded to any romantic impulse. She wanted something, and he decided to find out what it was.

Sitting cross-legged on the bed, she seemed to drink in everything Malko said, and she did a lot of talking herself. She peppered him with questions, as if he'd suddenly become the most fascinating of men.

Malko obligingly fed her answers, while awaiting the final thrust. It wasn't long in coming.

"Now tell me what you're *really* doing in Kabul!" she said at last. "I checked with the European Union delegation, and they've never heard of you."

Malko smiled.

"That was for Maureen's benefit," he said. "I don't want everybody to know my business. I'm actually here to discreetly contact some Taliban who want to pursue peace negotiations."

"On whose behalf?"

"I can't tell you that," he said, looking mysterious.

"Oh."

For a reporter, she was touchingly naïve.

This probe could be coming from only one person, he thought: Warren Michaelis. Apparently intrigued by Malko's contacting Nelson Berry, the CIA station chief was determined to find out what he was up to in Kabul. He couldn't confront Malko head-on, so he was using another, time-honored method.

Suddenly the reporter seemed no longer eager to stay. She stood up, stretched, and said, "I've got to go now. I'm interviewing one of Karzai's deputies. Let's get together soon, okay? Here's my phone number."

She put a business card on the table, slipped into her fleece coat, and kissed Malko good-bye more chastely than she had when she arrived.

Delilah had carried out her mission, but Samson still had his hair.

Musa Kotak had a guest, and Malko had to wait outside the building where the mullah received visitors. Finally a fat Afghan and a younger man came out, and Malko was ushered in.

As usual the cleric's face brightened when he saw him.

"Well, this is unexpected!" he said. "Can I give you some tea?"

They sat around the low table for the perennial tea ritual. Malko waited a few moments before asking his question. "What can you tell me about the person you're sending me to meet on the Salang Highway?"

Kotak didn't react, just calmly asked, "What person?"

Malko took out his phone and displayed the text message. Kotak read it carefully and looked up.

"I didn't send you that message."

Malko thought he hadn't heard right. Kotak immediately set him straight.

"I am afraid it is a trap," he said softly.

Malko was stunned. Not only was President Karzai trying to kill him and Warren Michaelis sending spies, but now strangers planned to ambush him.

"Who do you suppose is behind it?"

"I do not know," the mullah admitted. "But it must be someone who knows that you and I are close."

"Are they your people?"

"Perhaps."

"In that case, I'm not going."

Kotak shook his head. "I do not think that's the best approach. I would urge you to go; otherwise, we will never know who's involved."

Seeing Malko's dubious expression, he added, "I plan to take precautions, of course. I wouldn't want anything to happen to you."

Malko didn't answer. Even with "precautions," the mullah was sending him into uncertain battle.

"You have to trust me on this!" he insisted.

Malko didn't feel reassured. His mission impossible was becoming more and more complicated. On the Salang Highway the next day, he would once again be playing Russian roulette.

CHAPTER 17

Heading north in the armored Corolla, Darius and Malko were caught in the usual slow-moving traffic jam. They had taken the Salang Tunnel route—the only highway in the country safe from Taliban attack—toward Mazar-e-Sharif, the northernmost city in Afghanistan.

Malko scanned the roadside for the meeting place set by the mysterious correspondent who had impersonated Musa Kotak. This time he was carrying the Russian pistol Berry gave him. Darius had his folding AK-47.

A few years earlier, this highway had snaked over empty hillsides. Since then, the city had spread up their slopes, and thousands of houses thrown together without water or electricity now stretched as far as the eye could see. A miserable, sprawling urban fabric, inhabited by the wretched. The roadsides were jammed with wandering peddlers, carts, and open-air workshops.

Eight or nine miles from downtown Kabul, the highway divided, with separate lanes running on either side of a ravine with a thin trickle of water in its depths. Houses had been built down there as well, of brick or rammed earth.

Finally Malko spotted a big gas station on the left with a sign that read "One Star Petroleum."

"There it is!" he said.

Darius pulled over. The station consisted of six pumps under a wide roof next to a blue building. Parked along a wall was an old ambulance with flat tires. A mud-spattered SUV was stopped at the first pump.

Darius pulled up behind it. On the highway, cars continued to stream by.

Suddenly a Jeep Cherokee emerged from the traffic and stopped directly behind them. At the same moment, the first SUV's doors opened and three men with AK-47s jumped out.

"Back up!" Malko yelled.

Darius put the car in reverse but bumped into the Cherokee behind them. They were trapped.

The men from the first SUV started raking the armored Corolla with assault rifle fire. The bodywork rang with impacts and a dozen big stars appeared on the windshield, but the three-inch-thick bulletproof glass didn't shatter.

The attackers quickly realized that the Corolla was armored. One of them turned and shouted something. Now the SUV's back door swung open to reveal a fourth attacker with a long tube on his shoulder: an RPG-7 grenade launcher.

The Corolla's armor plate was no match for an RPG. Seeing the man aim his weapon at their car, Malko felt his mouth go dry. In moments, the warhead would hit, incinerating them in a four-thousand-degree fireball.

Mesmerized by the sight of the grenade launcher, Malko didn't notice when the back door of the old ambulance flew open and six men in black turbans with Kalashnikovs poured out. The first one fired a long burst at the RPG-7 shooter, practically cutting him in half. The man dropped his tube and collapsed.

The new arrivals continued firing short, accurate bursts, mowing down the three survivors from the muddy SUV.

The Cherokee behind the Corolla now raced off in reverse and vanished into traffic. The six men in black turbans ran past the blue building and disappeared down the ravine.

It was all over very quickly. The traffic on the highway hadn't slowed, and only people who had actually witnessed the firefight noticed anything. At the service station, Darius and Malko alone remained standing. The four men who had attacked them were lying on the ground, either dead or wounded. The entire incident had lasted less than three minutes.

Malko roused himself. The gunshots were sure to attract attention, and the police or the army would soon show up.

"Let's get out of here!" he shouted.

Darius quickly drove the Corolla out of the gas station. The armor plating on its radiator had held, and aside from the damage to the windshield, the car was fine.

They merged with the traffic and continued north. It took them a couple of miles before they found a place where they could cross the river and take the other lane south, back toward downtown Kabul.

"Let's go back to the commander's," said Malko.

He was feeling deeply troubled. Who had tried to kill them? And who had saved them? He was still stumped when they got to Berry's place.

The South African listened to his account, perplexed.

"Go see your mullah and shake him up a bit," he suggested. "This has Taliban written all over it. You're pissing some people off, and this has to be straightened out before we can go ahead.

"Darius will drive you there in an SUV, but after that, you're on your own. I have to find a new windshield for the Corolla."

"Try Maureen Kieffer," Malko suggested.

Musa Kotak was as unctuous as ever. When Malko entered his office, the mullah was sprawled on cushions like a big Buddha, drinking tea and eating pistachios.

"I heard what happened!" the cleric said in a serious tone before Malko had time to speak. "I put you in danger. I'm terribly sorry."

"If it weren't for the Corolla's bulletproofing, we'd be dead."

"I prayed to Allah for you," he said. "The men who saved you were excellent fighters, but a little slow to act."

"What exactly is going on?" demanded Malko. "I need to know!"

"One of the Quetta *shura* factions is against our project," Kota said. "The plan was approved by Mullah Omar, so they couldn't formally oppose it. Instead, they moved indirectly."

"So the people who attacked us were Taliban?"

"I'm afraid they might be, and I will know for sure soon."

"But it was your people who initiated this whole project!"

Kotak set him straight.

"That was just one of our factions. The Quetta *shura* isn't homogenous. Mullah Beradar, who met your friends in Doha, represents the major movement, but there are also two minority positions. The most extreme refuses any cooperation with the Americans. They have contacts everywhere, and I think they warned Karzai's people."

"In that case, this project is over as far as I'm concerned," said Malko. "I'm not committing suicide."

Kotak raised his hands soothingly. "Wait! I have decided to travel to Quetta and ask Mullah Omar to arbitrate the matter. Only he can order those who disagree to toe the line. Please don't go anywhere until I come back. Stay at the Serena, and remain on your guard."

The mullah paused. “Naturally, you might be tempted to leave Kabul, but that would be backing out of our agreement.”

Kotak certainly has some nerve! thought Malko. He’d come to Afghanistan as a predator, and here he was being hunted by Karzai and the Taliban, the country’s two biggest powers. And he’d already escaped death twice.

Malko looked up to find the mullah’s gaze full of goodness.

“You must believe me,” said Kotak. “Going to Quetta is a dangerous journey. I am only doing it for you.”

He rose and took Malko’s hands in his. “Enjoy life for a few days! It is a precious gift. I will contact you as soon as I return, and we will decide what to do next.”

Having made the effort to get up, he now led Malko outside.

“I will call a taxi to take you to the Serena.”

Malko followed him, still feeling very troubled. The mission that National Security Advisor John Mulligan had given him was already challenging enough. Now he faced an array of people hostile to it, people prepared to kill him to keep him from carrying it out.

A taxi pulled up and the cleric spoke to the driver in Dari.

“He’ll take you,” said Kotak. “Don’t give him more than a hundred afghanis.”

Instead of a taxi, what Malko really wanted was the first plane to Austria, but that would mean betraying the trust that Mulligan had in him. He decided he would stay on at least until Kotak got back from Quetta.

And was the Talib mullah really even going there? Malko wondered. There was no way to know for sure.

Entering the Serena lobby, he bumped into Alicia Burton, who was coming out.

"Speak of the devil!" she said. "I came to see you. I just left you a note."

"Why?"

"Come have a cup of coffee and I'll tell you."

Intrigued, Malko followed her to the hotel's nonalcoholic bar. Alicia walked in front of him, and the sight of her little round ass stirred him. Each time Malko escaped death, he experienced powerful sexual stirrings. As if she sensed this, Alicia leaned over the table to give him a panoramic view of her chest as soon as they sat down. Even in a heavy cashmere sweater, a tweed skirt slit up the side, and thick wool stockings, she was extremely sexy—and she knew it.

"Here's what I have in mind," she said. "I want to write a story about your kidnapping for the *New York Times*."

Which was just about the last thing he needed.

"I really don't feel like talking about it," he said carefully. "I'm not a public figure. Besides, I have some calls to make and I don't have much time."

The young woman persisted. "I'd like to chat with you a little, at least."

She was gazing at him very directly, in a way that went straight to his libido.

Malko pretended to agree reluctantly. "Well, if you insist. Let's go upstairs and talk."

"I'll go first. Let's not shock the natives!"

A mystified Parviz Bamyan was studying the report. The acting NDS chief was puzzled by the account of an attack by a group of Taliban on a foreigner named Malko Linge in the village of Kotali Khayr Kana two hours earlier. It was all very odd. Passersby had alerted the police about a fierce exchange of gunfire in a local service station. The police dispatched a patrol, which found a bullet-ridden SUV and the bodies of four armed men, one of whom had a grenade launcher.

They were almost certainly Taliban.

But the Taliban usually only attacked centers of power: the ISAF, the Americans, the police, or the Afghan army. In this case, they had shot up a gas station. There didn't seem to be any victims, in spite of the violence of the shootout.

Nor had the Taliban claimed credit for the action, as they normally did. In addition, some of the witnesses mentioned seeing a group of men in black turbans fleeing the scene. Given their clothes, these were likely Taliban as well.

A fruit seller claimed he saw a *khareji*—a foreigner—in a car at the gas station that had later disappeared: a Toyota Corolla, like tens of thousands of others in Kabul.

And there was one last curious fact: nobody had filed a complaint about the attack.

Bamyan decided to try to identify this foreigner, whom some Talibs had tried to kill and others had apparently protected. He sent the file over to his colleague in charge of monitoring Taliban groups in Kabul. Maybe he could make sense of it.

Alicia stepped into Malko's room, shed her coat, and leaned against a side table, smiling up at him. "I guess we know each other a little by now," she said.

The lower part of her body seemed drawn to Malko's like a magnet. He could feel the rough tweed of her skirt as she rubbed it against his alpaca suit.

She was offering herself on a silver platter.

He ran his hands over her body, moving from the roundness of her breasts to the flare of her hips, then stopping lower down, along the slits in her tweed skirt.

Alicia gave him an innocent look and asked, “Will you tell me about your kidnapping afterward?”

It was a free-trade-agreement proposal. The redheaded reporter knew how to use her charm.

“I don’t have much to say,” objected Malko, slipping his hands under the heavy cashmere sweater and finding the breasts without defense.

Without defense, but not without reaction. Under his fingers, the nipples were stiffening like brave little pencil erasers.

Alicia heaved a sigh and put her hands behind her back. With a faint zipping sound, her tweed skirt fell to the carpet. Malko was pleased to discover that her heavy wool stockings ended below her groin, at a lovely, snow-white string panty.

He now faced a painful choice. After due consideration, he abandoned the warm breasts for these tiny panties that seemed eager to be removed. Their owner helped with a slight shift of her hips, revealing her reddish, heart-shaped bush. Nor was she inactive. Skillful fingers lowered Malko’s fly, and he felt magic fingers clasping his cock and rousing it from its relative torpor.

Since her efforts weren’t producing results quickly enough, Alicia squatted on her heels and started performing a blow job, for which she had an obvious gift. Malko was fast forgetting his earlier worries. He hadn’t had many pleasant moments since arriving in Kabul.

The young woman’s red head rose and fell as smoothly as a well-regulated metronome. Malko now felt warmth spreading between his legs that demanded to be put into action. At that, Alicia looked up at him, her face softly aglow.

“I want it now,” she murmured.

Without waiting for an answer, she walked over to the bed. But instead of flopping down on her back, she wisely kneeled on the little bedcover carpet with her rump high, her chest on the quilt, and her arms stretched out in front of her.

Ready for the sacrifice.

Walking over to her, Malko couldn't help but admire this skillful woman who in a few moments had turned an anxious man into a buck in heat.

He didn't bother being gentle. He drove his cock into her, encountering purely theoretical resistance. Alicia's only reaction when he pinned her to the bed was to clutch at the sheets. Malko was in no mood for courtly love. Bracing himself with the young woman's shoulders, he started thrusting with all his might.

This drew gradually louder sighs from his partner. He was doing a kind of belly dance on her back, as if trying to split her in two. Suddenly, he became aware that Alicia was screaming. She clearly hadn't expected to get such energetic servicing.

Or to enjoy it so much.

Malko was on the verge of coming and was having trouble holding back. He was about to let it happen, but then his devilish instincts took over. First he surreptitiously withdrew from the slippery sheath. Alicia's cries subsided a little, but being polite, she didn't complain. But when Malko set his rigid cock against her ass, her screams resumed—on a very different tone.

Now she was sounding like a stuck piglet.

Undaunted, Malko again tried to enter her, but Alicia fought him like a wildcat. Irritated by this unexpected resistance, he was forced to return to his previous position. He sank all the way back into the young woman and came almost immediately.

All in all, a lovely bit of sexual recreation.

When she straightened out and turned around, he saw that the young woman's makeup had run and there was fire in her green eyes. The look she gave him was half-pleased, half-furious.

"You were fucking me just great, so why did you try to rape me?"

"I wasn't trying to rape you," he protested, "just enjoying your beautiful ass some more."

"Only sickos do that!" she spat.

To Malko, this suggested she needed some time in a good finishing school. But there was no point in arguing.

Alicia disappeared into the bathroom, and when she came out, she looked like a nice young girl again.

She was even more proper when she put on her panties and skirt. Then, with the same charming smile she'd shown when she arrived, she asked, "So what do you have to tell me, now that you've abused me?"

She had a gift for gab that would have done a politician proud.

Malko smiled back at her. "Not a thing," he said.

Her face instantly changed. The smile vanished, the corners of her mouth fell, and her eyes turned cold. If looks could kill, Malko would've been a little pile of dust.

"You bastard!" she screamed.

That was the only thing she said before grabbing her purse and going out, slamming the door so hard that plaster fell from around the jamb. The Serena had been built by a Turkish developer who'd pocketed half the construction budget.

Malko gazed at the door.

Whoever had sent Alicia Burton to debrief him wouldn't be getting their money's worth. They had lost whatever they invested in the operation, and the young woman had lost some infinitesimal part of her virtue.

Driving from downtown, Nelson Berry circled the Shah Massoud roundabout with the huge portraits of the late Tajik commander. He also passed a street on his right with checkpoints every twenty yards: one of the entrances to President Karzai's palace.

Beyond the roundabout, he took Airport Road, the wide avenue that led straight to the airport. Traffic was moving smoothly.

On the days when Karzai went that way, the avenue was closed off, allowing him to make for his destination at top speed. Policemen were stationed at regular intervals along the way to prevent demonstrations or assassination attempts.

The South African slowly drove up the avenue, which was lined by low houses. Suddenly he noticed a tall building under construction on his right, its facade hidden by sheets of green canvas. Workers were busy on the upper floors. Berry turned off onto the first street beyond it, which led to the Shaheen Hotel. He parked in the lot and walked back to the fifteen-story redbrick building. It bore a huge sign that boldly proclaimed: "Azizi Plaza. Completion: 2013."

They were running a little behind schedule.

Berry walked around the building, studying its access points. Then he returned to his car, thinking hard. He might have found a way to earn the CIA's money.

CHAPTER 18

A day after Mullah Kotak left for Quetta, Warren Michaelis phoned.

"I have what you asked for," he said. "Can I send someone to the Serena in an hour?"

"Sure, that'll be fine," said Malko, who badly needed a break. He'd been spending all his time watching television and had learned that the skeleton of Richard III had been dug up in England. Another twisted, paranoid ruler, thought Malko.

He had nothing else to do, having decided to suspend his activities until Kotak returned. Too many disturbing things had happened, including the recent gas station attack. Nelson Berry was still waiting for the five-hundred-thousand-dollar payment and hadn't contacted him. That didn't particularly bother Malko, who was staying on the sidelines for the time being. He didn't have any word from Maureen Kieffer either, and he hadn't called her. Until he knew exactly who was after him, he didn't want to put her in danger. The door-slamming Alicia Burton had probably gotten her knuckles rapped for failing to learn anything about his activities.

So when someone knocked on that same door a little later, Malko was startled. The case officer—a polite, distant young man—brought a briefcase with the money, but Malko didn't even bother opening it. He just initialed the receipt, as he had before.

When he was alone, he texted Berry: *I have your asset.* He got an answer a few minutes later: *Sending Darius to usual spot at noon.* Berry apparently trusted the Afghan enough to bring him half a million dollars in cash.

After giving Darius the money, Malko asked the front desk for a car and driver. As a change of pace, he felt like going shopping for semiprecious stones on Chicken Street—a totally ordinary outing for which he didn't need the CIA's help.

Malko was admiring the lapis lazuli and agate cats he had bought when his phone beeped with a text message. It was very brief:

I am back from Quetta.

So the fat mullah was showing signs of life! It was about time. Malko was starting to feel trapped. Between his mysterious kidnapping, Michaelis's honey trap, and the Taliban ambush, it was all a bit much. Especially since without the cleric's protection Malko would have joined Kabul's long list of unexplained deaths.

Mullah Kotak looked drawn and had lost some of his normal good cheer. After the usual preambles, he sat Malko down on the pile of cushions and served him tea.

"I thought I would never get there," he said with a sigh. "There was fighting near Spin Boldak and it was freezing in Quetta. But what wouldn't I do for a friend?"

The mullah fairly oozed unctuousness.

Malko was on pins and needles but was polite enough to drink some of his chai before asking, "Was your trip fruitful?"

"Completely!" said the cleric. "I had the great honor of an

interview with our sainted Mullah Omar, a man of great wisdom who loves justice."

Also an obscurantist, thought Malko. Omar was the man whose religious fervor led him to blow up the huge Buddhas of Bamiyan, destroying one of humanity's treasures. Once a simple village mullah, Omar had become the undisputed leader of the Taliban solely because of his rectitude and fanaticism.

"Was this meeting related to our business?" asked Malko.

"Yes, it was," said the cleric, nodding. "But first I spoke with Mullah Beradar, the man who traveled to Doha to reach an agreement with our American friends."

"And asked that President Karzai be killed," Malko reminded him.

"That's correct, though he was only transmitting the decision taken by our secret committee and confirmed by Mullah Omar, may Allah keep him in his holy protection.

"I told Mullah Beradar about the difficulties you encountered in Kabul even before you were able to put your plan into effect."

"Did you tell him that someone tried to kill me?"

"I had already sent a report to Quetta on that matter," said Kotak. "Mullah Beradar was very angry. He launched an internal investigation and arranged a confrontation between himself and Mullah Mansur in Mullah Omar's presence.

"After some reluctance, Mullah Mansur admitted that he disagreed with the secret committee's decisions. He felt that it wasn't worth the trouble to kill Karzai, that we should let him fall like a rotten fruit on the day we seize power. That his death would only complicate things by enraging the Tajiks and the Uzbeks."

"Did Mansur admit that he tried to kill me?" asked Malko.

Mullah Kotak waved the question away as if it weren't relevant, and went on.

"Following this confrontation, a *shura* was held with the various members of the secret committee, presided over by Mullah Omar.

"In the end, he settled the matter and decided the project should go ahead. That way, we avoid wasting our energy fighting the Americans. Once Karzai is dead, the regime will disintegrate and its most corrupt members will flee. We will have fewer people to hang. That will ensure a smoother transfer of power.

"Mullah Mansur promised to take no further action. He would never dare oppose Mullah Omar, our respected leader. Mullah Omar's only regret is that the task of killing Karzai has been given to an infidel."

Malko knew that Omar took matters of religion extremely seriously. The man had supposedly never in his life spoken to a non-Muslim, of any rank.

"Does this mean I won't have any more problems from within the Taliban?"

Kotak nodded.

"Mullah Mansur would never defy Mullah Omar. He put forth his point of view, and it was rejected. We are a democratic organization whose members are honest in the highest degree."

The chubby cleric wasn't above a bit of sly humor.

Malko felt relieved. He had taken this assignment reluctantly, and not to work with people who would stab him in the back.

"This sounds reassuring," Malko said.

But Kotak wasn't smiling. He merely fingered his amber tasbih—prayer beads—in silence. Malko sensed that he still had more to report.

The cleric leaned closer and said, "In my investigation, I had a long talk with Mullah Mansur. He and I may not always agree, but we fought the Soviets together, and that created a deep friendship between us. Mullah Mansur swore on our holy Quran that he didn't tell anyone about your presence in Kabul."

As Malko slowly grasped the implications of what Kotak had just said, his blood ran cold.

"Are you saying that the kidnapping had nothing to do with your people?"

"Nothing at all. The only action against you was the gas station attack by the people from Wendak, whom my fighters killed. May Allah forgive me for that, because they were good Muslims and brave men."

Malko was shaken. "You told me that the kidnapping came from the presidency."

"Absolutely," the mullah confirmed. "And I am positive about my information. It was a devious operation, using people who had no direct link to Karzai."

"So who tipped Karzai off?" asked Malko.

The mullah spread his fat hands. "I have no idea, but it didn't come from our side."

Which raised a whole new problem.

Malko could hardly imagine continuing a mission that was rotten at the core. Because there could now be only one source for the leak: the CIA. He didn't know who knew about the assassination project in Washington, where Hamid Karzai still had supporters. But Karzai had learned about it here in Kabul, so it was in Kabul that Malko would have to investigate.

"Thank you very much," he said to Kotak.

"I hope you are not going to give up your project."

"I don't plan to lift a finger until I know where the leak is coming from," said Malko firmly. "Otherwise, we're bound to fail. I will keep you posted."

They again exchanged a long handshake. Mullah Kotak seemed sincerely contrite.

"I have solved the problem on my side," he said. "It's now up to you to solve it on yours. But remember, you are not alone. I am continuing to protect you, discreetly."

In fact, Malko could think of only one person who could really protect him: Warren Michaelis, a man who was apparently already taking a great interest in him, by way of Alicia Burton. He would confront him in a day or so.

Michaelis was fairly dripping with goodwill. He'd immediately returned Malko's phone call with an invitation to lunch at the Ariana Hotel. An armored Agency SUV came to pick him up at the Serena.

As they ate, Malko let the CIA station chief do all the talking, without broaching any serious topics. Michaelis broke this tacit agreement with an innocent-sounding question.

"How is your stay in Kabul going?"

Michaelis apparently didn't know about the attack at the Salang Highway gas station.

"I have a big concern," Malko said as he finished his steak.

"Really? What's that?"

The American seemed honestly surprised—and interested. Malko gave him a totally innocent smile.

"You're aware that Langley gave me a mission with an extremely high need-to-know, right?"

"Yes, I am," said the CIA station chief with a frown. "I was instructed to steer clear of your activities, and I have."

"Not entirely."

"What do you mean by that?"

"I've been persistently approached by a freelance reporter

named Alicia Burton. She did everything she could to find out—somewhat clumsily—what I was doing in Kabul. I told her a few things that she probably passed on to you."

"To me? Why?"

Malko looked the American in the eye. "Because you sent her, Warren. Burton is a newspaper stringer. She has contacts in the Agency, and she depends on you for her livelihood. I'm not angry at what you did, but I need to be sure of what I'm saying. Once I am, I can abandon a lead I've been pursuing. You were probably just doing your job, but I have to know."

A long silence followed. If any pins were dropping, they would've been heard. At last, the CIA station chief spoke.

"I apologize, Malko," he said sheepishly. "What I learned, I kept to myself. I just wanted to stay informed and be sure you weren't taking any unnecessary risks."

Malko allowed himself a small smile. "Then we can consider the matter closed," he said. "But I have a much more serious problem. Did you know one of your predecessors, Mark Spider?"

"Of course. A remarkable man and very close to President Karzai, whom he's been following for the last twelve years. Spider did two tours as Kabul COS and is now in Washington."

"Do you know what he does there?" asked Malko.

"He's on the Strategic Committee for Afghanistan. It has people from the Agency, the Pentagon, the federal government, and the White House."

"Are they active?"

"Very. When President Obama decided we would withdraw our troops in 2014, it raised a lot of problems, and those issues are still on the table."

"Do you receive instructions on that subject?"

"Some, but our relations with President Karzai are very difficult. Even I sometimes have to wait several days before I can talk to him. He's very capricious and constantly complains about us to the media. Fortunately, one of my deputies is on good terms with him."

"Who is that?" asked Malko, sounding casual.

"Jason Forrest. He was number two when Mark Spider was COS. Mark introduced Jason to Karzai. He may even have the president's private cell number, which I don't."

Malko's face betrayed nothing. He might just have found the source of the leaks that had nearly got him killed in the kidnapping.

CHAPTER 19

"What exactly does Forrest do here in Kabul?" asked Malko.

"He runs the Office of Regional Affairs. It's a group of analysts that draws on Pakistani, Afghan, Iranian, and Indian sources to generate situation assessments."

"Does he meet with President Karzai in the course of his work?"

Michaelis paused before answering. "No, I don't think so. In any case, he's supposed to inform me if that happens. Why are you asking me all this?"

"For a very serious reason," said Malko. "I think someone told Karzai about the mission I've been assigned."

Michaelis's eyes widened. "How's that possible? Even I don't know what it is."

"I know, and I'm not accusing you. But I'm afraid that someone in the Agency—whom I can't name—has learned what I'm doing here and is keeping Karzai informed. I can't tell you how I know this, but I'm virtually certain that my kidnapping was a setup arranged by someone in his entourage to get rid of me permanently."

Michaelis looked as if he'd been punched. When he finally understood what Malko was implying, he asked in a horrified tone, "You don't really think Jason Forrest is informing President Karzai, do you?"

"Yes, I do."

"Why would he do that?" protested the station chief. "He's a respected senior officer of impeccable honesty, without a single black mark in his file. A man like that couldn't possibly be a traitor."

Malko smiled. "You know the four reasons for committing treason, don't you, Warren? Remember the acronym MICE: money, ideology, compromise, ego. In Jason Forrest's case, it would be ideology. Here's my thinking. I imagine that Forrest is still close to his former boss, Mark Spider, right?"

"Yes. They email each other quite often. Jason has mentioned it to me."

"Okay. Let's say that Spider, who has close ties with President Karzai, disagrees with American policy toward Karzai. He might very well want to inform him. That isn't *really* treason. Only, reactions here in Asia can sometimes be brutal. Trust me, I know."

Michaelis had been staring at his plate. Now he looked up—and went on the offensive. "That's just a theory," he said in a firm voice. "In my eyes Jason Forrest is completely loyal. I can bring him in and question him, if you like."

"That would probably be the worst possible thing to do," said Malko. "There's a much better way."

"What's that?"

"Discreetly get a listing of all calls made from his cell phone for the last month."

Michaelis blanched. "That's out of the question! It would be impugning the man! Anyway, counterintelligence handles that kind of inquiry. Otherwise, it would be casting suspicion on someone when it wasn't warranted."

"Come on, Warren!" Malko said with an understanding smile. "It's exactly what you would do if you thought a senior officer had been a little too chatty with unauthorized people. There's no shame in it. As COS, you'd just tell your security officer to keep his eyes peeled. And if it turns out that I'm mistaken, we'll forget all about it."

Michaelis shook his head vigorously, jowls flapping. "I just can't do it!"

When he met Malko's eye, the Austrian's gaze was icy. "As I see it, two very important things are involved here. First, the success of a mission given to me by Clayton Luger. Second, my personal safety. If you refuse, I'll be forced to turn to Langley. And I really don't want to do that."

A hush descended on the men, and it flew around the small dining room until Michaelis spoke.

"I'll launch the inquiry," he said dully. "And keep you informed."

His lunch with Michaelis over, Malko contacted Nelson Berry, who promptly sent him the same SUV with Darius at the wheel. They drove along the NDS complex, passing the Gandamack Lodge on their left. The moment they reached Berry's poppy palace, he bounded down the front steps and shook Malko's hand.

"Thanks for your little present," he said. "We're up to date now. Your timing's good, because I've made some headway. Follow me!"

He took Malko into a room next to his office. Standing on a wooden table was a long object wrapped in a blanket. Berry unwrapped it, revealing an enormous sniper rifle with a Zeiss scope on a tripod. It was a monster, with a barrel more than three feet long.

"This is a Degtyarov 41," he announced with a hint of pride. "A sniper rifle used by the Soviets. Fires a 14.5 mm cartridge, single shot. Accurate to eight hundred yards. The shell's kinetic energy is so high that if it hits a vehicle, it destroys it along with the occupants. I had it shipped from Dushanbe with some ammunition."

Malko gazed at the sniper rifle respectfully. You didn't see something like that every day.

Added Berry, "The shell will penetrate an inch and a half of armor plate."

The two men looked at each other, both thinking the same thing.

Malko broke the silence: "I assume you know how to shoot it."

"I've used it before," said the South African. "It's an incredibly powerful weapon. Of course, you can't afford to miss, 'cause there's no magazine. The advantage is that when you hit your target, your problem's solved."

"Have you chosen a kill zone?" asked Malko.

"Yeah, I have. I started looking into that while you were out of touch. I know how Karzai's people work. They sweep the route and get rid of all the cars along the way, but they don't go far beyond the perimeter. It would take too much manpower. I found a location I can shoot from, but there's still lots of problems to deal with."

"What about your exfiltration?" asked Malko.

"That shouldn't be an issue," said the South African. "I'll leave the rifle behind. It was stolen from a Russian unit in Tajikistan, so it can't be traced to me."

Berry rewrapped the Degtyarov, and the two men returned to his office.

"Has anybody else thought of getting rid of Karzai this way?" asked Malko.

"Maybe, but there are a couple of hurdles. First, you have to know how to use a rifle like that, and it isn't easy. I'm big enough, physically, because the recoil is terrific; 14.5 is the caliber of a Dushka, the heavy Russian machine gun. It's like firing an RPG, except the projectile travels much faster.

"Also, this kind of attack isn't in the Taliban mind-set. They'll swarm a building, break into it, then blow themselves up. I don't think they would conceive of this kind of tactic."

"Tell me more about your plan," said Malko. "Having the rifle is all well and good, but you still need a target."

"I've made some progress there, too," said Berry. "In a week or so, Karzai will be going to Lashkar Gah in Helmand Province. He's flying, so he'll be traveling from his palace to the airport, as he always does. The Airport Road route will be cordoned off, but not too far on either side. I've located a building under construction set back from the road that I can use as a hide site."

"What about Karzai's departure time?"

"I'm looking into that, but it shouldn't be too hard. Mainly I need a spotter at the palace so I can predict the time slot. There will be about ten minutes between the time he leaves the palace and when he enters my kill zone.

"The biggest problem is that when Karzai travels, his convoy always uses three identical Mercedes with tinted glass. He doesn't choose his car until the last minute. I don't need to see him, but I have to know which car he's in. I'm working on that.

"So what do you think of my plan?"

"It looks pretty good to me. But you're running a big personal risk."

The South African gave him a crooked smile. "That's what you're paying me for," he said. "What about you? You getting out of the country before D-Day?"

"No, I'm not."

If he left, he'd have felt like a coward. He rather liked the rough-hewn South African, even though he was a killer. He wasn't afraid to take chances.

"That should do it," said Malko. "Don't leave that rifle of yours lying around."

CHAPTER 20

It was raining in Kabul. Sheets of water fell from a leaden, grayish sky, turning rutted roads into muddy swamps. Thick fog hid the tops of the surrounding hills.

The change in the weather had been sudden and depressing.

Malko was in his room, staring out at the hotel's leafless garden. Kept indoors by the lack of action and the bad weather, he felt gloomy. This strange mission was lasting a very long time, and a hostile, invisible world seemed to be swirling around him.

By now, Hamid Karzai almost certainly knew Malko was in Kabul on a mission targeting him, even though he didn't know its exact shape. It would explain the attempt to kidnap and kill him. That could happen again, in some other form. Given the rocky relationship between Karzai and the Americans, anything was possible. The Afghan president's mix of smooth lies and public tantrums excluded overt action, but not dirty tricks. Malko probably wouldn't be arrested by the NDS, for example. Some other attempt would be made to discreetly get rid of him.

Hamid Karzai had far-reaching influence, lots of money, and many accomplices. And Malko's so-called Taliban allies weren't much help.

Just then, the rain stopped.

As if there were some connection, Warren Michaelis's number appeared on Malko's cell almost immediately.

"I'm sending you a car," announced the CIA station chief. "Are you available?"

"Of course," he said.

Malko practically wept with relief. At last, he would find out if the leak had come from the Americans, as he feared. Until the leak was plugged, it was impossible for him to make headway on his project.

Michaelis was looking grave when Malko entered his office. The station chief carefully closed the door and switched on the red light that meant he was not to be disturbed under any circumstances. Then he slumped onto his brown leather sofa and said, "You were right!"

"About what?"

"About Jason Forrest. We compiled a record of his cell phone communications. He called Karzai seven times since your arrival."

"Did you put a tap on his line?"

"No. That would have required a special security request."

"When was his first call?"

Michaelis went to his desk and returned with a printout of names and numbers.

"At nine thirty-five p.m. on the day after your arrival. The conversation lasted eleven minutes."

Malko did a quick calculation. That was two days after his meeting with Luger and Mulligan. Mark Spider hadn't wasted any time before racing to help his protégé.

So Malko had found the origin of the leak that had almost cost him his life.

A clearly tense Michaelis was watching him. "What do we do now?" he asked. "I can call Jason in and confront him with this list of phone calls."

"Why not give him a lie detector test while you're at it?" asked Malko sarcastically. "He hasn't done anything obviously wrong. He would come up with a perfectly good reason for those calls and immediately alert Spider. No, this calls for different countermeasures."

"Such as?"

"I'm going to make a quick trip to Washington. That's where the key to the problem lies. This leak has to be cut off at the source."

"So I shouldn't take any action?" asked Michaelis, looking somewhat disappointed.

"Whatever you do, don't tell anybody I'm going to Washington. You can hint that I left for Islamabad to visit some Taliban leaders in Quetta. I actually am going through Islamabad, to get a flight to the United States. It's not a very direct route, but I'm used to it."

Michaelis gave him a long, probing look. "Malko, someday I hope I find out what you came to Kabul for."

"Warren, I promise you'll be the first to know."

It was colder in Washington than it had been in Kabul. It had recently snowed, and an icy gale howled through the avenues. Malko had flown Kabul-Islamabad, then Islamabad-London, and finally London-Washington, and was exhausted.

The Willard InterContinental was as formal and low-key as ever. Malko phoned Clayton Luger the moment he checked in.

"I'm here," he announced.

"Great," said the deputy director. "Let's meet tomorrow for lunch at your hotel restaurant. It will be more discreet."

"I'll make the reservation."

What with the time difference and the changes of planes, Malko hardly knew where he was. He got undressed, took a long shower, and went to bed. He immediately fell asleep.

Warren Michaelis warmly welcomed Afghanistan's chief of police. The veteran cop knew the workings of the country like the back of his hand. Today, something was apparently bothering him.

After the ritual of tea and mutual politeness, Michaelis asked, "Is there something special you're concerned about?"

The older man answered with a question of his own. "Have you noticed an increase in local communications between various Taliban groups lately? I ask because your monitoring system is much more effective than ours."

Surprised, Michaelis answered, "I haven't been informed of anything, but I can find out. I'll get in touch with Bagram. Everything gets routed there. Why do you ask?"

"In the last weeks, the Taliban have launched several attacks on police stations and training academies. The most recent one was the day before yesterday. They seized a building and used it to attack a special forces barracks. We took some prisoners, and one said that his group came from the area south of Jalalabad. This means they crossed dozens of villages without anyone alerting us."

"That's not a good sign," admitted Michaelis.

"Oh, we're used to it," said the Afghan almost casually. "It's been this way forever. Officially we control big chunks of the country, but in fact our presence is just cosmetic. People have already gone over to the other side. But that's not what worries me. I get the feeling that Taliban combat units are taking up positions in the city, ready to start something."

"Like the Tet offensive in Vietnam?"

"Er, yes, something like that."

"As long as we're in the country, those groups can't stand up to our Apaches and Black Hawks," said Michaelis. "We don't have any troops in Kabul, but we have people in Bagram and elsewhere."

"That's true enough, but I'm still worried," said the old cop. "The Taliban never do anything without good reason. It's as if they're preparing for some sort of destabilizing event."

Michaelis escorted his guest out and returned to his office. He didn't know how seriously to take the police chief's nervousness. It was true that the Taliban often targeted Afghan police. That, plus desertions, was hard on morale. But he couldn't see why the Taliban would prepare a general offensive. Because if they came out into the open, they would be crushed.

Malko had been sitting in his booth for five minutes when Luger and Mulligan arrived, looking annoyed.

"I hope you have a good reason for calling this meeting," said the national security advisor. "I thought this project was already well under way."

"I didn't fly halfway around the world just for fun," answered Malko.

The three placed their orders: Caesar salads, racks of lamb, a bottle of California wine.

Malko knew the two men were anxious to get started, and he began with a simple question, "Who knows about our project?"

"Nobody except John, here," said Luger in surprise. "Why?"

"Because someone told President Karzai about it."

"Really?" Luger frowned. "Is this coming out of Kabul?"

"No," said Malko. "I'm sure it's not. The only person there who could have done it is Nelson Berry, the man you had me contact. And it's not in his interest."

Malko then described his recent misadventures, including the gas station attack and the mullah's intervention. He concluded,

"The leak came from Washington and we have to plug it. First, because it puts my life in danger, and second, because it might have serious consequences for the future."

John Mulligan shook his head and said, "It can't possibly be coming from here!"

Malko looked him in the eye. "Not only is it possible; I even have a lead."

"What?"

"Have you mentioned this project to the Strategic Committee for Afghanistan?"

A question they clearly hadn't expected.

"Why are you asking?" Mulligan snapped.

"Because it's at the heart of the leak problem. And you haven't answered me, John."

The White House advisor pretended to be thinking, then spoke reluctantly: "A passing reference was made to it, without any details. But the committee members are all senior officials, totally devoted to serving the United States."

"Aldrich Ames was also an outstanding CIA officer," remarked Malko. "Yet he betrayed all the Russians working for the Agency, and quite a few of them were shot. Ames did that for money, as I recall."

"That was the Cold War," grumbled Mulligan angrily. "What are you getting at, anyway?"

Malko continued. "Is a man named Mark Spider a member of the Afghanistan committee?"

"Of course! He's one of our best Afghanistan specialists. He did two tours in Kabul and his advice is invaluable."

"What else do you know about Spider, John?"

"Nothing but good things."

"Where were you eleven years ago, in 2002?"

"I was the head of the NSA. Why?"

"Because that's when Mark Spider got to know Hamid Karzai and helped make him America's proconsul in Afghanistan. Karzai is a Pashtun from a little tribe called the Popolzai. At the time, he was working for a Pashtun politician and didn't seem to have much of a future. Spider, who was one of the few Afghanistan specialists in those days, 'sold' Karzai to the Americans at the Bonn Conference in Germany. Karzai went in as an unknown and came out as a head of state. This created a bond between the two men. Since then, as you know, Spider has been Kabul COS twice, with unusual access to Karzai."

"Are you saying Spider is in his pocket?" asked Luger.

"No, it's a relationship of friends. Spider sees many good qualities in Karzai while ignoring his faults, namely that he's surrounded himself with deeply corrupt people and acquired a taste for power."

"What's the connection with our affair?" asked Mulligan.

"It's simple. During the Afghanistan committee meeting, Spider realized that the White House wanted to get rid of Karzai in a way that would maintain plausible deniability. Out of loyalty to Karzai, he warned him."

"He called Karzai?" asked Luger, incredulous.

"No, he called his former staffer Jason Forrest, who is still in Kabul. Forrest passed the warning on to Karzai."

Silence fell, broken by the White House advisor. "Can you prove this?"

Malko held his gaze. "Yes."

He summarized the inquiry he'd asked Warren Michaelis to conduct, which revealed the secret contacts between Karzai and Forrest. "I haven't figured out what the next steps are," he continued, "but as soon as Karzai was alerted, he reacted by having me kidnapped."

The two Americans were shaken when they heard the story of Malko's capture and eventual rescue.

"What should we do, in your opinion?" asked Mulligan. "Remove Mark Spider from the committee?"

"It's too late for that," said Malko. "The damage has been done. Karzai is now on guard. Since he can't take official action against me, he's trying to eliminate me."

"How does he know you're involved?" asked Luger.

"It's just a theory, but Warren Michaelis was informed of my arrival, and he must have mentioned it to his deputy Jason Forrest. My visit corresponded with Spider's warning, so Forrest concluded that I was the Agency's errand boy, sent to do the dirty work."

The mood at the restaurant table had become very tense.

"What do you suggest?" Mulligan asked again.

"One thing's for sure," said Malko. "If I return to Kabul, I'll be risking my life."

"So you're dropping the project?"

Malko was silent for a long moment, letting the Americans twist in the wind for a bit. When he finally spoke, it was to the national security advisor. "I can think of a way out of this, but it will require your cooperation, John."

"How so?"

"By easing Hamid Karzai's fears. Tell me: you convene the Afghanistan committee meetings, don't you?"

"Yes, I do."

"Are they held on a regular basis?"

"No, they're called in response to events."

"Very well," said Malko. "Let's say you call one of those meetings and Mark Spider attends. You announce that given the difficulties the project has encountered, you have decided to cancel it. You can be sure that Spider will immediately pass the good news to Forrest, who in turn will tell Karzai. He'll feel safe again and stop trying to kill me—at least I hope so. In addition, it could reduce some of his current hostility toward the U.S."

A heavy silence followed Malko's proposal.

"You're asking me to lie," said Mulligan in a reproachful tone.

"And you're asking me to kill somebody," Malko shot back. "This isn't a Boy Scout jamboree. It's your call. I'm not forcing you."

The coffees had arrived but remained untouched.

Mulligan looked at his watch and said, "I have to be going; I have an important meeting. I'll think about this and call you tomorrow."

The White House advisor shook hands and walked out, leaving Luger alone wth Malko.

"Do you realize what you're suggesting?" the CIA deputy director hissed. "You're blackmailing the White House!"

"I'm not blackmailing anybody," said Malko. "I'm just trying not to die prematurely."

"But this involves the president!"

"That's true," admitted Malko. "But I don't think his hand shakes when he signs the executive order to dispatch an armed drone to liquidate some Islamist. Same thing here. Compared to everything else, John's lie will be a pretty minor sin."

"So what do you plan to do now?"

"I'll wait for John's answer until tomorrow. Then I'll take a plane, either for Kabul or for Austria. Which one depends on you.

"And by the way, I hope John isn't tempted to lie to me. Not only would it be disloyal, but I'll find out, and it will end my association with the Agency."

Snow was falling lightly on Washington as Malko gazed across the park to the Capitol dome. It was ten minutes to one, and he still hadn't gotten the phone call he was expecting. He had decided to wait until the evening. To allay his nervousness, he turned on *NBC News*.

A few moments later, his cell rang. He recognized Luger's number—not a good sign.

"I didn't think you'd be the person to call, Clayton. You aren't a party to this decision."

"I'm calling on John's behalf. I just came from his office. We had a long talk. He's very upset."

"I'm sorry about that," said Malko. "Nobody could anticipate the way this turned out."

"John didn't sleep much last night," continued Luger, "but in the end he decided to do what you suggested. He's calling a meeting of the Afghanistan committee for tomorrow, and the person concerned will attend. Does that suit you?"

Malko was silent for a few moments.

"Is this absolutely definite?" he asked.

"You have my word," said Luger.

"Very well. In that case, I'll book my plane tickets."

CHAPTER 21

Malko waited for an hour at Islamabad for the arrival of a connecting flight and took the opportunity to text Michaelis and ask that a car be sent to meet him. He was dazed with fatigue.

On Malko's arrival in Kabul, the immigration officer spent a long time peering at his passport, as if he doubted its authenticity, which put him on edge. But he was eventually able to join Jim Doolittle in a white Land Cruiser waiting next to the terminal.

"I'll drop my bag off at the Serena and then we'll go to the Ariana," Malko said. He was anxious to wrap up his disinformation operation.

Fair weather had returned to Kabul, bringing a perfect blue sky and pleasant temperatures.

The men guarding the pedestrian entrance to the Serena watched an attractive woman with a slightly hooked nose and a silk head scarf walk up to the table on which visitors put items that might set off the metal detector. But instead of putting anything on the table, she flashed an NDS ID card with her photograph and name, Ashraf Nyadi. The guards recognized her, and let her bypass the metal detector and head directly for the lobby. At the front desk, she asked for Room 306, the one permanently reserved for NDS agents on surveillance assignments.

The moment Nyadi entered the room, she opened her large handbag and took out an automatic with a silencer. She unscrewed the silencer and put it and the pistol in the hanging closet safe.

She then got undressed, put on a Serena terry cloth robe, and headed for the sauna. That was one of the perks of this highly confidential mission: the hotel's sauna was the nicest in the city. Nyadi could relax while she waited for her target.

Malko didn't keep Warren Michaelis waiting.

"The problem has been taken care of," he announced the moment he entered the CIA station chief's office. "You don't need to say anything to Jason Forrest."

"So what happened?"

Malko merely smiled.

"I can't tell you, but things should get back to normal pretty quickly. On the other hand, I want you to start tapping Jason Forrest's cell phone."

"Why?"

"There's something I need to check. And I'm afraid I can't tell you about that, either."

Michaelis looked uncomfortable.

"All right," he said, "but you're making me do things that are illegal, and I don't like it."

Malko gave him a smile tinged with regret.

"I understand. I also wind up doing illegal things and they give me no joy. I'll need a daily listing of all the numbers Forrest calls. It's important."

In fact, it was vital. If Hamid Karzai wasn't completely reassured, he would remain on the offensive.

Just then one of Michaelis's phones rang—the Bagram Air Base was calling—and the station chief waved Malko good-bye.

Out in the fourth-floor hallway, Malko almost collided with Alicia Burton, who had a messenger bag on her shoulder and a burly CIA case officer at her side. So Alicia really was a CIA asset, Malko realized. They stared at each other, equally taken aback. She first put on a distant expression, but then her eyes lit up and she came over to him.

"I acted stupidly the other day!" she said. "Will you forgive me?"

Standing akimbo in jeans and a puffy down coat, she looked very sexy.

"Of course," said Malko.

With a glance at her American escort hovering a few feet away, she spoke quickly: "I can't talk now. Can we have dinner together tonight?"

"No problem."

"I'll come to the Serena," she said, and walked away.

After she left, it occurred to Malko that he might do well to kick his disinformation operation up a notch. He couldn't contact Nelson Berry until he was positive that Karzai believed the Americans wished him no harm. But this might be a good time to punch a few holes in his security cordon. He asked Doolittle to drive him to the Wazir Akbar Khan mosque.

The Land Cruiser eased into Kabul's demented traffic. Seated in the back were two Marines with M16s, hand grenades, helmets, and bulletproof vests; they looked distinctly uncomfortable. They kept glancing around as if they were crossing a city full of dangerous dinosaurs.

Kabul was no place they cared to be.

Mullah Kotak was working on his computer when Malko arrived. He stood up, showing a pleasure that might have been sincere.

"I was told you'd left Kabul! I see that wasn't the case."

"Actually, it was. I did some traveling and got back this morning. With some bad news."

The cleric's face fell so abruptly, it was almost funny. He led Malko to the back of the room and the pile of cushions. A ragged helper came in to serve them tea, then disappeared.

"So what is this bad news?" asked the cleric.

"I've identified the leak in our project. As you said, it didn't come from your side. It was inside the Agency. Someone warned Hamid Karzai that the Americans were plotting against him."

Kotak was no longer smiling.

"Who could have done that?" he asked, heaving a sigh. "This is very serious."

"I couldn't agree more," said Malko. "A number of meetings were held in Washington as to what to do next. And unfortunately the final decision wasn't along the lines that you hoped."

"Meaning what?"

"The Americans have decided not to pursue the project."

At first, Kotak showed no reaction. Then he spoke through clenched teeth. "This is very unfortunate. It means that evil, corrupt man will continue destroying the country."

"I'm afraid so. You might let the people in Quetta know."

"Do you think the decision is final?" he asked hesitantly.

"Yes, it is."

For a moment Kotak was lost in thought. Finally he said, "Mullah Omar will be disappointed. He is so honest, and he hates Karzai, who is so corrupt. Will you be leaving Kabul now?"

"Pretty soon."

"And your . . . preparations?"

"Are being dismantled. To succeed, the plan needed the element of surprise, and it no longer has it."

Malko now felt eager to get out of there. He had delivered the message and it would be quickly relayed to Quetta. Taking this step hadn't been essential, but he knew too well how porous Afghan circles could be. He was taking a belt-and-suspenders approach, just to be on the safe side.

Mullah Kotak seemed devastated. He gave Malko a long look, as if about to ask him something, but finally said only, "I will pray for you."

That could be taken in several ways, and Malko thought he detected a vague threat in Kotak's voice. Had he just made himself a new enemy?

Just the same, the cleric walked him out to the garden gate and said, "Be sure to come say good-bye before you leave Kabul!"

The phone in Malko's room rang, startling him. Without realizing it, he had fallen asleep on his bed fully dressed. Before picking up the handset, he glanced at his watch. It was 7:30 p.m. He'd slept for three hours.

"I'm downstairs in the lobby," said a woman's voice.

It took him a few moments to realize it was Alicia Burton.

"Give me fifteen minutes!" He had to take a shower.

He found Alicia waiting for him on a bench in the lobby, wearing a down jacket over a pair of long legs sheathed in black leather. She looked even more appetizing than Malko remembered.

She sat up and said, "My car's here, so we can go back to my place, the Gandamack. The food's pretty good."

A tan Corolla with an Afghan driver was parked out front. In ten minutes they were at the Gandamack Lodge, which was almost directly across from the NDS. The guesthouse had been named for Britain's disastrous final battle against the Pashtuns near the Khyber Pass in 1842.

Hidden behind another building, the guesthouse had no sign. Three night watchmen squatted nearby, AK-47s propped against the wall, sharing a bowl of rice *palau*. A metal door at the back of the courtyard led to the guesthouse proper. Malko and Burton walked through a patchy lawn to the tiny lobby, and from there to the three dining rooms. The place was pretty crowded; alcohol was served.

The waiter, who spoke only a little English, announced, "Today, I have lamb shops."

More than a gourmet dinner, what Malko most wanted was to find out what Alicia Burton was really all about.

"Tell me the truth," he said. "When you first approached me, were you acting on Warren Michaelis's orders?"

Alicia blinked.

"Yes, I was," she admitted quietly. "He occasionally asks me to do things for him."

"What did he want to know?"

"Exactly what you were doing in Kabul," she said after a slight hesitation. "He said you weren't an adversary but that he didn't like being left in the dark."

"And now?"

"He said there was no problem anymore. I'm here tonight because I wanted to see you again, and that's all."

Alicia's gaze was direct and expressive: basically, she wanted to get laid. As if to specify what she had in mind, she added, "I didn't like the fight we got into last time. I'm not in the habit of doing that sort of thing."

They had polished off a bottle of red wine from someplace or other, and Malko was finally beginning to relax. It was pleasant to be in the company of a young woman who was offering herself without any hidden agenda. He felt a little guilty about Maureen Kieffer, but the South African woman was off-limits for the time being.

When the bill came, Alicia snatched it up.

"This is my treat," she said. "You're on my turf."

They returned to the lobby and the night watchman gave her the key to Room 4. There was no elevator. It felt like being in an English boardinghouse.

Ashraf Nyadi was playing a video game on her cell phone when the phone in her room rang.

"He came back," said the front desk clerk, an NDS informant.

"Is he here now?"

"No, he went out again, with a woman who came to get him."

"All right, thanks."

Nyadi hung up and went to the little safe in the hanging closet. She took out her gun and fitted the silencer.

Her plan was simple. Her passkey gave her access to any room in the Serena, so she would enter Malko's room and wait. When he returned, she would shoot him and his companion. Then she would go back to bed.

Collateral damage wasn't really her concern.

CHAPTER 22

The room was small and cluttered, with a sleeping alcove and a minuscule bathroom. Alicia smiled apologetically.

"It's not the Serena, but it's cheap and convenient."

It was certainly warm enough, and Alicia took off her down jacket. She was dressed in a yellow sweater, leather pants, and boots.

"Want a drink? I've got whiskey and vodka."

"Vodka, please."

She stepped over to a tiny bar piled high with books and newspapers, and filled two small glasses with Stolichnaya. She handed one to Malko and raised her own in a toast.

"Do you realize this is the first time we've been together in an almost normal way?" she asked.

"Why do you play the Agency's games, Alicia?"

The young woman smiled somewhat bitterly. "To survive. I'm a freelance writer, remember. Without the Ariana's help, I wouldn't have any stories to sell to my papers. The Agency gives me leads in exchange for the occasional 'favor.'"

She abruptly bent over and pressed her lips to his.

"And by the way, it wasn't all just business last time," she breathed.

Alicia's tongue slipped into Malko's mouth, searching for his. For a moment, they flirted playfully, exploring each other. Then, as the room grew warmer, Malko moved to unbutton Alicia's sweater, revealing her small, perky breasts.

"Stretch out on the bed," she ordered.

When he did, she began to peel him like an orange, gently removing one item of clothing at a time. When he was naked, she put her mouth on his chest and murmured, "I like a man's skin."

She began delicately licking him like a cat, moving around his nipples, then lower. The silence in the room was total except for some faint noises from next door. Malko was almost paralyzed with pleasure. This was a welcome break in a delicate and dangerous mission. When Alicia's mouth gently closed on his cock, he felt something like a jolt of electricity.

From the corner of his eye, Malko saw that while she was sucking on him, Alicia had managed to twist around and take off her own clothes and was now naked as well.

Releasing his cock, she stretched out on top of him, rubbing her body all over his, like a Thai masseuse. Then she knelt on either side of Malko's hips, bringing her cunt directly over his cock. With a little thrust of her hips, she took him inside and began gently rocking back and forth. Malko let himself go. After the tension of the last days, this felt like a little piece of heaven. When he felt his orgasm rising, he wrapped his arms around Alicia's waist, pushing deep into her.

Afterward, they lay motionless, like a pair of cats purring in front of a fireplace.

After a while, Malko roused himself. "I've got to get back to the hotel," he said.

"Don't go! I like having you here. Anyway, my driver's gone and won't be back until tomorrow morning."

He didn't insist. A few moments later, he was sound asleep.

Ashraf Nyadi was struggling not to nod off. She glanced at her watch: 1:45 a.m. Kabul didn't have any nightlife, so the fact that her target hadn't returned meant he was sleeping somewhere else. No point in her hanging around any longer.

She forced herself to wait another fifteen minutes, then unscrewed the silencer and put it in her bag with the gun. She opened the door and slipped out into the empty hallway. As far as she was concerned, her "customer" was just getting a rain check.

Malko was heading down the stairs at the Gandamack when he got a text message:

Sending you a car at 9. WM.

Alicia was still asleep, but she'd mentioned that her driver came at eight. And in fact he was there, waiting in the lobby.

"We're going to the Serena," Malko said.

The car was parked in front of the big TNT building, and Malko got in. It was just past 8:00 a.m. and traffic wasn't too bad.

Ashraf Nyadi had slept badly. She hated failure, and the hours spent vainly waiting for her target had made her irritable. Since she didn't have any specific orders, she decided to improvise. It was only 7:30 a.m. If she went back to Malko's room right away, she thought, she could wait for him there and leave the hotel directly afterward.

Just then the cell phone in her handbag rang, its sound muffled. Nyadi's pulse sped up when she saw the number displayed: it was her boss. The conversation was brief, and when she hung up, she was furious.

Their project had been canceled, and she was instructed to leave the Serena immediately. A direct order, and not open to question. Feeling frustrated, she left the room without turning around. Nyadi felt no personal animosity for the man she'd been ordered to kill, just annoyance at not being able to do her job.

When Malko got to Michaelis's office, the CIA man had a cup of coffee in his hand and a smile on his face.

"Good news!" he said. "You were right!"

"Meaning what?" asked Malko.

"Security just gave me yesterday's call log. Forrest telephoned President Karzai at 5:28 p.m. The conversation lasted eleven minutes and twenty-seven seconds."

"That's quite helpful," said Malko, hiding his satisfaction. His ploy had worked. Warned by Spider, Forrest would have informed the Afghan leader that the operation against him had been abandoned. The pressure on Malko would now ease.

This was the time to strike.

"Thanks very much, Warren. That call confirms some good news. You can stop monitoring Forrest's phone. But whatever you do, don't mention this to anybody. When the time comes, I'll tell you the whole story."

He was now in a hurry to see Nelson Berry.

As usual, the South African was sitting at his desk with his feet up, talking on the telephone. When he hung up, he shot Malko an almost angry look.

"Where the hell have you been, *bra*?"

"I had to take a little trip. But I'm back and all's well."

Berry put his feet down and asked, "So is it a go?"

"If you're ready, it is."

"If you'd come back any later, we would've missed a perfect

opportunity," said Berry. "He's flying to Lashkar Gah in Helmand in four days."

"How does this affect our plan?"

"He'll take his usual route to the airport. Which means he'll pass within range of my position."

"That's not enough. You need to know which car he'll be in. You're only getting one shot."

Berry smiled coldly.

"That'll cost an extra ten thousand dollars. I have a source in the presidential palace who will pass me that information. This guy helps Karzai with all his travel. He actually opens the car door. Once Karzai's in, he'll call me. I'll already be in position."

"Can you trust him?"

"As much as you can trust any Afghan. His sister needs an operation and he doesn't have the money."

"Does he know how his tip will be used?"

"No, and he doesn't care."

The two men fell silent. It was an awful lot to put on a single roll of the dice.

"What if he betrays you beforehand?"

Berry shrugged. "It's a three-million-dollar bet, and I'm the one making it."

Malko quickly went over the plan in his head. Nelson Berry was taking almost all of the risk. He himself had been put in the clear by Jason Forrest's phone call. At this point, Karzai would be confident that the Americans had no ill will toward him.

"All right, it's a go," he said. "I don't think you and I need to have any further contact. Safer that way."

"Where will you be?" asked the South African.

"In Kabul, most likely. Once we know the result, I'll have your money sent."

"This place will be like an earthquake hit it," said Berry, shaking his head. "I don't plan to hang around long. And I won't be back anytime soon."

That's not a concern of mine, thought Malko. Nelson Berry was a dangerous man. No point in getting too involved with him. He didn't like this mission, and the sooner it was accomplished, the better.

He put his hand out to the South African. "Good luck!"

Their handshake was brief. Berry watched from the front steps of his poppy palace as Malko climbed back into the SUV.

It all almost seemed too easy. Yet the South African was serious, and his plan made sense. Afghans were so corrupt that the role to be played by the man who was going to precipitate the earthquake seemed normal. Heads of state were usually betrayed by the people they trusted most.

As Darius drove along Kabul's potholed streets, Malko reflected that in four days he would have done the impossible: assassinated the president of Afghanistan.

CHAPTER 23

For some reason, Malko had a knot in the pit of his stomach, and he didn't know why. Nelson Berry was no bluffer. He was a professional killer who had carried out many missions for the CIA. But Malko knew that if it weren't for his precarious finances, he'd never have taken on such a risky mission.

Just then, an unpleasant thought went through Malko's mind. What if the South African betrayed him to the NDS, either to get a reward or to make himself some friends? Or just took the CIA's money and did nothing?

Originally, Malko had planned to stay in Kabul until after the attack, but he now felt that would be unnecessarily risky. The NDS could react violently and turn on him. Best get to cover ahead of time.

At a downtown airlines ticket office, he booked a seat on an 8:10 a.m. PIA flight to Islamabad for the morning of the attack. That way, he could stay around to deal with any last-minute problems but be safely in the air when Hamid Karzai's Mercedes drove into Berry's sights.

It was the wiser course, all things considered.

With his SUV's headlights dimmed, Nelson Berry turned off Airport Road onto the side street that led to the Shaheen and parked near the hotel. He waited behind the wheel for a moment before getting out, but the dimly lit street was deserted. At two o'clock in the morning, everyone in Kabul was in bed.

From his trunk, Berry took out the Degtyarov 41 wrapped in a blanket, and carried it along a path that wound through empty gardens to the fifteen-story Azizi Plaza building.

From his scouting trips to the construction site, Berry had spotted a section of wall protected by rolls of barbed wire, directly opposite the main entrance. A small part of the wall had collapsed and was no more than six feet high.

He took a path around the site, moving soundlessly in almost total darkness. The chances of running into someone were close to zero. If the site had any night watchmen, they were probably fast asleep.

When Berry reached the place he had located, he stopped and listened. Not a sound. He hoisted the Degtyarov to the top of the wall and lowered it to the other side. Then he climbed the wall without too much trouble and jumped down into a small muddy area on the other side.

He was now only twenty yards from the main building.

Berry walked up to the green canvas that sheathed the entire structure. Taking a knife from his boot, he cut a three-foot slit in the canvas and slipped in. It was freezing inside the building.

Feeling his way in the dark, Berry tried to get his bearings. Everything was raw cement. He found a staircase and climbed to the fourth floor, the level he had selected for his shooting position. Once there, he again felt his way in the dark to locate the side of the building facing Airport Road. He went down some steps, came back up again, got turned around, and hit dead ends, but eventually he reached a room with windows blocked by the green canvas. When he slit it with his knife, he was hugely relieved to see the streetlights along Airport Road.

Finding a balcony with a rough cement guardrail, Berry set the Degtyarov on it, with just the end of the barrel showing. He adjusted the Zeiss scope for the anticipated distance and chambered a round. Then he set the rifle on the ground and sat down against a wall. He had eight hours to wait.

According to his source in the presidential palace, Hamid Karzai would be leaving for the airport around ten o'clock. Berry closed his eyes, though he knew he wouldn't be able to sleep.

A lone car drove by on Airport Road from time to time, and this gave him an idea. He stood up, got into shooting position, and waited for the next one. As the car passed, he found he had plenty of time to follow it in the scope, and he made a final adjustment. Then he hunkered down against the wall, fighting the cold.

Dawn had long since broken. Peering through the slit in the green canvas, Berry followed the preparations along Airport Road, which had been closed to traffic since seven o'clock. A line of cops was sweeping the avenue and its side streets; tow trucks were removing parked cars.

The usual routine.

Suddenly Berry started: he had just heard a noise in the stairway. At first he thought it was an animal, but the sound became more distinct: that of heavy steps climbing the stairs.

He stood up, hugging the wall. He had anticipated that the NDS would send someone into the Azizi Plaza but figured that the building was so big he wouldn't be noticed.

He listened carefully as the steps got closer. The man was coming to his floor. Very slowly, Berry drew the knife from his boot and waited, still pressed against the wall. The NDS agent was just as likely to go into some other room. That would be less of a problem, and only when he was leaving.

Unfortunately, the footsteps kept getting closer. He could now hear the hard breathing of a weary man.

After that, everything happened very fast.

A uniformed figure in a cap appeared in the doorway of Berry's room. He was young, with a mustache, and carried an AK-47 in a sling. Just as he spotted Berry, the South African jabbed the knife six inches into his belly and yanked it sideways. Eyes bulging, the NDS agent tumbled backward, his cap knocked off. Berry grabbed him by the throat to keep him from crying out, but there was no need. The man was already dead of a massive internal hemorrhage.

Berry lowered him to the ground and stretched him out on the rough concrete. When he stood up, his heart was pounding. If there was anyone else with the NDS agent, he was screwed.

Berry strained to hear any noise in the staircase. He heard nothing, and his pulse gradually fell back to normal. He dragged the body facedown over to the wall and retrieved his knife. Then he looked at his watch: 7:30 a.m. The NDS agent probably wouldn't have gone back downstairs until after Karzai's convoy had passed, so no one would miss him now. With any luck, Berry had overcome his last obstacle. Sitting with his back to the wall, he forced himself to breathe evenly. When he pulled the Degtyarov's trigger, he had to be perfectly calm.

The phone in Malko's room rang, jolting him awake. It was 4:15 a.m.

Thinking the operator had made a mistake, he snapped, "I asked you to wake me up at five thirty, not at four in the morning!"

But an Afghan speaking poor English said, "Sir, this is PIA. Today's flight for Islamabad is canceled. The airport is closed because of fog. I will let you know if the weather improves."

Malko hung up, now wide awake. He was stuck in Kabul.

Berry glanced at the cell phone lying next to him. It would give him the signal of Karzai's departure, and he switched it on and off to make sure it was working. The presidential convoy would take about ten minutes to drive from the palace to Berry's hide site above Airport Road. Plenty of time for him to get into shooting position.

All he had to do now was wait—and hope that nothing went wrong.

The South African remained completely motionless, head resting on his crossed arms. When the Nokia suddenly rang, it gave him a jolt of adrenaline. He grabbed the phone and answered. "*Baleh*?"

"Number three," said his source, and hung up.

Berry lifted the Degtyarov and rested its barrel on the cement railing. In the scope, Airport Road jumped into view, completely empty of cars. All traffic had been stopped for the convoy's passage.

He waited, forcing himself to breathe evenly, his cheek pressed against the chilly wooden stock, index finger under the trigger guard. He would have only a few seconds to shoot, he knew. But the fact that Karzai was in the third car made the job easier. He wouldn't be caught by surprise.

He was as motionless as a block of granite.

Malko was finishing his breakfast when his cell rang. It was the front desk.

"PIA has resumed flights to Islamabad," said the clerk. "There is a flight at two thirty-five p.m. Will you keep your reservation?"

"Yes, sure," he said, without thinking.

That would be too late. He felt as tight as a violin string. By now, President Karzai would have left the palace.

As if in a dream, Malko signed the check and went up to his room. He had no idea what to do next.

Berry held his breath as his pulse began to climb. His eye had become one with the Zeiss scope. A large black Mercedes had just appeared in his crosshairs. He resisted the temptation to follow it, for fear of spoiling his sight.

That lasted a few seconds.

Then another Mercedes appeared, the second one.

Berry was holding the Degtyarov tightly enough to snap the stock. He pressed the trigger slightly, to remove any play. When the hood of the third car appeared, he slowly and steadily pulled the trigger.

The detonation shook his entire body, and a sharp pain stabbed his shoulder.

It took less than a second for the shell to cover the three hundred yards to the car.

Berry saw a ball of fire and a cloud of smoke and knew he'd hit his target. He immediately put down the Degtyarov. He'd been wearing gloves, so there was no need to wipe away fingerprints. Abandoning the rifle, he grabbed his cell phone and rushed out and down the slippery stairs.

Racing through the building, Berry found the little open area and vaulted over the wall. In minutes he was back at his car near the Shaheen. He had passed a few Afghans, but they paid him no attention.

Malko was about to enter his hotel room when his cell rang. He recognized Michaelis's number and immediately answered.

"Do you know what just happened?" asked the CIA station chief, sounding frantic.

"No, what?"

"Somebody shot at President Karzai's convoy as it drove to the airport."

"Was he hit?"

"No, he was in one of the other cars. I've been summoned to the NDS. They're going out of their minds. I'll call you again later."

Stunned, Malko stood motionless. Nelson Berry had missed. The Afghans would quickly realize it was an assassination attempt, making him their prime suspect.

His first impulse was to rush to CIA headquarters at the Ariana Hotel. They couldn't get to him there. On the other hand, he wouldn't be able to leave, either. And he would be implicating the Americans in the attack, for which they would never forgive him.

Trying to board the flight to Islamabad was also out of the question. It would be tantamount to a confession, and the police might intercept him. And he couldn't stay at the Serena. They were sure to come looking for him here.

Mechanically, Malko walked over to the safe in the hanging closet. He took out the GSh-18 and strapped on the GK ankle holster. It was small consolation.

He was trapped in Kabul, with every intelligence agency in the country on his tail. And he now had a pressing problem: saving his skin.

PART TWO

CHAPTER 24

Malko's heart suddenly began to race.

A green police pickup was pulling into the Serena courtyard. Standing in the lobby, Malko was paralyzed. The failed attempt to assassinate President Karzai had taken place an hour earlier, and the investigation was under way. Karzai must be furious, and his rage would focus on Malko, whom he already suspected of being in Kabul to harm him.

The green police pickup turned right and headed for the parking garage.

Malko's pulse slowed as he realized that he was stupid for panicking. It wasn't the police he should be worried about, but the NDS. Either way, staying at the Serena a minute longer would be playing with fire. This was the first place they would come looking for him.

He headed for the exit, passing through the door manned by a bellman in a magnificent turban. Malko crossed the courtyard and exited to the street through the pedestrian gate. He felt more at ease out here, lost in the crowd. There weren't that many foreigners in Kabul, but there were some.

Where could he go now? His only asset was the pistol Nelson Berry had given him, a Russian GSh-18 automatic. If he phoned Warren Michaelis, he would get access to the Ariana, but the

Afghans would learn that he had gone to ground there, and it would compromise both the Agency and the U.S. government.

Who weren't likely to be pleased.

Malko would have to figure what to do on his own, at least for now. The problem was, there weren't many ways to get out of Kabul.

Showing up at the airport would be suicide. The overland routes to Jalalabad, Herat, Kandahar, and Bamyan were all in Taliban hands. That left the highway to Mazar-e-Sharif through the Salang Tunnel, but the only way to travel it was by bus, and a foreigner on a bus in Afghanistan would be noticed. Besides, there were checkpoints on the highway out of Kabul, which made the trip too risky.

What had happened to Nelson Berry? he wondered. If the South African had been arrested, Michaelis would have mentioned it. Berry knew Afghanistan well and had plenty of cash, so he had probably escaped. In any case, it would be too dangerous for Malko to contact him.

By then Malko had reached the Massoud memorial roundabout, and he stopped for a moment. He thought briefly of Clayton Luger back in Washington but knew that the CIA deputy director would probably tell him to just do the best he could.

A loud noise made him jump, but it was just the honking of a truck that had clipped a fruit and vegetable stand, sending oranges rolling all over the street. Passersby gathered and shouted, taking sides in the dispute. The greengrocer picked up a stick and started pounding on the truck cab. A policeman with a white cap tipped back on his head sauntered over.

Malko melted into the crowd as it moved along Zarnegar Park. Above all, he had to remain at large. If he fell into Afghan hands, he was finished. They probably wouldn't bother throwing him in jail, just quietly torture and execute him.

That route was definitely out.

Malko thought of going to Maureen Kieffer but immediately dismissed the idea. It would put her in danger and might not even be safe. The NDS knew he was friendly with her and would be waiting on her doorstep.

The deafening traffic noise was making it hard for Malko to think clearly. CIA headquarters came to mind again, but that posed a major obstacle, too. The Afghans could well be stationed in front of the Ariana Hotel to intercept him. The Americans and their Nepalese guards didn't have the right to act outside the Ariana perimeter. So that was out as well.

Abruptly, Malko realized he was at the turnoff to Wazir Akbar Kahn Road and the mosque. There he might find Musa Kotak, the Taliban mullah with enough influence to protect him from Karzai's thugs.

The only man able to help him.

But it was too early. Kotak came to the mosque only in the afternoons.

At the NDS, it was all hands on deck.

Before flying to Lashkar Gah, President Karzai had been told about the assassination attempt. He ordered Parviz Bamyan to find the shooters at any cost.

The targeted Mercedes had been destroyed and its driver killed. The wreck stood on the side of Airport Road, protected by a ring of policemen and yellow crime scene tape. The force of the impact had slammed the car against a building and crushed it, in spite of its armor.

The search for gunmen started within minutes after the convoy passed. A swarm of NDS agents combed the building the shot was fired from, but it took two hours before a team found the Degtyarov 41 and the body of the murdered NDS agent nearby.

An examination of the rifle produced nothing. It bore no fingerprints or DNA evidence and held just one empty shell, also clean. Only an experienced sniper could have used such a weapon, which was extremely rare in Kabul. The NDS immediately sent the serial number to Moscow to try to track it, but without much hope.

At the NDS, Bamyan started going through his files. Kabul had people of every persuasion who would love to take a shot at President Karzai, but none of the usual suspects jumped out at him.

Eventually, he came to Malko Linge's file. The CIA operative was already suspected of gunning for the president, and a female NDS agent had been sent to the Serena to kill him. In the file, a note in red ink indicated that the order had been canceled.

Bamyan phoned Ashraf Nyadi, the agent originally charged with the sanction.

"Go back to the Serena," he ordered. "See if your customer is still there."

"Same instructions as before?" she asked.

"No! Just keep me informed; that's all."

This was hardly the time to kill the only person who might be able to lead them to the shooter.

He absolutely had to locate this Linge person. He had his secretary call their informant at the Serena to see if the Austrian was still there. The informant called back a few moments later. The guest in Room 382 was still registered and his room was made up, but he hadn't been seen since that morning. Bamyan got his passport number and began the tedious process of alerting everyone who might be able to prevent Malko from leaving Kabul.

Linge might just come back to the hotel at the end of the day, of course, but he might also try to make a run for it. Bamyan had his deputy dispatch two agents to the Serena to search his room and wait for him. Then he tackled the list of people to alert, starting with the airport. He drafted all-points bulletins for the police and the Afghan National Army and had them transmitted to all checkpoints, both in the city and on the roads leading out of Kabul.

With his net now in place, Bamyan sat back and thought. It wouldn't be easy for Linge to get out of Kabul, so it was more than likely that he was still in the city.

He ordered up the file that had been assembled at President Karzai's request. Studying it gave him an idea: What about the Ariana Hotel, CIA headquarters? Minutes later, an unmarked car went to take up surveillance opposite the hotel complex.

Bamyan then turned to study Linge's known contacts. Maureen Kieffer was first, and he immediately sent an agent to her place, to ask her to keep them informed. Her business depended on the NDS's goodwill, so she was sure to be cooperative.

Which left the most puzzling part of the file, a strange incident in the village of Kotali Khayr Kana. An old armored Corolla in which Linge was riding had been ambushed there by persons unknown, probably Taliban.

Bamyan sat at his desk, absorbed in reading the file. Where could such an armored car have come from? he wondered. Given the car model and its age, it wasn't likely to be the CIA. But Linge had been in touch with one Nelson Berry, a former South African mercenary who might well own an armored Toyota.

Bamyan decided to bring Berry in on some routine pretext.

Maybe I'm worrying for no reason, he thought. Linge might appear at the Serena later in the day and they could simply pick him up for questioning. They would treat him with all due deference, of course. After all, he was a known CIA operative and was probably in Kabul on assignment.

When Jason Forrest entered his boss's office, he looked grim. He had requested an urgent meeting a few minutes earlier.

"I have some serious things to tell you, sir," he announced. "Can I be sure this won't go any further?"

"Of course," said the CIA station chief. "What's on your mind?"

"This morning President Karzai was the victim of an assassination attempt."

"I understand that he wasn't hit, just one of the cars in his motorcade."

"Yes, but he was the target. You know that as well as I do."

"But that's not our concern. It's the NDS's problem. The shooters were probably Taliban."

Forrest gave him a long look. "Are you sure of that, sir?"

Michaelis got the feeling that his case officer knew more than he was letting on.

"Who else would get involved in something like that?" he asked with apparent candor.

Forrest's expression showed that they were getting to the heart of the matter. "Do you know what a certain Agency contractor named Malko Linge is doing here in Kabul?"

Michaelis's toes clenched in his shoes. "No, he didn't tell me. Why?"

Forrest looked him in the eye. "You know that I've remained on good terms with your predecessor, Mark Spider," he said tensely, "who is now in Washington."

"I'm aware of that. So what?"

"I got a message from him this morning. Mark has an important position in the policy group that deals with Afghanistan. He says it's possible that Malko Linge was part of the assassination attempt."

A chill ran down Michaelis's spine. "That seems highly unlikely," he managed to say. "Linge has been working with the Agency for years and would never carry out an action that was contrary to U.S. interests."

Forrest's smile was razor thin. "Except that in this case, the action was carried out on orders from the White House."

The CIA station chief slowly shook his head. "Jason, I don't know what you're talking about," he said. "I'm sure that Linge isn't involved in this business. Thank you for sharing your concerns. It was the right thing to do and I appreciate it. I will report them to Langley."

"Will you be meeting with Linge?"

"I'm not due to, and I don't even know if he's still in Kabul. He was here on a mission given to him directly by headquarters and outside of my authority."

The station chief stood up to signal the end of the meeting, which was making him ill at ease. Forrest took the hint and left.

Michaelis slumped in his leather armchair, his head in a whirl.

Jason Forrest had just given him the last piece of the puzzle he was missing. He now knew why Malko had come to Kabul, and he understood the questions he had been asking.

He also realized he was in the middle of an internal policy conflict, which made him extremely uncomfortable. But his first thought was for Malko, whom he liked. Where was he? If Forrest was telling the truth, the Austrian operative was in grave danger. Michaelis reached for his cell phone but stopped himself. The NDS monitored all their communications, he knew. If he phoned Malko now, he might precipitate a catastrophe.

Michaelis closed his eyes and said a prayer for him.

CHAPTER 25

Malko was shivering. He'd been pacing up and down Wazir Akbar Khan Road for the past hour, waiting for Musa Kotak to appear at the mosque. An icy wind was blowing through the city, and the sky was clouding up. Malko resolved to walk at least a mile before turning back toward the mosque.

If Kotak didn't come, he would go back to the Serena and act innocent. After all, no material evidence linked him to the assassination attempt. But it would be a desperation move.

His last resort would be to call Warren Michaelis and have an Agency car pick him up—with the reactions that would trigger. Could the CIA afford to take in a man who was hunted for an attempt against President Karzai's life?

Malko still hadn't answered that question when he again found himself in front of the mosque where Kotak received visitors. He was frozen stiff.

Heart pounding, he walked across the garden and headed for the outbuilding where the cleric's office was located. The young guard he had encountered before was standing out front. As soon as he saw Malko, he went inside and immediately came out again, holding the door for him.

The mullah was back!

Malko was grateful for the room's heat, but what really warmed his heart was the chubby cleric's welcome.

Musa Kotak waddled over and took Malko's right hand in both of his. In his unctuous voice he said, "I've been expecting you!"

"I came by earlier," said Malko, "but you weren't here."

"I'm never here in the morning," Kotak reminded him. "Did you drive?"

"No, I walked."

"Better that way," said the mullah, clearly relieved. Seeing that his guest was shivering, he immediately added, "Come over here. You need some hot tea with honey."

They walked to the pile of cushions where the mullah liked to sprawl and sat down. Warming his chilled hands on a glass of tea, Malko gradually began to unwind.

The cleric's slightly sarcastic tone gave him a start. "You know, I actually believed you the other day when you said you had abandoned your project." Kotak laughed briefly. "You are learning to lie like an Afghan."

"I have to be very careful," said Malko, sipping his tea. "I don't know who I can trust."

He was cursing himself for accepting this crazy mission. Everyone had dropped him, leaving him alone in Kabul.

The cleric nodded. "You are being hunted, my friend! I have known it since this morning. Word spreads quickly in town. I do not know why your plan failed, but the agencies that answer to Karzai are all looking for the man who tried to assassinate him."

"Then I'm putting you in danger," said Malko.

"No, you are not," Kotak said smoothly. "No one will come after me, and nobody knows you are here."

"Your guard does."

"He would hold his tongue even under the worst torture. And in any case you are not going to be staying here."

"What do you have in mind?"

"I am going to get you out of the city."

Malko thought the cleric might be boasting. The Taliban controlled many things in Kabul, but not the immigration service at the airport.

"How do you plan to do that?" he asked. "I'm sure they're watching the airport."

"We do not fly when we need to travel," said Kotak with a smile. "There are many roads out of Kabul."

The reason foreigners couldn't use those roads was because of the Taliban, but of course the Taliban themselves could travel wherever they pleased.

"I think you should leave the country," said Kotak. "Hamid Karzai has a lot of money and he still wields power. Even people who do not like him would be happy to capture you and sell you to his cronies."

"How do you plan to get me out?"

Kotak sipped his tea before answering.

"Personally, I control only one route, the one from Kabul to Kandahar and then on through Spin Boldak to Baluchistan. My contacts are in Quetta, where our *shura* is, so I can guarantee your safety that far. My Quetta friends will take you in hand and put you on a flight to Islamabad. From there you can return to Europe."

"That's a terribly long trip!"

"That's true, but it is the best I can offer. I do not have the necessary contacts on the route through Jalalabad over the Khyber Pass, and there are too many checkpoints. Whereas we are on home ground in Kandahar."

"Assuming the trip is possible, I would still have to deal with the Pakistani authorities. And I don't have a visa."

The cleric smiled again. "Crossing into Pakistan is no problem. And our contacts there will take care of your status. You will board the plane for Islamabad with a proper passport."

Malko still felt hesitant but recognized that the scheme was workable.

Mullah Kotak was looking at him with his beatific smile. "You cannot stay in Kabul," he repeated. "The NDS will be going crazy. I do not know who your sniper was, but he was just following orders, whereas you are the link between the U.S. administration and the attempted assassination. You would be very valuable to the Karzai regime. It would give them leverage over the Americans. We cannot let you fall into their hands."

Knowing the methods the NDS used, Malko knew that they would almost certainly extract a confession from him. To dispel this unpleasant prospect, he asked, "Specifically what do you have in mind?"

"Your trip will be in several stages. First to Ghazni, where we are well established, and from there to Kandahar."

"Will you be coming with me?"

"Alas, no," said the cleric with a sigh. "But I will give you an escort: my nephew. He speaks good English and will watch out for you. He will accompany you all the way to your Islamabad flight. With him, you will be in no danger."

Kotak seemed to have thought of everything. In any case, Malko had no alternative. Without a car or place to hide, his options in Kabul were pretty limited.

"It will take two or three days to prepare the trip," Kotak continued. "My nephew will take you to a safe place nearby where you will not be in any danger. I will call him."

Kotak took out two cell phones, one white and one green. Using the green one, he had a long conversation in Pashto.

"He will be here in two hours," he announced, hanging up.

"Until then, you can relax. I have some visitors I need to see, so I will put you up in one of my other rooms. Are you hungry?"

Malko said that he wasn't. Recent events had made him lose his appetite. All he wanted was to stretch out and sleep.

In safety.

Nelson Berry was walking up the main street of Panjsad Famili, a northern part of Kabul. As in any working-class neighborhood, the flat-roofed cob and mud-brick houses were modest, and the place was crowded and lively.

Night was falling as he strolled through the bird market, where the sellers were starting to put away their cages. Even poor Afghans bought these little balls of feathers and kept them in tiny cages.

But the South African wasn't seeing the birds; he was totally consumed by his fury. When he'd pulled the Degtyarov's trigger, he'd had the satisfaction of seeing President Karzai's armored Mercedes explode three hundred yards away. He'd abandoned the sniper rifle, sprinted down the raw concrete steps of the building under construction, and made his way to his SUV parked near the Shaheen Hotel, propelled by this happy thought: he had just earned three million dollars.

It was only when he turned on the car radio that he learned the truth. He had fired at the wrong car, and Karzai was still alive. At that moment he didn't think of the three million dollars slipping through his fingers or even the danger he faced, but only of the betrayal by the man he had paid ten thousand dollars to tell him which Mercedes was the right one.

That was Sangi Guruk, a Pashtun who swore on the Quran that he told the truth.

Berry hadn't liked having to trust Guruk, but he was the only person who could tell him what car Karzai was getting into.

And that had been the key to the whole attack.

The South African glanced around as he made his way along the narrow, muddy street, but he saw nothing suspicious, just street vendors, shops with acetylene lamps, women in burqas running errands, and men walking home from work.

Rage sat like a hard knot in his gut. Not only had Guruk cheated him; he was now a mortal danger, as the only person who could connect Berry to the assassination attempt.

If Guruk were clever, he would alert the NDS so its agents could set a trap for the South African. Of course, in doing that, he would be admitting that he participated in an attempted assassination, and that would cause him a lot of trouble.

But Guruk was stupid and probably figured that Berry would panic and run away from Kabul. He would also assume that since he wasn't an Afghan he wouldn't think the way Afghans did.

What he didn't know was that Berry had lived in Afghanistan for so long that he had adopted the country's habits, including the rule that revenge had to be fast and ferocious, even disproportionate. A family with women and children might be shot dead over a debt of ten thousand afghanis, without a thought for the consequences. For his part, Berry was thinking of the consequences: he had to eliminate the only man who could cause him trouble.

He stopped for a moment, ostensibly to light a cigarette but in fact to carefully look around. He was almost opposite Guruk's house. There was no one in front, the passersby were unremarkable, and nobody seemed to be waiting around. Just the same, Berry took the precaution of passing the house and walking up the hill for some distance before turning around and coming back.

By now night had fallen and no one was paying him any attention. He stepped up to the wooden door and rapped on a panel, once, twice, three times.

A woman's voice, probably muffled by a burqa, eventually answered. "What is it?"

"I've come to see Sangi," Berry yelled through the door.

"He isn't home yet," said the woman.

"I'll wait for him. Open up!"

The woman cracked open the door and he slipped inside. The living room had a goat-wool carpet on the floor and was warmed by an old wood-burning *khali* stove. The woman in the burqa pointed Berry to a bench covered by a worn carpet and fled to the back of the house to join Guruk's second wife. If she had been at home alone, she would never have opened the door to a man, for fear of being repudiated.

The South African sat down and unbuttoned his leather coat, loosening the holster that held an old Makarov automatic with a silencer. He didn't know how long he would have to wait, but he was prepared to spend the night. There was no point in asking the woman when her husband would come home; she wouldn't know.

Lulled by the room's warmth, Berry didn't notice the time passing, and he started when the door creaked open and his onetime friend Sangi Guruk appeared.

The Afghan stopped on the threshold and began to back away. He immediately stopped when the gun and silencer emerged from Berry's leather coat.

"Stick around!" said Berry. "Don't you think we should have a little chat?"

Guruk was at a loss, his panicky eyes darting this way and that.

"You swore on the Quran," Berry hissed, "you dirty son of a bitch!"

The frightened Afghan stammered, "I—I made a mistake, may

God forgive me. I got scared at the last minute. I'll give your money back. I haven't spent any of it."

"Good idea!" said the South African almost cheerfully.

From under a bed, Guruk hurriedly pulled a colorful, hand-painted box in which he kept his valuables. He opened it with a little key on his key ring and took out a roll of hundred-dollar bills.

"It's almost all here!" he said. "I was saving up to buy a piece of land."

"You're right. Real estate is always a good investment."

Standing in the center of the room, Guruk was shifting from one foot to the other.

"So are we okay?" he asked. "Would you like some tea?"

The man honestly thought he was in the clear. But when he met Berry's eyes, he realized he was wrong. Without bothering to get up, he aimed the Makarov at Guruk's chest and fired.

A first soft *pfut!* was heard, followed by a second.

Guruk fell where he was standing. Berry glanced at the curtain that separated the living room from the kitchen. No one had noticed the shots. He crossed the room and pushed the curtain aside.

Two women in burqas were chatting in Pashto, with three small children playing on the floor nearby. The oldest, a boy with large dark eyes, was probably about eight.

Berry calmly shot both women, who collapsed without a sound. Surprised, the three children stopped playing and looked at the South African wide-eyed. The oldest one started to cry.

Berry promptly put a bullet in his head while the two others stared, puzzled. The South African stepped back and let the curtain fall. He hadn't killed the boy out of cruelty, only because he was old enough to tell the police that a *khareji* had killed his mommy.

He left the way he'd come and strode down the hill toward his car. He was still furious but was feeling relieved. There was now nobody left to trace the assassination attempt back to him.

He was going out of town the next morning, providing security for a big drug deal in Logar Province. He would be protected by his client, a major Pakistani trafficker with ties to Karzai's clan. Berry would stay away from Kabul for a week, to give things time to settle down.

Once back in his car, he checked his cell phone. There were no calls from Malko Linge, which was smart. Malko was probably safely holed up at the Ariana Hotel, so Berry wasn't worried for him.

Which left the loss of the three million dollars.

And that really hurt.

CHAPTER 26

The mood was tense at the NDS complex, where finding the president's attackers was the top and only priority. Hamid Karzai had returned from Lashkar in a lather of fear and fury. To people who suggested the Taliban were to blame, he snapped, "It wasn't them, I can feel it!"

But uncertainty gnawed at him. If it wasn't the Taliban, then it could only be the Americans, which meant the tensions between them had risen to a new level. He summoned Parviz Bamyan, who was heading the investigation. After being announced, the acting NDS chief bowed his way in and humbly took the seat the president offered him.

"Do you have any news?" asked Karzai.

"I might," said Bamyan cautiously. "The weapon didn't give us any clues, but when we examined our various surveillance and monitoring reports, I learned that Malko Linge, the CIA operative, has been in contact with a South African doing business here named Nelson Berry. He's a former mercenary who runs a security agency. He has worked for the CIA on various occasions and we know he's in financial difficulties."

"Have you arrested him?" snapped Karzai.

"No. When we went to his place, he had already left with his driver, an Afghan named Darius Gul."

"Where did they go?"

"His employees said that they were going to Logar Province for a few days, but they didn't know why. We searched the place without finding anything connected to the attack. We took his people in, and they're being interrogated."

Having their fingernails ripped out might help them remember some useful details.

"It's only a slim lead, sir," concluded Bamyan. "We don't have anything concrete."

"It's a *good* lead," said Karzai. "What about this Malko Linge?"

"He left the Serena this morning and hasn't come back yet. We've stationed some agents there."

"Arrest him, too," said Karzai, "and find the South African. Interrogate them, and keep up your surveillance. I want results!"

"I will do the impossible, sir."

Bowing his way out of the room, Bamyan fled the president's fury.

Bamyan was now beginning to think that Berry might be the shooter. It would certainly fit his profile, and the South African was even registered as a sniper. But Berry would only be a hired gun. If he had fired at the president, it was because he'd been ordered to. An order that could have been given by Malko Linge, the man Bamyan absolutely had to find.

He was sure Linge hadn't left Kabul by plane. Bamyan had threatened the immigration officers with such horrible punishment if they let someone slip past them that no one would dare disobey.

Every place that Linge might go was being watched. The checkpoints on roads out of town had been alerted, and the same threats made. Besides, it was difficult for a foreigner to drive anywhere. That was even more dangerous than staying in Kabul.

One possibility remained: that Linge had taken refuge at CIA headquarters.

Back at the NDS, Bamyan called the interior minister, the only person who could intervene with the CIA. At the very least, the station chief must be told that the NDS considered Malko Linge a person of interest.

Which might put a chill on their relations.

Mullah Kotak's office door opened to admit a young bearded man in a turban with slender tortoiseshell glasses. He was holding an ankle-length brown coat and a chestnut-colored turban with a hanging fold.

Malko had just reentered the quarters of the former Taliban minister. His wait had turned out to be longer than expected. It was nearly 9:00 p.m., and the mullah had gone home.

The young man walked over to Malko. In rough but perfectly understandable English, he said, "I am Nadir, your friend the mullah's nephew. He asked me to look after you. I swear by Allah to do everything in my power so nothing bad happens to you."

"Thank you," said Malko. "What do we do now?"

"I am going to take you to a safe place where you can rest before your trip. A house that belongs to us. But first, please put these on. It would be best if you did not attract attention."

Nadir held out the coat and turban. When Malko put them on, he looked like a typical Afghan.

They crossed the mosque garden and went out onto Wazir Akbar Khan Road. Night had fallen and they saw few people as they made their way to a narrow dirt alley lined with thatched-roof stone houses. Nadir stopped at one and unlocked the door.

Malko was pleased to find it warm inside, where a big traditional stove was blazing. He shed his coat and turban and looked around. A wooden staircase led to the upper floor.

"There is a bedroom upstairs," explained Nadir. "A woman will come to do the cooking. It is Afghan food, of course, but she is pretty good. Stay here, don't go out. I will come back tomorrow. Do you need anything?"

"I don't think so."

When Nadir left, Malko went up to the bedroom, which was also pleasantly warm. There was a tiny bathroom and shower with an antediluvian Russian water heater. Everything, in fact, except a razor: the Taliban didn't shave.

As Malko stretched out on the low bed, the weight at his right foot reminded him that his only piece of survival gear was the pistol and ankle holster that Berry gave him.

"The president is very concerned about Afghanistan," said John Mulligan, the national security advisor.

"I can imagine," said Clayton Luger.

They were sitting in leather armchairs in the soundproof, bugproof room on the second floor of the East Wing of the White House. Nicknamed "the Tank," this was where the most secret conversations took place.

Two days earlier, these men had tried to assassinate the president of Afghanistan, with Malko's help. Karzai was bound to learn that someone in the White House had given the green light to the attack. The Afghan ambassador had asked to meet President Obama to deliver a personal message from President Karzai. Given the tensions between the two countries, the situation had to be defused.

Mulligan broke the silence. "I just met with the president, and we agreed on the following course of action. He'll tell the ambassador that rogue elements were plotting to kill President Karzai and that we had to put a stop to it. Karzai's buddy Mark Spider can confirm this."

"But the attack already took place!" said Luger.

"We'll say that events got out of hand before we could intervene. The ambassador may not believe us, but it's the best we can do. We'll probably also yield on some other point, like the number of troops left in place after 2014. If we don't get a status-of-forces agreement, Congress won't let us leave a single soldier in Afghanistan."

"I know," said Luger, "but in that case it won't be our problem anymore."

"Have you heard anything from Malko?"

"Not a peep. He hasn't called me, I haven't called him, and the Kabul station doesn't have any news. Since the attempt, he's simply disappeared."

"You think he could have left Kabul?"

The CIA man shook his head. "If he'd done that and was in a safe place, he would've given some sign of life. We don't know what really happened, except that Malko almost certainly didn't pull the trigger. That was much more likely to have been Nelson Berry. He hasn't called either, but I've disconnected the voicemail box he used to reach me. That's less important, because there's no direct connection between Berry and us. Which isn't the case with Malko."

"Right now, Malko's a problem for us," said Mulligan soberly. "We absolutely have to find out where he is. Do you have any way of knowing if the NDS has picked him up?"

"I'll see what the station people can find out, but it won't be easy. The NDS isn't going to shout it from the rooftops."

"If they capture Malko and make him talk, we're going to be in deep shit vis-à-vis Karzai," said Mulligan with a sigh.

"Malko is a first-class mission leader. He'll find a way to go to ground and send word."

"I hope to hell that's true. We were crazy to try this thing."

A hush descended on the men, hiding its face in shame.

Mulligan spoke again. "What I'm about to say is awful, but I would rest easier if Malko were dead."

The deputy CIA chief didn't blink. "It *is* awful, but I understand you," he said. "If Karzai ever got a confession out of him, he'd have us by the short hairs."

"Still, heaven help him. He's a good guy and has always served the Agency loyally."

The two men knew that when it came to reasons of state, one man's life didn't count for much. History was full of such examples. The people sacrificed were rehabilitated, of course, but posthumously.

"Let's wait until tomorrow," said Mulligan, standing up. "And find a way to contact Malko. We have to know!"

"I'll put together a communications hookup through Austria that can't be traced to us."

"Here's hoping you reach him."

Luger said nothing, well aware that the national security advisor thought exactly the opposite.

Dead, Malko was a hero. Alive, he was a liability.

CHAPTER 27

Malko watched the falling rain through the high window that illuminated his room. The streets near the house had turned from muddy paths into running streams.

After two days of inaction and anxiety, he was feeling as if he'd been exiled to another planet. Morning and evening, a figure in a blue burqa came in and bustled about in the kitchen. In the morning she made him tea and chapatis with honey and ghee, and sometimes a kind of yogurt.

In the evening it was *palau*—spiced rice with chunks of lamb—or flat *chelow kebab*, served with rice and fruit.

The woman never spoke to him; besides, she almost certainly didn't know English. Meanwhile, Kotak's nephew Nadir hadn't given any sign of life.

Malko was cut off from the world. The house didn't have a radio or TV, of course. He was feeling bored, and there was nothing he could do about it. He was safe, and the NDS agents must be wondering where he'd disappeared to. But he was getting anxious to leave Kabul, dangerous though that might be.

To pass the time, he daydreamed.

Suddenly his cell phone rang, and he jumped.

It hadn't rung in the last two days, and when he looked at the screen, his heart began to pound: Alexandra's number!

He was so flabbergasted, he let the phone ring and ring.

Alexandra *never* called him when he was on assignment. It was an absolute rule.

Finally he roused himself and grabbed the phone. "*Putzi*?"

The connection wasn't very clear, but through the static he heard a man's voice. "Malko?"

"That's me. Who are you?"

"We've been worried," said the unknown man. "We haven't heard from you."

Malko immediately understood: the CIA had routed the call through Alexandra's cell phone or was using her number. In a way, it cheered him; he hadn't been completely abandoned.

"I'm fine," he said.

"Do you plan to come home soon?" the man asked in a level tone. "Where are you?"

"I'm still in Kabul, but not at the same place."

He didn't want to say more on the phone. There was a long silence on the other end; then the man ended the conversation:

"Very well. I'll call you again."

The message was clear: Malko was not to phone, either Langley or the White House.

He gazed at his now-silent phone. He would have loved to talk to Alexandra, but the call was a trick that she surely didn't know about. Her number was in his CIA personnel file, and they must have used it without her knowledge.

Malko stretched out on the bed and let his mind wander. People at the CIA were worried about him, but probably more worried about themselves. On the loose in Kabul, Malko was a live hand grenade: the link between the United States and the attempt on President Karzai. If he hadn't answered, his CIA backers would probably be resting easier, but when he saw Alexandra's number, he couldn't resist.

Hearing footsteps downstairs, he figured the blue burqa was back. But then the steps creaked on the wooden staircase, and Kotak's nephew Nadir appeared. His arms were full of presents, which he tossed onto the bed: a new suit of Afghan clothes, heavy boots, and a long brown coat.

"We are leaving tomorrow morning at six!" he announced. "We are going to Ghazni, the first stage in your trip." This was a town about ninety miles south of Kabul, a Taliban stronghold.

"Won't it be risky, with the checkpoints?"

"No," said the nephew with a slight smile. "Taxis drive that route all the time, and the soldiers at the checkpoints do not bother them. With your clothes and turban, they will not even realize you are a foreigner, and you will not be noticed. In Ghazni you will be taken in by a cousin who will handle the rest of your voyage."

John Mulligan stared at the encrypted message that Clayton Luger had just sent him. So Malko was alive and still in Kabul! The national security advisor felt reassured, because he liked Malko, but also anxious. How would he survive in the Afghan capital? Also, what would happen if he were captured?

Parviz Bamyan still hadn't located Malko Linge, and Nelson Berry was out of reach. There was no question of going after him in Logar Province, and interrogating his staff hadn't produced anything. Maureen Kieffer was busy at her workshop, where surveillance continued. And word had come back from the CIA. The station claimed it had had no contact with Malko. It was as if he'd vanished into thin air.

Hunkered down in his palace, President Karzai exploded when he learned that the investigation wasn't making any progress. On his orders, security measures on every road out of town were reinforced, and NDS informers constantly patrolled the few restaurants and guesthouses frequented by expats.

Without result.

Nor did Bamyan know quite what to make of a piece of new information from the Kabul police. The day after the assassination attempt, a man named Sangi Guruk had been shot at home along with his two wives and one of his children. No one had seen or heard anything. The police figured the killer must have used a gun with a silencer.

Guruk had been in charge of the palace garage and vehicles, and whoever shot at the president's Mercedes must have had information about his motorcade. The murdered Guruk could have tipped the person off, which was probably why he'd been killed.

By whom?

The NDS chief couldn't imagine Linge venturing out to Guruk's neighborhood, so it must have been whoever had fired at the president.

The party was in full swing.

There were only men in Baber Khan Sahel's house, along with a covey of adolescent singing and dancing boys. Dressed like women, with bright clothes and sequined bracelets at their wrists and ankles, they swayed to the rhythms of a tambourine trio, entertaining the lord of the manor and his guests.

Baber Khan Sahel was the biggest drug lord in Pul-i-Alam, the capital of Logar Province, and he had a good reason for throwing this party. He had just bought a large share of the poppy crop and was reselling it to traffickers. Their laboratories were located to the south, along the Pakistani border, as the chemicals needed to turn poppy into heroin came from Pakistan. Because of the rapacity of the participants, these transactions occasionally turned violent.

So Baber Khan Sahel hired Nelson Berry to make sure everything went smoothly. Berry and his partners, Rufus and Willie, were professionals, in no danger of being turned or intimidated, and they had enough firepower to keep even the most vicious traffickers in line. The guests included two representatives of the local Taliban, which levied a tax on the lucrative trade.

Outside, the house was guarded by Baber Khan Sahel's sentinels, and no one would have thought to disturb this family get-together.

In the euphoria, the master of the house gave an order and the young dancers obediently stepped onto a large table to continue dancing to the sound of the tambourines.

One of the boys started gyrating in front of Berry, who was leaning on a bench strewn with cushions. He immediately started clapping in time with the young dancer's undulations. Flattered at having caught this *khareji*'s attention, the boy thrust out his hip and clicked his ring cymbals. His eyes made up with kohl, he had slender arms and legs and moved with a kind of feminine grace. In Afghanistan it was said that women were for making babies, but boys were for pleasure.

The eyes of the guests were beginning to glisten. Though Berry was the only person drinking alcohol—and discreetly, at that—the men sitting around the table didn't hide their mounting excitement.

Somewhat reluctantly, the local Taliban representatives quietly left the party.

The boy was now dancing for Berry alone, swinging his hips like a woman, thrusting his stomach out, and giving the South African ever more explicit glances.

In turn, Berry could feel his senses coming alive. It was almost impossible to find an available woman in Afghanistan, but there were any number of accommodating, handsome young boys. It wasn't politically correct to say so, but parties like this one happened in every village, sometimes organized by the local mullah. Raping a woman was a crime punishable by death, but sodomizing a teenager was a minor sin. After all, it didn't have any consequences.

On a final note, the three musicians finished playing.

A hubbub followed.

Some of the guests left, for various reasons. Others hastened to help the young dancers down from their improvised stage. Baber Khan Sahel didn't have to move. The most heavily made-up boy gracefully jumped to the floor and came to kneel in front of him. The dancer who had excited Berry did the same, curling up at the South African's feet while giving him a seductive look, well aware of what would happen next.

Soon every turbaned, bearded guest had his boy. The only light in the room came from thick, smoky tallow candles.

Berry and the young dancer exchanged a long look. They didn't need to speak. The South African calmly stood and took the boy by the hand, leading him to the bedroom Baber Khan Sahel had provided. It was pretty basic, furnished only with a *sharpoi* bed with a blanket, clothes hooks on the wall, and a copper tray on a tripod. The dancing boy went to sit cross-legged on the bed.

Berry left him for a few moments to open the shutter and look out at his SUV parked in the courtyard. Darius had rigged a bed in the back and was asleep, guarding a leather bag with half a million dollars that no one else knew about.

Which was just as well.

The South African closed the shutter and stretched out on the bed. He didn't have long to wait.

The boy crawled over and slipped a small hand into Berry's open shirt, stroking his chest and nipples with feminine delicacy.

Berry happily closed his eyes and started thinking hard about Elena, one of the Russian waitresses at the Boccaccio who sometimes sold her charms to him.

When it was over, Berry gave a sigh of delight.

All in all, it was just as good as with Elena.

Drained and happy, he took a thousand-afghani bill from his trousers and stuffed it into the boy's hand.

"Now, get out!" he said in Dari.

The young dancer didn't need to be told twice. Clutching his clothes in one hand and the money in the other, he silently disappeared.

They hadn't said a word to each other, but what would have been the point? They came from two different worlds.

When he was alone, Berry became thoughtful. The glow of pleasure gradually faded as black clouds of anxiety moved in. He couldn't stay in Logar Province forever. Eventually he would have to go back to Kabul—a Kabul where Hamid Karzai was still president and where Berry might well be a suspect. He knew the Afghans. Even without any proof, they could still stick him in an NDS cell.

He wondered what had happened to Malko. If he had fallen into the hands of the NDS, Berry's future was in serious jeopardy.

Before he realized it, he was asleep.

It was five thirty in the morning, and Malko was finishing getting dressed. He put the *shalwar kameez* on over his Western clothes, keeping the ankle holster and pistol. Wearing a turban, he wouldn't attract any attention. Many Afghans were light skinned.

He heard the door downstairs open, then footsteps on the staircase. Nadir came in, gave Malko a quick once-over, and smiled approvingly.

"That is perfect," he said. "No one will notice you sitting in the back of the taxi. I will take care of everything."

Malko had some tea and a chapati, then followed Nadir outside. An old Corolla was parked nearby, with a young bearded man at the wheel. Malko and Nadir got in the back. Emerging onto a wide, potholed avenue, they reached the outskirts of Kabul in about half an hour.

The driver pulled into a big Ensalf service station on their right. Besides the cars at the pumps, some twenty blue and yellow taxis were parked around the gas station.

"They all go to Ghazni," Nadir announced. "Follow me."

One of the drivers got out and gave Nadir a hug. The men exchanged a few words, and Nadir said, "This is one of my cousins. We will go in his taxi."

Three minutes later, they were heading for the mountains. The car's seats sagged and its shocks were shot, but it rode well. They constantly passed overloaded trucks and minibuses. Malko was starting to relax when they reached the first curves leading up to the pass.

"Aren't there any checkpoints?" he asked.

They were just then passing a roadblock stopping cars bound for Kabul.

"Not in this direction," said Nadir. "Anyway, they know my cousin, and they do not bother him."

A layer of fog forced the taxi to slow to twenty miles an hour. Reaching the pass, they drove by a long military barrier that featured bundled-up soldiers, an old Russian armored personnel carrier, and a few coils of barbed wire.

Ahead, the soldiers had stopped a minibus, making its passengers get out and searching them.

When Malko and Nadir's taxi reached the chicane, their driver said a few words to the soldier on duty. He waved them through, and they started down from the pass. Malko heaved a mental sigh of relief. He was out of Kabul!

The Taliban methods were working.

"There are no more checkpoints before Ghazni," said Nadir.

Malko dozed as the monotonous landscape rolled by. They pulled off the bumpy highway into a truck stop for tea and biscuits, then went on. Ghazni was much lower than Kabul, and the temperature gradually rose.

"We will be there in twenty minutes," announced Nadir.

Suddenly their driver slammed on the brakes. Leaning forward, Malko saw a dozen men standing in the middle of the highway. At first, he thought it was an accident but then realized that the men were carrying AK-47s; one had an RPG-7 on his shoulder. They had set up an improvised roadblock and were checking the cars.

They were probably Taliban.

In spite of having Mullah Kotak's nephew with him, Malko felt an unpleasant shiver run down his spine.

"What's happening?" he asked.

"It is just a Taliban roadblock," said Nadir, who didn't seem especially concerned.

They were now moving at walking pace. Cars were being stopped for a few moments, then allowed to drive on. When their turn came, the taxi driver rolled his window down to speak with a fierce-looking bearded man who was checking the cars. They exchanged a few words, and the man put his head inside the car. He immediately jerked back and started screaming at the driver. Malko caught just one word: "*khareji*!"

In seconds, their taxi was surrounded by a dozen hostile, bearded men who made them pull to the side of the road. Nadir went over and had a tense conversation with their leader.

The men were toothless, unkempt, and filthy and had AK-47 magazines jammed into their pockets. They were all glaring menacingly at Malko.

"What the hell is going on?" he asked.

"Something stupid happened," said Nadir. "An Australian ISAF patrol shot two boys from the village, mistaking them for Taliban. These are their cousins and their friends. They want revenge. But do not be afraid. I told them who I was and said that you are under my protection, in the name of *pashtunwali*"—the Pashtun hospitality code. "But they are very angry and we have to talk with them."

Just then, shouts arose nearby. Armed villagers were dragging a man out of his car and beating him with their rifles while yelling and swearing. His hands in the air, their unfortunate victim tried to explain himself.

Suddenly a bearded man with bulging eyes, more agitated than the others, burst from the crowd and screamed at the man at length. Then, without warning, he raised his AK-47 and fired a burst full in the man's face, tearing off his lower jaw. He fell to the ground in a shower of blood. The shooter then calmly finished him off with a short burst to the chest.

Nadir had turned pale. To Malko, he said, "He was an Afghan National Army officer in civilian clothes. They say he was an accomplice of the coalition."

Several of the men kicked the body into the roadside ditch. Malko was starting to feel very uneasy. Even without alcohol, these villagers were as worked up as a bunch of angry drunks.

Now the man with bulging eyes was standing in front of Malko and yelling at him in Pashto. Nadir immediately intervened. Speaking quietly, he managed to calm him somewhat. But suddenly the man turned on Nadir, seeming even angrier than before. The young man was as pale as death, but he stepped in when the man tried to haul Malko aside. A new discussion followed. Nadir again calmed things down, but he turned to Malko. "They say you are a spy."

Better and better, thought Malko.

Hunched behind the steering wheel, their driver tried to make himself inconspicuous as he watched the scene unfold. Suddenly a tall old man in a turban cut through the crowd, a Lee-Enfield rifle on his shoulder. His face was gaunt, and a few snaggled teeth showed in his bushy beard.

Putting his hand on his heart, Nadir greeted the old man at length and started a conversation in a much quieter tone. But Malko could see that Kotak's nephew was getting upset.

"What's going on?" he asked again.

"This is the village chief," Nadir explained. "He is in charge. He has decided to hold a *shura* with the elders to decide your fate. The villagers are very upset. Two innocent boys have died."

"My fate? What does he mean by that?"

They were now surrounded by armed men who were looking at Malko and speaking more and more angrily.

"What are they saying?"

"Some of them want to let you go in the name of *pashtunwali*," said Nadir. "Some of them want to kidnap you and sell you to the Taliban. And others want revenge for the blood of the two young boys shot by the Australians."

"How?"

"By killing you."

CHAPTER 28

At first, Malko experienced an odd feeling of detachment. It took him a few seconds to fully realize that it was *his* life they were talking about. He was somewhere in the wilds of Afghanistan, in a place he couldn't name, among people he couldn't communicate with and who lived in another world.

But their logic was implacable; two boys from their village had been killed, so they would take revenge by killing a foreigner. It just happened that the foreigner was Malko, who had nothing to do with the blunder by the Australian soldiers.

He exchanged a look with Nadir. The young man seemed overwhelmed, his eyes panicky.

"Do they know you're with the Taliban?"

"Yes, of course, but they do not care. I do not belong to their clan or their village. Blood has been spilled and it must be paid in blood. It is Pashtun tradition."

"Do you think this *shura* might really condemn me to death?"

"I will defend you," Nadir said shakily. "I will tell them that you are under the protection of Mullah Omar. They have great respect for him."

"Will that be enough?"

"I—I hope so," he stammered.

In other words, Nadir was asking him to gamble with his life.

Malko looked around. The crowd had shuffled off the highway, and traffic was moving normally again. AK-47s slung over their shoulders, the men were heading to their vehicles to drive to the village, where they would decide Malko's fate.

Suddenly the toothless old man turned and shouted something at them.

"What did he say?" asked Malko.

"We are to follow him in the taxi."

"That's fine. It'll give us a chance to escape. All we have to do is let them get ahead of us."

Things were looking up.

Malko climbed back into the taxi, followed by Nadir, who gave the driver his instructions. The driver, who understood the situation perfectly, said something in a plaintive voice.

"He is asking if we can pay him now," explained Nadir.

The driver apparently had no illusions about the outcome of the *shura*.

As Nadir was looking for his money, they suddenly saw the most agitated of the villagers, the one who had threatened Malko, exchange a few words with the toothless old man, then come striding back toward the taxi.

He looked as hostile as ever, and Malko was sure he would vote to kill him without hesitation. If only the Australians were still here! But they had probably gotten into their armored vehicles and taken off.

The angry man climbed in next to the driver, the barrel of his Kalashnikov poking against the car roof. He spoke sharply to the driver, who looked even more terrified.

"We are going to the village together!" Nadir translated. "It is three miles from here."

Which meant they had less than five minutes to decide what to do. After that, it would be too late.

They passed the army officer who'd been killed and whose body had been rolled into the ditch.

A sinister omen.

For a couple of minutes, nothing happened. They passed rocks, a few sheep, a shepherd. They were in the middle of nowhere. Suddenly Malko turned to Nadir. He had made up his mind.

"We can't go to the village," he said firmly.

"What do you mean?" said the young Afghan. "The driver is doing what the man in front tells him to. You must not try anything foolish!"

"Don't worry," Malko reassured him.

He slid his right hand down along his leg, reaching the grip of his GSh-18. He tore the pistol from the ankle holster, chambering a round as he raised it to his lap.

Nadir was now gaping at him in horror.

Malko pressed the barrel of his automatic against the bearded villager's neck. To Nadir he said, "Tell him not to move, just to give us his rifle. We'll stop the car and let him out."

When the man felt the cold steel on his neck, he started violently and turned around with a roar, his features twisted in fury.

Half-dead with fear, the taxi driver braked and stopped the car without being told.

The villager feverishly tried to free his AK-47, its barrel banging this way and that. Malko yelled to Nadir, "Tell him to settle down! I'm not going to shoot him."

Nadir stammered a few words, but they failed to calm the man. The threat of the pistol clearly wasn't enough. With the taxi stopped, he suddenly yanked the door open and jumped out, still tangled in the strap of his Kalashnikov.

"Get us out of here!" Malko yelled at the driver, forgetting that he didn't understand English.

Rigid with fear, his hands clamped on the steering wheel, the driver didn't budge. Malko turned to Nadir.

"Tell him to drive away, fast!"

Nadir blurted something, but the driver still didn't react. Suddenly, Malko looked out the open door to see the bearded man getting up, looking enraged. The moment he was on his feet, he slipped the AK-47 off his shoulder and chambered a round, clearly intending to shoot them.

The terrified driver now threw his door open and ran off down the road. Malko found himself staring into the wild eyes of the bearded villager, who was aiming his AK-47 at the car. In a second, he would empty his magazine at them. Malko couldn't hesitate: it was his life or theirs.

He fired the GSh-18 as the villager was bringing his rifle to bear. The first bullet hit him in the chest, sending him stumbling backward, finger still clenched on the trigger. Its barrel now pointed at the sky, the AK-47 loosed a long burst that went over the car. Malko had already fired again, this time hitting the man in the hip. He tumbled to the ground and lay sprawled in the dust.

"You killed him!" said Nadir dully.

Standing not far from the taxi, the driver was wailing like a banshee.

Pretty emotional, for a Talib.

Malko got out, the automatic still in his hand.

The motionless villager's eyes had glazed over. Fortunately there was nobody else on the road. Now as white as a sheet, Nadir came over to Malko.

"What are we going to do?" he moaned. "They are going to come after us!"

"We aren't going to wait for them," said Malko, still shocked by the sudden turn of events. He'd never thought he would have to kill this frenzied villager, but if he hadn't acted, they would all be dead.

"Tell the driver to turn around," he ordered. "We can't stay here."

He had no desire to battle any villagers who came to see what had happened. But the driver stood rooted to the spot, arms hanging by his sides. In the distance, Malko could see a car coming their way. This was no time to dawdle. He pointed his gun at the driver. To Nadir, he said, "Tell him that if he doesn't get back in, I'll kill him!"

Nadir didn't need to translate for the driver to finally move. He came back and slid behind the wheel as Malko climbed in. The man was so rattled that he stalled the engine three times before getting it going.

"Turn around!" yelled Malko.

This time, Nadir translated.

The driver made a clumsy U-turn and they headed back the way they'd come.

The only evidence of the incident was the villager's body lying in the middle of the road.

As they drove, a shaken Malko went over the series of events that had led him to shoot the man who was about to kill him. It made him sick, but fate had given him no choice.

Suddenly the driver spoke up in a whining voice.

"He says he can't let us stay in his taxi anymore," translated Nadir.

"Where does he want to go?"

Nadir asked the question, and the Afghan answered in the same plaintive tone.

"He has to go back to Kabul now. If he shows his face in the village, they will kill him. This is very serious because he will never be able to drive the Kabul-Ghazni route again. He wants a lot of money in compensation."

Malko still had ten thousand dollars on him, the equivalent of half a million afghanis. An enormous sum, and more than enough.

"Okay, tell him I'll give him five hundred thousand afghanis, but he has to take us back to Kabul."

Nadir passed this on, but the driver didn't seem satisfied. He made a long speech, which Nadir translated:

"He says that when the villagers find the body, they are going to alert the whole region. He's risking his life by letting us ride with him. He says he's going to drop you off at the next town, whether or not you give him the money. Otherwise, it's too dangerous."

This was a disaster.

Thinking quickly, he asked Nadir, "Are we expected in Ghazni?"

"Yes, why?"

"Is there some other way to get there that doesn't go through the village?"

The idea of going back to Kabul was wrenching.

After a long talk with the driver, Nadir finally said, "He does not know the way, and it would be too risky. If he is stopped in a village, his life would be in danger."

"Aren't there any coalition troops around here?"

"No, they are based much farther away, beyond Ghazni."

Meanwhile, they were still driving north, toward Kabul. Going back to square one enraged Malko. Without the stupid accident caused by the Australians, they would have reached Ghazni by now, and he would be on his way to Quetta.

They drove for another twenty minutes, until the first houses of a village appeared. The driver pulled into a parking lot below a small restaurant, stopping next to a white SUV that was being washed. A few trucks and private cars were parked there, and a dozen truckers were sitting up on the terrace.

The taxi driver turned around and had a long conversation in his usual plaintive tone with Nadir, who summarized it for Malko.

"He apologizes but says he is afraid. The villagers are sure to tell everybody what happened. They will be looking for him at the checkpoints. He is going to try to get back to Kabul as soon as possible, but he will not be able to work anymore."

"I thought he was a member of your organization," said Malko.

"Not really," Nadir admitted. "He is a sympathizer. He does favors for us. Because of what happened he will not be able to drive a taxi anymore. He is afraid somebody will remember his license number. Out here in the provinces, the villagers are in charge, not the president."

The driver then said something brief.

"He wants his money."

Malko realized that there was no point in arguing. Pulling hundred-dollar bills from his pocket, he counted off eight thousand dollars, keeping two thousand for himself. He handed the wad of bills to the driver, who pocketed the money without counting it.

The moment they got out, he raced off as if he had the devil on his tail.

Malko watched thoughtfully as the taxi drove away and disappeared in traffic. "Aren't you worried that he might turn us in?"

Kotak's nephew looked shocked. "Oh no, he is my second cousin! He would not do that. It would lead to reprisals."

"What do we do now?" asked Malko.

Nadir pointed at the restaurant. "Let us get something to eat. No one will mind us."

It was lunchtime. They climbed the wooden stairs and sat at a table next to an orange seller. Nadir was right; nobody paid them any attention.

Just then a minibus stopped down below, let out some passengers, and drove off in a cloud of dust.

"Couldn't we take one of those back to Kabul?" suggested Malko.

The idea didn't exactly fire Nadir with enthusiasm. "It is risky," he warned. "You are a *khareji*, and foreigners never travel that way. They would spot you at the first checkpoint.

"I have a better idea: I will get in touch with my uncle and have a car sent from Kabul. Only it will take some time. We need someone trustworthy."

A skinny, bearded young man came to take their order and looked at Malko in surprise. Nadir chatted with the waiter for a moment, and he left.

"I ordered *palau* and fruit juice," he said. "They do not have much here. To keep the waiter from wondering, I told him you were an agricultural engineer and our taxi had to drop us off. Do you like dahl, lentil soup? He recommended it."

"Dahl it is, then!"

The situation looked none too promising. Malko had been forced to kill a man, he was stuck out in the boonies, and his only real option was to go back to Kabul, where he'd started. Plus, he imagined that all the restaurant customers were staring at him. You didn't see many foreigners in the Afghan countryside.

Nadir was on the telephone. When he hung up a few minutes later, he looked annoyed.

"I was not able to reach my uncle," he said. "I talked to his secretary. He will try to solve the problem, but we will not have a car for several hours."

"So what are we going to do?"

"Wait here," said Nadir with an apologetic smile. "There is nothing else we can do."

Malko looked at the cars passing on the road below the restaurant.

What was he going to do when they reached Kabul? He would be even more vulnerable than when he'd left. And he now had the killing of an Afghan on his back.

Malko felt caught in a web, and it was getting tighter all the time.

CHAPTER 29

A secretary put an emailed report from the NDS supervisor in Ghazni on Parviz Bamyan's desk. He tossed it onto a stack of papers and went on writing his memo for President Karzai's chief of staff. Bamyan didn't pay much attention to incident reports from provincial officers.

A single assignment filled his entire calendar: track down CIA operative Malko Linge, who was a suspect in the attempt on the president's life. Karzai was putting terrific pressure on the Directorate to produce results, as a matter of both honor and safety. While officially blaming the Taliban for the attack, he was privately convinced the Americans were behind it. But he needed proof.

The NDS chief finished his memorandum summarizing the measures taken to find Linge, listing the places under surveillance and the people interrogated. He had even ordered the people manning the roadblocks to note all vehicles driving in and out of the Ariana Hotel. He couldn't stop them, of course, but at least he would know who they were. More than thirty NDS agents had been assigned to the investigation.

Feeling weary, Bamyan decided to take a break and asked his secretary to bring some tea.

As he sipped his tea and ate some orange slices, he picked up the last file to come in and quickly perused it.

Suddenly his pulse quickened.

The Ghazni NDS officer had reported an odd incident.

ISAF troops had mistakenly killed two young villagers, and their cousins and friends set up a roadblock, hoping to seize governmental officials or soldiers in retaliation. Nothing unusual about that.

In checking cars, they had stopped a taxi headed for Ghazni with a *khareji* of unspecified nationality in it. They tried to detain him, but in a series of confused events, the foreigner's group shot one of the villagers and escaped. The taxi had driven off toward Kabul and parts unknown.

Bamyan gave the report a long look.

Why in the world would a foreigner take a taxi on such a dangerous highway, instead of flying? Suddenly Bamyan thought of Linge. What if it were him?

He absolutely had to know more.

Bamyan found his list of provincial NDS officers and phoned Ghazni. He was soon talking to the writer of the report, who confirmed the events and said they had taken place in a village called Yusuf Khel.

"Get up to Yusuf Khel right away," he said, "and call me back from there."

Bamyan no longer felt like drinking tea. He didn't have any proof, of course, but he had a hunch he was on the right trail. And that raised other questions. Whoever had helped Linge take an Afghan taxi, it wasn't the CIA. Which meant he was getting help from somebody local. Pushing aside his other files, Bamyan took the one that listed Linge's contact in Kabul and noticed several visits to the Wazir Akbar Khan mosque. According to an agent, the *khareji* had called on Musa Kotak, the former minister for the promotion of virtue and prevention of vice—a man shielded by President Karzai to keep an open channel to Quetta.

It was obvious: Linge had used the Taliban network to get out of Kabul.

So when President Karzai fulminated about the Taliban and the Americans ganging up on him, he wasn't far wrong. Bamyan now had to confirm what so far was just a theory. He called one of his deputies and had the surveillance around the mosque increased. If Linge came back to Kabul, that was where they should be looking for him.

Malko glanced at his watch: it was 4:30 p.m.

He and Nadir had been hanging around the restaurant for more than four hours. Customers had come and gone, never staying long, and the two of them were now part of the landscape. From time to time the young man ordered tea, but otherwise, the waiters ignored them. In Afghanistan, the notion of time was flexible.

"What the hell is taking him so long?" hissed Malko angrily.

"My uncle told me that they found a car. But at this time of day it takes almost two hours just to get out of Kabul."

"Can't you phone them?"

"No. They know where we are. The driver is someone we can trust; he is close to my uncle. Maybe he had trouble getting his car. We just have to wait."

In any case, there was nothing else to do.

An hour earlier, a police car had pulled over below them, and Malko's heart had jumped into his mouth. But the two cops just drank some tea and left without even glancing at him.

Suddenly he saw an old VW bus coming from the Kabul direction in the middle of the highway, its turn signal blinking, clearly headed for the restaurant. It made the turn and parked below the terrace. A young man in Western clothes got out, and Nadir exclaimed, "It is Koshan! He is here to pick us up!"

The man climbed the wooden stairs and came over to their table. The two young men embraced, and Nadir explained the situation: "First he had to repair the car, and then had a lot of trouble getting out of Kabul. Traffic, you know."

Malko glanced at his watch: it was 5:15.

The old white VW bus didn't look too speedy, but it was better than nothing.

"Okay, let's go!"

He was seething with impatience. He had no idea what he would be facing in Kabul, but anything seemed better than this endless wait out here in the sticks.

"I am getting in front," Nadir announced. "Lie down on the backseat as if you are asleep. It will be better for the checkpoints. We will tell them you are sick."

Malko did so. The VW bus had seen better days, and its interior was pretty dilapidated. He stretched out as best he could behind the front seats, his feet against the sliding door. Within minutes, they were driving toward Kabul.

Bamyan grabbed his ringing cell phone: it was the Ghazni NDS officer calling him back. After the usual politenesses, he brought Bamyan up-to-date. He was in Yusuf Khel, he said, where he'd gotten a very unfriendly welcome. He had just been talking with the village chief, who was still in shock, and had been gathering information.

"What information?" barked Bamyan.

"The villagers stopped a taxi that was driving from Kabul to Ghazni. There were three men inside. One of them was a *khareji* wearing Afghan clothes. A tall man with light-colored hair. His companion claimed that the man was under Mullah Omar's protection and wasn't to be interfered with. He said he himself was a Taliban commander."

"What was his name?"

"They don't remember. But they were very angry, so they seized them anyway. A villager named Abdul Zuhoor Qamony got into the taxi with them, and they started driving toward the village. When the other villagers didn't see the taxi arriving, they went back and found Qamony's body; he'd been shot twice. The taxi and its passengers had disappeared, probably heading toward Kabul."

Bamyan could hardly contain himself. The description of the *khareji* more or less matched that of Malko Linge, who was clearly traveling under Taliban protection.

"Is that all?"

"No, Commander. The head of the village knows how to read, and he got the taxi's number."

"Give it to me!"

He wrote it down, got off the line, and immediately started phoning all the checkpoints on the Kabul highway with the license number. Finding the taxi driver would be a big step: the man might know where Linge was hiding in Kabul. Bamyan decided he wouldn't leave his office until he had further news.

When the VW reached the town of Maidan Shahr, traffic slowed considerably, even though they were still twenty-five miles from Kabul. Hordes of Toyotas jammed the bumpy highway, zigzagging between the ruts and holes in wearying confusion.

Lying in the backseat, Malko glanced out the window from time to time. They had passed only two casual checkpoints, where nobody took much interest in the dirty old VW bus. Now that they were nearing Kabul, he had to think of the future. He didn't much like returning to the little house Mullah Kotak had given him, but it was better than nothing. At least he would be safe from Karzai's goons. And he wasn't eager to make a fresh attempt to reach Quetta.

Afghanistan was too unstable for such an expedition. Short of turning himself in—which would be crazy—he felt trapped.

The VW was making its way through the crowded streets toward a casual roadblock where soldiers were lounging around, letting the cars through.

Malko sat up and asked Nadir, "What do we do when we get to Kabul?"

The young man turned around and said, "I will ask my uncle for instructions. We are not going to abandon you."

"Am I going back to the same place where I was before?"

"I do not know. I have to talk to him directly."

Soon they were heading out of town, and the VW sped up a little. Malko was tired of rattling around in the back of the bus, but he also felt apprehensive about being in Kabul.

His impossible mission seemed far away. Right now he had only one objective: saving his skin.

They drove on for about another thirty minutes, until traffic slowed to a crawl. A minibus coming the other way grazed them, and its driver yelled something at the VW driver.

A few moments later Nadir turned around, looking anxious.

"Koshan says traffic is bad because there is a checkpoint on the pass before the descent to Kabul, and they are checking all the cars coming from the south. They are looking for somebody."

Malko felt an icy chill. This wasn't good news.

"Isn't there another road?"

Nadir shook his head.

"No, this is the only way through the mountains."

CHAPTER 30

When his deputy ran into Parviz Bamyan's office yelling, "They've got him!" he gave a shout of joy.

Thanks to the license number given by the village chief, the checkpoint at the Kabul city limits had stopped the taxi driver, who unfortunately was alone in his cab. He was immediately handed over to the NDS, who were bringing him into town in a police car, lights flashing, followed by an agent driving the taxi. He would arrive in half an hour.

Bamyan could hardly contain himself. With a little luck he would now be able to locate Malko Linge. But he cautiously decided not to alert his superiors just yet. He wanted to question the taxi driver first.

The VW bus was crawling along at two miles an hour. At the pass, traffic slowed to a trickle as cars threaded their way between chicanes guarded by soldiers hunkered down behind sandbags, Kalashnikovs at the ready.

Every car was being stopped, and everyone's papers checked. The policemen were on edge and, for once, motivated. They had stopped a minibus ahead of the VW and were frisking its occupants for weapons. There were now just a dozen cars between

Malko's VW and the checkpoint. He was struggling not to let anxiety overwhelm him.

"What should we do?" he asked Nadir.

The young Afghan looked nervous.

"Koshan's papers are in order," he said. "We will say you are sick. Stay stretched out on the seat. We will tell them you have appendicitis and can't be moved. Be sure to keep your turban on!"

Fortunately, night was falling. In the darkness, you couldn't tell that Malko wasn't an Afghan unless you got very close.

"What if they arrest us?" he asked.

Malko was painfully aware of the weight of the GSh-18 automatic at his ankle. A weapon that had killed a villager, which could get him sent to jail for a long time. He considered tossing the gun out the window but changed his mind. He might still need it. Besides, he was in so deep already . . .

The minibus passengers were now climbing back in, and the VW moved forward a few yards. In a quarter of an hour at the most, they would know their fate.

The NDS agents shoved the taxi driver into Bamyan's office so hard that he slammed into the far wall. His hands were cuffed behind his back and his face swollen from the beating he'd received when he was arrested.

The agent escorting him tossed a plastic bag with the contents of the driver's pockets onto Bamyan's desk.

"He was carrying eight thousand dollars and four hundred and fifty afghanis," he said.

Eight thousand dollars! Bamyan's brain snapped into high gear. Allah was on his side. A poor bastard like this taxi driver would never have so much money unless he was involved in something crooked.

"Put him in the chair!" he ordered.

He walked over to the driver and asked, "What's your name?"

As encouragement, Bamyan slapped him hard twice, bloodying his nose. It was difficult to make out his answer, but it didn't actually matter. He snatched the roll of hundred-dollar bills and waved it in the man's face.

"Who did you steal this from?"

To drive the question home, he punched him, knocking him and the chair over backward. In Afghanistan, the presumption of guilt had replaced the presumption of innocence. It made things much easier.

When the driver had been propped upright and the blood wiped off his face, he plaintively told his story.

He hadn't done anything wrong, he said. He was just an ordinary taxi driver on the Kabul-Ghazni run. That morning, he'd been waiting at the Ensalf station in the Ivan Begi neighborhood, when a young Afghan asked to be driven to Ghazni. He was accompanied by a *khareji* wearing Afghan clothes. As encouragement, the man offered him a thousand afghanis instead of the usual six hundred, so he couldn't very well refuse.

Everything went well until just before Yusuf Khel, where they were stopped by a group of armed villagers.

Bamyan listened to the rest of the story with only half an ear. It matched what the Ghazni NDS officer had already told him. But he sat up when the driver said it was the *khareji* who had fired the two shots at the villager riding with them.

"What happened next?" he barked.

"They made me turn around. I was very scared. They wanted me to take them back to Kabul, but I made them get out at the first village."

"What about the eight thousand dollars?"

"I told him that I couldn't work as a taxi driver anymore. If I went near Yusuf Khel, I might be recognized and killed. I must have compensation. So the *khareji* gave me that money. It's the truth, I swear by Allah."

At bottom, Bamyan didn't care about the eight thousand dollars.

"What happened to your passengers?"

"I don't know, I swear by Allah. I left them in front of a restaurant. I don't even remember the name of the village. They must've taken a shared taxi or a minibus. They wanted to go back to Kabul."

"Weren't you surprised that a *khareji* would be taking a taxi to Ghazni?"

The driver shook his head.

"In talking with the villagers who stopped us, the Afghan man explained that the *khareji* was under Mullah Omar's protection. He said he was the nephew of a very respected mullah, Musa Kotak."

For Bamyan, that did it. Malko Linge had visited Kotak several times. He had an officer bring some photographs of Linge taken by NDS agents during their stakeouts and showed them to the driver.

"Do you recognize this man?"

Malko wasn't in disguise in the pictures, of course, but the driver didn't hesitate.

"That's the *khareji* I drove, I swear by Allah."

Bamyan felt a surge of optimism. He'd taken a giant step forward. He still didn't have the proof that Linge was behind the attack on President Karzai, but he now had a solid charge against him: murder. And he had a witness.

All he had to do now was find him.

"You're going to give a deposition," he told the driver. "You may eventually have to identify this *khareji*. You'll have to be sure you recognize him."

The Afghan swore he would.

The agents took his statement, which he signed without reading. He didn't notice that the eight thousand dollars had disappeared from the list of his personal effects. NDS agents were poorly paid, and they had to make ends meet somehow.

Bamyan found one thing in the interview especially encouraging: Linge and Kotak's nephew had wanted to come back to Kabul. Here in the city, he could get his hands on them. All he had to do was set the trap. If Bamyan succeeded in this matter, he would be a strong candidate for the head of NDS.

The VW bus stopped at the chicane and was immediately surrounded by soldiers, fingers on the trigger. One of them spoke to Koshan as he handed over his papers. After a brief exchange, the soldier asked, "Do you have any weapons?"

"None, I swear by Allah. You can search me and the bus."

"What about the guy asleep on the backseat?"

"He's sick," said Koshan. "We're taking him to the hospital for an operation." Then he added, "He's my cousin."

The soldier hesitated, glancing at the man stretched out on the seat with only his coat and turban visible. Fortunately, Afghans take health matters seriously. He handed the papers back and waved the bus on.

Koshan smiled and thanked him before taking off.

"*Tashakor*!" he said.

Malko waited until they were in the switchbacks descending to the Kabul plain before sitting up. He was less likely to be spotted in the city, though he still faced plenty of problems.

"Are you going to telephone your uncle?" he asked Nadir.

The young man shook his head.

"No, that would not be wise. We will go directly to the mosque. He is waiting for us there. I do not know what he plans to do with you."

Malko had to accept that.

The traffic was terrible again. It would take them another hour to get downtown.

As Maureen Kieffer pulled up in front of her guesthouse, she noticed a black Corolla parked next to the gate. When she went to open the gate, a man got out and walked over. Hand on heart, he greeted her politely in Dari and asked, "Are you expecting a visitor this evening?"

"What visitor?" asked the young woman in surprise.

The man mumbled something and headed back to his car. Suddenly Maureen thought of Malko. She hadn't had news from him in a few days and didn't even know if he was still in Kabul. But the attack on President Karzai had brought him and his odd attitude to mind. Something told her there was a connection, but she didn't know his exact role.

The stranger's presence at her door suggested that Malko was probably still in Kabul and might be in trouble. Resisting an urge to phone him, she climbed back into her SUV and drove to the guesthouse.

Looking around the streets, Malko began to recognize where he was. They soon took the big roundabout leading to Wazir Akbar Khan Road and were getting close to the mosque. More than fourteen hours of driving and danger, he thought, only to wind up back at their starting place.

The VW bus was passing along the fence around the mosque, its minarets visible in the darkness. But as they slowed down, Nadir suddenly shouted something, and Koshan stepped on the gas and passed the mosque entrance without stopping.

"What's going on?" asked Malko.

Nadir turned around, looking tense.

"There is an NDS car in front of the gate! They are waiting for you."

To Malko, this felt like a karate chop to the neck. His last few allies in Kabul were vanishing. How had the NDS found his hiding place?

The VW bus continued, turned right onto a narrow, dark street, and stopped. Nadir turned around and said, "We cannot go in there."

That much, Malko understood. But he felt rattled and was having trouble gathering his thoughts.

"Can't you go in to see your uncle?"

The young Afghan was rigid with fear.

"I am afraid they will arrest me," he stammered. "I do not know what is happening."

"So what are we going to do?"

Kotak's nephew seemed just as distressed as he was.

"I can drive you somewhere," he suggested. "Where would you like to go?"

The problem was, there was no place he could go.

CHAPTER 31

Malko was silent for a few moments. Then he asked Nadir, "Can't you take me back to the house where I was this morning?"

The young man's face fell. He looked frightened.

"They might be waiting for you there, too."

"Then go see your uncle! Ask his advice!"

"I am afraid to," Nadir admitted. "I am afraid they will arrest me. They will not do anything to my uncle, for political reasons, but it is not the same for me."

They were at an impasse.

Malko desperately racked his brain, trying to come up with a solution.

Going back to the Serena was suicide. He didn't know the way to Maureen's house and didn't want to telephone her. He had to buy some time. Suddenly, he had an idea. It was dicey, but he didn't have any choice.

"All right, then. Take me to the Iranian embassy."

Kotak's nephew looked astonished.

"The Iranian embassy?"

"That's right. Do you know where it is?"

"Yes, of course."

After a long silence, the young man said something to Koshan, who started the VW bus. A quarter of an hour later they were driving along the NDS complex wall, then stopped at the next roundabout.

"There is the embassy," said Nadir.

"I know, thanks," said Malko. "Tell your uncle to send me a text if he can still help me."

He took off his turban and shed the *shalwar kameez* he'd been wearing over his Western clothes. Sliding the side door open, he stepped out onto the empty sidewalk. Sharpoor Street was deserted.

The VW bus immediately took off, and Malko waited for it to be far away before turning around and retracing his steps. He walked about a hundred yards past the big TNT building. He knocked on a heavy wooden door, which was promptly opened by a man with a straggly beard. As usual, three guards were camped out in the forecourt with their AK-47s.

"The Gandamack Lodge!" said Malko with a smile.

They immediately let him in, and he walked to the second gate, the one that led to the guesthouse proper. There, too, he had to ask to be admitted, but his Western face was as good as any passport. He walked around the empty garden to the entrance.

It was out of caution that he hadn't had himself dropped off in front of the guesthouse. Who knew what might happen to Nadir? This way, if he was interrogated he could only say that Malko's destination was the Embassy of Iran, which would baffle his questioners.

Malko entered the small lobby and walked over to where the night clerk sat dozing at his desk. He looked up blearily as Malko studied the keys on the board.

His stomach tightened. The key to Room 4, where Alicia Burton stayed, was on its hook. The young American wasn't in. There was no point in quizzing the clerk; he probably didn't even know her name. So Malko made for the dining room. There were quite a few people there: journalists, NGO staffers, and a few Afghans.

British expats, especially, liked the Gandamack. Malko sat down at an empty table.

At this point, only Alicia could possibly bail him out, at least for the short term. He couldn't very well sleep in the street.

Tomorrow would be another day. For now, he was too tired and his brain wasn't working.

He ordered dinner but ate without appetite, praying that the young reporter wasn't away overnight. If she was, he would really be out of luck.

An hour had passed, and the diners were starting to leave. Some had rooms at the Gandamack; others were heading home. Nobody had asked Malko anything.

He paid the check and went back to the front desk.

This time his pulse started to race. The key to number 4 was no longer on its hook! The night clerk didn't even lift his head. Without hesitation, Malko walked by him and started up the staircase, his heart pounding. The stairs creaked and the hallway was dim. He got to door number 4 and knocked very gently. He heard noises inside, the sound of a key turning, and the door opened.

On a woman in a black burqa!

Malko stood rooted to the spot, thunderstruck. All he could think was that Alicia had moved out and some Afghan woman had taken her room! He was about to back away when a voice emerged from the burqa.

"Malko!"

The sound was music to his ears. Hesitantly, he asked, "Alicia? Is that you?"

"Of course it's me," said the somewhat muffled voice. "Come on in!"

He slipped into the room.

The young woman grabbed the hem of the burqa and pulled it off, revealing an ordinary dress underneath. Her hair disheveled, Alicia said, "You're lucky to catch me. I just got back from Jalalabad. When I go, I wear a burqa; it's safer. The road isn't secure."

She flopped down on the bed.

"What brings you here at this hour of night? You look kind of wasted."

"It's a long story," said Malko. "The NDS is after me, I can't go back to the Serena, and I can't take a plane. I tried to leave Kabul by road, but that didn't work out."

He told the young woman his misadventures, concluding, "I had to kill an Afghan, and I'm still carrying the gun that shot him. You're running a risk by taking me in."

"Well, I'm not about to turn you away," Alicia said with a smile. "No one's going to come looking for you here this evening. The desk clerk is convinced that all Western women are prostitutes, so he won't be surprised at my having a male guest, if he even noticed. Tonight, at least, you're in no danger.

"After that, I don't know. There are snitches in the hotel, and they might wonder about your presence here."

"We'll see tomorrow," said Malko.

Alicia had undressed and was now down to bra and panties. She was sexy as hell, but Malko was too tired to be interested; his libido was running on empty.

"You look exhausted," she said. "Get into bed."

He did so, with pleasure. In moments he was under the sheets, soon joined by Alicia, who had shed her last garments. Sweetly, she climbed into his arms and murmured, "I'm glad you came here to hide out."

The warmth of the young woman's skin did Malko good. He put his arms around her, feeling her breasts pressed against his chest.

Touched by her kindness, he kissed her neck and said, "I'm sorry."

Alicia merely said, "The bed's pretty narrow. I hope you sleep well."

Malko was so exhausted, he could have slept on a bed of nails.

As he slowly awakened, Malko found himself lying on his back, with pale light filtering through the curtains. He reached out to his sides without touching anything. The bed didn't seem that narrow. And he had it all to himself.

Suddenly he became aware of a weight pressing on his stomach. Reaching in that direction, he encountered warm flesh: Alicia's hips. Now fully awake, he realized why he hadn't found the young woman beside him: she was astride him, kneeling on the sheets.

His fingers moved up and encountered two small, firm breasts. At that, Alicia began to rock very gently, pressing down on his still-soft cock. She leaned close and murmured:

"You seem less tired this morning."

Her rocking movement was now frankly erotic, and Malko felt his desire stirring. The scene was unreal. He closed his eyes and let nature take its course. Without exchanging a word, they gradually excited each other. Malko could feel himself swelling. He took Alicia's nipples and gently twisted them, drawing little sighs from their owner. He stroked her hips as she raised herself to give his cock some freedom to move.

Glancing at the now rigid prick rising along her belly, she took it in her left hand and raised it to vertical.

"See? All you needed was a good night's sleep."

In fact, all Malko needed now was to be inside this beautiful, more than consenting woman. His libido was completely aroused. As he did each time he escaped danger, he felt a furious desire to make love.

Eros and Thanatos. An old, very comfortable couple.

"Come on!" he said.

Alicia obligingly lifted herself, like a rider posting in a trot, and seized his prick. The moment it brushed her burning folds, Malko gave a savage grunt, seized Alicia's hips, and pulled her down, entering her in a single thrust.

He felt as if he was coming back to life.

The young woman gave a little cry. "Hey, easy does it!"

Initially, she set the tempo, sliding up and down on his cock, her eyes closed, nipples erect. But Malko accelerated the rhythm, raising and lowering her more each time, until she gave a shout and collapsed onto him.

He could feel her heart pounding on his chest. They enjoyed a long, delicious moment together; then Alicia slipped off and ran into the little bathroom.

Leaving Malko appeased.

Just the same, his anxiety quickly returned. He had won a few hours of freedom, no more. Staying on at the Gandamack would be insanely risky, but he couldn't think of what else to do.

When Alicia emerged from the bathroom, he was no further along in his thinking.

She gave him a bright smile and said, "Take a shower; then we'll go down and have some breakfast."

It was in the shower that Malko dreamed up the outline of a solution. It was an option he would have preferred to avoid, but he was at the end of his rope. He waited until they were in the dining room to ask Alicia the question that was now on the tip of his tongue.

"Are you going to be contacting the Ariana Hotel?"

"Yeah, they're interested in what I saw in Jalalabad. Why?"

"How do you go there?"

"My driver takes me. I let the Ariana security services know I'm coming, and they give my license number to the various checkpoints around the Green Zone. That way I get through with no sweat."

"Could you take me with you, but without anyone knowing ahead of time?"

"Sure," Alicia said promptly.

Malko had just found a reliable way of reaching the CIA.

"I don't want to show up at the Ariana by myself. What time do you plan to go there?"

"I have to call and have the guard station give my number to the checkpoints; it'll take about an hour."

"Good," said Malko approvingly. "But whatever you do, don't mention me."

They went back upstairs to Alicia's room, and she got on the phone.

"It's all set," she announced a few minutes later. "We'll go at ten. I'll be seeing Warren Michaelis."

"He's going to be surprised," said Malko. "I'm sure he doesn't expect to see me."

Alicia's car stopped at the roadblock just before the French embassy, the first of three checkpoints. In the distance, the Ariana Hotel with the watchtower on its roof was visible. A soldier checked her papers, made sure the old Toyota had a Green Zone permit, and let them through.

Alicia and Malko sat silently in the backseat.

Same procedure at the second checkpoint.

At the third, a soldier ran a mirror under the chassis, checking for explosives. They then dealt with the Gurkhas guarding the Ariana Hotel proper. Malko had to show his passport, but given the color of his skin, they didn't ask any questions.

Still, he didn't breathe easy until the barrier protecting the hotel courtyard was finally lowered. Alicia's driver parked the Toyota in front of the building, and she and Malko went over to the Marine guard station. Telephone calls, verifications.

Five minutes later, a young case officer emerged from the elevator.

"Mr. Michaelis is expecting you, Miss Burton," he said. "Are you with her, sir?"

"Very much so," said Malko.

"Do you also have an appointment?"

"Mr. Michaelis isn't expecting me. I wasn't able to call ahead. But he'll be happy to see me."

The case officer hesitated but finally said, "I seem to remember seeing you here before. Okay, come along. I hope I don't get chewed out for this."

"I doubt it," said Malko.

On the third floor they were ushered into a small waiting room with sagging chairs. Malko's stomach was tight. How would the station chief receive him?

A few minutes later, Michaelis opened the door in his shirtsleeves. On the threshold, he stopped dead and said, "Holy cow, Malko! Why didn't you tell me you were coming?"

"I'll explain in a moment," said Malko. "I think you have a few matters to settle with Miss Burton first. I can wait."

"Go down to the cafeteria and I'll meet you there," Michaelis suggested. "One of my deputies will take you."

Malko knew the station chief had a lot of questions for him.

CHAPTER 32

Malko was working on his second cup of insipid coffee when Warren Michaelis joined him. Sitting down, the station chief gave him a long, searching look.

"The last time we spoke was five days ago," he finally said. "I haven't heard from you since. Why haven't you called?"

"I can't tell you that yet. I have to consult with Langley first."

"Where have you been?"

"In Kabul, and outside it, for a while."

The men were both ill at ease. Michaelis spoke again. "After the attack on President Karzai, I had a disturbing conversation about you, and I have to admit that it bothered me."

"With who?"

"Jason Forrest. He hinted that you were somehow involved in the attempt to kill Karzai."

"Did you believe him?"

"No, but he raised some troubling points." Michaelis sounded hesitant.

"What is known about that attack so far?"

"Not very much," Michaelis said. "It was carried out by a trained sniper using a Russian weapon that nobody's been able to trace. I'm sure he was helped by someone on the inside, but the Afghans haven't said anything about that."

"And nobody's been arrested?"

"Not yet."

"Did my name come up?"

"No."

A long silence followed, eventually broken by Malko. "Besides the attack, what's been going on these days? I've been out of the loop."

Michaelis gave him a strange look. "What do you mean?" he asked.

"How are various people reacting to events?"

"Well, Karzai is angrier at us than ever. He's hinting that the Taliban tried to kill him with our support. He even refused to meet with Secretary Hagel, claiming he had the flu. Our relations are at the lowest point ever."

Malko's disinformation pipeline had worked apparently. But Karzai was no longer fooled.

"Is that all?" he asked.

"Concerning Karzai, yes. Aside from that, the NDS tell me they have evidence that the Taliban have called off a major military operation. My opposite number at the Directorate learned that armed groups from Logar and Wardak were secretly entering the city. They now seem to have pulled back out. That would lend Karzai's claim some credibility. If he'd been killed, the Taliban were apparently ready to launch uprisings in Kabul to take advantage of his death. Of course, this is just a theory."

"Of course," said Malko. "By the way, have you mentioned this to Langley?"

"Not yet. I'll put it in my weekly brief tomorrow."

Malko was now on pins and needles, with an additional reason to talk with Clayton Luger—urgently.

"Warren, I have to contact Langley on an absolutely secure line. Is that possible?"

"Of course. Come with me."

When they got to the third floor, Malko realized that with the eight-and-a-half-hour time difference, it was 3:00 a.m. in Washington.

"I'm going to have to wait until the end of the day to call," Malko said. "Until it's nine o'clock at Langley."

"Do you want to be driven back to the Serena?"

"Thanks, but I'd rather stay here."

"No problem," said the station chief. "We have a room on the fourth floor set aside for visiting operatives. I'll have you taken up."

While they were waiting for a deputy to escort him upstairs, Malko said, "For the time being, nobody must know that I'm here."

Michaelis took this in. "Not even Langley?"

"I mean the Afghans. I don't think anybody noticed my arrival. Alicia Burton is the only person in the loop."

Malko was shown to a sparsely furnished room whose single window faced a concrete wall topped with razor wire.

He stretched out on the bed and tried to relax. He was still being hunted by the NDS, he knew. They couldn't get to him here, but he couldn't stay at the Ariana forever.

It was time to start winding this insane mission down.

His eyes half-closed, Musa Kotak listened to the ritual blandishments from his visitor. The high NDS official was charming and polite, and his short beard showed that he was religious, unlike most of the NDS agents from the procommunist Khalq political faction.

It was a visit Kotak had been expecting.

The evening before, his nephew Nadir had been picked up by NDS agents staking out the mosque and taken to Directorate headquarters. Kotak had cautiously refrained from reacting, preferring to wait and see. Koshan, the driver of the VW bus, had then told him what had happened during the aborted Ghazni trip. Kotak himself was protected by President Karzai, so he wasn't worried; nothing could happen to him.

The politeness ritual over, the NDS officer explained why they'd had to take Kotak's nephew in and assured him that the young man was being well treated. He then recounted the incident in Yusuf Khel and the role played by a foreigner in killing a villager there. Finally the NDS officer quietly asked, "Maulana sahib, do you know this foreigner, whom you put in your nephew's care?"

"Of course. He was sent to me by our beloved leader, Mullah Omar."

The officer stiffened. Now they were getting somewhere. Like everyone, he knew that Karzai had extended immunity to the former Taliban minister as a way of keeping a channel to Mullah Omar open. He would have to handle the affair with kid gloves.

"Maulana sahib, why was your nephew accompanying this man?"

"He asked for my help to travel to Quetta, to meet with members of our *shura*. As you know, the Americans shower us with kindnesses, so after consulting a friend in the *shura*, I decided I would do well to assist him."

Kotak spread his chubby hands. "Needless to say, I had no way of knowing that the trip would end in such tragic fashion. I would be amazed if my nephew Nadir were in any way responsible. He is a quiet and gentle man."

The NDS agent immediately spoke up. "Maulana sahib! Your nephew is absolutely not involved. In fact, he will be released this evening. I only wanted to know if you knew where this foreigner might be now."

"I have no idea," said Kotak, his eyes still half-closed. "I never saw him again. My nephew might know more."

"He told us that he dropped him off yesterday evening at the Iranian embassy."

The cleric couldn't hide his surprise.

"I didn't know that he had any connection with our Iranian brothers," he said. "But then again, he didn't tell me about all of his activities. I'm afraid I don't see how I can help you. I must now go pray, but I am always at your disposal.

"I hope my nephew will be released quickly. I asked him to accompany this foreigner into an area that isn't very safe. Because of the Taliban, of course."

A touch of black humor.

The NDS officer didn't insist. He stood up and handed Kotak his card. "Maulana sahib, if you hear anything about this man, could you please contact me?"

"I'll be glad to," said the cleric, escorting his visitor out.

As soon as he was alone, Kotak drafted a message for Quetta, describing all that had happened. The careful scheme they had put together with the Americans was collapsing. Worse, Karzai might well make the connection between the Taliban and an attack that almost cost him his life.

Which could complicate things.

He ended his message by stressing that the only link between the attack and the movement was Malko Linge, who therefore represented a threat to their cause. As long as the Afghan president was alive, they would have to deal with him. It would be best, he concluded, to erase all traces of the aborted operation.

Kotak now had to find Linge. He was reluctant to call him, knowing that the NDS was almost certainly tapping the phones. He would use his networks instead.

Nelson Berry left Pul-i-Alam around noon, after a final meal with his host. Having weighed the pros and cons, he was heading back to Kabul. After all, he couldn't stay in Logar indefinitely.

The attempt on Karzai's life was no longer the main topic of conversation. In Afghanistan, so much happened every day that people soon moved on from the failed attack, which had killed just a single person, one of the president's drivers.

As he and Darius drove toward Kabul, Berry wasn't feeling too worried. He had eliminated the only man who could testify that he was involved in the attack, and he knew the Degtyarov 41 couldn't be traced. All that remained was his connection with Malko.

Berry had already prepared a story to tell the NDS, of course. He would say that Linge had asked him to carry out some CIA operations in areas that were too dangerous even for the Agency, eliminating members of the Haqqani network, but that he'd turned him down.

The story's main advantage? It couldn't be checked.

Berry felt confident that he could resist an eventual NDS interrogation. They weren't as brutal when questioning *khareji*.

Which left him with only two concerns.

The most immediate one was the five hundred thousand dollars he was carrying. He couldn't risk the NDS finding it. He would have to explain where it came from, and they would probably steal it.

There were plenty of hiding places in his poppy palace, but none good enough to resist a determined search. However, Berry owned an abandoned farm outside of Kabul that he used as a firing range and storehouse. It was guarded by an old one-armed mujahideen fighter grateful to be given food and shelter. Berry decided to hide the moneybags among his stores of weapons. Nobody would think to look for them there. That way, if the NDS picked him up when he reached Kabul, he would be clean.

His other concern was Malko Linge.

If the CIA operative had left Afghanistan, the problem was solved. If not, Berry's wisest course would be to kill him.

CHAPTER 33

Malko dialed Clayton Luger's number at exactly 5:30 p.m., which was 9:00 a.m. in Washington. The deputy director got to his office around eight o'clock and would have reviewed his most urgent files. Luger lived near Langley in McLean, Virginia, and made it a point of pride to be among the first to pull into the CIA's purple parking lot.

"Luger here."

"Clayton, it's me, Malko."

There was a brief moment of silence, then a crisp question. "Where are you?"

"In Kabul, at the station. I'm calling on a secure line."

"We haven't talked in a long time," Luger said. "What's been happening?"

"A problem that I haven't been able to sort out."

"That's not important anymore. We've gotten very bad blowback on this. Karzai wants to skin you alive."

"How did he connect me to this business?"

"Because of a son of a bitch whose name I won't mention on the phone," Luger said bitterly. "Karzai is especially angry because we passed the word that the operation was off. We're going to have to negotiate away a few points with him. This whole business is a disaster."

Luger continued. "We have to make nice, so we're all palsy-walsy again, regardless of how we actually feel. In any case, it's a real cluster fuck. Do you have any news of our other man?"

"Nothing," said Malko. "He's disappeared. I don't think he's been arrested; otherwise, Karzai would be parading him through the streets because of his connections with the Agency. Anyway, you can give John one piece of good news."

"Good news? Really?"

"This screw-up is actually a stroke of luck. Your Taliban friends were planning to double-cross you. Your whole scheme was to get them to stay on the sidelines, wasn't it?"

"That's right. Why?"

"Once Karzai was killed, they intended to put Kabul to the torch. A number of fighting units had secretly gathered in the city. We don't know exactly what would've happened, but they were certainly planning a takeover."

There was a long silence; then Luger asked, "How do you know this?"

"Tomorrow your COS will send you an in-depth report based on NDS analyses. In the confusion following Karzai's death, anything could have happened. The only people expecting it were your so-called allies. They were planning to betray you up and down the line. Let you do the dirty work, then pull their chestnuts out of the fire."

"Are you positive about all this?"

Luger was clearly having trouble believing it.

"Just ask Warren," said Malko. "I think we dodged a major bullet."

"Thanks to you," said the CIA deputy director.

"Thanks to luck," Malko corrected him. "So what do we do now?"

"Has the Agency officially taken you in?"

"No, I'm here undercover. But I don't plan to stick around. Warren suggested exfiltrating me through Bagram and Dubai. That's probably safest. I don't dare show my face in town anymore. The NDS is after me, and it would be awkward if I fell into their hands."

"That's out of the question," said Luger. "But your leaving Kabul is also out of the question."

"Why?"

"As I told you, we're working on Plan B. We still don't want Karzai, but we have to handle him very gently. I'm coming to Kabul in a few days. The president wants us to wrap this business up, and I'm going to need you. Keep a low profile in the meanwhile, okay?"

"I don't have much choice."

Malko was perplexed as he left the code room. What exactly did the Americans want?

Returning to Michaelis's office, he could immediately tell from his face that something was up.

"I have bad news," announced the station chief.

"Concerning me?"

"Yes. I just received a message from the number two at the NDS. Officially neutral. Asking me if I knew how to reach you. It seems the Directorate plans to charge you with the murder of a villager in the Ghazni area. There are witnesses, apparently. What's that all about?"

"I didn't have time to tell you earlier. It's true, unfortunately."

Michaelis listened in silence as Malko told the story, then said, "That's very awkward. I claimed I didn't have any word from you, of course. I'm going to have to ask Langley for instructions, and I'll do what they tell me."

The station chief seemed to be washing his hands of him.

"In other words, I'm under house arrest."

"You mustn't put it like that," Michaelis protested. "You're safe here."

But Malko wasn't kidding himself. The Afghans would use his killing the villager as a pretext to interrogate him about the real issue, the attempt on Karzai's life.

So for now, he was trapped. Which was ironic, considering the risks he had taken on behalf of the White House! But the world of intelligence is merciless, and it grinds individuals into dust. He of all people should know this, but it took him by surprise each time.

Parviz Bamyan reread the report of the interrogation of Mullah Kotak's nephew implicating Malko Linge in the villager's murder. This was proof that the Taliban had stopped supporting Linge. They knew there were some lines you didn't cross.

His secretary came in and put another report on his desk. Bamyan read it and cursed under his breath.

An NDS informer at the Gandamack reported that a foreigner had spent the night with one of the guests, an American woman named Alicia Burton who had close ties to the CIA. She and the unknown man had left the hotel in her car the next morning. From the license plate, the NDS suspected they had driven to CIA headquarters at the Ariana Hotel.

So Warren Michaelis had lied to him.

Bamyan's only consolation was that he now knew where Linge was, albeit in a place as inaccessible as the far side of the moon.

But Michaelis's lie gave him a hold over the Americans. After all, Linge was being charged with murder. Bamyan immediately drafted a report for the president's office. It wasn't going to improve Karzai's mood, since they now had definite proof that the CIA was protecting Linge and surely knew he was involved in the attack against the president.

Nelson Berry immediately spotted the two men sitting in an old green Corolla parked at the corner of Street 15 and Sharpoor Street near his poppy palace. They didn't stir while his guards opened the front gate, which meant they hadn't been given orders yet.

The South African was feeling more comfortable. He had dropped off his treasure at the farm two hours earlier, hiding the money in a pit filled with crates of ammunition. Even his old one-armed caretaker hadn't noticed. Berry now strolled into his office, turned on the computer, and made a few phone calls. Outside, Willie and Rufus were unloading the car.

Nothing happened for a couple of hours; then he heard the honking of a horn. Almost immediately, Darius walked into his office.

"There's a man who wants to see you," he said.

"Who is he?"

"He says he's General Abdul Raziq of the Interior Ministry. He's in a white Land Cruiser, license plate Thirteen Kabul Police."

"Show him in," said Berry, "and bring us some tea."

A ministry special advisor, Raziq was a person worthy of respect. He belonged to a prominent family and was fairly close to President Karzai, so Berry expected the worst. Raziq was in uniform; this was an official visit. The two men had met several times before, and they embraced with the usual expressions of goodwill.

Then, having sipped the usual tea, they moved on to serious matters.

"It seems you just came back from Logar," said the general, who had excellent information sources.

"That's right," said Berry. "I was in Pul-i-Alam, doing a favor for a friend who—"

"I know," said Raziq with a smile.

Berry didn't try to avoid the subject. "It's harvest time, and Baber Khan Sahel had a big transaction he wanted me to safeguard because he doesn't quite trust his partners. I was able to earn a little money. Business is bad these days."

The general nodded understandingly and said, "Don't worry, that isn't the reason for my visit."

The opium and heroin trade was a sensitive matter in Afghanistan. It brought in about three billion dollars a year, of which more than seven hundred million went to the poppy growers. Nobody wanted to upset such a large sector of the country's economy.

"So what can I do for you, General?"

"Do you know a man named Malko Linge?"

Now we're getting down to brass tacks, thought Berry.

"A little," he said. "He came to see me a couple of times. You know he's a CIA operative, right? He wanted me to carry out gray operations in dangerous areas, getting rid of Taliban commanders. I turned the job down because it was too dangerous and didn't pay enough."

"You were right to do so," said the Afghan general. "It's not wise to get involved with the Taliban and the Americans' problems. Do you know where he is now?"

"Not the slightest idea," said Berry honestly. "I don't even know if he's still in Kabul. But I have his cell number."

"So do we, but he isn't answering."

"Why does Linge interest you?" he asked, trying to sound casual.

The general lowered his voice. "You remember the attack against President Karzai? We have reason to believe he might have been mixed up in that."

Berry felt he should protest. "But Linge works with the CIA!" he said. "The Americans wouldn't want to assassinate the president. He's their ally."

The general allowed himself a private smile. "I can't tell you more, but our suspicions are well founded. Let me ask you something directly: if this man is still in Kabul, can you help us find him?"

He was gazing at Berry with large, soft eyes. With his white hair, Raziq looked like a kindly grandfather.

The South African didn't hesitate. "If I can be of service, it would be a pleasure. Your department has always been very fair with me, General."

The Interior Ministry was the agency that issued weapons permits. If Raziq wanted to, he could put Berry out of business with the stroke of a pen.

"I know you're a resourceful man," said Raziq. "We would be extremely grateful if you could help us."

He took out a business card, wrote some numbers on it, and handed it to Berry. "Here are my four phone numbers," he said. "I underlined the one I always answer. I hope I hear from you soon."

To Berry, the quid pro quo was perfectly clear. Give them Malko Linge, and they would leave him alone. The Afghans were interested in Berry only as a means to an end. Even if the general were sure the ex-mercenary had participated in the attack, he was willing to overlook it. But Linge was another matter. The CIA operative led directly to the White House. And there, the political stakes were much higher.

Berry walked the general out to his Land Cruiser, which was guarded by a tiny old man with a forked beard, an AK-47 on his shoulder.

"That's my bodyguard!" said Raziq. "He's a former Taliban leader who took up farming but got bored. I'm very satisfied with him."

Berry waved the general good-bye as the Land Cruiser pulled out onto 15 Street. He was thinking that he had better find Linge before the Afghans did.

And silence him permanently.

CHAPTER 34

After his first night in the Ariana billet, which felt as cozy as a hospital ward, Malko went downstairs for breakfast. He was about to head back up when Warren Michaelis walked into the cafeteria.

"Big news!" said the station chief, sitting down at his table. "Clayton Luger is arriving tomorrow on an Agency jet—private trip, top secret. He asked to see you as soon as he arrives."

"Will he be staying here?" asked Malko.

"No, of course not. He'll stay at the embassy. I'll let you know as soon as he arrives. Right now, let's go to the embassy PX so you can buy whatever you need."

"All my things are at the Serena," said Malko with a groan. "Isn't there some way to get them?"

"Not now," said the American dryly. "It would be like hanging a banner on the front of the building announcing that you're here."

Later, Malko was finishing a cup of coffee in the cafeteria when a young intercept operator handed him a note. A number associated with one Nelson Berry had been repeatedly dialing Malko's phone, without success. To keep anyone from picking up the phone's signal, Malko had removed the battery and wrapped the phone in foil. They were crude steps, but they would have to do until he got a new, secure phone, with a number the Afghans didn't know.

He wondered why Berry was trying to reach him. Berry was taking a big chance in calling, given that the Afghans suspected Malko in the attack on Karzai. Malko decided he would postpone getting in touch with the South African.

Musa Kotak greeted his visitor with all due deference. Hadj Mohammad Himmat was a member of the Quetta *shura* and close to Mullah Omar. Though a sworn enemy of Hamid Karzai, he was able to travel freely in Afghanistan because he sometimes carried secret messages to the president.

"Did you have a good trip, brother?" asked Kotak, seating his guest and offering him a glass of tea.

"Allah was with us," said Mullah Omar's envoy. "We didn't have any flat tires and we weren't stopped at any roadblocks. But it's still a long voyage."

"Do you bring good news?"

"A letter from Mullah Mansur for you."

Himmat rummaged in the pocket of his long *kameez* and took out a rolled sheet of paper. Kotak accepted it respectfully, put it on the table, and resumed their conversation. He knew it was the answer to the question he had asked. The two men chatted for a while, until Himmat excused himself to get some rest. Kotak didn't ask where he was going. For security, movements among the Taliban were extremely compartmentalized.

The moment Kotak was alone, he unrolled the paper. Written in a beautiful hand, it was very brief: *Nothing should remain of our intentions, if Allah so wishes.*

Allah would certainly so wish, thought Kotak, since he was on their side. All he now had to do was to get rid of Malko Linge, and do it in a way that wouldn't attract suspicion. But first he had to find him, and that wouldn't be easy.

When the waitress at the Boccaccio brought Nelson Berry his pizza, he gave her a long look—a look the young woman smilingly reciprocated. Mariana's passport was Kirghiz, but she was one hundred percent Russian, with big gray eyes and a chubby body squeezed into a fitted top, black tights, and a miniskirt. Seeing her running around the restaurant, Berry could feel himself getting a hard-on.

It was only at the Boccaccio that you found women like her. A notorious crook, the restaurant owner paid off the police to leave him alone. Everyone in Kabul knew you could find any liquor on earth at his place and that the waitresses really knew how to serve the customers. Three of them took turns, wearing provocative outfits and doing business only with expats.

Every so often a table full of Afghans showed up, all men. After eating and drinking their fill, they left without ever being presented with a check. The top echelon of the Kabul police.

This evening the restaurant was full, as usual, with a fair number of Afghans who couldn't help ogling the sexy women you saw nowhere else.

Berry was feeling good. General Raziq's visit had greatly cheered him. It was nice not having to worry about being picked up on a whim. For the time being, his unwritten deal with the general protected him. Of course, he had to fulfill his end of the bargain: find Malko and, more than that, convince the Afghans to accept a dead man in satisfaction. That would be a lot harder, because Malko dead wasn't worth an afghani to them. But while he was alive, the operative represented a clear danger to Berry, who knew that no prisoner handed to the NDS could resist interrogation.

So he had to make contact with him. Malko now knew that the

South African wanted to reach him. The moment he answered, Berry would be ahead of the game.

Mariana—not exactly a Kirghiz name—brought Berry his check with the same cool smile as before. The South African's libido, already lubricated by the beer, rose to the occasion. The dancing boy in Pul-i-Alam had certainly given him pleasure, but he wasn't a woman, a rare species in Kabul.

"Two hundred," he murmured.

Two hundred dollars, meaning ten thousand afghanis: an enormous sum. But the young woman just stood there, eyes downcast, gauging the desire radiating from this husky young guy.

"No, I'm tired," she said.

Suddenly Berry really wanted her. He put three fingers on the table. After all, it would barely dent his five hundred thousand dollars. This time, she said a few words in Russian:

"In the lot at the end of the alley. In a quarter of an hour." Then she carried his check to the cashier.

Berry serenely made for the restaurant's entrance, crossed the small garden, and climbed into his Land Cruiser. It was just as well that he hadn't brought Darius. Once behind the wheel, instead of turning left to leave the alley, he continued right, to a small vacant lot, and parked the SUV so as to be able to leave immediately.

As a precaution, Berry took the pistol out of his boot, chambered a round, and put it in the central console. There were robbers in Kabul, and everyone knew that rich expats frequented the Boccaccio.

Mariana appeared twenty minutes later and got directly into the backseat. Berry walked around and joined her, immediately seizing her breasts, a delicious sensation.

The woman stiffened and quietly said, "*Valuta*"—the cash.

Berry peeled three hundred-dollar bills from his wad. She stuffed them in her right boot and relaxed.

Putting his hand on her knee, Berry noticed that she had taken off her tights. Her skirt was so short that he quickly found her crotch without encountering the slightest impediment. She wasn't wearing panties.

As he was getting excited, caressing her all over, Mariana asked, "How you want?"

"Like this," said the South African. He seized her hips and made her kneel on the seat, her face against one of the doors. Fortunately, the SUV was roomy enough to handle this kind of recreation.

The moment she was in position, Berry unzipped his pants and shoved his underwear aside, freeing a cock as stiff as a baseball bat. He lifted Mariana's miniskirt from her hips, admiring her shapely ass. Gripping the door handle, the young whore waited stolidly.

But when the huge prick plunged into her, it still came as a shock.

Berry was hung like a bull, and he wasn't into gentleness. In two thrusts he penetrated Mariana to the hilt. He, too, was kneeling, with his feet firmly planted against the other door. As he started energetically working her over, the Land Cruiser began to rock.

The young woman's head banged against the bulletproof window while her energetic partner grunted like a lumberjack. Now sliding smoothly, he went at it with a will.

Alas, all good things must come to an end. With a final thrust, Berry clutched her hips and emptied himself in her. Mariana waited a decent interval before pulling free.

"*Spasiba,*" she thanked him politely. "Was very good."

Her tone was completely indifferent, but Berry didn't care. This was a red-letter day.

The two got out of the SUV at the same time. Mariana headed back to the Boccaccio, and Berry went around and got behind the wheel.

Malko answered his new cell phone, which was secure, like his old one. Michaelis was on the line.

"Mr. Luger is in my office," he said.

"I'll be right down."

He'd been waiting in his room for an hour and was getting restless. When he entered the station chief's office, he found Clayton Luger sprawled on the leather sofa. The deputy director looked jetlagged, and no surprise. A seven-thousand-mile trip would exhaust anyone. He must have showered and shaved, because he otherwise looked quite presentable.

Luger managed a smile and said, "I'm starving. Let's go have dinner."

"I reserved the embassy dining room," said Michaelis.

They had to cover only a couple of hundred yards, but it was studded with checkpoints and took them nearly twenty minutes. There weren't any Afghans here, only Americans and Gurkhas in bulletproof vests.

The dining room looked out on a garden, its windows protected by netting against hand grenades. A Marine waiter served them and poured a Bordeaux. The three men's conversation was casual, focusing on the difficulties the United States was having getting its matériel out through Pakistan, an operation that was costing a hundred and fifty million dollars a month. Luger was clearly waiting to be alone with Malko to talk seriously.

Michaelis disappeared as soon as coffee was over, having settled Malko and Luger in the sitting room of the ambassador, who was away from Kabul for a few days. When he closed the door behind him, Luger visibly relaxed and gave Malko a warm smile.

"I'm very relieved to see you, Malko! We were worried. Exactly what happened?"

"I really don't know," Malko admitted. "I haven't seen Nelson Berry since before the day of the attack. I know he hit the wrong car, he hasn't been arrested, and the Afghans are blaming the Taliban. He phoned me yesterday, but I didn't pick up. I was waiting to see you."

"That was smart," said Luger. "We're in deep doo-doo, and the president has decided to get us out of it. This isn't your fault, of course. Maybe it's nobody's fault. But regardless, we have to defuse the situation. John and I have devised an exit strategy.

"First of all, John thanks you. He read the report Michaelis sent. Those damned Taliban were planning to screw us six ways from Sunday. But that's past, and we'll settle our scores later. My trip here today has just one goal: make peace with President Karzai."

"That isn't going to be easy," remarked Malko.

"I'm coming hat in hand," said the CIA deputy director. "But there isn't any other way. Here's the approach we decided on.

"Tomorrow morning I have an appointment with Karzai's chief of staff, Hadj Ali Kalmar. I won't be going alone. Jason Forrest will accompany me. He's been briefed by Mark Spider, who himself was briefed by John." Luger smiled bitterly. "Forrest is my guarantee."

"What are you going to tell them?" asked Malko, intrigued by this strange visit.

"Part of the truth," said Luger. "That an extremist group, which I won't name, convinced the White House that for the security of the United States, President Karzai had to be eliminated."

"Are you going to mention the Taliban?"

"Hell no! This is an internal American affair."

"What then?"

"That after due consideration, we decided to cancel the operation, which is why the Afghanistan committee met for a second time. Unfortunately the operation was already under way, so it was lucky it didn't have any consequences. Needless to say, I will apologize abjectly and offer the president an arrangement whereby we keep some troops in Afghanistan to protect him."

"You think the Afghans will buy that?" Malko was dubious.

Luger heaved a sigh. "I'm going to take a double dose of Prozac."

"I wish you luck," said Malko. "And what happens to me?"

"We'll talk about that later. First, I have to go bury the hatchet."

"The Afghans are going to demand compensation. They have the advantage."

Luger dismissed the objection. "If it's a matter of money, we have it. If it's breaking with the Taliban, we'll do it. Now that we know they planned to fuck us, we won't have any regrets."

He fell silent and lit a cigarette. To Malko, it felt unreal to be talking this way in the U.S. ambassador's quiet, well-appointed living room.

"All right, I'm going to bed!" said Luger. "I need a good night's sleep. See you tomorrow!"

The white Land Cruiser flying the American flag on its left fender was as armored as a tank. It stopped at the checkpoint off the Massoud roundabout. Ahead stretched a long straight avenue interrupted by three more checkpoints. This was the Green Zone, which protected the presidential palace and its outbuildings.

A young Afghan woman wearing glasses was waiting at the checkpoint and climbed into the Land Cruiser next to Luger.

"I am Mariam Azibullah," she said. "I will escort you to Mr. Kalmar's office."

They went through the three checkpoints. Despite the presence of Karzai's staffer, each was more thorough than the last. There was another roundabout at the end of the wide avenue, then a second avenue leading to a kind of fortress with ramparts, a tower topped by the Afghan flag, and a passageway for vehicles.

"We get out here," said the young woman. "Cars aren't allowed any farther."

They passed through a metal detector, and a soldier then politely searched all of them, even the CIA deputy director. They emerged onto an esplanade worthy of Versailles. Azibullah pointed to a group of buildings on the left. In a profoundly respectful tone, she said, "That is where President Karzai lives."

Luger's group headed to a matching group of buildings on the right. Armed men were everywhere. Climbing a flight of stairs, they entered an attractively furnished office with a low table for tea. Their guide made Luger and Forrest comfortable and disappeared.

The CIA men waited nearly twenty minutes before a young man with glasses wearing a Western suit opened the door. Without the hint of a smile, Kalmar shook their hands and ushered them into his office.

His face could have been carved in ice, and it was hard to catch his eye.

After a few moments of silence, Luger gathered his courage and said, "I've come from Washington to have a straightforward talk with you. I think there's a serious misunderstanding between our two countries."

Kalmar didn't stir, only giving Luger a sharp glance. In perfect English, he said, "I hope you have come with the best of intentions, because you have a lot to apologize for. I won't hide the fact that I had to beg the president to be allowed to receive you. I don't think the relations between our two countries have ever been more"—he hesitated, choosing his word carefully—"threatened."

Luger bent his head. He had expected a chilly reception and he wasn't disappointed. Seeing his guest's dismay, Kalmar softened the blow a little.

"An Afghan proverb says that fair weather always follows a storm. So please, speak your piece."

"Mr. Luger wants to see you in my office at six o'clock," said Michaelis. "I'll leave you alone, because I think he has a lot to tell you."

It was 5:30, and Malko hadn't heard from Luger since their conversation the evening before. All he knew was that he had gone to the palace and met with President Karzai's right-hand man. Since then, he had been closeted in the embassy.

When Malko entered Michaelis's office, Luger was already there. He was looking better than he had the previous evening but had big bags under his eyes. He greeted Malko with somewhat forced warmth. Michaelis already had his hand on the doorknob.

"Should the three of us have dinner together?" he suggested without much conviction.

Clearly preoccupied, Luger didn't bother answering. He was looking at Malko.

"Which do you want first, the good news or the bad news?" he asked in a dull voice.

"The bad news, of course."

The American nodded.

"I'm afraid I'm going to ask you to do something very unpleasant."

CHAPTER 35

For a few seconds, Malko wondered anxiously what Clayton Luger could ask of him that was so unpleasant—short of surrendering to the Afghan authorities, that is. His mission had become a nightmare. Even his American backers were turning on him.

"I'm listening," he said.

Luger took a deep breath and began.

"I just had the most uncomfortable hour of my life," he said. "Kalmar began by threatening to make public the CIA plot to assassinate the president of a supposedly friendly country.

"That could have been devastating, because the Afghans have concrete evidence, including your and Nelson Berry's names. There's also the matter of the murdered villager, which aggravates the charges against you, and the fact that you tried to get out of the country afterward. The nephew's testimony is especially damning. He says you tried to reach Quetta clandestinely when you knew you were wanted by the Afghan authorities."

At this, Malko exploded. "You know very well that I was trying to avoid causing you problems! I could easily have taken refuge here at the Ariana, but I didn't want to drag the Agency into it."

"That didn't ultimately do any good, but I appreciate it," said Luger. "Anyway, what's done is done. I'll spare you the rest of the conversation. In the end I was able to convince Kalmar that a public break would hurt both our countries. So he moved to his fallback position. He asked for your head."

"Is this what you meant by 'something unpleasant'?" asked Malko, alarmed in spite of himself.

"Don't worry, I immediately refused. I explained that you were acting under orders—my orders—and that you were a vital Agency asset. There was no question of handing you over. That was a deal breaker. Kalmar knows you're here under our protection and that we can exfiltrate you through Bagram, so he didn't press the point."

"In other words, I'm in the clear," said Malko.

Luger made a cautious gesture. "Wait, it's not as simple as all that! Kalmar then laid out his own bottom line, which came straight from President Karzai. And he considers it nonnegotiable as well.

"Karzai is prepared to wipe the slate clean of our 'misdeeds' on one condition: by Afghan tradition, a blood price must be paid."

"You mean the driver who died in the motorcade attack? That shouldn't be a problem."

"No," said Luger, shaking his head. "Kalmar didn't even mention him."

"Who then?"

"The blood price is that of the man who committed the assault, the guy behind the gun."

"Nelson Berry?"

"That's right. They want him so they can show the Afghan people a concrete result: a mercenary paid by a hostile entity—namely, the Taliban—to kill their president."

"I understand, but what role do I play in all this?"

"You're the only person to have contact with Berry. Your job will be to convince him to turn himself in and confess."

Malko jerked upright in his chair. "That's disgusting!" he cried.

"*I'm* the one who dragged him into this mess, using *your* money, and now you're asking me to betray him!"

"It's not a betrayal," argued Luger. "In Vietnam, officers were asked to abandon their soldiers in Vietcong territory, even though it meant condemning them to death or imprisonment. It was in the national interest, for diplomatic reasons."

"And some of those officers committed suicide instead," Malko angrily pointed out. "During all the years I've served the Agency I've managed to maintain a minimum standard of ethics. I don't plan to stop now."

"I'm not asking you to commit suicide or to compromise your values—"

Interrupting him, Malko went on, "Besides, the first thing Berry will do if he's arrested will be to implicate me. He can prove I gave him money. Your plan isn't just amoral; it's idiotic!"

For the first time since the start of their conversation, a thin smile crossed the American's face.

"You're forgetting that we're in Afghanistan," said Luger. "This is all playacting! Karzai wants to show the public that the Taliban tried to get rid of him. And that's what Berry will tell his interrogators."

"But he'll have to talk about me."

"Of course, but only as an intermediary between the Taliban and us. He can claim not to know who in the Taliban put the plot together. Do you see what I'm getting at?"

"Perfectly," said Malko. "And the way this little piece of theater plays out, Nelson Berry dies. Sorry, I won't do it."

"Actually, we reached an agreement to cover that," said Luger. "Once Berry has confessed along the lines that implicate the Taliban, he'll be transferred from NDS custody to the prison in Bagram."

"Won't he go to trial?" asked Malko, surprised.

"Afghan justice works very slowly," said Luger. "At the Bagram prison, detainees are held for months or even longer before being tried. So here's the deal I struck with Kalmar. Berry will spend a few months behind bars in Bagram—no sinecure, but the lesser of two evils. Then he'll be quietly moved to the part of the prison we still control and flown out of the country."

"Where to?"

"Wherever he likes. We have military flights to Dubai, Europe, and the United States. And you're authorized to offer him one million dollars in compensation for his stay in prison. That's a small cost for getting ourselves out of this catastrophic situation with our heads high.

"Karzai is due to go to the United States to meet with President Obama in a month. Everything has to be settled by then. They'll be discussing the departure of coalition troops, and those talks can't be poisoned by this sort of problem."

Luger paused.

"So what do you think of all this?"

"How much faith do you put in the Afghans' word?" asked Malko.

"As a rule, none. But in the present case, the risks are limited. Berry won't be tortured, because he'll confess what we tell him to. I'm sure he'll go through some bad times, but he's a tough cookie. And after all, he did try to assassinate Karzai. He took a chance, and he'll pay a price for it.

"Then, when he's moved to Bagram, he'll be more on our turf. We've transferred the prison to Afghan control, but we're keeping an eye on it."

"How do things stand with Kalmar right now?" asked Malko.

"I have until this evening to call him, to confirm or reject our agreement."

"What if you reject it?"

"Then I'm finished," said Luger flatly. "John warned me that there would have to be a scapegoat."

A hush descended on the men. It was laughing heartily at the sight of the Americans being hoisted by their own petard.

Luger glanced at his watch. "You have two hours to think this over, which should be plenty of time. As soon as I have your answer, I'll communicate it to John."

Malko stood up and asked a final question. "What if Nelson Berry refuses my proposal?"

Luger shook his head. "I don't see how that would be in his interest. His career in Afghanistan is finished. If the Afghans arrest him outside of our agreement, he'll go through some very rough times. By signing on with us he gets a million dollars and can go make himself a life somewhere else after a few months in prison. Anyway, it's up to you to convince him."

Luger put out his hand to shake, signaling the end of their meeting. Clearly, Malko thought, the Americans were ready to do practically anything to extricate themselves from the mess they'd gotten into. He just hoped the CIA deputy director wasn't hiding anything from him.

Parviz Bamyan was having tea with General Raziq, who was in civilian clothes. The NDS chief had just come from the presidential palace, where he'd been briefed on the proposal put to the Americans.

"The whole trick is to quietly get hold of Nelson Berry and extract his 'confession' implicating the Taliban," he told Raziq. "Then we'll pull out our secret weapon."

"What's that?"

"On the day of the attack, Berry killed an NDS agent in the Aziz Palace construction site, so as to act undisturbed. But until he confesses to shooting at the president, we don't have enough evidence to charge him.

"We also want Berry to tell us how he got the Degtyarov 41. The president insists on that. It will be a key piece of evidence at the trial."

"What happens after that?"

"Then we extract his *real* confession, implicating Linge and the Americans. That way we'll have something to hold over their heads."

"Let's hope this all works," said Raziq with a sigh.

"And another thing," continued Bamyan. "We said we would transfer Berry to the Bagram prison. We aren't going to do that. He killed our agent, so we can keep him in one of our cells, beyond the Americans' reach."

The plan was a tortuous one, but it had a number of advantages. The more evidence the Afghans had of U.S. involvement in the attack against Karzai, the stronger their position in the future. The Americans had no idea that their Afghan counterparts were so skilled at playing double or triple games.

A difference of culture.

Malko lay on his bed in the Ariana. Since leaving the CIA deputy director, he'd been going over the American proposal in his mind, looking for pitfalls. Because there had to be one. He had decided not to leave the protection of the CIA until he was sure that he wasn't at risk.

The stakes were too high for a single individual to have much importance in matters of state. And this affair had started at the top, with the president of the United States.

Malko's cell rang. A hidden number. He answered anyway and recognized Luger's voice.

"I'm still at the embassy," he said. "I'm sending you a car in fifteen minutes."

He hung up before Malko had time to answer.

He rested for a few more moments, then went down to the Ariana guard station, where a case officer drove him to the American embassy.

They quickly passed through the various checkpoints. An operative was waiting for Malko at the embassy entrance.

"If you'll follow me," he said, "I'll take you to the residence."

Luger was sitting on a blue sofa smoking a cigar. He smiled at Malko and got right to the point.

"Have you thought it over?"

"If I said yes, what would my status be, as of right now?"

Luger's features relaxed slightly. "That's a point I settled with the palace. In that case, I give Kalmar a call, and all surveillance of you is dropped. You can move back into the Serena, and an Agency car will be at your disposal."

"Can I leave the country?"

"Not right away, but when this problem is dealt with, sure," said Luger with a smile. "The Afghans won't object. By the way, you originally told John that you didn't want to be paid for this assignment, for ethical reasons. Considering what's happened to you, that clause is canceled. You'll be generously rewarded for your efforts, and you will have earned John's and the Agency's esteem."

"I hoped I already had it," said Malko.

He was silent for a few moments. The CIA was putting everything in the balance to get free of a trap of its own devising. He again cursed himself for accepting this outlandish assignment, but there was no point in crying over spilled milk. And he thought longingly of the Serena, which now seemed as desirable as the finest hotel in the world. The last few days of life on the run had exhausted him.

"Very well," he said. "I accept your proposal."

Luger's face brightened. "Great!" he exulted. "I expected no less of you. And now, to get the ball rolling, we'll start with a little formality."

"What's that?" asked Malko.

"You're going to phone Nelson Berry."

CHAPTER 36

Nelson Berry gazed thoughtfully at the unfamiliar number displayed on his cell phone. He hadn't heard from Malko since his first attempt to reach him, but that didn't mean much. He decided to risk answering the call. When he did, the Austrian's accent came as a breath of fresh air.

"I know you called," said Malko, "but I wasn't in Kabul then."

"It's good to hear from you. Want to have a *dop* with me tomorrow?"

"Where?"

"My place. Noon, if that works for you. I'll send Darius."

After hanging up, Berry poured himself a whiskey. He had done a lot of thinking since his initial call to the CIA operative and had come up with a plan.

He had decided to leave Afghanistan for good, but he didn't want to leave a troublesome witness like Malko behind. If he talked, the Afghan authorities might get Interpol to issue an international arrest warrant against Berry, which would cause him no end of trouble. He intended to go to Dubai first, and the Dubaians were sticklers about international regulations.

Thanks to General Raziq's intervention, he was free of surveillance, and this had allowed him to plan his departure.

Before leaving Kabul he would swing by his farm and dig up his five hundred thousand in cash. Then he would drive north on the Mazar-e-Sharif highway to Tajikistan. The highway was safe, and Berry felt sure he would reach the border without any trouble. In Dushanbe, he would sell his car to some drug traffickers he knew and catch a flight for Dubai.

Thanks to Malko's telephone call, Berry could now finalize his arrangements.

The next morning, he would pack his computers and whatever else he needed from his poppy palace, drive to the farm, and have his caretaker dig a grave in a nearby field. Darius would pick up Linge and bring him there. Berry would shoot him at the first opportunity and leave him for the old man to bury. That way, he could head for Dushanbe with an easy mind.

Having drunk his whiskey, he went to get Darius. The two of them had to deliver an SUV he was selling to Maureen Kieffer to earn some extra money. Berry was sick and tired of Afghanistan. The sunshine in Dubai would revive his taste for life.

Riding in an Agency SUV, Malko gazed out at Kabul's anarchic traffic. He felt as if he were in a new city, yet nothing had changed: the same pedestrians in turbans and *pakol* hats hurried along the sidewalks, and the same yellow taxis, aging buses, and omnipresent Toyotas jammed the streets.

His heart soared a little when he passed through the Serena Hotel's sliding armored gates.

The lobby was empty, as usual. The desk clerk handed Malko a new room key—his old one had expired—without inquiring about his absence.

Room 382 was in perfect order. To Malko, it felt like coming home.

He got undressed and raced to the shower. The hot water felt so good, he didn't want to leave. When he was finally clean and dry, he felt like himself again. His Russian GSh-18 was still in the GK ankle holster. He had almost forgotten it.

Malko suddenly realized that it was after eight o'clock and he was famished. He hated the idea of eating alone, so he phoned Alicia Burton but got no answer. She must not be in Kabul.

Then he thought of Maureen Kieffer, whom he'd stayed clear of, for her safety. The young South African woman wasn't off-limits anymore. He dialed her number, but she didn't pick up.

He had resigned himself to eating at the hotel buffet when Maureen rang him back.

"Malko!" she cried warmly when she heard his voice. "I thought you were dead!"

She wasn't far wrong.

"I was away, but I'm back in Kabul again, and a lot of my problems have been solved. I'd really like to see you. Would you like to have dinner?"

"I'd love to, but I can't. I invited a bunch of friends over, and I can't cancel. Why don't you join us? I can send my driver. He'll come at nine o'clock and wait outside the hotel; it's too complicated for him to come in."

"That's perfect. I'll be out front at nine. I would bring you a bottle of champagne, but they don't have any here."

"Don't worry, I have some!" she said, laughing. "See you later!"

At Maureen's, Malko was greeted by a smiling young Pakistani with a neatly trimmed beard. He put his hand out and said, "My name's Parvez. I run the UN Humanitarian Air Service. I'm a pal of Maureen's. She's in the kitchen. Come on in!"

There were a dozen young expats in the living room, draped across armchairs or sitting on cushions. Al Jazeera was playing on a big flat-screen TV with the sound off, and a CD of vaguely Indian music filled the room. Malko walked through to the kitchen.

"Malko!" Maureen cried.

She quit stirring a big pot of spaghetti and ran to his arms.

She was wearing a very short black dress and looked extremely sexy. She ground her hips against his in a silent invitation, then giggled and said, "We're going to have to wait for a while. My pals like to drink and talk a lot."

She apparently wasn't angry at Malko for whatever may have happened with Alicia Burton.

"I'll leave you to your cooking," he said.

Back in the living room, the champagne was flowing freely. Malko poured himself a glass and went to sit next to Parvez, who seemed the most interesting person there.

"I just got to Kabul," he said. "What's the situation like?"

"Not great," said the young man, grimacing. "We don't know what will happen after Karzai goes. The Americans are pulling out, and that's leaving a lot of people unemployed. There's no money. The Afghans would like to emigrate, but where can they go? Nobody wants them, not even Dubai. There are more and more beggars in town."

"What about the Taliban?"

The young Pakistani smiled sarcastically.

"Oh, they're doing just fine! We don't see them much in Kabul. They only launch occasional suicide attacks against the police or the army, but they're on a roll in the provinces. They don't control any cities, but they're everywhere in the countryside.

"Also, they're systematically cutting the highways. You can't go to Bamyan overland anymore. You have to fly. Which is making a man out in the Band-e-Amir Lakes crazy." These were a chain of spectacular lakes on a fourteen-thousand-foot plateau a hundred miles west of Kabul.

"Why is that?" asked Malko.

"Believe it or not, he built a ski resort there. For rich people from the city."

In the middle of war-torn Afghanistan? Malko was amazed.

"A ski resort! How?"

"Oh, he jury-rigged it somehow," said the Pakistani. "He wasn't able to build a ski lift, so he uses donkeys to haul the skiers up the mountain on a tow rope. But people love it. There aren't many places to have fun in this country."

Just then Maureen emerged from the kitchen with a huge plate of spaghetti.

"Soup's on!" she cried.

Maureen's living room was littered with dirty dishes and empty bottles. She had just seen her last guest to the door. She flopped down next to Malko on the sofa and sighed.

"To make them leave, I told them there wasn't any more champagne."

"They do drink an awful lot."

The young South African shook her blond locks.

"I'm liquidating my supply. I can't take it with me."

"You're leaving Afghanistan?"

"Soon as I can find someone to buy my business. Everyone's leaving. Pretty soon there won't be any more expats here. Most of my customers have already closed up shop."

She crossed her legs high enough for Malko to glimpse her white panties, then stood up and ran into the kitchen. She came back with a bottle of Roederer Cristal and started to open it.

"This one's for us!" she announced.

She filled two glasses and came to stand in front of Malko, provocatively thrusting her full breasts at him.

"Do I still turn you on?" she asked playfully.

Instead of answering, Malko slipped an arm around her waist and caressed her breast with his other hand. She promptly pressed her crotch against his and started to move.

But not for long.

Freeing herself, she slipped her dress over her head, keeping only her panties. Then she said, "It's been a long time since I hosed you down. Get undressed!"

Since Malko didn't react fast enough, she started unbuttoning his shirt, then attacked his alpaca pants. When he was completely naked, she took his cock in her right hand and gently stroked it until it was as stiff as she liked.

As she did, she gazed into Malko's eyes, her upper lip drawn back a little from her dazzling white teeth.

As before, she drenched Malko's belly with champagne, then knelt in front of him on the rug. First she licked the champagne from his stomach, then moved down to his cock, lapping the wine up like a little cat. Finally, she took his cock in her mouth and deep in her throat. Sighing with pleasure, she then settled back on the sofa, her legs apart.

Malko needed only to push her white panties aside to slide into her warm pussy.

A delighted Maureen bounced beneath him, squeezing his hips with her thighs, giving a little cry with each of his thrusts. Meanwhile, she licked the champagne from his chest each time she was able to. Eventually, he gave a yell and came deep inside her.

When she caught her breath, Maureen gave a peal of joyous laughter.

"I'll always love sucking off a man with a big hard-on and a little champagne."

The woman's tastes were simple, though difficult to indulge in a country like Afghanistan.

She lit a cigarette and suddenly said, "By the way, d'you remember that guy you once mentioned, Nelson Berry? A South African, like me? He's leaving town, too."

Malko's heartbeat picked up.

"How do you know that?"

"He came by this afternoon to sell me one of his cars. He's leaving tomorrow morning."

CHAPTER 37

Maureen Kieffer had clearly made the remark casually, without anything special in mind. Her meeting with Berry didn't conflict with Malko's, and there was no reason for Berry to have given Malko his schedule when they'd spoken. But it felt worrisome, somehow.

When Malko didn't respond, Maureen asked, "Have you seen him?"

"We talked on the phone, but he didn't say what he was up to. Why is he leaving Kabul?"

"He doesn't have enough clients. At least that's what he told me."

"I should know more tomorrow," said Malko. "I'm due to meet with him. And now I think I better get back to the hotel. Can you have your driver give me a lift?"

"Of course," she said. "If you stay on in Kabul, I hope we can see each other again."

Ten minutes later, Malko was riding through the darkened streets of the city. He was intrigued by what Maureen had told him, but he wasn't able to say why.

It was 11:30 a.m., and Malko was due to be picked up by Berry's driver at the usual place. As he was about to leave his room, he hesitated. The automatic and ankle holster lay on his night table, and he couldn't decide whether to take them. Finally, he strapped them on, first making sure a round was already chambered. The GSh-18 was the kind of weapon that had to be ready in an instant.

Taking it felt a little silly, given the conversation he was going to have with Berry. He would try to get him to throw himself to the wolves in exchange for a million dollars. And Berry would probably tell him to forget it, especially if he was leaving the country.

The sun over Kabul was brilliant. As before, Darius had parked the Corolla beyond the police checkpoint and was waiting for him. At first, Malko didn't pay much attention to their route. But he soon noticed they hadn't passed the NDS compound. Instead, they were heading north to the Jalalabad highway.

"Aren't we going to Mr. Berry's place?" he asked.

"The commander will see you at one of his properties," said Darius. "It isn't far."

They soon left the highway for a bumpy track that wandered between barren hills, past flocks of sheep and isolated farms. Three-quarters of an hour after leaving downtown, they reached a large farm surrounded by a high wall. Berry's SUV was parked in front of the farmhouse.

As Darius pulled up, a smiling Berry appeared in the doorway. He gave Malko a warm handshake and led him inside to a big wooden table.

"This is my annex," he explained. "I store a lot of my stuff here. Want some chai?"

"So what happened?" asked Malko.

They hadn't spoken since the attack.

"I was sold out by my source," said Berry with a scowl of disgust. "The wanker pointed me to the wrong car. I only found out later, of course."

"What did you do then?"

"I went to Logar Province for a job. I didn't know what kind of shit was going to come down in Kabul, but fortunately nothing did. When I got back, life went on as usual."

"A lot has happened in the meantime," said Malko. "For one thing, the Americans have decided to make peace with Karzai."

Berry looked surprised. "Did they admit what they'd been planning?"

"No. They were betrayed by someone on the inside, in Washington."

"That takes the cake!" he said, whistling softly. Then he frowned. "What about me?"

Malko looked him straight in the eye. "I'm afraid your involvement has been discovered. But we've come up with a solution that will satisfy everybody, including you."

The South African stiffened. "Tell me about it," he said carefully.

Malko outlined the tricky plan they had hatched with the Afghans, the million dollars Berry would get for his cooperation, and what would happen after that.

The South African looked as if he'd been turned to stone. "Your Washington friends are pretty fucking naïve," he finally said. "The Afghans are going to screw you, and then they'll screw me. Once I'm in the hands of the NDS, they'll do whatever they please."

"But it's the only possible solution," argued Malko. "Otherwise they'll have our hide."

"They'll have *your* hide, because I won't be around. I don't even plan to return to my poppy palace. From here I'm heading to Mazar and then Dushanbe, where I'll take a plane to Dubai."

Which tallied with what Maureen Kieffer had said, thought Malko. But why had Berry wanted to meet him out here in the sticks?

"Still, it's not a bad offer," he said. "You're going to need money, even if you leave."

Berry's mouth twisted into a kind of rictus. "I'll never see your million dollars because the NDS will never let me go." He paused. "Too bad. I wish this business were ending some other way."

Something in his tone set off an alarm in Malko's brain. "Since you're leaving Afghanistan, why did you have me come out here?" he asked.

The South African smiled slightly. "I'll explain, *bra*. Follow me."

He stood up and led Malko out into the yard, then another hundred yards farther to an orchard. Berry was walking slowly in front of Malko. Just before reaching the perimeter wall, he stopped.

Malko did too, suddenly feeling very tense.

He barely noticed Berry's right hand move, but the sight gave him a jolt of adrenaline. Without pausing to think, Malko crouched and tore the GSh-18 from the ankle holster. He was straightening up when Berry turned around, aiming a big pistol at him.

Malko immediately fired. The shot's rising trajectory caught Berry under the jaw and tore into his neck, exiting through the back of his head—along with a mass of bone, blood, and brain.

The South African didn't even have time to pull the trigger. Knocked backward by the impact of the 9 mm shell, he collapsed, still clutching the gun in his right hand.

It all happened so fast that Malko had trouble gathering his wits. Berry lay bleeding from the neck, stone-dead. Malko turned to see an old one-armed man come out of the house, shouting something. The man slowly walked closer but stopped when he realized he wasn't talking to Berry, and scuttled back inside.

Malko looked up at the perfect blue sky, a taste of ashes in his mouth. He hated the idea of taking a human life yet had now killed for the second time since coming to Afghanistan. And for the second time, he'd been forced to do it. If he hadn't reacted so quickly, it would be him lying there in the orchard, dead.

Silence had fallen.

Why had Berry wanted to kill him, when he'd just offered him a million dollars? Now he would never know. The plan the CIA and the Afghans had concocted was collapsing. The blood price had been paid, but not the way anyone expected.

Malko took a few steps and noticed a hole in the ground near a large orange tree. Berry certainly had foresight: he'd even had his grave dug.

The sound of an engine made Malko turn around, and he saw Darius driving the Corolla out the gate, fast. He was now without a car somewhere far from Kabul. Taking out his cell phone, he dialed the CIA station chief.

"Come and get me, Warren. I'm somewhere outside the city. I don't know where and I don't have a car. Please locate me with my phone's GPS. I'll be waiting."

He went back into the farmhouse and sat down on the bench. He felt very, very weary.

More than two hours later, a convoy of three white Land Cruisers and a green police pickup pulled into the farm.

A man in a general's uniform with a kepi stepped out of the lead SUV, which bore a red police license plate. He was followed by a tiny old man with a long gray beard, barely taller than his AK-47. The man in the kepi—it was General Abdul Raziq—walked over to Malko and in excellent English asked, "Where is Nelson Berry?"

"Over there at the end of the garden."

Emerging from the second Land Cruiser were Clayton Luger,

Warren Michaelis, and two armed Marines. The four joined the general and his diminutive bodyguard.

Taking the big automatic from Berry's hand, Raziq remarked, "He didn't have time to shoot."

"If he had, I'd be dead," said Malko. "Berry brought me here to kill me. A woman friend told me last night that he was leaving Afghanistan. He wanted to do some housekeeping before he left."

"This isn't good," said Luger. "The Afghans are going to be furious."

"If I had died and Berry had left the country, they would be just as furious," Malko responded.

"Search the property," Raziq ordered the policemen. He and the others gathered near Luger's Land Cruiser.

A half hour later an officer brought over a big leather satchel that he'd found in the South African's SUV. Malko's pulse began to race. It was the bag with the five hundred thousand dollars he had given Berry.

The general opened it, glanced at the bundles of hundred-dollar bills, and returned it to the officer.

"Put that in my car," he said coolly.

The CIA didn't have much chance of ever seeing its money again.

They stood around chatting while the policemen hauled crates of ammunition, pistols, and RPG-7s from the farmhouse.

Raziq then took Luger aside for a long conversation, which ended with a vigorous handshake. The general climbed into his Land Cruiser, leaving the police officers behind.

To Malko, Luger said tersely, "Let's go."

As they made their way down the bumpy track, he turned to Malko and said, "Here's what General Raziq and I agreed on. Thanks to a tip from us, the Afghans caught Nelson Berry trying to escape from Afghanistan. He fought back and was shot. Searching his place, the police found the sniper rifle used in the assassination attempt."

"But that's not true!" said Malko.

Luger merely smiled. "The NDS already has the rifle. All they have to do is bring it here and pretend it was found on the farm."

Presto, the "blood price" was paid—and there was no risk of Nelson Berry naming the people who had given him his orders.

As they drove down toward Kabul, Malko wondered what awaited him. He still had a heavy sword of Damocles hanging over his head: the killing of the villager. If the Afghans wanted to harm him, it would be easy to do.

CHAPTER 38

Mullah Kotak typed out a short text to send to Malko. Now that he had the green light from the Quetta *shura* to kill him, there were a few things he had to make absolutely sure of.

They had come within an inch of success, he reflected. The moment Karzai was assassinated, members of the police and army would shoot their officers, roadblocks would be thrown open, and targeted killings would destabilize Kabul. By the time the Americans realized what was happening, it would be too late, and the Taliban already would be in charge.

Now they would have to start again from scratch.

A small Kiowa helicopter was parked in front of President Karzai's residence, across from the path where Luger was walking with his guide. Despite General Raziq's assurances, the CIA deputy director was ill at ease. The business with Nelson Berry hadn't gone as expected. The Afghans could certainly claim a success, but it wasn't the clean sweep they would have liked.

When Luger entered the presidential suite, Kalmar was leafing through some papers. He gave the American a perfunctory handshake, set his files aside, and got right to the point.

"General Raziq sent me his report," he said. "Mr. Berry's death is a positive development, and it will help us conclude this matter in the eyes of the Afghan public. However, there are still things we don't have yet."

"Such as?"

"The link between the person who ordered the attack and the one who carried it out. We've been wondering whether your operative Malko Linge might have shot Berry to keep him from naming him."

Luger practically fell out of his chair. "What? Berry had a gun in his hand and was about to kill him!"

"The scene could have been arranged after the fact."

Luger felt he should keep the discussion on track. "Mr. Kalmar, everything happened exactly the way Malko Linge described it. The issue is settled. I came here to confirm that in our eyes this unfortunate business is finished. A poor decision was made on our side, followed by a rogue action that fortunately had no undesirable consequences. I now hope that our relations are restored."

The Afghan was silent for a few moments, then said, "To completely conclude this affair, it would be useful if we had a signed statement by Mr. Linge explaining how he recruited Berry to assassinate our president."

Luger had to struggle to keep his cool. The man was asking for nothing less than written proof implicating the U.S. government in the attack. It would be an invitation to endless blackmail.

"That's out of the question," he said firmly. "I would never authorize Linge to make such a statement. As a matter of fact, I plan to take him with me when I fly back to Washington this evening."

He had made up his mind on the spot. I have to put an end to the Afghans constantly jerking me around, he thought.

After a brief silence, Karzai's chief of staff said, "That's too bad, because Mr. Linge isn't allowed to leave Afghanistan for the time being."

Luger was startled. "Why not?"

"Because of the regrettable matter of the villager he shot. We know he was acting in self-defense, but local Afghan customs are different from ours. A blood price must be paid to appease the spirits."

It was getting to be a habit.

"What do you mean?" asked Luger guardedly.

"The dead man's family is demanding twenty thousand dollars."

"That's not unreasonable," said Luger, brushing the request aside. "They'll get the money."

"I don't doubt it," said Kalmar smoothly. "Except that custom demands that the killer pay the blood price in person. Until that is done, the case will remain open."

This asshole really is shitting me, thought Luger. Aloud, he said, "Given your position, don't you think we could dispense with the formalities?"

The chief of staff shook his head, looking apologetic. "It's a delicate matter for us. As you know, President Karzai is often accused of covering up 'missteps' by the Americans and the coalition. If we offend the *pashtunwali* code, we'll be again accused of siding with the United States. It would be bad for the president's image. I've discussed this with him, and he insists that the full ceremony be performed."

"So this means Malko Linge can't leave Afghanistan," said Luger, inwardly fuming.

"Temporarily," said Kalmar with an appeasing gesture. "Only temporarily. As soon as he pays the blood price, he will be free to leave. I realize that you could use the Bagram Air Base to fly him out of the country, but that would be seen as an insult to the president. There are enough problems between us not to create more."

Luger was in a bind. He knew that the blood-price business was bogus but couldn't afford to trigger a fresh conflict with Karzai. He wondered what John Mulligan would do in his place.

"Very well," he said wearily. "I'll fly back to Washington without him."

"I think that's a wise decision," said Kalmar, "and the president will appreciate it. Particularly since Mr. Linge has a great deal to apologize for, even if he was acting under your orders."

Luger understood that there was no point in insisting and stood up. "In that case, I'm entrusting Malko Linge to your care," he said in a tone heavy with implications.

"Have no fear," said Kalmar easily, a Pashtun as comfortable in treachery as a fish in water. "We consider him a friend again, as we have always considered you."

Luger was fuming as he made his way across the presidential grounds. There was no question of flying Malko out now. It would be a casus belli with the Afghans. But in a way, he realized, it might help advance a plan he had in mind.

Malko came out when he saw a Land Cruiser pull up to the Serena awning. At the wheel was Jim Doolittle, accompanied by a couple of Marines.

"We're going to the embassy," said the case officer. "You're expected there."

They endured the interminable checkpoints and the wary looks of the Nepalese soldiers. It felt like entering a besieged fortress. A young Marine greeted Malko in the embassy reception area and led him directly to the residence. There he found a worried-looking Clayton Luger, whiskey in hand. The American looked up and gave him a faint smile.

"Afghans suck!" he said.

"What's going on?" asked Malko with some concern.

"You've become a hostage. You can't leave Afghanistan, at least not for the time being."

Malko felt a chill run down his spine. Here we go again, he thought.

"Have a drink, and I'll explain."

The Marine poured Malko some vodka. A sip of the ice-cold liquor did him good.

"Are the Afghans still angry at me?" Malko asked. "I thought this morning's meeting had put the matter to rest."

"I thought so too, but those people are as nasty as a skilletful of rattlesnakes."

He explained the proposed blood-price ritual, then said, "It's a pretext to keep you from leaving the country. Afghan peasants are being blown to bits every week by coalition bombs and drones, and all Karzai ever does is to file verbal protests."

"So what are they really after?"

"Hell if I know!" Luger admitted, sipping his whiskey. "I think they're still smarting from what we did to them. With Berry dead, you're the only actor in the operation still alive, and I'm sure they'll try to somehow extract a confession from you. It would be a powerful weapon against the U.S. government."

"In that case, why not fly me out with you? We can easily travel to Bagram, and they don't control our flights."

"I know," said Luger thoughtfully. "But I have specific instructions from the White House: I'm here to appease the Afghans, not fan the flames. The wounds are still too fresh.

"I doubt they would attack you directly, but I'd watch out for dirty tricks. I've given orders for you to be properly protected when you go to deliver the blood price. By American troops, not Afghans."

"Will I be able leave the country then?" asked Malko, who still felt worried.

"I imagine so," said Luger enigmatically. "Come on. Let's go have dinner."

Efficiently served by a pair of silent Marine waiters, the two men looked a bit lost in a dining room designed for twenty. At the start of the meal Luger changed the subject, talking instead about recent events in Washington. Malko felt tense because he sensed the CIA deputy director wasn't telling him everything.

The idea of staying on in Kabul made him ill.

By the time they were eating their apple pie, they still hadn't broached the main topic again. Eventually they returned to the residence living room for a cup of coffee.

Luger discreetly dismissed the two Marines, then turned to Malko.

"I have something to tell you," he said. "As far as we're concerned, your mission in Kabul isn't finished."

CHAPTER 39

Malko was taken aback.

"You aren't thinking of trying to kill Karzai again, are you? Because if you are, I don't want any part of it!"

Luger put up his hands. "No, no, of course not! But we still want to put him out of action, at least politically. The man's been a disaster for the country. We know he's determined to hang on to power any way he can, and that risks plunging Afghanistan into a bloodbath. My orders from the White House are to stop him."

"I've already done my part," said Malko. "You have plenty of good people at the station here in Kabul to deal with it. I want out, Clayton."

"I understand," said the American soothingly, "but from our standpoint, you're uniquely positioned to help. First, you know the country. Second, you have local contacts that our station people don't. Besides, this wouldn't be an overt action but an operation behind the scenes."

"With everybody in Kabul watching me? You really must want me to die here."

"Certainly not! What we'd like is for you to promote an anti-Karzai front. That way, if he tries to stuff the ballot boxes or run one of his henchmen, he won't succeed."

"How do you expect to achieve that?" Malko asked skeptically.

"By getting the Taliban on board."

Malko gave Luger a sharp look. "You know they don't want to participate in elections. It's against their culture, Karzai or no Karzai."

"I realize that, but you have a direct connection with Mullah Musa Kotak, and he's the unofficial representative of the Quetta *shura*—the real Taliban power. He won't do business with anyone but you."

"What do you expect of them?"

"Persuade the people in areas they control to vote for the candidate of our choice."

"By offering them what?"

"A share of power when our candidate wins."

"They'll never believe you," said Malko flatly.

"It'll be your job to convince them. The Taliban actually have everything to gain, because legislative elections will follow the presidential ones. They can have their say then, by running candidates who embrace their ideas.

"There's a lot of work to do, of course. The Taliban are shrewd, fanatical, and stubborn. But some of them want to return to power, even without an Islamic emirate in Afghanistan. We already discussed this in Doha."

"Let me be sure I understand what you're saying," said Malko. "You want me to launch a crusade against Hamid Karzai when he and the NDS already have me in their sights."

"No, this would be a much more subtle operation," said Luger. "We can't just sit on our hands, Malko. Nobody can persuade Karzai to step aside. Since we weren't able to eliminate him, we have to beat him at the ballot box."

At least the CIA deputy director took responsibility for his actions.

"And who will your candidate be?" asked Malko.

"We haven't decided yet, but I'll tell you as soon as I can."

"That's the first question the Taliban are going to ask me! You know how suspicious they are."

"I would start by finding out if they're prepared to buy into our project. Will you agree to do that much?"

Malko didn't answer immediately. What he was being asked to do fell within the purview of an Agency mission leader. It involved persuading people, not killing them. The problem was that it was taking place in Afghanistan, where people tended to shoot first and ask questions later. And the moment Karzai realized that Malko was again plotting against him, he would have just one idea: eliminating him once and for all.

But Malko was too tired to argue. All he wanted was to forget the stress of these last days.

"All right," he said. "I'll contact Kotak again, after I'm finished with this ridiculous blood-price formality. I hope he'll listen to me."

"Great! The station will be at your disposal for logistics. As far as keeping in touch, you'll report directly to me on a secure line. I'd like to see you succeed."

Malko didn't reply. He was thinking not of succeeding but of sleeping.

"I'll call you a car," said the deputy director. "Until we see each other in Washington again, be careful. By the way, Karzai's office will contact you tomorrow for the blood-price ceremony."

Ten minutes later, Malko was in yet another of the CIA's white Land Cruisers, heading for the Serena.

As he got undressed, Malko glanced down at the GSh-18 strapped to his ankle. It had twice saved his life already. He took off the holster, slipped under the sheets, and immediately fell asleep.

A photo of Nelson Berry's body surrounded by smiling policemen was splashed across the front page of the *Afghanistan Times Daily*, a Kabul English-language newspaper. The accompanying story was worthy of the picture, describing how a careful investigation led the NDS to the author of the attempt against the president. The article said the Taliban were obviously behind the attack but didn't specify exactly who.

Malko was finishing his breakfast when an Afghan woman came into the dining room by herself, an event rare enough to be noteworthy. She had long black hair, partly covered by a silk head scarf, and was dressed Western-style in a classic blue dress.

Malko watched as the woman chose a table across from him, then went to serve herself at the buffet. She didn't look like a journalist or an NGO staffer. When she came back to sit down, their eyes briefly met. Just then, Malko's cell phone rang.

An unknown voice with a strong Afghan accent told him that the blood-price ceremony would take place in forty-eight hours at Yusuf Khel, in the presence of the village chief. Malko was to bring twenty thousand dollars and give it to the chief after a brief speech.

Malko would be picked up at the hotel at eight o'clock by a military escort, because the road wasn't completely safe.

As soon as he'd hung up, he called Warren Michaelis.

"Luger told me about it," said the CIA station chief. "We're going to give you a *real* escort, of course. I don't trust those sons of bitches. I'll notify Karzai's office. We'll bring you the money at the same time."

That was one problem taken care of, at least.

Malko felt wary of this whole blood-price setup, because he knew the ceremony was rarely held. Coalition authorities generally arranged to pay compensation to the families of those killed by drone or bomb attacks, but without getting personally involved. Why had the Afghans insisted so strongly on his presence in this case?

“Nelson Berry’s dead,” said Malko.

Maureen Kieffer was silent for a few moments, then asked, “Do you know what happened?”

“Yes. I shot him to keep him from killing me. It’s a long story.”

“I read about it in the papers,” said the South African woman. “It’s too bad. Nelson was an okay guy, and he wasn’t afraid to take chances.”

“He took one too many,” said Malko. “Anyway, I think your warning probably saved my life.”

“Was he really the person who shot at Karzai’s car?”

“If you have dinner with me tonight, I’ll tell you all about it.”

“You know that’s always with pleasure. Shall I come get you?”

“Nine o’clock. We’ll go to the Boccaccio.”

Malko wasn’t outside for more than three minutes when Maureen pulled up to the Serena’s sidewalk blast wall in her old SUV. The young woman was alone, and her car smelled of perfume.

She had put on a skirt, a red cashmere sweater, and high heels. The good weather was back, and the streets were finally free of mud.

“Nice of you to dress up for me,” said Malko, laying a hand on her black-clad thigh. “I haven’t had much relaxation these days.”

“Maybe not, but at least you’re still alive,” she said, giving him a knowing look. “That’s not true of everyone.”

She was driving toward the Boccaccio, through traffic that was moving well at that hour.

“Are you thinking of Nelson Berry?” he asked.

“Yes. It’s upsetting to think that you shot him. He wasn’t a bad sort.”

Everything's relative, Malko thought.

"I can explain what happened," he promised. "I don't like killing people, but I've sometimes been forced to."

Malko had left his GSh-18 in the hotel safe for the evening. He almost felt like he was on vacation.

They were nibbling on a big naan in the middle of the table while waiting for their spaghetti with clams. Malko was wrapping up his account of the Karzai attack and Berry's death.

"I'll never know why he wanted to kill me, but I didn't have any choice. He had it all planned. He'd already had my grave dug."

The South African woman nodded. "Nelson must've been afraid you would turn him in. I can't think of any other reason. At least the Afghans now know who carried out the attack."

"They also know I'm the person who ordered it."

The spaghetti arrived and they dug in.

After a while Maureen said, "You haven't told me why you're staying on in Kabul, since this business is over."

"I still have to pay the blood price."

"Yeah, but that'll be quick. Will you be leaving right afterward?"

Malko almost said yes, then realized it was silly to lie to her. "I don't know yet. I'm talking with the Taliban."

She gave him an anxious look. "That's dangerous, you know. Karzai gets hysterical over contacts between the Americans and the Taliban. And you're vulnerable. They've already targeted you."

"That just means you won't be able to see me," he said lightly.

Maureen scowled at him. "Don't be a bonehead, Malko! It's you I'm worried about, not me. They've got a thousand ways of getting rid of you."

"I'll be careful," he promised.

They sat talking about his problems until the end of the meal.

Driving back through Kabul's poorly lit streets, all Malko could think of was being in Maureen's arms. They drove directly to her guesthouse.

When they embraced, Malko knew they would make love in an unusually intense way. An interlude that would restore his sense of himself.

Hugging each other in Maureen's living room, they began to sway. Malko pushed the young woman against a wall, put his hand under her skirt, and slid her panties down. Maureen agreeably let him have his way.

She was wet by the time he led her to the big sofa where they had made love before. As evidence of her mounting excitement, she didn't suggest hosing him down.

She wasn't playacting anymore.

When Malko slowly entered her, she lifted her legs so he could penetrate her deeply. They made love slowly, almost without moving, until the young woman's whole body shuddered and her arms clutched him.

Sometime later, she murmured in his ear, "Come see me again after you've paid the blood price."

CHAPTER 40

A young Afghan approached Malko's table as he was eat-ing breakfast. A small man, he had long hair and was wearing gold-rimmed glasses, a tan *shalwar kameez*, and a black vest. He looked like a frightened weasel.

"Good morning," he said in hesitant English. "I am Nassim Madjidi, your interpreter. I will accompany you to Yusuf Khel. Are you ready?"

"Are you a police officer?" asked Malko.

"No, of course not," said Madjidi with a hapless smile. "I work for the Culture Ministry. The president's office assigned me to make sure everything goes good there. Can I think you don't speak Pashto or Dari?"

"That's right."

Malko went to pay his check and found himself standing next to the unknown Afghan woman he had noticed the day before. She had a handsome face and wore very little makeup. She was wearing a pantsuit and carried a computer case slung over her shoulder. They exchanged a glance and a slight smile. Malko would have liked to pursue the matter, but Madjidi was standing right next to him, silently insistent.

Out in the corridor, the interpreter asked, "Do you have the money?"

"I'll be getting it from my escort. They're waiting for me."

"But I have a car and driver!" protested Madjidi.

"Did you bring an armed escort?"

The Afghan's eyes widened. "Whatever for?"

Malko gave him a chilly smile. "Hasn't anyone told you that the road to Ghazni isn't secure?"

Madjidi looked astonished. "But you're under the protection of the Culture Ministry! This is a peace operation. We are going to resolve a dispute. I am certainly not carrying a weapon."

"Well, I am. This is a dangerous country."

Parked under the Serena awning was the interpreter's car, a tan Corolla displaying an Afghan flag. Malko and Madjidi climbed into the back, and they headed for the exit.

"That's my escort over there," announced Malko, pointing to three Land Cruisers crammed with special forces soldiers pulling away from the sidewalk. Because of their weaponry, they weren't allowed into the courtyard. One SUV was in constant contact with headquarters in Bagram, which could send a rescue helicopter if needed. Warren Michaelis had arranged the operation.

The moment Madjidi's Corolla emerged from the hotel, the lead SUV pulled in behind it. Malko thought the little interpreter was going to have a heart attack.

"Those are ISAF troops!" he squeaked. "They are going to frighten the villagers. Those are the soldiers who cause bad events. They must not come with us."

"If they don't go, then neither do I. You better call your superiors for instructions."

The interpreter was already on the telephone. The call lasted a long time. Eventually, Madjidi said, "The soldiers come along, but they cannot get out of their vehicles. They must remain in cars during all the ceremony."

"That's fine," said Malko. "They're only along for my protection. I also want this to go well."

They had reached the highway west and were already caught in the usual huge traffic jam. Malko's cell beeped. It was Jim Doolittle.

"Is everything okay, sir?" he asked. "I have the money. And don't worry, we aren't letting you out of our sight."

Yusuf Khel's central square lay under a broiling sun, surrounded by quite a few local cars. Arrayed on carpets in front of a mud-brick building were wooden chairs and cushions, and tables bearing pots of tea, cakes, and pieces of chicken.

A half dozen fierce-looking villagers in turbans were already squatting nearby, holding AK-47s. An Afghan flag stood in a corner of the square.

Malko got out of the Corolla and said to Madjidi, "I'm going to go get the money."

He headed for the Land Cruisers on the far side of the square. The three armored SUVs probably held eighteen heavily armed soldiers among them.

Doolittle came out holding an envelope. He was wearing a helmet and bulletproof vest and had grenades at his belt, magazines in various pockets, and an M16 on his shoulder. Not exactly a picture of peace.

"Here's your money, sir. Be careful!"

Malko took the envelope and went back to Madjidi, who was staring at the white vehicles in dismay.

"I hope this does not make the ceremony to fail!" he said. "People in villages get very upset when they see foreign soldiers. There have been many incidents in the area."

"These particular villagers wanted to kill me," Malko pointed out. "They aren't exactly pacifists."

The young interpreter didn't seem to realize that the place was ruled more by the Kalashnikov than by the olive branch. Thirty years of civil war will do that to people's outlook.

Malko and Madjidi walked toward the villagers, who were sitting in a semicircle. In the center sat their chief, the toothless old man with the fierce eyes and forked beard who had originally wanted to submit Malko's fate to the local *shura*.

Malko sat down facing him, and the two men stared balefully at each other.

The chief immediately started speaking angrily to Nassim Madjidi, who translated for Malko:

"He wants to know why you bring armed men to a peaceful meeting."

"Tell him that I see that the Yusuf Khel people are armed as well," Malko retorted. "Everyone in Afghanistan carries weapons. It's not a sign of aggressiveness."

The answer seemed to satisfy the old man, who launched into a long peroration. Madjidi translated as he went along.

"He says the person you killed was good, fair, and very devout. He left two widows and seven children. He never did anyone any harm. You have committed an exceptionally cowardly crime, and he says he is not sure he will accept the blood price."

"If he doesn't want my money, I'm leaving!" snapped Malko, now thoroughly exasperated by the whole charade.

"Pay no attention to that!" Madjidi hissed to him in English. "It's traditional language! I will tell the chief that you regret the man's death greatly, and want to provide a decent living for his family."

This was rendered in Pashto, and the Yusuf Khel leader gave another speech in reply.

"They will assemble in a *shura* to decide if they should accept the blood price."

The villagers gathered around their chief for a lengthy discussion. After about ten minutes, he resumed the meeting and said something.

Madjidi's face brightened. He turned to Malko and said, "They will accept the money for the benefit of the widows and the orphans. Now you go over and give it to him."

Malko went and put the envelope containing the twenty thousand dollars on the chief's knees. He opened it and handed wads of bills to his neighbors to count. This lasted quite a long time. The silence was total, broken only by the rustling of bills. Finally the money was all put back in the envelope, and the chief started speaking in a loud voice.

"The blood price has been paid," he announced. "The offense is washed away, and we can celebrate reconciliation in the name of Allah the all-powerful and the all-merciful."

The old man now seemed in high good humor. Boys circulated through the crowd serving tea and food. Everyone ate heartily as the hot sun beat down on Malko's back and shoulders.

At long last, the chief stood and walked toward him, hands outstretched. He took Malko's hand and squeezed it hard, while delivering a long, emotional speech.

"He wishes you happiness and prosperity," Madjidi translated. "You will always be welcome in Yusuf Khel, where you will be shown all the respect due an honored guest. May Allah watch over you!"

The old man was practically sputtering with happiness.

Malko wondered how much of the twenty thousand dollars would actually go to the family, which was nowhere to be seen.

As people began to disperse, a delighted Nassim pulled Malko away.

"That went very, very good," he said. "You are now all forgiven, and I will report this to the president's office. We can go back to Kabul now."

Malko glanced at the interpreter's old Corolla.

"If you don't mind, I'm going to let you go back alone," he said diplomatically. "I'll travel faster in a Land Cruiser."

Madjidi looked terribly disappointed. "That is too bad," he said. "I would enjoy telling you about Afghan culture during the voyage."

"We'll do that another time," promised Malko, heading for the nearest SUV. Doolittle moved a Marine to the rear so Malko could sit up front with him. The village square was emptying.

"Okay, back to Kabul!" said Malko.

They had driven through Maidan Shahr and were now within twenty miles of Kabul. The landscape had changed, the dusty, yellowish plain replaced by the mountains around the capital. They'd been forced to drive much more slowly because of the many old trucks on the road and buses that stopped in the middle of the highway to let out passengers.

Nassim Madjidi's aged Corolla, which had preceded them through the traffic jams, was bouncing along some distance ahead. Malko thought about the future as he struggled not to fall asleep. Normally, he would be booking a flight for Dubai or Turkey the next day, since he was free to leave the country and had no further official role in Kabul. Instead, he had to put together yet another undercover operation.

He glanced up, admiring the dramatic landscape.

The road wound between barren cliffs beneath the occasional snow-covered peaks. There wasn't a village in sight. The three Land Cruisers were driving more and more slowly. In front of them, an overloaded minibus lumbered along. It was driving in the middle of the highway, and impossible to pass. There were almost no cars coming the other way.

Suddenly Malko was aware of the tension in his car. The soldiers were checking their weapons and peering anxiously out the windows.

He turned to Doolittle.

"What's going on, Jim?"

"Nothing, sir. But this is a bad stretch. There have been ambushes here."

"So close to Kabul?"

"The Taliban come up the far slope, from territory they control."

He had barely stopped speaking before Malko noticed little flashes of light, like tiny fireworks, amid the jumble of black rocks on the hillside to his right. At first he didn't understand what was happening. Then Madjidi's Corolla started zigzagging, as if its driver were drunk. Its gas tank exploded in a ball of flame as the car skidded across the road, rolled over the embankment, and disappeared.

CHAPTER 41

Inside the Land Cruiser, the only sound to be heard was of weapons being loaded. Malko stared in disbelief at the place where the Corolla had gone over the cliff. If he had accepted Nassim Madjidi's invitation to ride with him, he would be dead.

The minibus that had been driving slowly in the middle of the road for some reason now suddenly sped up and disappeared around a curve.

A number of dull thuds shook the Land Cruiser's armored body; the convoy was under fire. The bright flashes flared among the black rocks on the hillside. It was a classic ambush.

Jim Doolittle braked hard, pulling the SUV to the side of the now-empty highway. The vehicles behind them had heard the gunshots and were cautiously hanging back.

"Everybody out!" he yelled.

Malko followed him, exiting on the side sheltered by the car. The soldiers piled out of their vehicles and took positions behind them. Several fired M16s at the part of the hillside the shots were coming from. Malko could make out the characteristic chatter of a Russian Pulemyot machine gun.

Doolittle pulled him away from the Land Cruiser.

"Don't stand too close to the vehicle, sir. They might have an RPG."

Behind the third SUV, a team set up a 60 mm mortar, and its first shell raised a cloud of dust in the black rocks. Both sides were steadily firing now. The Taliban fighters were about two hundred yards above them, shooting down at the highway.

After loosing a long burst, Doolittle yelled, "I alerted Bagram. They're sending choppers."

Thanks to GPS, the helicopters would be able to pinpoint their location. Malko was sorry he wasn't carrying his GSh-18, though an ordinary automatic wouldn't do much good in these circumstances.

Just then a shell dinged the SUV's windshield.

The Taliban were careful not to come down to the highway. They knew they were facing heavily armed soldiers who were probably calling for backup.

Word of the ambush must have spread, because no other vehicles appeared.

The 60 mm mortar was now launching a steady rain of shells as the Marines raked the hill with small-arms fire.

After a while, the rate of fire from the hillside seemed to slow. The muzzle flashes were diminishing. Hunkered down behind their three armored vehicles, the Americans started to hold their fire. Suddenly, silence fell.

"They're falling back," announced Doolittle.

The American soldiers fired a few last bursts and got to their feet. The acrid smell of cordite filled the air. No sound came from the hillside, and the highway was still deserted. Malko spoke up.

"I'd like to see where the interpreter's car went over."

Four Marines surrounded him as he crossed the road. Standing at the edge of the ravine, they could see a burning vehicle a few hundred feet below. It didn't look as if anybody had gotten out alive.

Stony silence reigned on the highway for a moment, then was

broken by a growing *whump-whump-whump* of approaching helicopters. Two Black Hawks appeared, threading their way through the canyons. They overflew the men's position in a deafening roar and went off in the direction of the attackers.

They came back a few moments later and hovered above the highway. Doolittle radioed them and summarized their conversation for Malko.

"They didn't see anyone, but they say that the terrain's very rugged. They plan to escort us back to Kabul. Let's head out!"

Everybody climbed back into the vehicles, leaving the highway littered with spent shell casings. Beyond the curve, they could see a long line of stopped vehicles waiting for the firefight to end.

Malko and his group were no longer in danger.

Twenty minutes later, the Kabul plain appeared. They passed through an Afghan police checkpoint without stopping and began their descent toward the capital. The highway was completely empty.

The Taliban had probably seen the three ISAF vehicles heading for Ghazni and decided to hit them on the way back. But if so, why did they start by shooting at the Corolla that Malko was supposed to be in?

Parviz Bamyan was baffled as well. He had been studying Malko Linge's file, and the report of the attack in which Nassim Madjidi died was on his desk. At first, the NDS thought Linge had also been killed, but when they reached the wrecked car, they saw he wasn't in it.

Why not?

Only Linge knew.

What bothered Bamyan was that the ISAF and local Afghans positively identified a Taliban group that had already launched similar attacks in the area. The CIA operative had clearly been their target, which undercut the NDS's theory that he had renewed his contact with the Taliban in plotting against President Karzai.

You don't kill the people you're negotiating with.

Something in this business didn't make sense.

In any case, Bamyan would soon see if Linge was leaving Kabul. If he didn't, the NDS leader would be in a sticky situation.

He couldn't take any action against Musa Kotak, who was protected by the president—unless the mullah was only a stalking horse, and the real contacts were taking place elsewhere.

Bamyan had to draw his net around Linge tighter. That operation had begun, but it would take time. And the CIA operative was sure to be on his guard.

The next day, Malko had himself driven to the mosque, determined not to let Musa Kotak off the hook this time. Before he took another step, he had to know who in the Taliban wanted him dead.

A dozen men were praying on the mosque's forecourt, taking advantage of the last rays of the setting sun.

When Malko was shown in, Kotak greeted him with his usual good cheer. But Malko began coldly, "Were you told that someone tried to kill me yesterday?"

Kotak's eyes widened.

"In Yusuf Khel?"

"No, on the way back. A group of Taliban fighters attacked our convoy. A car I was supposed to be in was destroyed and its occupants killed."

"How can you be sure they were Taliban?" asked the cleric.

Malko glared at him.

"Because they were identified by the ISAF, that's why. Besides, there aren't that many armed groups around."

"If that's true, they could be members of the Haqqani network," said Kotak, sounding puzzled. "They take their orders from the Pakistanis and they don't obey us."

"Either way, I have to know the truth," insisted Malko. "Your sources can find out. You've always stressed that the Quetta *shura* is the one running the movement. Now is the time to prove it."

Kotak looked embarrassed. For the first time, Malko felt the cleric had been knocked off-balance.

"I'll make inquiries," he said somewhat uncertainly.

"When you get results, text me. I have a proposal from Washington to put to you."

After Malko left, Kotak closed his eyes and addressed a long, silent prayer of thanks to Allah. If the CIA operative hadn't decided to change cars, he would now be dead, something the Americans certainly wouldn't have liked. And they apparently still hoped for Taliban political support.

So Kotak had to come up with a convincing explanation to prove that he hadn't played any role in the ambush—which, in fact, he had organized at the request of the Quetta *shura*. The failure of the Karzai attack had so traumatized the *shura* that its sole focus was on eliminating anything linking it to that act of war.

Now he had to repair the damage.

An idea occurred to him: once Linge told him what Washington's intentions were, they could have a representative of the *shura* come to Kabul for a meeting. Someone like Abdul Ghani Beradar, who knew the Americans. This would show they were serious about the talks. Kotak immediately started drafting a long email to be sent by a secure channel.

It would depend on Beradar being willing to risk entering Afghanistan, of course.

Malko was still in a foul mood by the time he got back to the Serena. His meeting with Kotak had left him with a sour aftertaste. He knew perfectly well that Taliban fighters had attacked him, so it was up to the cleric to clear things up. Malko didn't feel like going to his room, so he walked past the front desk and made his way to the nonalcoholic bar.

The room was empty except for the attractive Afghan woman he had noticed twice before. She had a glass of fruit juice in front of her and was typing on a laptop. When she saw Malko, she gave him a shy smile, then returned to her screen.

He sat down at the next table and ordered a cup of coffee, enjoying the beautiful stranger's presence. For a moment, nothing happened. Then the woman closed her laptop and asked for the check. She signed it, which showed that she was staying at the hotel.

As she was getting up, Malko took the plunge and asked, "Are you a journalist?"

The young woman stopped and smiled. "No, I work for the Aga Khan Foundation, which owns the hotel. We're studying other sites and amenities."

She seemed glad to have someone to chat with.

"Do you have time to have coffee with me?" he asked.

She shook her head. "I'm afraid not. I'm going to go unwind in the sauna. I've worked hard today. Maybe another time."

Disappointed, Malko watched as she walked gracefully away. Since she was staying at the Serena, he figured he was bound to see her in the hotel dining room. In Kabul, a woman alone wouldn't go out to eat. He might as well get to know her. Until Kotak told him the result of his inquiry, he didn't have anything to do.

Musa Kotak's text message reached Malko at 3:10 p.m. *Come have tea with me.*

At four o'clock, he was crossing the mosque's sunlit garden. He found Kotak reading the Quran. On seeing Malko, he set the holy book aside and came toward him, aglow with apparent pleasure.

"My investigation was quick because we have informers within the Haqqani network," Kotak announced. "I now know that the attack was launched by one of their commanders, who has no ties with Quetta. As I told you, they only take orders from Pakistanis. I thank Allah that you escaped death."

Those last words were probably Kotak's only sincere ones, but Malko chose to believe him. After all, the cleric's story was almost plausible, and he wasn't in a position to prove otherwise.

"So you're sure that nobody on your side wants to do me harm?" he asked.

"Quite the contrary," said Kotak. "I myself pray for you very often. If you could help rid Afghanistan of Karzai . . ."

Malko sat down next to the cleric and said, "As a matter of fact, Washington has given me a second assignment along the lines of the first, but with a different approach."

"What does it involve?" asked Kotak.

"Next year, when Karzai can't be a candidate in the presidential elections, Washington is convinced he will either rig the election or run one of his cronies. If the man's elected, he'll do whatever Karzai tells him to."

"That is quite likely," said Kotak. "Do you have a way of preventing that?"

"Our American friends are thinking of supporting another candidate."

"Which one?"

"I don't have a name to give you yet, but it would be a person of integrity."

Which in Afghanistan was as hard to find as a diamond in the rough.

Kotak nodded, then asked, "A Pashtun?"

"As I said, I don't know," Malko admitted. "But I'd like to discuss this with someone high in your *shura*."

The cleric was silent for a few moments. "That can be arranged, but for a *shura* member to travel here, he would have to be given the candidate's name. That's not negotiable. We have very strict criteria for supporting a candidate. He must be honest, devout, and have no ties with Karzai. When you can give us that name, come back and see me. I will then see what we can do next."

Parviz Bamyan finished examining the list of passengers flying out of Kabul in the next three days. Fortunately, there weren't many flights, and people always booked in advance.

Malko Linge's name didn't appear anywhere.

Bamyan had also checked with the Serena, which the CIA operative had shown no evidence of leaving.

If Linge stayed on in Kabul, it would have to be for some reason. He wasn't here on vacation. And if Bamyan didn't learn that reason, he might lose his job, or worse.

He phoned the president's chief of staff. He needed specific instructions to know just how far he could go.

CHAPTER 42

Out of the corner of his eye, Malko watched the attrac-tive brunette serve herself at the buffet. He had figured correctly that she would be eating at the hotel.

A handful of Japanese were in the dining room, along with a few Americans and a table of Afghans. The menu was the same as usual: *palau* and its variations. If you didn't like rice, you were out of luck.

The woman finished her coffee and went over to the cashier to sign the check. Malko was already on his feet. He was careful not to approach her in the restaurant, catching up with her only as she was walking down the hall. When he drew level with her, she turned her head and politely said, "Good night," without slowing down.

"Would you like to talk for a few moments before you go up to bed?" asked Malko. "The hotel doesn't offer much entertainment."

"That wouldn't be proper," she said without stopping. She gave him an apologetic smile. "The staff here is very strict. Besides, we don't know each other."

"Well, we do a little, now," argued Malko.

She shook her head.

"You Westerners don't understand our customs. I'm very sorry."

Having reached the lobby, she turned left, as did Malko. She glanced back at him.

"Are you following me?" There was a touch of irritated mockery in her voice.

"No, I'm not," he said, annoyed. "I'm just going to my room. Are you in this wing too?"

"Yes," she said.

They reached the elevator together and Malko stepped aside to let her pass. In the confined space of the cab, he was able to study her more closely. She had regular features, a somewhat large mouth, dark, almond-shaped eyes, and a slightly hooked nose. A jacket and cashmere turtleneck set off her large breasts.

A very pretty woman.

They stepped out of the elevator together and she preceded him down the hallway. To Malko's surprise, she stopped at the room next to his.

"We're neighbors!"

"I didn't realize that," said the woman, sliding her key in the slot.

Malko did the same, then returned to the charge. "Why don't we stay here and talk for a minute? There's no one around."

Instead of refusing, the young woman raised a surprising objection. "Somebody might come. There are people in the hotel."

"In that case, let's talk in my room. I don't feel like going to sleep yet."

He had opened his door. Seeing hesitation in her eyes, he decided to take the initiative. Leading the woman gently by the arm, he propelled her inside and closed the door. He then walked across to an armchair and sat down, leaving his guest standing in the center of the room, arms akimbo.

"What's your name?" he asked.

"Shaheen Zoolor," she said shyly.

"I'm Malko Linge. I work for the European Union, and I'm here to review the work of some NGOs. Please, sit down."

After a brief hesitation, Zoolor came and perched on the edge of a chair.

"Would you like some fruit?" he asked, pointing to the basket on his coffee table.

"No, no. I'm not going to stay. If anyone saw me here, it would be very bad. I would be fired immediately."

Shaheen Zoolor seemed quite unnerved, but she didn't get up. As they talked, she gradually relaxed. After twenty minutes, she looked at her watch and said, "I'm going to my room. I hope nobody sees me!"

"I'll check the hallway."

He went to open the door. The hall was empty. "Come on," he said.

As she passed by him, her chest lightly brushed his alpaca jacket. Their eyes met for a moment.

Smiling, Malko said, "I hope you'll come back and see me sometime."

Without replying, Zoolor walked quickly to the door of her room and vanished inside like a ghost. But the smell of her perfume lingered in Malko's room—a pleasant sensation.

The sun was shining on Kabul. The city had celebrated Nowruz, and spring had officially begun.

Malko was eating breakfast when he got a text message:

Come see me at 4. Kotak.

He wondered what line the chubby cleric would feed him this time.

When he called Michaelis to ask for a driver later in the day, the CIA station chief sounded upset.

"We lost a helicopter in the south, with five guys," he said. "The

Taliban were hiding in a village where we'd organized a militia, and they turned on us."

From the vantage point of the peaceful, luxurious Serena Hotel, such an image of the war felt incongruous, but this was Afghanistan. Everything seems calm, and then suddenly a suicide bomber blows himself up.

In fact, the country had long been the subject of a power struggle between different factions, each more determined than the next. And Malko was in the middle, representing the only group that really was outside the struggle, yet was being taken in by everyone. The Americans were doing their best, but the Afghans were always cleverer than they were.

With nothing to do, Malko killed time watching television. In a brief foray to the lobby, he didn't see Shaheen Zoolor.

The hotel felt deserted. The guests, including a lot of Japanese, left early in the morning and came back late at night.

When he went outside, he was struck by the warm weather. The Land Cruiser showed up in a few moments, and Malko directed Doolittle to the mosque.

He was sure he was being followed, but he couldn't very well make himself invisible.

The two bearded men in front of the mosque glared at Malko, who clearly wasn't a Muslim.

The flowers in the garden had bloomed, and a dozen men were kneeling on the worn carpets of the forecourt, facing Mecca.

When Malko arrived, Mullah Kotak looked unusually serious. Carefully closing the door, he led his guest to the cushions of his sitting area and served him tea.

"I have very good news," he announced sententiously.

"What's that?" asked Malko.

"I forwarded your request to Quetta, and our leader, Mullah Omar, has reached a decision. He is sending Mullah Abdul Ghani Beradar to discuss your proposal. It is a great honor, and Mullah Beradar is taking a serious risk by coming here. He has not traveled to Kabul in a decade. He is at the top of the NDS's most-wanted list, and they have already tried to kill him three times, in Quetta and Karachi. The Americans know him, and you can give them his name."

"If it's so dangerous for the mullah to come here, I could meet him somewhere else," said Malko. "In Pakistan, for example."

"No. If you met in Pakistan, the ISI would immediately know about it and start asking questions. They distrust the Americans."

Everyone distrusted everyone.

"I'm looking forward to meeting him," said Malko.

"But wait, there's a condition. Mullah Beradar will only come here if you are prepared to reveal the name of the person the U.S. will support for the presidency."

"I don't know it myself."

"But the Americans do. They must authorize you to tell us; otherwise, there can be no negotiations."

"I'm sorry, but I can't make that commitment right now," said Malko. "It's not in my hands."

"Then come back and see me as soon as you know. Only then will I arrange Mullah Beradar's trip."

Warren Michaelis didn't ask any questions when Malko requested a secure line to Langley. Within minutes, Malko was describing his meeting with Kotak to Clayton Luger.

"That's terrific!" said the CIA number two. "I'll ask for the candidate's identity right away. It's a White House decision. Call me back in an hour!"

Malko was forced to go down to the Ariana cafeteria and its undrinkable American-style coffee. Apparently the Nespresso machine hadn't reached this corner of the world yet. Twenty minutes later he was joined by Michaelis, who'd heard he was there.

"I have a break and thought I'd have a cup of coffee with you. Are you making progress?"

"Slowly," said Malko. "What's the news on your end?"

"Word has it that Karzai is working hard to find a candidate for the presidential election. He's pushing a member of Hezb-e-Islami."

"What's that?"

"A strange group, midway between Karzai and the Taliban. I think he's pulling the strings, but it includes some former Taliban members. It's his latest secret plan."

"Does it have any chance of success?

"On paper, no, but here, you never know. It depends how much money gets put on the table."

Michaelis's cell phone beeped, and he glanced at the text message.

"It's my secretary," he said. "Langley just called back. Let's go upstairs."

Luger was on another call, and Malko had to wait ten minutes for him to be free. When they connected, the CIA deputy director sounded excited.

"I just talked to John," he said. "He's giving you the go-ahead. He finds it very encouraging that the mullah is coming to meet you in Kabul. The man's taking a hell of a risk."

"That's his problem," said Malko.

"But it might become yours," said Luger with a brief laugh. "If Karzai learns that you're dealing with Beradar in Kabul, he'll go apeshit. It's his worst fear. Be *very* careful!"

"I'll try," promised Malko, "but unfortunately, the situation's not under my control. So what's the story?"

Luger didn't answer immediately.

"Before I tell you the man's name, you have to make sure it stays within an extremely restricted circle. This is information nobody can have yet, and that includes the person involved. No point in getting his hopes up. Once the negotiations with the Taliban are under way, you can tell him the news."

"But I have to give his name to Mullah Beradar," said Malko. "That's a bottom-line requirement."

"Of course, and I'll give it to you. But you can only share it with Beradar. Not even Kotak.

"He's the guy who ran against Karzai in the 2009 presidential election and got 30.5 percent of the vote, which is huge. His father is Pashtun and his mother, Tajik. Also, he was Shah Massoud's right-hand man. Needless to say, the Taliban don't like him very much. In fact, I hope Beradar doesn't choke when he hears his name.

"Our candidate is the former foreign minister Abdullah Abdullah."

CHAPTER 43

Malko had himself immediately driven back to the mosque. Night was falling and a dense crowd had gathered for evening prayers. He made his way to the cleric's office between bearded men in turbans.

He was announced by the guard and promptly shown inside. Kotak seemed surprised to see him back so soon.

"I have the answer for you," Malko announced. "It's yes."

The cleric's face brightened. "That's very good news! I'll immediately pass it on to Quetta. Do you really know the man's name?"

"I do, but it's so confidential I'm not even allowed to tell it to you."

In an almost comical gesture, Kotak clapped his fat hands over his ears. "I do not want to hear it!" he cried. "I am just a humble go-between. As soon as I know when Mullah Beradar is due to arrive, I will let you know."

"Will I meet with him here?"

"Certainly not!" Kotak exclaimed. Then he lowered his voice, as if afraid of being overheard.

"It would be too dangerous for him," he said. "The NDS watches us around the clock. We have to find a safer meeting place. I do not need to be present, as Mullah Beradar speaks English perfectly. Do you have any suggestions?"

Malko was startled. "Why ask me? You know Kabul much better than I do."

"Karzai's people have infiltrated many branches of our organization," the cleric explained. "Ideally, you should meet Mullah Beradar somewhere you can go without arousing suspicion. Then he could discreetly join you there."

Only one place occurred to Malko: Maureen Kieffer's guesthouse. The NDS knew he was friends with the young woman, and she had no connection with the Taliban. He would need to ask her permission, of course.

"Let me think about it," he said cautiously. "Meanwhile, try to come up with someplace at your end."

Maureen was busy when he called but suggested meeting at eight o'clock at the Serena Hotel bar, where she was due to see one of her customers. Malko had just enough time to get back to the hotel. As often happened, the lobby was full of Japanese women connected to some NGO or other. Malko ran into Shaheen Zoolor near the elevator.

"Would you like to have dinner with me?" he suggested. "Somewhere outside the hotel?"

"No, no!" she said. Looking frightened, she practically bolted for the elevator.

When he reached the bar, Maureen was already there, talking with a tall, redheaded man with massive forearms. She gave Malko a wink and he sat down at a nearby table. She joined him a moment later.

"I can't stay long," she said. "We haven't finished talking. Did you need to see me about something in particular?"

"Yes, to ask you a favor."

She smiled. "With pleasure, if I can do it."

Malko explained. "I'm due to meet with someone who isn't very popular in Kabul. It would be convenient if we could meet at your guesthouse. You don't need to be there."

"Sure, just let me know when, and we'll arrange it."

"Problem is, I don't know how to get to your place."

She smiled and fetched a business card from her purse. "Here you go," she said. "The address is written in Dari; it isn't hard to find." Then she added with a grin, "I'm guessing it isn't a woman. Women here don't do that sort of thing. When you know for sure, phone and tell me the day and time of your meeting. *Ciao!*"

Which left Malko to face the depressing dining room, where he once again saw Shaheen Zoolor alone at a table. He did as he had before, except that he didn't approach her in the hall, but followed her to the elevator.

When they were alone in the small cab, she broke the silence. "You were with a very pretty blond woman at the bar earlier," she remarked.

"I didn't see you," said Malko.

"I just peeked in. It was too crowded."

The elevator stopped and they got out together. This time Malko went directly to his room, and Shaheen followed. She entered without hesitation when he stepped aside, and walked over to the chair she'd occupied the evening before.

"I'd like to watch some television," she said. "I enjoy MTV videos."

She seemed to be getting used to being with him. Malko turned on the TV and observed as the young woman watched it in delight. This went on for a while, until she looked at her watch and jumped.

"My God, it's late!"

She was already on her feet and on her way out, but he caught up with her at the door. They were facing each other.

Looking away, she asked in an even tone of voice, "Why do you keep pursuing me?"

"Because you're very pretty."

They were within inches of each other. Malko didn't want to scare her off, but platonic friendships weren't really his style. He lightly put his hand on the young woman's hip and brushed his lips against hers. Then he opened the door and said good night.

He expected her to flee. Instead, she stood rooted to the spot, as if thunderstruck. Her gaze wavered, and she blushed. Her lips were trembling.

Suddenly finding her voice, she said, "This is the first time I've ever kissed a man!"

It certainly wouldn't be the last, Malko thought. Anyway, it wasn't a real kiss. He decided there was no point in pushing things. He opened the door wider and glanced out into the hallway.

"Run for it!" he said. "There's nobody there."

She slipped out, but this time he was sure she would be coming back.

The episode was such a contrast with the violence that surrounded him, it almost made Malko feel young again. He sat back down and watched a few more MTV videos, in which chaste Indian dancers mimed love in the most innocent possible way.

The man who showed up at the main NDS pedestrian entrance could have been anybody. He was wearing a grayish turban, a tan *shalwar kameez*, and a grimy vest. He handed the guard a piece of paper with a telephone number.

"Call this number and say that Khalid is here."

The guard did so. After exchanging a few words, he hung up and said, "Stay here. Somebody will come get you."

A few minutes later, he was led across the large inner courtyard, into a small building in the rear, and up to a second-floor office.

There, a man dressed Western-style stood up from his desk

and embraced him. NDS agent Mudir Rassul was Khalid's handler.

"Chai?"

"*Baleh.*"

When Khalid finished his tea, Rassul casually asked, "So what's the latest from Quetta?"

Khalid was one of the most effective moles ever to infiltrate the city's large Pashtun population. He had been living in Quetta for five years, working as a handyman for Mullah Omar's *shura.* He never attracted attention, had a faultless work history, and slept in a corner of the mosque. Everybody liked him, and nobody knew that one of his cousins worked for the NDS, recruiting informers.

It was very dangerous for Khalid to contact his handlers, so he rarely came to Kabul. For his good and loyal services, he was paid five hundred afghanis a month—about ten dollars. He was saving his money to someday buy a farm.

Khalid wiped his mustache and hesitantly said, "I overheard a conversation, and I think I have some good information."

"What's that?"

From his pocket, he took a piece of paper with some words written on it. He unfolded it and gave it to Rassul.

"This man is supposed to come to Kabul very soon."

When Rassul read the note, his eyebrows shot up. "Are you sure of the name?"

"Yes."

"Do you know him?"

"No, but I've seen him. He's young, has lots of hair. Big nose, neat beard. He often dresses like a foreigner."

Rassul stood up and said, "Have some more tea and wait for me here!"

He practically ran to the neighboring building and into the elevator. On the third floor he strode over to the two guards outside Parviz Bamyan's office.

"I'm Mudir Rassul," he said. "Tell your boss I've got something important to tell him."

One of the guards disappeared behind the upholstered door. He came back a few moments later and gestured for Rassul to enter. Bamyan was at his desk, working his way through a pile of documents he had to sign.

"What do you have for me?" he asked irritably.

"I just got a terrific tip, Commander. Abdul Ghani Beradar is coming to Kabul."

At that, Bamyan put down his pen. Beradar was one of the regime's bitterest enemies, and he was careful never to come to Afghanistan. The NDS had already tried to kill him several times, in vain.

"Who told you that?" he asked.

"My source in Quetta. He just got here."

"Does he know where Beradar will be going in Kabul?"

"No, I don't think so."

"Then how the hell do you expect us to find him? Your tip isn't worth a wormy goat. Get out of here and let me work!"

Bamyan angrily waved him away and went back to signing papers. Feeling sheepish, Rassul returned to his office. He pulled a hundred-afghani note from his pocket and handed it to Khalid.

"Here, treat yourself to a good *palau*. If you learn anything more, come back and see me. But I'll need details."

When Bamyan finally finished signing his papers, he decided to take a break. Lighting a cigarette, he thought back to the information his subordinate had delivered. Suddenly it clicked in his mind. They knew that the Quetta *shura* had appointed Beradar to hold discussions with the Americans, and an NDS agent was almost sure he had spotted the cleric in Doha.

If Beradar was coming to Kabul, it could only be for a serious reason. Bamyan again thought of Malko Linge.

For the past few days, the NDS chief had been wondering why Linge was still in the city, and he now thought he knew. And it meant he no longer had to search for Beradar in the various Taliban circles. All he had to do was to keep a close eye on Linge.

Even if the tip turned out to be wrong, the surveillance would cost little enough. He immediately gave appropriate instructions, emphasizing discretion.

Beradar was a professional—an educated, clever man. In coming to Kabul, he was sure to take a number of precautions. Bamyan's challenge was to defeat them.

It had by now almost become a ritual. As soon as Shaheen Zoolor left the dining room, Malko followed her at a respectful distance.

Like the evening before, they again wound up waiting for the elevator together. Practically an old couple.

But just as the cab arrived, a boy sprinted down the hallway toward them. Without so much as glancing at Zoolor, he put a folded piece of paper in Malko's hand and ran off.

Startled, he unfolded it. It was a handwritten note:

> Tomorrow at six pm in front of number 69 on Street 15, off the Wazir Akbar Khan roundabout.

CHAPTER 44

Startled, Malko stuffed the paper in his pocket. This was the first time Kotak had arranged to meet with him somewhere other than the mosque. Malko had until the next day to investigate the area.

When they were in the elevator cab, Shaheen asked, "Am I keeping you from something?"

"Not at all," said Malko, who wasn't about to mention the message he'd just received.

Without being too obvious, he looked the young woman over again. She was still wearing her pantsuit and had no makeup. She radiated a low-key, very natural sensuality.

She stepped out of the elevator first, and the gentle swaying of her hips aroused Malko's libido. He was living under such constant stress that the slightest distraction tended to go right to his head.

They reached his room at the same time, and she waited while he put the door key into the slot. They were making progress.

He didn't let Shaheen get as far as her usual armchair. Instead, he gently took her arm and turned her around until they were face-to-face. Their eyes met. The young woman's gaze was less limpid than usual, and slightly quizzical. Malko had decided to skip a few stages. He slipped his arm around her waist and drew her close.

She yielded without struggle or protest, just calmly said, "I know what you want, but there's no point in trying."

"And what is it that I want?" asked Malko, intrigued by this pseudosubmission.

Shaheen smiled slightly.

"When I became a woman, my mother showed me the opening between my legs. She said that all the men I met would try to put their penis into that opening. She said I had to prevent them until I found a man to marry me. Otherwise, I would be cursed with misfortune. You're a man, so it's normal that you would want to do that."

She was so matter-of-fact, and her tone so neutral, that Malko nearly burst out laughing.

"So you haven't found a man?"

"I don't want to get married yet. I'm working and I'm happy. If I have a husband he will beat and rape me. If I don't submit, he will throw acid at me or kill me."

She had a pretty radical concept of human relationships, thought Malko, who was somewhat knocked off his stride. He certainly didn't intend to rape her.

"Aren't you afraid of me?" he asked.

"No," she said, quite seriously. "There's no reason for you to be interested in me. I have never been with a man, and I know nothing about sex. I only know not to let anyone take advantage of me; that's all."

She was looking at him confidently, without aggressiveness.

Suddenly Malko yielded to an irresistible impulse. Leaning close, he put his lips on hers. He expected her to pull back, but not only did she not retreat, but her lips parted and her body pressed slightly against his.

Pushing his advantage, he slipped his tongue into her mouth. To his astonishment he promptly felt a delicate, warm tongue meeting his. Within seconds, they were sharing a passionate kiss that lasted until Shaheen freed herself, slightly out of breath.

"It's just like in the Indian videos!" she exclaimed. "The people kiss almost like that!"

Looking down, Malko noticed that her nipples were straining against her sweater. Their kiss apparently hadn't left her indifferent.

Rousing herself, she abruptly said, "That was very pleasant. I'm going off to bed now."

Shaheen clearly didn't connect that which was forbidden—having sex—with innocent physical pleasure.

He walked her to the door, knowing that he would get a little further next time. A conquest of this wise virgin would make a pleasant change from covert intelligence operations.

The CIA Land Cruiser stopped along the Wazir Akbar Kahn roundabout near a checkpoint at Street 15, which was the continuation of Wazir Akbar Kahn Road. The roadblock at its entrance was on the boundary of the heavily guarded Green Zone around Hamid Karzai's palace.

"Drive up the avenue a ways," Malko told Doolittle. "I'll call you when I'm finished." If the white SUV parked in the roundabout itself, it might attract attention.

Once the car was gone, Malko walked through the black-and-white barrier across the avenue under the gaze of a bored Afghan soldier concerned with cars, not pedestrians.

Malko saw that Street 15 was lined with private residences, with another checkpoint at its far end. Also, the houses had numbers, which was unusual in Kabul. He walked as far as number 69, stopping at a brick wall on his left with a black gate through which he could see a garden.

There was no one in sight.

He'd been standing in the dark for ten or fifteen minutes when a slim, bearded man walked up from the end of the street. He gave Malko a slight smile and said, "You come!"

Malko followed him to the end of Street 15, passing through the second checkpoint as easily as he had the first. A dark Corolla was parked in the shadows. The young man opened the rear door for Malko, revealing Musa Kotak sprawled on the backseat. There was no one at the wheel, but Malko could see a man standing a little distance from the car.

"Thank you for coming," said Kotak. "It's safer than at the mosque. Were you followed here?"

"To be honest, I don't know. Not since I turned onto the street, anyway."

"We posted a lookout at the entrance," said the cleric. "He would have warned me of anything suspicious. I have good news: Mullah Beradar is in Kabul and wants to meet with you. Were you able to find a location?"

"I have the use of a friend's guesthouse," said Malko. "All you have to do is set the time."

"How about tomorrow evening at seven?"

"That's fine," said Malko. "The owner of the guesthouse gave me her business card with the address printed in Dari. Will that do?"

"Let me see me the card."

Malko handed it over, and Kotak took a look.

"I will give the card to Mullah Beradar," he said, pocketing it. "He should find the place without any trouble. Will you be alone?"

"Yes, except for the guesthouse watchmen."

"That's perfect," said Kotak. "We will talk again later, after your meeting. Remember, Mullah Beradar is a very important man. He will be speaking on behalf of Mullah Omar, who trusts him implicitly. So weigh your words carefully."

As he usually did, Kotak took Malko's hand in his and murmured, "May Allah watch over you."

All Malko needed to do now was to alert Maureen. Neither he nor Doolittle knew how to get to her place, so Malko phoned from the car. The young woman was in her workshop, thank God.

"Could you swing by the hotel?" he asked.

"I can come around dinnertime, but just for a minute."

Parviz Bamyan was now receiving hourly reports of Malko Linge's movements. He had detailed fifteen agents to round-the-clock surveillance.

He cursed. It was nine o'clock at night and he'd just received his latest report. Linge had gone to a street off the Wazir Akbar Kahn roundabout, but the two NDS agents tailing him hadn't been able to see whom he was meeting. Many foreigners lived on that street.

Bamyan was on edge. If the information from the Quetta mole was accurate, Mullah Beradar was certainly coming to Kabul to meet Linge. That had been Bamyan's private hunch, but he was now inclined to think he was right.

If he could capture Beradar dead or alive, he would earn President Karzai's gratitude.

Maureen got to the Serena at seven and left her car and driver outside, to avoid the checkpoint hassle. Malko was waiting in the lobby.

"Do we have time for a quick cup of coffee?" she asked. "I have another meeting with a customer."

They went into the still-empty bar and Malko gave her the scheduled time of his meeting the next day.

"No problem," she said. "I'll be at my shop until about nine. I'll send a driver to pick you up, and he can take you back afterward. You'll find whatever you want to drink in the bar."

Malko smiled. "I doubt the person I'm meeting is into alcohol."

Five minutes later, Maureen was gone.

Everything was set for the meeting with Beradar, and Malko could report the good news to Washington.

"When you and Mr. Luger are finished talking, we can have a bite in the cafeteria," said Michaelis.

Malko had shown up at the Ariana Hotel with Doolittle in the afternoon, because of the time difference with Washington. His meeting with Beradar was now just a few hours away. From Michaelis's office, he called Clayton Luger's number. It was 8:10 in the morning in Washington.

"That meeting is very important!" Luger said after hearing Malko's account. "You have to convince Beradar that our approach is the only one with a real chance of countering Hamid Karzai. If Abdullah Abdullah can get even tacit Taliban support, he could be elected in a landslide. It would avoid a bloodbath with the Tajiks and also keep Karzai from returning to power in some other form."

"I'll do everything I can," Malko promised, "but I doubt Beradar will give me an answer right away. Still, the fact that he's risking coming to Kabul shows the Taliban feel your project is very important."

"We have to save Afghanistan, and there are only so many ways of doing it," said Luger seriously. "If Karzai manages to hang on, it'll spark a civil war worse than in 1992."

It was really unbelievable, thought Malko: the United States and the Taliban, sworn enemies since 2001, were now acting in concert.

Strange bedfellows, indeed.

Sitting on the big sofa in Maureen's living room, Malko listened hard for sounds from the outside. Her driver had brought him from the Serena, and he'd been waiting at the guesthouse for more than an hour. The meeting time had come and gone long ago.

No one showed up.

Could Beradar not have found the place? Had he been arrested? Anything was possible.

Malko resolved to wait another half hour before heading back to the hotel. He would have liked to contact Musa Kotak, but it was too risky.

At eight thirty, Malko finally went to find the driver, who was waiting in the kitchen.

He felt terribly let down.

There were no messages waiting for him at the Serena, and he didn't see Shaheen Zoolor. He was reduced to eating alone in the depressing dining room, surrounded by Japanese.

It wasn't until 11:00 p.m. that his cell beeped, with a very short text from Kotak:

Tomorrow noon same place.

Maybe he would learn what had gone wrong.

CHAPTER 45

Malko didn't have long to wait this time. An old Corolla pulled up in front of number 69, and the man at the wheel gestured to him to get in. They immediately took off down Street 15, merging with the traffic on the roundabout.

Malko soon lost track of their route. They entered the Shahr-e-Now neighborhood and negotiated a maze of alleys before finally turning into a courtyard. Two young Afghans immediately closed the gate behind them. A young bearded man led Malko to a living room with furniture covered with plastic slipcovers. There was just one person in the room: Musa Kotak, looking worried.

"There was a problem," said the cleric, rising to greet his visitor.

"Wasn't Mullah Beradar able to find the place?" asked Malko.

"He was able to find it, but when he got close, he sent someone ahead to check it out. The man reported that the guesthouse was being watched, almost certainly by the NDS. Mullah Beradar did not want to take any chances, so he left."

To Malko, this was very disturbing news. How could the NDS have learned about the meeting? It hadn't involved phones or email; everything had been arranged orally.

Kotak provided an explanation. "I think the NDS suspect you of being in contact with us, so they are watching all the places you normally go. There was no way they could have known about the meeting."

"What should we do now?" asked Malko.

"Mullah Beradar wanted to leave Kabul immediately, but I convinced him to try a second time to meet you, this time using our connections. He will be expecting you today at four o'clock in a store run by one of our sympathizers, an extremely devout man. You know Chicken Street, don't you?"

"Yes, of course."

"Go to store number 276. It sells newspapers, scarves, and clothes. There will be a young man behind the cash register, to the right of the door. Ask him if he has any *shahtoosh*."

"What's that?"

"Extremely fine scarves woven from the fur of Tibetan antelopes. The fibers are ten times smaller than a human hair. The sale of *shahtoosh* is forbidden because the antelopes are endangered. That is the password. The man in the store will take you to Mullah Beradar."

A nervous Jim Doolittle dropped Malko off at the start of Chicken Street, a main Kabul business thoroughfare that, oddly enough, turned into Flower Street halfway down. Malko had gone shopping there before, so his presence today shouldn't arouse undue attention from anyone who might be following him.

As he walked along the street, he made a point of entering a half dozen stores selling lapis lazuli carvings, jewels, and carpets, examining several items each time. It was easy to identify the shops; each one had a number on its facade. Eventually, he reached number 276. It was long and narrow, like the others. Malko opened the door and saw that its walls were hung with cashmere scarves. A young man with steel-rimmed glasses and a small goatee gave him a salesman's smile.

"Welcome, sir," he said in English. "What are you looking for today?"

"*Shahtoosh*," he said quietly.

The Afghan shook his head. "I'm sorry, sir, but selling *shahtoosh* is against the law. But we have some very nice cashmere shawls. Let me show them to you."

From the man's confidential tone, Malko knew that he had understood.

Slipping off his stool behind the cash register, he led Malko to the back of the store and up a small flight of stairs. The first floor was given over to carpets, and there was a changing room at the far end. The shopkeeper lifted the curtain aside, revealing a youngish Afghan man seated on a stool. Dressed in *shalwar kameez*, he had a full head of hair and a prominent nose.

"My name is Abdul Ghani Beradar," he said, extending a hand. "I am the person you asked to see. I know Mr. Clayton Luger and I know that I can trust you. Mullah Kotak has told me something about your project. Can you tell me more?"

Malko sat down on a stack of carpets facing him and started laying out the details of the American proposal, but the mullah quickly interrupted him.

"Before you go any further, you must tell me the name of the person the United States wants to support in the presidential election."

"The man himself doesn't know about this," said Malko. "Nobody knows, aside from a few people in Washington."

But Beradar would not be put off. "I must know his name," he said. "Some people are not compatible with our values."

Malko could see that the mullah was going to insist. And after all, he had been authorized to tell him. "You'll be the only person to know," he said. "The candidate would be Abdullah Abdullah, who ran in the presidential elections in 2009."

Beradar scowled. "A Tajik!" he exclaimed, in a way that clearly wasn't intended as a compliment.

"Half Tajik," Malko pointed out. "His father is Pashtun." Then he quickly added, "He's a declared enemy of Hamid Karzai and an honest man, I think."

Beradar nodded. "His reputation is not bad," he admitted. "But does he really have a chance of being elected?"

"That will depend on you. The last time, he got almost 31 percent of the vote without Taliban support. You have enough influence in the Pashtun community to get people to vote for a half-Pashtun. After all, in 2000 you persuaded the farmers not to plant poppies, even though it was against their interest."

"That was a religious matter," said the mullah. "Our peasants are very devout. We explained to them that Allah did not approve of the cultivation of opium. What we have here is a cultural problem. In the last election, Pashtuns who feel only hate and contempt for Karzai still voted for him, because he is Pashtun."

"But what do you think of the general idea?" asked Malko.

Beradar evaded the question. "This is not a decision I can take by myself. I have to submit it to the *shura* and to Mullah Omar, who will surely demand certain guarantees."

"Abdullah can't openly boast of Taliban support," said Malko.

"We would not ask that of him," said Beradar. "But if we are able to reach an understanding, he must make a formal commitment to our leadership. We do not want to help him at our expense. I do not trust Tajiks. They have no love for us and they have fought us. Abdullah was the right-hand man of that dog Massoud, whose picture today defiles the walls of the city."

There was clearly lots of work ahead, thought Malko. Aloud, he said, "If an agreement could be reached, it would help national reconciliation and give your movement a way to return to power. At least partly."

The Taliban mullah gave him a chilly smile. "We will return to power sooner or later in any case. But we want to spare our country any more suffering."

Malko was about to respond when they heard hurried footsteps on the stairs. The shopkeeper burst into the room, breathless. He blurted something to Beradar, who jumped to his feet and said, "The police are in the street! I have to leave!"

He turned and pushed a small partition, revealing a narrow staircase leading to the roof, and disappeared.

The young store owner grabbed two scarves from a pile and thrust them at Malko.

"Take these! You can say you bought them. Quick, get out of here! They are coming!"

Malko didn't need to be told twice, and he rushed down the staircase. Downstairs, the shop was empty. When he stepped out into the street, he understood Beradar's panic: it was full of cops in and out of uniform, and they were going into all the stores.

Malko had come within an inch of being caught with Beradar—which wouldn't have helped his relationship with Hamid Karzai.

He walked along Chicken Street, trying to ignore the policemen, who were out in force. Who had tipped them off? Malko wondered anxiously. He considered and dismissed the idea that he had been followed. The betrayal must have come from the Taliban side.

Just as he spotted Doolittle's white Land Cruiser at the entrance of Flower Street, he heard gunshots from the other end of the street. Climbing into the SUV, he said a silent prayer that Beradar would escape his pursuers.

Mullah Beradar frantically sprinted across the roofs of the Chicken Street shops, finally diving down a trapdoor into a souvenir store. He didn't know the people there, but he shouted, "May Allah protect you! Karzai's dogs are after me! Don't tell them you saw me."

Saying that sort of thing was pretty safe. Everybody hated Karzai.

When Beradar emerged into the street, the police seemed to be everywhere. Without hurrying, he walked along the broken sidewalk toward the supermarket across the way, where he could lose himself in the crowd.

Beradar's heart was thudding in his chest, and he cursed himself for taking the chance of coming to Kabul. But it was a little late for regrets.

Suddenly he heard a shout behind him. Instinctively turning around, he saw a pair of plainclothesmen running his way. He hesitated, briefly considered staying where he was, but realized that would be a bad choice.

The bulk of the policemen were far away. Beradar pulled a Makarov from his *shalwar kameez* and fired at his pursuers. He emptied almost the whole clip, and the two men fell. Putting the gun away, he strode quickly toward the store. But the shots had attracted attention, and he now heard cries and shouts behind him. He lunged for the supermarket doors.

A fraction of a second too late.

Something hit his left thigh, and the leg suddenly folded under him. He didn't feel any pain, but he stumbled and fell across the doorway. People hurried to help him up, and a wave of pain overwhelmed him as he half stood, supported by two passersby.

Soldiers and policemen appeared, swinging the butts of their rifles to knock the men holding Beradar aside while yelling orders and insults.

The mullah collapsed on the ground and lay sprawled on his back, drenched in sweat. Terrible pain was shooting through his leg. Looking up, he saw a soldier's face contorted with rage, and the black circle of a Kalashnikov barrel. He closed his eyes and prayed to Allah that the man would kill him right away.

It was the best thing that could happen.

But through his half-conscious haze, he could hear someone screaming, "Don't shoot him!"

He was still conscious when he saw someone leaning over and shaking him. Opening his eyes, Beradar could vaguely make out the shape of a man.

"You're Abdul Ghani Beradar, aren't you?" the man yelled. "You're under arrest, you Talib bastard!"

To back up what he said, the policeman kicked Beradar's thigh where he'd been shot. The pain was so intense that he passed out, so he didn't see the military ambulance pulling up in front of the supermarket.

The mullah's hell was about to begin.

CHAPTER 46

"This is awkward," said Clayton Luger, sounding dismayed. "Very awkward."

The moment Malko got back to the Ariana Hotel, he'd rushed to a secure phone line to warn Langley of the disastrous turn of events.

"Did you give him Abdullah's name?" asked Luger.

"Yes, just before he had to make a run for it."

The CIA number two heaved a deep sigh. "Then let's hope to hell they don't catch him. Otherwise you've painted a big fat bull's-eye on Abdullah's back. Karzai hates him already, and if he finds out he's hooking up with the Taliban, he'll do everything he can to bump him off.

"Well, there's nothing left to do but hope for the best. Keep me posted!"

Malko was reluctant to return to the Serena, but staying holed up at the Ariana would amount to a confession. Trying to get rid of Hamid Karzai brings me nothing but bad luck, he thought.

Beradar's stretcher was set down in Parviz Bamyan's office, and the jubilant NDS chief looked him over.

The prisoner had been given a shot of morphine, his wound

roughly bandaged, and he'd been handcuffed to the stretcher. He was lucid, though still groggy.

Bamyan leaned close and asked, "You're Abdul Ghani Beradar, aren't you?"

"You know very well who I am, you communist dog!" snapped the cleric, staring at him coldly. "May Allah curse you!"

Bamyan had indeed been a member of Najibullah's old Khalq faction. Unruffled, he said, "Save your energy, because we're going to have a lot to talk about in the coming days. I'm sure you have many, many things to tell me. Starting with why you came to Kabul, since it's been so long since you visited our beautiful country."

Beradar closed his eyes without answering. He knew what awaited him. He had no fear of becoming a *shahid*—a martyr—but he was afraid of what would happen before he ascended to Allah's paradise. Nobody had ever successfully resisted NDS torture, he knew. And he had so many secrets that his interrogators were sure to reserve special treatment for him.

He could hear people entering the office, and the NDS leader gave them orders:

"Take him to the first subbasement. And don't beat him. Let him get his strength back. He'll need it."

Haji Shukrullah, who owned the Chicken Street shop where Malko had met Beradar, looked up to see two plainclothes policemen entering his store. Without a word, they yanked him from behind the cash register and started to beat him.

By the time they tossed him into the green police truck, his collarbone was broken and his face smashed. And this was just the start of the softening-up process.

A good Muslim who had made the hajj, Shukrullah prayed to Allah to give him the strength not to be too cowardly. He didn't want to be a *shahid*, but neither did he want to betray his friends.

It was a fine line.

Malko was having coffee at the Serena's nonalcoholic bar, trying to settle his nerves. He had returned from Chicken Street without incident and was starting to feel hopeful again. Kabul didn't have any real media, so he had no way of knowing if Mullah Beradar had managed to escape.

The ringing of his phone pulled him from his thoughts.

Without preamble, Warren Michaelis asked, "Are you at the Serena?"

"Yes, I'm at the bar."

"Okay, I'll be there in half an hour."

There had to be a serious reason for the CIA station chief to come to the hotel. Malko hoped it wasn't a bad one.

He had drunk two more cups of coffee by the time Michaelis showed up. The station chief was accompanied by a pair of Marine "babysitters," who sat down at the next table. He looked tense and drawn.

"Mullah Beradar is in the hands of the NDS," he immediately said. "He was wounded and arrested."

"Are you sure?" asked Malko.

"Yes. My NDS source confirmed it. This is a major problem, because they'll make Beradar talk—about you."

Malko had no illusions about the cleric being able to resist torture. Blowing yourself up with a suicide vest was one thing, but having your fingernails ripped out was quite another. An obvious solution occurred to him.

"This operation is obviously terminated, so why not fly me out now? I'm of no further use in Kabul."

Michaelis gave him a long look and said, "Actually, you are. I got a message from Mr. Luger. We have to assume that Beradar will give them the name of Abdullah Abdullah, which puts him in Karzai's line of fire. You have to warn him."

"What?" Malko was taken aback. "Why me? I don't even know Abdullah!"

"Officially, the Agency can't get involved in the presidential election, as you know. So the station isn't allowed to approach someone like Abdullah Abdullah. But you're a free agent and can go talk to him. And that will wrap up your mission. Once you've delivered the warning, you can leave Afghanistan."

Naked except for underpants and a bulky bandage on his thigh, Mullah Beradar was strapped to a metal table with his arms above his head and his ankles handcuffed to the side bars. An NDS agent had stuffed a rag in his mouth and was steadily pouring water from a pitcher onto it.

The relentless flow kept bringing the cleric to the edge of suffocation.

He gasped like a fish out of water. His head thrashed around, trying to escape the torment, which had begun hours earlier.

They hadn't asked him any questions yet, only half asphyxiated him at regular intervals. A very effective way to weaken him.

The last of the water from the pitcher flowed into Beradar's mouth, and he expected his tormentor to refill it from the big bucket nearby. Instead, he set it on the ground and took the wet rag from between his victim's teeth.

Beradar hungrily sucked air into his lungs, grateful for this unhoped-for respite.

It didn't last long.

The interrogator sat down on a stool and lit a cigarette. He blew out the smoke and leaned close to his victim.

"Now I've got a few questions to ask you, brother," he said in a gentle voice. "Who did you come to see in Kabul?"

The cleric realized he still had some willpower left.

He didn't answer.

The man didn't seem bothered by his silence. Then he took a drag on his cigarette to heat the tip and pressed it onto Beradar's left nipple.

Eyes bulging from their sockets, Beradar let out a loud scream as the smell of burned flesh filled the room. The pain was excruciating. The interrogator removed the cigarette so it didn't go out, but the pain continued.

When Beradar stopped screaming, the man said, "You should answer my question, brother. Otherwise it's going to be a very long day."

Bamyan was turning Maureen Kieffer's business card over and over in his fingers. They had found it in one of Beradar's vest pockets.

The NDS leader was puzzled.

None of his men had reported Beradar visiting the woman, yet her card hadn't wound up in his pocket by accident. To Bamyan, the link between them was immediately obvious: Malko Linge. Though he still didn't have any concrete proof, he was now positive Linge was the man whom Mullah Omar's envoy had come to Kabul to meet.

He didn't need the South African woman to apprehend Beradar anymore, of course. But having her in custody might be a good way to put pressure on the Americans.

Just then someone knocked at his door: one of the interrogators from the Beradar cells. He'd been assigned to question the Chicken Street shopkeeper suspected of arranging the meeting between Linge and Beradar.

"He talked," the agent said briefly. "I showed him the photo of the *khareji*, and he recognized him. One of his cousins asked him to arrange the meeting, but he claims not to know what it was about."

"Very good," said Bamyan. "Now he has to admit that it was Beradar."

"No problem, Commander," said the interrogator before heading for the basement.

A shopkeeper didn't have the moral fiber of a Talib.

Feeling satisfied, Bamyan stepped into his deputy's office and handed him Maureen Kieffer's card.

"Go to this woman's place and bring her back here. Don't tell her why. Shake her up first. I want her to talk of her own accord."

It didn't take the interrogator long to "persuade" Shukrullah that he was sure that it was Mullah Beradar he had welcomed into his shop. When the NDS agent started gently slicing the shopkeeper's penis with a razor, he signed whatever was put in front of him without arguing.

Shukrullah definitely didn't have the soul of a *shahid*.

Signed confession in hand, the interrogator returned to Bamyan's office, where he was given a five-hundred-afghani bill for his promptness. Then Bamyan said, "Send him to Bagram, in solitary."

The Afghans had regained control of the prison, where they could now do whatever they pleased.

CHAPTER 47

When Malko entered his office, Warren Michaelis looked as if he was having a bad day.

"Luftullah Kibzai just gave me some pretty lousy news," he said.

"Did Mullah Beradar talk?"

"I don't know about that. But the NDS arrested your friend Maureen Kieffer this morning, and they're interrogating her. Do you know why?"

At first, Malko didn't know what to say. If the NDS had wanted to arrest Maureen because of her relationship to him, they would have done so long ago. But then in his mind's eye he suddenly saw the young woman handing him her business card at the Serena. He had given that card to Kotak, who must, in turn, have given it to Beradar.

Malko was horrified. Maureen couldn't possibly know why she'd been arrested, because she didn't know whom he was meeting at her guesthouse.

Malko turned to Michaelis and said, "I think I know why the NDS arrested her."

Michaelis listened to his explanation in silence, nodding. Then he said, "It's awful, and I don't know how we can get her out of there. They're going to ask her if she knows Beradar, and she'll honestly say no."

Malko cursed himself. It was his fault that Maureen was in this hellish situation. "What can we do?"

"For the time being, nothing," said Michaelis. "I'll try to have Luftullah Kibzai keep me posted on what's happening. Let's just hope they don't treat her too badly."

The second slap landed while Maureen was still recovering from the sting of the first. They were delivered by a stocky, broad-shouldered Afghan because she answered no to the question, "Do you know why you're here?"

She had been living in a nightmare since three men showed up at her workshop and bundled her into an unmarked Corolla, without even giving her time to get her purse or keys. They took her directly to a little basement room with walls oozing humidity. Since then, the men kept asking her the same question, for which she didn't have an answer.

Sitting on a chair, cheeks burning and eyes full of tears, Maureen faced her interrogators.

"I don't know why I'm here," she said in English. "I want my embassy notified. I haven't done anything wrong."

This last statement enraged the stocky one, who spoke English. Rummaging in his pocket, he pulled out a business card and waved it under her nose.

"So what about this?"

"It's one of my business cards."

"Do you know where we found it?"

She shook her head, and he continued, "On a fucking Talib, Abdul Ghani Beradar. He says he knows you."

The name meant nothing to her. But then she visualized herself handing the card to Malko for his meeting at her guesthouse. Everything was clear now, but she couldn't tell them this.

"I don't know that man," she said. "I don't know how he got my card."

The stocky Afghan rubbed his hands. "You are a tough one," he said. "A tough one and a liar. Well, we know how to deal with that. Let's go!"

They dragged her into a cell that held only an adjustable X-shaped metal table with tie-down straps.

"Take your clothes off," said the stocky man.

When she didn't move, he grabbed her sweater and tore it in half, with incredible strength. Leering at her large bosom, he seized her bra and ripped it off, baring the young woman's breasts.

As she tried to cover herself, he shredded her pants. In seconds, she was stripped to her white panties. The stone floor underfoot was cold. She shivered, her mind reeling.

The two men forced her down onto on the steel X, securing her hands and feet. The icy metal against her back came as a shock.

Standing next to her, the stocky Afghan started stroking her breasts and belly. When he got to her panties, he yanked on the elastic until it broke, revealing her blond bush.

"Listen here," he said. "If you answer my questions, in an hour you will be in a nice comfortable cell and we will leave you alone. Where did you meet Mullah Beradar?"

Maureen was so frightened, it took her several seconds before she could speak.

"I don't know that man!" she cried. "I've never heard his name in my life!"

The man walked to the foot of the table, took the two ends of the X, and spread them wide apart. That way, he could stand between his prisoner's naked thighs.

Shaking his head, he said in a mock-casual voice, "So you will not answer, eh? In that case, my friends and I are going to have a little fun with you. We have plenty of time."

In bed, Malko tossed and turned. He couldn't stop thinking about Maureen, imagining the worst and raging at his powerlessness.

With no solution in sight.

He'd passed Shaheen Zoolor in the lobby but had barely glanced at her. She must be wondering why his attitude toward her had changed so much. He looked at his watch: 3:45 a.m. Time was passing with exasperating slowness, without relieving his sense of helplessness. He was well aware that the Americans couldn't do anything. Nobody could do anything.

As he did every day, Parviz Bamyan got to NDS headquarters at eight o'clock. He looked over the files placed on his desk but didn't see anything of interest. The presidential palace had already congratulated him for capturing Beradar, and he was in a very good mood.

When the Talib bastard downstairs had yielded all his secrets, things would be even better, Bamyan thought. He might officially be named head of the service at last.

He was still toying with that pleasant thought when one of his deputies entered his office. It was the head of the Beradar interrogators.

"Salaam alaikum, Commander," he said. "I have good news for you."

Delighted, Bamyan said, "Sit down and have some tea. What's the news?"

"We worked very hard," said the man, almost as a complaint. "Well into the night. He's a tough son of a bitch, but he eventually told us everything. We now know why he came to Kabul: to meet with that CIA agent, Malko Linge. Also what they talked about."

"*Baleh*?"

"The Americans and the Taliban plan to support a candidate together in the presidential elections."

"Who?"

"Someone we know very well: Abdullah Abdullah!"

"That Tajik dog!" Bamyan exploded. "Are you sure?"

"I'm about to write my report, Commander. It'll be ready in an hour."

Bamyan could hardly contain his excitement. "How's your customer doing?"

"He's in pretty bad shape, sir. He had a very rough time. Do you want to see him?"

"Yes."

They went downstairs together and crossed the courtyard to the small interrogation building. The stench hit them as soon as they started down to the subbasement: a mix of urine, filth, and sweat, and the stale smell of blood.

The glare of a bare bulb lit the room where Beradar lay.

He was motionless, eyes closed, but his chest still rose and fell weakly. Studying him, Bamyan saw the neat cuts made at the especially sensitive parts of his body. On a table nearby lay the metal saw that had made them, its blade still bloody.

The NDS chief straightened up and said evenly, "Make sure you haven't overlooked anything. Then strangle him and burn the body."

A corpse so badly mangled could never see the light of day, he knew. If the Taliban ever found it, their vengeance would be terrible.

Bamyan headed back upstairs feeling proud of himself. He held some strategically important information, and Hamid Karzai's enemy now had a name: Abdullah Abdullah.

Without his usual CIA resources, it had taken Malko some time to discreetly contact the people around Abdullah Abdullah, and even more time for them find him a trustworthy escort, a minor Tajik drug runner.

To make sure they weren't followed, Malko and the man changed cars twice before even heading to the Parwan neighborhood where Abdullah lived. The only access to the Afghan political leader's street was a narrow passage between two enormous concrete blocks guarded by armed men. Thirty yards beyond the chicane, guards patrolled the little house where Abdullah lived—and had, apparently, been born. There were still more armed men inside.

On the threshold, Malko was greeted by a smiling man wearing a black Mao jacket, whose large eyes sparkled with intelligence.

"Welcome," Abdullah said in excellent English. "It's a pleasure to have you in my modest home. Please, have some tea."

They sat on a sofa in an attractive living room with modern furnishings and a large flat-screen TV.

"To what do I owe the honor of this visit?"

Malko gave him a pained smile and said, "I would have liked to meet you under other circumstances. I'm here to warn you that you may be in danger."

"What do you mean?"

"Do you know Mullah Abdul Ghani Beradar?"

"Only by name. He's an important member of the Quetta *shura*. But I've never met him and I don't think he's in Afghanistan anymore. Why?"

Malko explained. "You're aware that the U.S. government views your running as a candidate in the presidential elections favorably, aren't you?"

"Yes, I am. The ambassador said as much at lunch recently. I was very flattered."

"The Americans had the idea of getting the Taliban movement to support you, as a way of encouraging Pashtuns to vote for you."

Abdullah smiled. "That wouldn't be a bad idea, provided the Taliban accepted me. I fought them for a long time, but they include people of value who are nationalists."

"How do you suppose Hamid Karzai would react if he learned that you and the Taliban were considering an alliance?"

"He would try to have me assassinated," Abdullah said calmly.

"Well, I'm afraid he may have just learned it," said Malko. "Let me tell you why." At some length, he described Mullah Beradar's trip to Kabul, their meeting in Chicken Street, and Beradar's capture by the NDS.

"I'm not naïve," Malko concluded. "Nobody resists NDS torture. So we have to assume that Beradar has talked and that Karzai now knows everything."

A long silence followed, eventually broken by Abdullah. "I agree with your thinking," he said in the same calm voice. "Those people are animals. I'm glad you warned me, because I will redouble my precautions. Karzai would have found out sooner or later, but this gives him more time to try to kill me."

"I'm really very sorry," said Malko. "I still don't know how the NDS learned that Mullah Beradar was in Kabul. I may never know. I must have slipped up somewhere."

The Afghan waved his concern away.

"It doesn't matter. What's done is done. If Mullah Beradar dies, I don't think his death need be an obstacle to the plan, provided the Taliban agree."

Abdullah stood up, signaling the end of the meeting, and said, "It would be a good thing for Afghanistan, which needs peace. We've been at war for more than thirty years."

The two men exchanged a warm handshake. Malko found his

Tajik escort waiting, and they exited through the barricade to the street beyond.

Finally, his work was done.

Relaxing back at the Serena, Malko had reason to be satisfied. He'd been impressed by Abdullah's poise and intelligence. Also, he appreciated the politician's tact in not making him feel too responsible for attracting Karzai's wrath. But most of all, Malko was relieved that this crazy mission was finally at an end, knowing that the Agency would put him on a plane anytime he wanted.

But could he fly out of Afghanistan while leaving Maureen Kieffer in the hands of the NDS? He would feel like a deserter.

Staying on in Kabul was dangerous, he knew. Karzai would soon learn about his role in connecting Abdullah with the Taliban, making him doubly vulnerable.

Abdullah Abdullah was well protected, and Mullah Beradar was in custody. Which left Malko as the number one target of a regime not in the habit of turning the other cheek.

CHAPTER 48

Parviz Bamyan bounded up the steps to Hadj Ali Kalmar's office, a thick folder in his hand. The news he was bringing was practically all good.

After extracting the last scrap of information from Beradar, they had killed him, burned the body, and scattered the ashes in the mountains. Mullah Abdul Ghani Beradar had traveled to Kabul, but no one would ever know how he left. No mention of him appeared in any NDS records.

Beradar's confession told them a great deal, including the exact role played by the Americans and Malko Linge, who was the key to the whole assassination plot. As a bonus, Beradar also revealed the name of the candidate the Americans—and maybe even the Taliban—would back in the coming elections. Which gave them some time to get rid of him.

Only one shadow darkened this otherwise sunny picture. Despite very rough treatment, the South African woman Maureen Kieffer still hadn't admitted to knowing the mullah, even though her business card had been found on him. But that was secondary. They would get her to confess sooner or later.

Kalmar, who already knew the general tenor of Bamyan's report, was waiting in his office. After a long handshake, he sat back and carefully read it.

When he finally looked up, his vulpine face was alight with joy.

"This is first-class work!" Kalmar exclaimed admiringly. "I'm sure the president will be very grateful. Since Asadullah Khalid still hasn't recovered from the bomb attack, I'm going to suggest that you be named NDS director in his place."

"That would be a great honor," Bamyan said modestly.

"I will be seeing the president right away."

The newly anointed NDS head bowed his way out of the office, his heart singing.

As soon as Kalmar was alone, he phoned President Karzai on his direct line and asked if he could bring him a very important dossier.

Three minutes later he was crossing the wide esplanade between the two groups of buildings.

President Karzai was in his office. He was wearing a black vest and green pants, and his bald head gleamed in the light from a halogen lamp. He looked through the dossier carefully but didn't display his joy openly, merely congratulating his chief of staff.

The information in Bamyan's report gave Karzai a big leg up in his struggle with the Taliban and the Americans. But he now had a personal score to settle with this Malko Linge. And he knew just the man to do it.

"So what do you want to do?" asked Warren Michaelis. "I can fly you home through Bagram and Dubai whenever you like. I know Langley will approve. It would be very risky for you to stay in Kabul."

"I know," said Malko, "but . . ."

"You're thinking of Maureen Kieffer, aren't you? I can inform the South African authorities, but I'm afraid the Afghans will just stonewall them. This involves state security, and they don't kowtow to anyone except the United States."

"Can't you intervene?"

"No, I can't," said Michaelis, slowly shaking his head. "Not on my own authority. And if I ask Langley, I'm sure they'll say no. She isn't American, and she doesn't work for the Agency."

Malko felt worse and worse. It was because of him that Maureen was in the clutches of the NDS, and all for wanting to do him a favor.

"Give me forty-eight hours to think this through," he said, standing up. "And I want you to promise me something: to give Maureen Kieffer my payment for the mission, whatever happens."

Michaelis looked anxious.

"Don't push your luck, Malko! This business has been screwed up pretty badly already. In a situation like that, you don't charge ahead; you pull back."

"I know, but I want to be able to look myself in the face in the mirror when I shave."

Shaheen Zoolor smiled at him when they once again found themselves waiting for the elevator after dinner. Malko stepped aside to let her get into the cab.

"I've decided your mother was right," he said with a tight smile. "I think you should be very careful with men. You are a beautiful woman and you will have many temptations."

Not understanding what he meant, Shaheen didn't answer. When they reached the door to his room, she clearly intended to follow him inside.

Instead, Malko took her hand and kissed it.

"I hope you have a very happy marriage," he said. Then he entered the room and gently closed the door, leaving the young woman in the hallway. He would never know if she would have yielded to him, but Maureen Kieffer felt too present in his mind to give free rein to his libido.

Twenty-four hours later, he still hadn't come up with a solution.

He'd been in the room for only a moment when his cell beeped with a text:

Langley is ordering you home. WM.

If he was going to pull something off, he was running out of time. He went to bed and lay in the dark, his eyes open.

Malko had just walked into the lobby from the breakfast room when four Afghans in civilian clothes approached him. They were husky, self-confident men with expressionless faces and thick mustaches.

"Are you Malko Linge?" one asked.

"Yes."

"We're with the Interior Ministry. Our commander wants to talk with you. It won't take long."

"What have I done?"

The Afghan smiled apologetically. "Nothing, sir. You'll be back around noon. This is just for a quick chat."

They had surrounded him, clearly determined not to let him get away. Malko reached into his pocket for his cell, but the Afghan immediately spoke up.

"No need to telephone," he said curtly. "This won't take long."

They were already hustling him toward the door held open by a turbaned bellhop. A black SUV was parked in front of the hotel. They helped Malko into the back and seated him between two of the policemen.

Not a word more had been said.

After a few minutes' drive, Malko spotted the long wall of the NDS complex, but the SUV didn't stop. They circled the roundabout beyond and turned into the street leading to Kabul's poppy palaces. Intrigued and now increasingly uneasy, Malko asked, "Aren't we going to the Interior Ministry?"

"No, sir," said one of the men placidly. "We're going to our commander's home."

A few hundred yards farther, the car slowed and the driver honked his horn. The black gate of a large house promptly opened, and they entered the courtyard.

Malko got out and the officers escorted him up the front steps. A ragged guard with an AK-47 opened the door; another man could be seen behind him. Releasing Malko, the four cops went back down the steps and disappeared.

The foyer was decorated in ornate Pakistani style and smelled of incense. Two scruffy men appeared, grim-looking Afghans with AK-47 magazines in their shirt pockets. One grabbed Malko by the arm and led him away. They searched him, taking his cell phone. One of the Afghans slid a heavy wooden door aside, unleashing a furious concert of deafening barking.

They shoved him into a tiny room and slid the door shut. Malko then saw the source of the barking. One wall of the room was a grill separating it from a kennel containing five huge dogs. They were enormous mastiffs with an odd peculiarity: their ears and tails had all been cut off.

These monsters, which probably weighed a hundred and fifty pounds apiece, circled and growled, apparently ready to attack. Malko realized that without the grill they would tear him to shreds.

He sat down on a bench. Deafened by the barking, he tried to stay calm.

Michaelis dialed Malko's number for the tenth time in a row, but it immediately went to voice mail. Now seriously worried, Michaelis called one of his informants at the Serena.

At the mention of Malko's name, the Afghan lowered his voice and said, "Officers from the Interior Ministry came to get him earlier. They asked me where he was."

The American felt his blood run cold. "Thanks," he said curtly.

Within minutes, Michaelis had placed a formal call to a senior official at the ministry. Half an hour of stormy phone calls later, Michaelis knew only that none of the security services had arrested Malko. It wouldn't be the first time that fake policemen had grabbed someone in broad daylight.

There were only two things for him to do.

First, he sent a message to Langley announcing Malko's disappearance. Then he called Hamid Karzai's office. He told them what he knew and said how concerned he was and that he held the Afghan government responsible for Malko's fate. This was mere hand waving, he knew, but better than nothing. It did nothing to relieve his anxiety.

Who had kidnapped Malko, and why?

The day passed very slowly, punctuated by the dogs' nearly constant barking. It was enough to drive a person crazy.

The door suddenly slid open, and a guard with a Kalashnikov gestured to Malko to follow him. He hastened to do so, grateful to escape the deafening racket. The Afghan pointed him down a long hallway, and they entered a room full of carpets, cushions, and gilded chairs, with incense burners everywhere.

At the far end, Malko saw a fat man in *shalwar kameez* sitting in a big armchair. He had a puffy face, prominent eyes, and a thick mustache whose ends drooped on either side of his mouth. He was smoking a cigar, and a bottle of whiskey with a glass stood on a tray nearby. After giving Malko an appraising look, the man waved him to a smaller chair nearby.

The ragged guard with the AK-47 went to crouch on the carpet in a corner of the room.

The man puffed on his cigar and blew out the smoke. "You must be wondering why you're here," he said in rough but serviceable English.

"I was told I was going to the Interior Ministry."

The man burst out laughing. "They do not even know you are here! Nobody does except the men who brought you, and they work for me. And of course the person who asked me to do this. He is a very powerful friend, and he asked me to get rid of you. Because I have the means."

"What means?"

"You have seen my dogs. They are real beauties, are they not? They are fighting dogs. They weigh nearly seventy kilos and are very fierce. Those won several fights this year. I bought one of them for fifteen thousand dollars. Now, after Nowruz, the season is over, and they are resting. But they still must be fed. Each one needs several pounds of meat a day. Otherwise they become weak.

"Right now they are starting to be hungry.

"If I opened the grill that keeps them from your room, they would tear you to pieces in a few minutes. By the end of the day there would be nothing left of you. This is what I was asked to do. I think you have caused my friend harm, and you must pay. I wanted to warn you."

He fell silent and puffed on his cigar, watching Malko through half-closed eyes.

Despite the man's measured tone, Malko knew he was talking seriously. A long silence followed.

"Aren't you afraid this might cause you trouble?" Malko finally asked. "I work with the CIA, and they take revenge seriously."

"We are in Afghanistan," he said, shrugging. "Nobody can do anything against me. So that is all. I just wanted to meet you and say good-bye."

Malko couldn't think of anything to say. The fat man didn't look like someone whose better nature could be appealed to. The silence went on, this time broken by the dogs' owner.

"Actually, I have a proposal that maybe will allow you to save your skin."

"I thought you were under an obligation," said Malko, on guard against bad surprises.

The fat man made a vague gesture. "It is always possible to reach an agreement. I will explain my problem. Do you know the American DEA, the Drug Enforcement Administration?"

"Yes, of course."

"They do not like me. They claim I have shipped several tons of heroin to the United States. So they put me on a blacklist. If I leave Afghanistan, there is an Interpol arrest warrant in my name. I would be immediately arrested and transferred to the United States, probably for the rest of my life."

He gave a sigh of annoyance. "This bothers me. I like to travel. If you are able to lift this prohibition, you maybe can get out of here. What do you think?"

A wave of hope surged through Malko, but he didn't let it show. "I obviously can't solve the problem alone, but I can discuss it with the CIA authority in Kabul. For starters, I'll need your name."

"Farhad Naibkhel."

"So how do I proceed?"

The fat man took a cell phone from his vest pocket and handed it to Malko. "Call whoever you like. But I warn you, if anyone tries to rescue you, you will be torn apart by the dogs before they get up the front steps. And another thing: I want an answer in three days. And not just words, a document. Otherwise I will have to do the favor my friend asked me."

CHAPTER 49

"And you're actually inside Farhad Naibkhel's place?" asked Dale Weles incredulously.

"That's right," said Malko. "He's right here. Do you want to talk to him?"

"God no!" cried Weles, the head of the DEA in Kabul. "A grand jury in the Southern District of New York indicted him for bringing heroin into the United States. He's one of Afghanistan's worst traffickers. He used to be connected with Hamid Karzai's half brother, who controlled heroin production in Kandahar and was assassinated. Just a month ago, he shipped two thousand pounds of heroin out of Dushanbe on a Kam Air plane."

"What is his legal status?" asked Malko.

"He's got an international warrant on his ass. If he takes one step outside of Afghanistan, he'll be arrested and extradited to the United States."

"Okay, thanks. Can you pass me Warren Michaelis again, please?"

Malko had spent the last two hours on the phone with the CIA and the American embassy. The CIA station chief's initial reaction to Malko's kidnapping had been brutal.

"Give me an hour, and I'll send a task force for you," he said. "We don't tell the Afghans anything and we attack the house. No bunch of flea-bitten guards is going to stop the Marines."

Malko calmed him down.

"That's not the right thing to do, Warren. By the time you get inside, the dogs will have killed me. We have to make a deal, if we can."

Once Malko explained the situation, it had taken Michaelis an hour to get hold of the DEA man.

Michaelis now came back on the line.

"Is Dale Weles gone?" Malko asked.

"Yes, he is."

"Do you think he can help us reach an agreement?"

"I doubt it. Naibkhel is one of the drug lords the DEA absolutely wants to take down. They just arrested another big trafficker in Guinea-Bissau by luring him outside of territorial waters. He's facing at least forty years in prison." Michaelis paused. "In any case, Weles doesn't have the authority to negotiate this."

"I suspected as much," said Malko. "We have to go higher. Try Clayton Luger first, then John Mulligan. The solution can only come from the White House."

"And you're sure you don't want us to take action here?" asked Michaelis.

"Absolutely certain. It would condemn me to a horrible death."

"Jesus! I'll call Langley right away. What are Naibkhel's demands?"

"The DEA has to get the international arrest warrant lifted, so he can travel. And he needs proof in writing."

"That shouldn't be hard," said Michaelis. "The DEA just has to contact Interpol. Okay, that's it for now. Try to hang in there."

When Malko handed the cell back to Naibkhel, the trafficker gave him an ironic smile.

"You are very convincing," he said. "That is good. Let us hope they value you. Meanwhile, we will have something to eat."

While Malko was on the phone, a servant brought in an enormous copper tray loaded with various dishes and bottles of soda and mineral water. He and Naibkhel sat on the carpet. Having not eaten anything since the morning, Malko was ravenous.

Naibkhel took a piece of lamb, dipped it in a spicy sauce, and remarked, "I do not have anything against you personally. I hope we can make this deal. It has been two years since I have been able to leave Afghanistan. And it would be better for you also."

That had to be an example of Afghan humor, Malko thought.

Twenty minutes later, Naibkhel went back to his armchair and said a few words to one of his bodyguards. Knowing what was next, Malko stood up of his own accord. What was the point of resisting?

He had barely been shoved into his room when the dogs started barking furiously.

It was nerve shattering.

He curled into a ball on the cot and tried to ignore the horrible noise. Praying that the CIA and the White House wouldn't let him down.

"David Hoffman is on the blue line, sir," said Mulligan's secretary.

The national security advisor picked up the phone. Hoffman was the head of the DEA, and the two men knew each other slightly. Mulligan quickly got to the matter at hand.

"Did you give the instructions to Interpol?"

"Yes, but they're dragging their feet. They don't understand."

Mulligan exploded.

"A man's life is involved, for Christ's sakes! One of our best operatives! Interpol has to knuckle under, and that's all there is to it. And you have to lift your indictment. We have only a few hours left. Interpol must take Naibkhel off its list. The president wants this."

"I'll call France again," said Hoffman, "but I'm not going to cancel the U.S. warrant on Naibkhel. If that scumbag sets foot in this country, he'll be arrested."

"That's fine," said Mulligan. "I doubt he feels like coming here."

"It'll be a done deal by tomorrow!" said Michaelis. "I just got a message from the White House."

"How will we know?" asked Malko.

"Naibkhel can go to the Interpol website and type in his name on their wanted list. He'll still be forbidden from entering the United States, of course."

Malko hung up and handed the phone back to Naibkhel.

"The DEA agrees!" he said.

The Afghan gave a joyous shout. "So I'll be able to go to Dubai?" His ambitions were modest.

"I think so," said Malko. "As of tomorrow morning, you can start checking the Interpol website."

"This we have to celebrate," said Naibkhel. "I've had a delicious *palau* prepared."

Malko was able to force himself to eat.

When he was returned to his room, the ear-splitting barking assaulted him again. It took the dogs an hour to settle down.

Time passed very slowly.

The moment the door slid open, the dogs again started barking. The Afghan with the AK-47 gestured for Malko to come out, and he fled from the din. His watch read 10:00 a.m.

When Malko entered the office, Naibkhel was standing next to his desk, looking furious.

"There is nothing on the Interpol site!" he shouted. "You are fooling me and you are going to pay for it!"

Malko felt a chill run down his spine.

"I have the White House's word," he said. "I told you that yesterday."

"But I am still on the list," said Naibkhel. "If I am still there at six o'clock, you are going to be dinner for my dogs. I knew you damned infidels cannot be trusted!"

Something suddenly occurred to Malko. "Wait a minute! Interpol's headquarters is in Lyon, France. It's only seven in the morning there! There's a three-hour time difference between France and Afghanistan!"

The Afghan dismissed this with a wave, sending him back to the mastiffs.

Malko stared at the hands on his watch: it was already 5:30 p.m. He had a half hour to live.

Suddenly he heard the door slide, and the dogs started barking. The Afghan guard gestured to him.

It was double or nothing.

When he got to Naibkhel's office, he immediately knew from the man's smiling face that he'd been saved.

The drug trafficker embraced him, grinning widely.

"I'm going to spend next weekend in Dubai!" he said. "You are free to go whenever you like," he added, "but the authorities here must never hear of this. So phone your American connections, and never, ever come back to Afghanistan."

A bodyguard entered the room and spoke to Naibkhel, who turned to Malko.

"Your friends are here," he said.

Three white Land Cruisers were parked in front of the house.

When Malko came down the steps, Michaelis emerged from the first car and hugged him.

"We're going straight to Bagram," he said. "I haven't told the Afghans anything. You take off in two hours."

Malko climbed into the lead SUV. He began to relax only when Naibkhel's poppy palace was out of sight behind him and the barking of his dogs stopped ringing in his ears.

They had turned onto the Salang Highway and were climbing the switchbacks to the pass when Michaelis spoke.

"I have good news for you," he said.

"What's that?"

"The South African authorities put maximum pressure on the Afghans, and they're going to release Ms. Kieffer and send her home."

"Thank God!" said Malko. With the money from his CIA mission, Maureen would be set for life and he could leave Afghanistan with some peace of mind.

Even though he had nearly wound up in the jaws of Naibkhel's mastiffs, Malko had a strange feeling that he would miss this crazy, fierce country.

About the Translator

William Rodarmor (1942–) is a journalist and veteran French literary translator in Berkeley, California. Before *Chaos in Kabul*, he translated *The Madmen of Benghazi*, also by Gérard de Villiers, and *The Yellow Eyes of Crocodiles*, by Katherine Pancol (Penguin, 2013). Rodarmor was a fellow at the Banff International Literary Translation Centre, served as a Russian linguist in the Army Security Agency, and worked as a contract French interpreter for the U.S. State Department.